Exile Music

EXILE MUSIC

JENNIFER STEIL

WHEELER PUBLISHING
A part of Gale, a Cengage Company

GALE
A Cengage Company

**LIBRARY OF CONGRESS CIP DATA ON FILE.
CATALOGUING IN PUBLICATION FOR THIS BOOK
IS AVAILABLE FROM THE LIBRARY OF CONGRESS**

ISBN-13: 978-1-4328-8056-9 (hardcover alk. paper)

Published in 2020 by arrangement with Viking, an imprint of Penguin Publishing Group, a division of Penguin Random House, LLC

Printed in Mexico
Print Number: 01   Print Year: 2020

For all who live far from home
and in between

And for Tim and Theadora, who gave me
the first two sparks of this story

Re-creating your entire life is a form of reinvention on par with the greatest works of literature.

— EDWIDGE DANTICAT

Tradition is not the worship of the ashes but the preservation of fire.

— GUSTAV MAHLER

OVERTURE

When I think of Austria, I remember what a child remembers — details as vivid as the bright shards of a dream. The coffee-warmed air of the kitchen. The rough fabric of my father's suits against my cheek. The chalk dust of my classroom tickling my nose. The ice-crusted snow in the Jesuit-enwiese meadow that cut my eyebrow open when I fell off the toboggan halfway down the slope. My Anneliese. My parents' voices in the kitchen as I hovered still and silent by the door, secretly listening. It was important then, to listen.

I remember the tang of my mother's apricot jam spread over a thick layer of butter on crusty bread. The fungal stink of my older brother's dirty sports clothing on the bathroom floor. The earthy scent of the square olive-oil soap that was always slipping into the sink.

I remember a plum tree in our small communal courtyard that dropped its sour-sweet fruit onto our terrace. They were a dark, dusty purple, more oval than the green ones we would eat in Bolivia. In Vienna, Anneliese's mother collected the dropped fruits and used them to make tortes.

I remember my mother's voice in our parlor, starting off low and gathering the energy to soar. I remember the scent of rosin on horsehair, the vibrations of my father's viola, how I could feel the notes on my skin even after he stopped playing and I was in bed, listening only to the silence.

I remember the inky smell of my school-books as I cracked their spines. The sound of Frau Fessler's ruler smashing into my desk when she caught me with a book on my lap during math class. The way the fruit gummies from Weiss's got stuck in my back teeth so I had to pick them out with my fingernails. I remember the damp heat of Anneliese's hand as she folded it with mine for the last time.

I remember our neighbors' long coats decorated with flocks of badges saying only *Ja*. The swastikas on every armband and flag, pinned to every lapel, painted on our sidewalks. They even fell from the sky, flurries of paper spiders dropping onto our heads. I remember the newspapers my

10

parents hid from me under sofa cushions.

I remember lying awake, twisting the satiny border of my blanket in my fingers, until my mother came and curled around me. I remember her breath on my neck, the ice of her fingers on my spine, stroking my skin until I drifted into dreams.

The bland quotidian details, the textures of ordinary days, seared themselves most permanently.

Except for Anneliese. Anneliese, who was neither bland nor ordinary. Anneliese, who was more a part of me than not. Our mothers had birthed us in the same building a week apart and from then on there were no divisions between us. The three syllables of her name were my first song.

I remember Friedenglückhasenland.

We imagined the place into existence long before the Anschluss, when we were small and preliterate, as we lay sprawled on our stomachs on the floor of her kitchen, scribbling with our pencils on the back of brown paper from the grocer's.

"Where do you think we lived before this?" She looked up at me with large dark eyes.

"We have always been here, Ana. We've never been anywhere but here." Our families

11

had lived in the same apartments in the same small building owned by my grandfather since we were born. I thought for a moment. "I guess before here we were in our mothers' bellies?"

"No, I mean before we lived in our mothers' bellies."

"Nowhere," I said. "The belly is where we start."

Anneliese shook her head, the ends of her long hair dancing across the paper. "How could we not have existed? We must have been somewhere." She traced the outline of her lips with the rubber end of her pencil as she gazed up at the ceiling. At the left corner of her mouth, a faint scar curved upward so that even at rest her lips suggested a smile. "I know where *I* was," she said definitively. "I was in Friedenglückhasenland."

Friedenglückhasenland. Peace, Happiness, and Rabbits, all stuck together in a single word to make a place.

I stared at her. I was pretty sure that I hadn't existed before I emerged from my mother in some bloody and uncomfortable way she described in only the vaguest of terms. But I wanted to have always been with Anneliese. I wanted to have come from the same place, to belong to the same land. "Was I there?" I looked at the rabbit lying next to me. "Was Lebkuchen?"

She looked at me, her eyes drifting to a world only she could see. "Don't you remember? We lived in a palace with Mutti Hase. The mother of all bunnies. She was the queen. She still is. She's about a million years old. No — a billion. She is the wisest person in the world. She knows the names of all of the dinosaurs and has lived on all of the planets. She can talk to trees and turn herself invisible. She has two other children, Alezia and Nicholas. Do you remember them?"

I closed my eyes. "I remember Alezia's red hair." She began to take shape in my mind, tall and thin. "They were both dancers. Russian dancers."

"Until Nicholas starting drinking too much wine. He could have been so famous but he started putting wine on everything. He even put wine sauce on his vegetables." Anneliese glanced toward the bottles clustered near her family's waste bin. Her father's bottles. "He couldn't balance on his toes anymore."

"But not Alezia," I added quickly, anxious to save one of them.

"Not Alezia."

"There was a Vati Hase, too, wasn't there?"

13

"Yes. Only he died. But not of old age."

My belly tightened as I thought of all the ways I was discovering that daddies could die. "He died of silliness," I offered.

"Yes. He decided to be a soldier but didn't kill anyone, so they killed him."

"It was silly of him to become a soldier." My brother Willi wanted to be a soldier, and the prospect of his absence was gnawing away at me like a hungry rat.

"Your daddy was a soldier."

"I know, that's what I just said."

"No, your real daddy. Your Vienna daddy."

"I know." Like most Austrian men his age, my father had served in the Great War. He'd even received a medal, the Kriegserinnerungsmedaille with crossed swords on the back, reserved for frontline troops or the wounded.

"Aren't you proud of him?"

I shrugged. My father never talked about the war. "I guess. I'd just rather there were no soldiers. None at all." My father made sense only as a creator of music, not as a uniformed killer.

Anneliese bent her neck so our foreheads touched. I could feel the warmth of her breath against my lips, her eyes so close they blurred together. "There are no soldiers in Friedenglückhasenland," she whispered.

14

"No one can get in. The country is surrounded by stone walls and when invaders try to get in the wind just blows their hands off the doorknob."

"There are no cars either," I whispered back. "That way we can run across the streets whenever we want without looking. It's so quiet there you can hear the apples dropping off the trees. We can hear the moles tunneling into the earth. We can even hear the hairs of the rabbits brushing together when they hop." I closed my eyes. I have never wanted to be anywhere as much as I wanted to be in Friedenglückhasenland then. "No one is lazy and everyone walks everywhere."

We lay there, eyes closed, our foreheads pressed so close I felt our skin would grow together. That we could become one girl. "Orly. We have always existed."

■ ■ ■ ■

FIRST MOVEMENT:
VIENNA

■ ■ ■ ■

ONE

In May 1928, the Nazi Party gains twelve seats in Germany's elections.

My parents fell in love when they were still students at the Universität für Musik und darstellende Kunst. While women were unwelcome in the Vienna Philharmonic and in the music world at large, opera required them. For this reason, my mother trained her voice rather than her fingers, even though her fingers had always been rather good at piano.

On a rare warm spring day my father had stopped on the shores of the canal to play to the lilacs, the passing boats, and the birds. My mother, who recognized him as well as the song he played, had paused to add her voice. "I couldn't help it," she told me. "I love that song."

But they can never agree on what he had been playing. She says it was Handel's

19

"Flammende Rose," while he says it was definitely Brahms's "Zwei Gesänge."

"It can't have been," she argued. "I didn't even know 'Zwei Gesänge' then."

"But 'Flammende Rose' wasn't written for viola," he pointed out.

Ultimately, the song didn't matter.

They were so young. They had Willi when my mother was still a girl of seventeen. After that, they figured out how to avoid having another child for a decade.

I was born on Friday, January 13, 1928, the same year Wolpe's satirical opera, *Zeus and Elida,* premiered, the same year the curtain rose on Weill and Brecht's *Die Dreigroschenoper,* and the same year Schoenberg composed *Von heute auf morgen.* Jewish musicians of Europe were busy creating.

It was a happy year for my parents. While their salaries were modest, they had the good fortune of relatives who had chosen more practical careers. My mother's parents were flourishing bakers in a village near Graz. My father's father, an ophthalmologist, owned our three-story apartment building on Seegasse. My grandparents spent the early years of their own marriage in what would become our apartment, but once their children were grown they moved a block away to a smaller apartment on

Pramergasse, over my grandfather's practice. Anneliese's family lived directly above us on Seegasse, the rooms of their apartment mirroring ours. On the top floor were the Windens, an elderly couple with no children who often invited Anneliese and me in for cake or a strudel. It was a quiet building, except for us.

Anneliese and I were the laces that tied our two families together, though our parents had never been close. Her banker father's mind was occupied with figures and balance sheets while my father's preoccupations rarely ventured beyond the body of his viola, of the orchestra. My mother, whose concerns were with cavatina, recitative, and cabaletta, had no shared vocabulary with Ana's mother. Once in a while they happened upon a shared enthusiasm for a pastry recipe, but beyond that they regarded each other warily across the borders of our doorsills.

As children, neither of us thought much about money, the privilege of having enough not to have to think about it. A privilege, like so many others, that I failed to appreciate until it was lost.

My very first memory is a sound: the long shimmer of my father's bow across the strings, the upward flight of my mother's voice, filling the air of our apartment in 4 Seegasse as I lay on the living room floor, drawing.

My second memory is tactile. When I was old enough to stay silent and still, my father took me to the Musikverein before one of his rehearsals with the Vienna Philharmonic. My mother must have been there, too, or my nanny, Stefi, to whisk me away when the musicians finished tuning their instruments, but I don't remember anyone except my father, who hoisted me into the air, his hand over mine as he pressed my fingers against the belly of one of the golden women whose heads propped up the first balcony. The long sides of the rectangular room were lined with these figures growing out of pillars, their arms folded across their ribs, their cone-shaped breasts pointed toward the ceiling. A pianist and a cellist were warming up onstage, and under my fingers I could feel the women tremble along with the notes, the oscillations of the music. "Wood vibrates with sound," my father explained. "Almost everything here is wood, even the parts painted to look like stone."

"Or gold," I whispered, stroking the shuddering belly.

"Or gold," he agreed, lowering me to the ground.

I looked around me at all of the gold that was not gold, the stone that was not stone, the seemingly stable floor that hid a trap door. Even the organ was fake, my father had told me, created to disguise a series of changing organs installed behind its façade.

"Isn't there anything here that is real?"

My father laughed, but low, so only I could hear him. "Only one thing in this building is real, Liebling: the music. All else is deception."

That room was the Golden Hall, the jewel box where my father became part of a larger instrument, a larger organism: the Philharmonic itself.

My third memory was my brother Willi's fault. He was the one who taught me to whistle, neglecting to mention to me the prohibition of the practice within the hallowed Musikverein. I had thought I was making music, that my lips were an instrument I was learning to play, so I was shocked at the pressure of my father's fingers on my arm, the force with which he marched me to the closest exit and literally tossed me through the doors onto the street. "Nie! *Never in here.*"

Willi claimed he hadn't known. "I thought

23

it was just for theaters," he said of the superstition. Because backstage workers often used coded whistles to send messages to each other during scene changes, a whistling actor could cause the premature lowering of a set. "But concerts don't have sets."

When I was older, I learned that for many years there had been gaslights in the Musikverein and other concert halls. If a flame flickered out, leaving behind a lethal stream of gas, it made a whistling sound, signaling danger.

"Whistling causes evil things to happen," my father explained flatly. "It curses us."

There were times, even years later, I would wonder if it had been my whistling that caused it all.

Two

In 1933, Hitler is appointed chancellor of Germany. The Dachau concentration camp is established near Munich.

December 21, 1933
When I was nearly six, my parents decided I was finally old enough to attend the opera. I wasn't yet old enough to begin school, but for my parents, music was more essential than words or numbers. Ever since I had learned how to speak, ever since I had first understood what it was my parents did for a living, I had wanted to see them onstage. Opera stories — tragic though most of them are — had been my bedtime reading, alongside stories from Greek mythology and the Brothers Grimm.

Why she chose Meyerbeer's *Les Huguenots* I will never know. It's not a very festive opera. Something light and funny — *The Bartered Bride* or *The Abduction from the*

Seraglio, for example — might have better suited a child's sensibilities. Perhaps it was simply to hear Rose Merker singing Valentine or Marie Gerhart singing Marguerite, though neither was her favorite. Perhaps that is just what happened to be on the day she decided to take me.

Or perhaps it was intended as an early warning: the god you choose to worship could get you killed.

My opera dress, pale blue with white lace along the hem and at the edges of the sleeves, made me feel grown-up. My mother brushed my hair until its pale, coppery strands shone like a one-schilling coin and gathered it up on top of my head. Her hair was curlier and darker than mine, glossy like the horse chestnuts we found on the ground in early September. She twisted my hair like hers, and even dabbed a bit of her lilac perfume on my wrists. "There," she said, stepping back to admire her work. "Pretty as a china doll."

I twirled, watching my skirt catch the air. "As pretty as you?" My mother looked glamorous in her floor-length, cream-colored silk gown. Embroidered leaves and flowers in the same color spilled down the bodice and over the curve of her hips.

"Prettier!"

This was not possible. No one was as beautiful as my mother.

The opera house was even grander than the Musikverein. I was so busy staring around me that I tripped going up the stairs and my mother had to catch my arm. Above us, tucked into the corners near the ceiling, were statues of children clutching instruments or theater masks, gazing down on us as we ascended. Dozens of chandeliers dangled from the ceilings like upside-down fountains.

"There's Meyerbeer," my mother said, pointing to one of the busts carved into the top of one of the walls. "Who wrote this opera. And there's Mahler." She nudged me toward a black marble head perched on a pedestal in front of a mirror.

"Shouldn't he have combed his hair before he let someone carve him into a statue?" My question was sincere: Mahler's hair looked lumpy and long.

My mother laughed. "We don't love him for his hair," she chided.

"Do we love him because he's Jewish?"

"We love him for the same reason we love everyone in this building. We love him for his music."

27

Just as in the Musikverein, everything in the opera house was gilded. Music for me was always associated with elegance, gold, and crystal.

My mother had gotten us seats on the left side of the second balcony so that we could look down at our fellow operagoers filing into their seats. I leaned over the railing staring at the ladies' dresses and furs until my mother told me to look up. From the middle of the ceiling was suspended the largest chandelier I had ever seen. I wasn't struck so much by its beauty — it looked like a gigantic shiny pastry — as by its mass.

"It weighs eleven tons," my mother said. "Fifteen cows. Or twenty grand pianos."

Gazing at it, I was glad we were not sitting underneath. "How come it doesn't pull down the roof?"

"Well, the roof is even heavier."

All of this was making my chest tight.

"Orly," said my mother, sensing my discomfort, "this building has been standing for a very long time. And it will be standing for a long time more. I promise you, Schatz.

"Now, do you remember the story of *Die Zauberflöte*?" While we waited for the curtain to rise, my mother entertained me with opera stories and bits of gossip about the composer and singers. When she got to *Lo-*

28

hengrin, I made her tell me the story three times. I loved to hear how the knight turned into a swan, how the lady married a man whose name she didn't know. It all seemed very romantic and mysterious, except for the end. Insatiably curious, I found it maddening that the women of opera, of legend, of myth, were so often forbidden to ask questions of their men, and punished when they did. Psyche, not allowed to see the face of her beloved. Elsa, not allowed to know even the name of her husband, Lohengrin. How terrifying it must have been to marry someone you didn't know. "I'm going to marry Anneliese," I announced to my mother. "She lets me ask her questions. And I already know who she is."

My mother laughed and squeezed my hand. "What a silly duckling you are." The lights dimmed, and I pulled my spine up as straight as I could and firmly crossed my ankles, locking my feet together to keep them from mischief.

There was no chance of me squirming during *Les Huguenots.* Stunned by the heady mixture of music and violence, I sat like a stone. I didn't cough, I didn't swallow, I didn't change the crossing of my ankles. (Later, when I undressed for bed, I would notice an indentation remained on

29

the top of my right foot, so hard had I pressed it into the buckle of my left shoe.) I imprisoned my mother's hand in mine.

I had thought, somehow, that music was meant to tell only beautiful stories, love stories. But here was a story in which every single character was murdered, in which a father murdered his own daughter. I felt sorry for both the Catholics and Protestants — even though it was mostly the Protestants who got killed — because they were not allowed to fall in love with each other.

During the interval, I shook out my stiff legs as we walked to the lobby bar. My mother ordered me an apfelspritz and herself a glass of champagne, which she explained was a grown-up version of the same drink. I looked longingly at the cakes, but my mother said we could go to a café afterward. As she was paying, a woman with long, glittering earrings and a spiraling tower of fair hair touched her elbow. "Julia? I thought it was you!"

My mother turned to greet the woman, introducing her as a singer she knew from work, but I failed to catch her name. I was distracted by another woman — was it a woman? — just behind her. Dressed in what looked like a man's tuxedo, she had combed her short, dark hair straight back. Instead of tipping her weight into one hip or wobbling on heels, she stood with her legs a foot apart, comfortable like a man. When she saw me staring, she smiled.

"I'm Odiane," she said, her voice warm and low as she offered me her hand.

I took her dry fingers in my damp ones. "Are you a girl?"

Odiane laughed, but my mother reached for my elbow and pinched it. "Orly! That's not polite. Odiane, please forgive my daughter." She turned back to me. "Odiane is a pianist. And a composer."

"Pleased to meet you." I curtsied, hoping it might make up for my rudeness. I didn't know that girls could dress like that. I didn't know that women could stand that way.

The bell chimed while we were still drinking, and we had to finish quickly before the lights went down. I wanted to follow Odiane back to her seat, but she and the blond woman quickly disappeared in the throng.

"Mutti, how do you know her?"

"I told you. From work. She's a mezzo."

"No, Odiane."

"Ah." My mother glanced down at the program in her lap. "She lives with Ilse."

"They're sisters?"

"More like roommates, I think."

I thought about this. I wondered if Anne-

31

liese and I could be roommates. "Why does she dress like that? Odiane, I mean?"

"Some women like to wear trousers. Even the First Lady in the United States sometimes wears trousers. And Marlene Dietrich, the film star. Though I don't recommend that you start. Frau Fessler would not approve."

"Do you think Odiane wears trousers all the time? Are there girls who do that?"

My mother took my hand. "Erdnuss, you'll find a bit later in life that there are all kinds of girls."

"Listen to her," my mother said, rapt, when Rose Merker was onstage. "Just listen."

But I could not absorb anything other than the massacre unfolding before me. Near the end of the opera, three of the characters sang about their visions of heaven. Which sounded nice. But then at the very end, the soldiers were all shouting: "God wants blood!"

By the final act, my right foot was asleep and I had to limp out of the opera house. The sky was a painting, smudged blue and black on one of the longest nights of the year. I was grateful to be outside, away from the sadness still ringing in my ears, despite the frigid air that numbed them. The shops and cafés around the plaza radiated light and life, letting out bursts of cinnamon- and chocolate-scented air every time a door opened.

It was a treat to be allowed out so late. Elegant women in long gowns swept past us, on their way to assignations at the Café Sacher or the Imperial Hotel. I looked around for Odiane and Ilse, but they had vanished. Men in long, dark coats began emerging from the back of the opera, carrying instrument cases. My mother wrapped her scarf twice around her neck. Vocal cords worked best when they were kept warm.

"What do you think angels look like?" I asked my mother, my mind adrift in a kind of fugue state. "I think they look like that woman in the blue coat, with the furry hat."

My mother looked where I was pointing. "Angels have such expensive tastes?" She smiled. "I don't know if I believe in angels. For that matter, I am not so sure I believe in heaven."

"But everyone believes in heaven." So many of the Catholic children in our neighborhood, on the playgrounds, referred to heaven as if it were the country next door. Anneliese believed in heaven.

"Not Jews," said my mother firmly. "Jews don't believe in heaven."

"We don't?" I thought about this. "So what happens when we die?"

My mother turned to me then and crouched down to hug me, even though it meant that her dress dragged on the ground. "Liebling. What do you say to some hot chocolate?"

"At Café Sacher?" Visions of that chocolate cake were already dancing in my mind. I was easily distracted.

"What about Café Sperl?" Café Sperl was one of the oldest in Vienna and my mother's favorite. She liked the fact that the waiters still wore the same suits they wore when she was a child, that the café still had the same marble tables, the same crystal chandeliers. She started going there when she was small, because it was close to the Theater an der Wien, where her parents would take her to performances.

I hesitated. It was a long walk to Café Sperl. "Come on, we'll take a taxi," said my mother, smiling.

As soon as one of the familiar, tuxedoed waiters had greeted my mother and settled us on one of the soft, embroidered banquettes, I returned to my preoccupations. "Do you really not believe in heaven, Mutti?"

"I think maybe I am afraid to believe in

34

heaven, because then I will have to believe in hell." She turned her face from me, as if checking to see who could overhear us, the glow of a chandelier turning strands of her hair into a rosy dawn. The elderly couple to our left continued to dig into their strudels, and the table on our right was vacant.

"Do no Jews believe in it?"

Her eyes found mine again, their dark centers reflecting my pale face. "I'm sure many Jews do believe in a kind of afterlife. But your father and I are focused on the life we are in. Because no one knows what happens after this one. So why not think about what we have?"

"But what if we are wrong and there is a heaven and hell?" I stroked my fingers across the cool marble of the tabletop.

"Then we are wrong. But as long as we do our best in this life, we don't have anything to worry about." She picked up a menu and glanced at it, though she must have known it by heart. "Now, Topfenstrudel?"

I nodded, accepting the change of topic. Topfenstrudel, with its layers of pastry and soft cheese dotted with raisins, was one of my favorites. We never had Topfenstrudel at home; it was too tricky to make. The emperor's cook once said that you have to stretch the dough so thin you can read a love letter through it, and my mother didn't have that kind of patience.

Because she was in a generous mood and I was, after all, about to turn six, my mother let me take three small spoonfuls of the whipped cream on the top of her Franziskaner and dab it into my hot chocolate. "Would you like to go hear your father play one day this week?" she asked, as if this were not a rhetorical question.

"Oh, Mutti!" I sat up straighter than ever before. "And you too? The next time?"

"The very next time."

It wasn't until my mother had finished her Franziskaner and I was halfway through the strudel did I remember, with a tight feeling in my chest, the very end of the opera. "Is it true what the soldiers in the opera said about God?"

My mother looked up from the newspaper she had gone to fetch from the selection spread out on the table by the door, her brow creased. "Is what true?"

"That God wants blood."

My mother pushed the paper aside, almost as if she were angry with it. "Meine liebste kleine. What kind of god would that be? If there is a god, Orly, he would want nothing but peace. We have had enough of war.

Now, no more religion talk. It's bad for the soul."

Anneliese was at our door the next morning, wrapped up in her red woolen coat and hat, before I had finished getting dressed. "Did you really go? Did you see the whole thing? Were the singers very good? Were they as good as your mother?" Anneliese had never seen my mother perform — even I hadn't yet seen her — but she loved when my mother sang us "My Gorilla Has a Villa at the Zoo" as we walked to the park or when we finished our homework. My mother sang all the time, even when she wasn't singing opera.

"Close the door, you're letting the cold hallway air in!" I was still on the floor, lacing my boots. Ana stepped into the apartment, pulling the door shut behind her. "It was magical and scary and I got to go to Café Sperl after, in the middle of the night. I wish you could have come!" Anneliese's parents didn't let her stay out late at night.

"Me too." Ana sat down next to me, pulling her knees into her chest.

"When my Mutti sings, then you can come to see her, can't you?"

"Maybe."

I finished lacing my boots and stood up.

"Don't forget your bunny!" Stefi emerged from the kitchen to pass me Lebkuchen soft and cinnamon-brown like the cookies he was named after. She was taking us to the Riesenrad. "And your hat."

"I don't need a hat! I'm never cold!"

"Me, too, I never get cold!" Anneliese echoed, leaping up and twirling in the hall. "Even when we're sledding or skating and having snowball fights and —"

"I don't care if neither of you ever gets cold, you're wearing hats or we don't go. Come on, get moving, both of you." Stefi handed me my scratchy wool hat and pulled on her coat.

I grabbed Ana's arm and dragged her out the door. Not until we got down to the street and had raced ahead of Stefi did I tell her the most interesting thing I had discovered.

"Ana, I met a woman last night who was dressed as a man."

"You mean in trousers? Lots of women wear trousers now." She skipped ahead of me.

"No, not just trousers, she was all dressed up, in a tuxedo. And she had short hair." I jogged to keep up. Stefi was a whole block behind us, calling our names.

"Really? Did she really look like a man?"

I considered this. "You could tell she was a woman. She was pretty, but in a different way." I didn't know how to express the way Odiane had carried herself, the way she walked and talked as if she had every right to be like she was. "She lives with a singer who works with my mother."

"Was the singer dressed in a tuxedo too?"

"No. She had long blond hair up on her head and a green dress. My mother said they were roommates."

"Maybe they didn't have a man to go with so they were pretending to be married."

"Maybe. But they live together."

"Maybe they are married!"

"Can girls marry girls?"

"I don't know." Anneliese took my mittened hand in hers and we stopped to allow Stefi to catch up. "But if they can, I'm marrying you."

I laughed, my boots slipping over the snow. "That's what I told my mother. Will you wear the tuxedo or shall I?"

THREE

In February 1934, members of the Social Democratic Workers' Party rebel against Austria's Fascist regime. Four days of violent clashes end with the deaths of several hundred and the dissolution of all political parties other than the Patriotic Front.

During the four days of conflict and general strikes of February 1934, we had no school and my parents made us stay inside. Police were attacking the workers, they told us. It wasn't safe on the streets. Willi sprawled on the sofa with a book, sulking, as my parents had also forbidden him to join the socialist paramilitary Schutzbund to fight against the right-wing Heimwehr.

While my parents were theoretically socialists, they had little time for political activism. I think they thought that music somehow protected them from politics, that as artists they were beyond earthly concerns. But Willi was fourteen, full of unspent passion and idealism. He and my Viennese grandmother were the fiercest socialists in our family, though all of my relatives were staunchly anti-Fascist. Willi closely followed Hitler's rise in Germany and was perhaps the only one of us with foresight enough to worry.

Anneliese and I sat on the carpet with our rabbits, Marmalade and Lebkuchen, quarreling about which one of them was going to be the socialist and which the police officer.

"They should both be socialists." We looked up in surprise. Willi didn't often join in our games. "They should join forces to fight against the foxes." He returned to his book.

Anneliese and I glanced at each other, unsure whether to tolerate this intrusion.

"We don't have foxes. There is no one for them to fight against," I pointed out.

Willi heaved himself off the sofa and disappeared into his room. A moment later he dumped a cardboard box in front of us, spilling leaden soldiers onto the floor. "Here you go. Heimwehr for you."

Anneliese looked at them all, her dark eyebrows raised. "We need more socialists."

She ran up to her apartment to gather all the rest of her stuffed animals. I raced to my room to collect the rag doll I had been given at birth, a china-headed doll with a cloth body, and one stiff porcelain doll too pretty to be any fun.

Willi settled back onto the sofa with his book, but after a few minutes he threw it aside. "I mean no insult to Mahler, but if I have to hear that Adagietto one more time I am going to lose my will to live." He stood and walked to the window.

"He's practicing." It would never have occurred to me to criticize my father for playing. While the strikes had kept them from going to work, neither of my parents neglected their practice. I thought the Adagietto was pretty. It made me think faraway thoughts, as if it were stretching what I knew about the world toward the horizon.

"I know he's *practicing,* Peanut. I just wonder if there's something more important he could be working on."

"I don't understand."

"Of course you don't. Never mind, Erdnuss. Oh, I feel like a trapped animal!" He began circling the room, swinging his arms wildly.

Anneliese chose that moment to come crashing back through our front door, arms full of plush socialists, and I returned to the welcome distraction of our game.

Predictably, the socialist herbivores won the battle and dragged their captive soldiers off to Friedenglückhasenland. There, the soldiers drank too much wine with Nicholas, chased each other with knives, and fell in love with wood nymphs, who escaped their advances by turning into trees. The queen turned the men into women and outlawed soldiers.

When my mother came home from rehearsing a duet from *Giuditta* with a fellow singer who lived nearby, she looked pale and strained. The soldiers we'd been playing with lay strewn about the carpet, surrounded by knives I had taken from the kitchen when Stefi wasn't looking. "What are you playing?" she asked in surprise.

"Opera," I said, as if that should be obvious.

Willi paused in his pacing of the room. "I thought it was politics."

My mother unwound the scarf from her neck and began tugging off her gloves, one finger at a time. "The difference between the two is increasingly negligible."

FOUR

After the death of German president Paul von Hindenburg in 1934, Hitler merges the roles of chancellor and president and declares himself Führer, immune to all laws.

Stefi, a blue-eyed nineteen-year-old girl from Lutzmannsburg, was in many ways a third parent to me. She was given the worst of the jobs: toilet training, mashing my early foods, and wiping jam and egg yolk from my face. By looking after our basic needs, she freed my parents to focus on teaching me to read music and books. My room was off the kitchen, next to Stefi's, so that if I woke in the middle of the night I wouldn't have to disturb my parents. Sleep, my mother told me, was essential for vocal quality and for steady hands. When my mother was singing out of town, Stefi took over parenting entirely. Several times during my earliest years my mother was away for months, singing roles at the Oper Köln, Hamburgische Staatsoper, and Berlin's Städtische Oper. Once she sang in Paris. I always wanted to go with her, but she told me it wouldn't be any fun for me because she would be working.

I never did get to see Paris.

When my mother went away, she always brought me back a memento. Sometimes it was an ordinary gift, like a fancy postage stamp or a book of opera stories, but sometimes it was something more unusual, like a piece of chipped crystal from a chandelier at the Paris Opéra that was being replaced, or a silk rose from the set of *Arabella* in Dresden. I liked these best, because no one else had them and they were secretly famous, having been seen by thousands of people. Even more, I loved them because they meant my mother had been thinking of me while she was working.

Stefi was off on September 3, 1934, the eve of my first day of school. My parents had sent me to bed early, and a new dress was laid out on the armchair by the door. I was looking forward to school, and to showing off that I already knew how to read. Perhaps I would have been more nervous had I not known that Anneliese was to be in the same class. With Anneliese, I was never afraid. Still, my heart was beating too fast for sleep, and my mother had left my door — which Stefi usually shut — wide open.

"What bothers me most," I heard my father saying to my mother in the kitchen, where they sat at the table drinking their after-dinner coffees, "is that they don't even seem to be trying to hide it."

"But it's illegal."

"I know it is, Julia. That doesn't stop them from joining." I heard the strike of a match and the sizzle as the flame met the tobacco of my father's pipe. "Don't think there aren't plenty of singers in the party as well."

"But I don't know any. I can't imagine — Do they talk in front of you?"

"There are few secrets in the orchestra, Liebling. They're in the air. We can hear them in between the notes."

"Seriously, Jakob." My mother's spoon clattered into her saucer.

"I am serious. I can hear them in the trumpeting of Helmut Wobisch."

There was silence for a long moment. I tried to imagine my mother's face. "You've suspected him for a while."

"And I've been right. I just wish it were only him."

"How many do you think there are?"

Another silence. A long exhale. "Eleven? More? Hard to say exactly. Wilhelm Jerger's been in the party for years."

"Are you in danger?"

"It's hardly a secret what I am. Wouldn't they have done something about me already?"

More silence.

"If they *do something* about the Jews in this country, they'll have no music left." My mother's voice had turned bitter. "Even *Walter* is a Jew! Can they seriously eradicate him?" Bruno Walter often conducted the Philharmonic. I had met him several times when my father took me to the Musikverein.

"I don't think anyone's saying anything about *eradication.*"

"They are across the border. Have you even looked at a paper?"

I heard the legs of my father's heavy chair scrape across the kitchen floor as he pushed it back to stand. "I don't have time to read the papers."

It was my mother's turn to sigh. "You know, Jakob, if you had been on the *Titanic,* I think you would have been the last one to set down his bow." But there was a smile in her voice.

My father laughed. "I wouldn't have set it down at all. The Rahab would have had to take me playing." The Rahab, I knew from my father's bedtime stories, was a demon of the sea. It was this demon the God of the Torah had to crush in order to separate land from water.

"The Rahab might take you yet, if you don't take seriously what's happening around you. Around all of us."

"You can't think that that horrid little man is a real danger to Austria."

"I don't know what to think, Jakob. The things I heard when I was in Germany . . ."

"It's true that you probably won't be getting any work in Germany anymore. Not with —"

"I know that. That's what I'm trying to say —"

"So what do you want us to do? Just pack up and leave? Julia, Schatz, you're rehearsing a solo show of Lieder at last, and you want to leave? What about our parents, would we take them? Thekla? Klothilde? We need time to think. Besides, they can't get rid of all of us. *They can't.* Imagine what that would do to our sound."

"You think Hitler cares about our *sound*? Jakob, I don't *want* to do anything but continue our lives. But I'm not thinking

48

about what we *want* to do." I imagined them staring at each other over the table, their words failing.

"Please, darling, no decisions tonight." My father's voice was weary. "We've got time to think about all of this. I promise I'll read the newspaper on Sundays if it will make you happy."

There was the rattle of china cups against the sink, and then nothing but their footsteps as they retreated to their room.

I pulled the quilt over my head and curled around my rabbit Lebkuchen, trying to make sense of my parents' words. Was my mother right, would Hitler try to come here? Did my father work with people who might endanger him somehow? I was confused. I wished Anneliese were here, or Stefi. Someone to reassure me. Apparently there was more to worry about in the world than impressing the other students with my ability to sound out words.

Friedenglückhasenland. I whispered the word out loud. That's where I needed to go.

FIVE

On September 15, 1935, Hitler announces the Nuremberg Laws, which strip German Jews of their citizenship and prohibit relationships between Jews and other Germans.

On September 26, 1935, Klaus Barbie joins the SS.

There was only one year Anneliese and I were not in the same class at Volksschule. Our teachers separated us in our second year, when we were seven, in the vain hope that we would make other friends. It wasn't healthy to have just one friend, our teacher Frau Fessler told us. "It takes many poles to hold up a tent."

Anneliese stifled a snort. "We're a tent?" she whispered, kicking me under my desk. "I always thought of us more as a castle."

She and I started school on the same day

and in our first year we shared a table, our pencils, and our books. When the teacher wasn't looking, one of us would draw the head of a bunny and then fold the paper down so the other couldn't see it. Without looking at the head, the second person drew the bunny's stomach, and then the first person drew its legs and feet. Sheets and sheets of folded paper bunnies, hatted or crowned, dressed in finery or swimsuits, holding baskets or flowers, piled up on our table. Everything I did — every math problem, every verb conjugation, every recitation of history — I showed to Anneliese for her approval before turning it in. Her opinion mattered so much more than the teacher's.

Frau Fessler was not the only person irritated by our constant togetherness. Heinrich Müller, a thuggish little boy with fair hair and fat cheeks who went to the boys' school nearby, often stalked after us on our way to school, delighting in interrupting our games. There have always been bullies, after all, even before they started wearing the official badges of the SS. Heinrich threw rocks into our marble games and stole the pictures we drew. He yanked out strands of my bright hair yelling, "Look, Orly's on fire!" One morning on the sidewalk outside the school gates, he emptied a bucket of water on the chalk map of Friedenglückhasenland we'd been sketching on the pavement. Furious, and without thinking about the repercussions, I stood up and slapped his fat face, as hard as I could. "What is *wrong* with you?" I shouted at him. "Why can't you just leave us alone?"

He stood there for a moment, his pink face growing pinker, stunned that a girl had had the audacity to hit him. I could tell he was tempted to hit me back, but he was too clever. He knew he would get in just as much trouble as I would, if not more. "Because you're a Büchsenmasseuse." He hurled the word at us as if it could pierce our intimacy.

I couldn't move. The word slipped around in my brain; I couldn't grasp it. It had something to do with us, with our bodies, with how we were together, but I wasn't sure how it was meant to wound.

This time it was Anneliese who hit him. "And you're nothing but a Bürger von Krokodilland!"

I turned to her, astonished. "He's a *what*?"

At that moment, Frau Fessler appeared at the gate to drag us both away by the arms.

It didn't surprise me that Anneliese would

strike a boy. After all, she had learned punishment young. The previous summer, when my family took us out of Vienna to Zell am See, she swam with something over her suit, a blouse or even a dress. I teased her for this — I cringe when I remember it, but it's true — prancing around her in my skimpy suit, trying to pull the blouse from her shoulders. As she twisted away from me, I glimpsed the raised stripes of angry pink welts underneath. "Ana?" I had started, unsure of what they were.

She wrapped her arms around her rib cage. "Doesn't your father hit you?"

Mute, I shook my head. I knew that many fathers hit their children. Even some mothers. But I'd never seen such scars on someone my age.

Anneliese squinted into the sun. "They'll get better."

I couldn't think of what to say. "But why? Why does he do it?"

She shrugged her small bony shoulders and looked away. "I don't listen?"

That night while she slept next to me I lifted her nightdress to kiss that blameless flesh of her back, my lips barely brushing her skin. How soft and small she was. Letting her nightdress fall, I curled beside her like a sentry, careful not to press too close against her wounds.

Later on the afternoon that Anneliese and I smacked Heinrich, after Anneliese's father had taken a belt to her again and my mother had told me I would be going to bed without stories for a whole week, we sat at my kitchen table drawing on the backs of sheet music my father no longer needed. "I think my father might be from Krokodilland," she said in a low voice so Stefi wouldn't over-hear.

When I thought of Anneliese's father, a fat banker whose only role in the household other than funding it seemed to be to mete out punishment, I felt like throwing up. I wished I were brave enough to slap *his* face. I had given Anneliese my pillow to sit on, feeling very grateful that my father didn't hit me.

"What's Krokodilland?" The question had been burning a hole in my tongue.

She looked up. "You know. The country next to Friedenglückhasenland. The one with all the mean people. The Krokodills. I figured I couldn't get in trouble for calling Heinrich a citizen of Krokodilland. We're the only ones who know what it means."

"Oh, I know, I remember. The country that doesn't have any trees." I leaned for-ward and trapped one of Anneliese's feet between mine, anxious to contribute. Friedenglückhasenland was circular, a belt of a country with a hole in the middle. A vast sea filled that hole, and three large islands. But surrounding it all, I reminded her, was Krokodilland. "The Krokodills always want to start wars against Friedenglückhasenland."

"But Friedenglückhasenland refuses to fight. It has never fought a war."

"Because the bunnies would rather pick cherries." I plucked another from the bowl between us.

"Or learn ballet steps."

"Or go ice-skating."

"It has magical protections, because the Krokodills are always trying to get in."

"Everyone wants to get in."

"Yes, because in Krokodilland people eat nothing but lederhosen." She smiled at me, her teeth stained pink by the cherries we were eating. My mother had said no sweets before dinner, but Stefi whispered to us that we weren't really breaking a rule because the cherries were sour.

"And the children never get to celebrate their birthdays."

"And it is against the law to celebrate holidays or have a peaceful time together."

"Where there are no vegetables. All there

55

is to eat are stinging nettles that tear at your throat when you swallow and burn forever."

"And all of the animals are poisonous."

"Even the humans!"

"Yes, especially the humans."

We grinned at each other, and spit the pits of our cherries into the bowl between us.

The following year, the school separated us.

The distance between our second-year classrooms infuriated me. I did my work but refused the advances of the other children, only interacting with them when it was strictly required. No matter how many times the teacher spoke to my parents, I remained on the periphery of my classroom.

At every recess, Anneliese and I raced each other to the playground to meet by the swings. Pushing our toes in the dirt, we told each other stories of our life elsewhere, our adventures in a country where rabbits nibbled pomegranate seeds at the movies and solved arguments with poetry contests or football matches.

In the mornings, I slipped new pages of our story into her school satchel where it hung on a hook outside of her classroom. Friedenglückhasenland was part of a nearby planet called Rose of Erta, I wrote. Its allies included the countries of Katzenland, Stein-

56

land, and Hamsterhimmel. These were those three islands inhabiting its inner sea.

The next morning there would be a new page slipped into my own satchel. "In Katzenland everything is made from apples," Anneliese wrote. "There is apple tea and apple cookies and roasted apples and apple juice. All of the music is created from sounds that apples make falling, which is the most beautiful sound in the world."

At the bottom of the page was an addendum: "P.S. — In all of Rose of Erta there is no Herr Kahn to slam his ruler down on your desk when you are trying to read something far more interesting than he is."

When I was separated from Anneliese, I resolutely refused to be happy. My mother had always said I was a stubborn child. When I was eighteen months old, she says, she took me with her to the post office to send a few letters and a parcel to her aunt in Graz. The postal clerk, apparently feeling festive, held out a tin of cookies to me, gingery Lebkuchen baked for Christmas. Clearly, this man had never had children, or he would have known better than to hold out an entire tin of Lebkuchen in front of a toddler. Despite my mother's admonition to take just one, I reached in and grabbed a fistful. Furious and embarrassed, my mother ordered me to put them back. But the harder she tried to pry them from my fingers, the more tightly I clutched them, until they crumbled into a damp dust in my hand. If I couldn't have them, no one would.

The postman was apparently unusually forgiving of my rudeness, but my mother never forgot that particular incident, reminding me of it every time I resisted a parental command.

Whenever I felt angry with my mother, I reminded myself that I came from somewhere else. I convinced myself that I had formed in Friedenglückhasenland. Anneliese and I agreed we had shared the womb of Mutti Hase, been born together, and lived in her palace for many years. We had only been born to separate mothers in Austria by some clerical error. "But it doesn't matter," Anneliese said. "Because we landed in the same building."

I wasn't cross with my mother very often. My mother was everything beautiful and good in the world. She smelled like lilacs and lemons. Her voice sent delicious shivers across my skin, even when she was singing something as simple as Brahms's "Wiegenlied."

When I explained to my mother that even though I first existed in Friedenglückhasenland, I eventually chose to be born a second time in Vienna, she smiled.

"Why Vienna?"

The answer was obvious. "You were here."

"Erdnuss," she said. "I'm honored. Of all the mothers you could have chosen."

The following year the school gave up keeping us apart. "You'd think you're Ianthe and Iphis, you two," my mother said, half exasperated, half amused. It was entertaining to imagine myself as Iphis, a girl brought up disguised as a boy. Her father had sworn to kill her at birth if she wasn't a boy, so her mother had kept her sex a secret. I thought of all the freedoms that granted Iphis — she could wear trousers and walk the streets alone, like my brother Willi. Like Odiane. I wondered if people on the street made fun of Odiane for the way she dressed, or if they just thought she was a boy and left her alone.

When Iphis was very young, she became close to another girl named Ianthe. Like Anneliese and me, they were always together. They studied together and played together and — I liked to think — invented worlds together. Eventually, they fell in love. When they became betrothed, Iphis's mother Telethusa panicked. What would happen on the wedding night when Ianthe realized her love was a woman? She wept in despair, praying to the goddess Isis for rescue. And because two girls cannot be married, the night before the wedding the gods took pity on Iphis and changed her into a boy.

This ending had always bothered me. While I envied the freedom of boys, I didn't want to actually *be* one. I did not want to become hairy and thick, with a scratchy beard. I liked the smooth curves of my face. If Isis was so powerful, why couldn't she just make Ianthe happy that Iphis was a girl? Perhaps Ianthe had fallen in love with Iphis because she sensed her feminine nature, and would be repulsed by her abrupt maleness, by the coarse hairs sprouting on her face. Just as in so many fairy tales, we never got to find out what happened after that marriage. This was a serious flaw. Think of all of the things that could go wrong with a marriage! What if you discovered you had married a man who would hit his own daughter?

SIX

In July 1936, Hitler orders mass arrests of Jehovah's Witnesses and Roma. The SS establishes the Sachsenhausen concentration camp near Berlin.

The first time I heard my mother sing, I took Anneliese with me.

My grandparents chaperoned us that day in December 1936. My father's father didn't often make it to the opera, overwhelmed as he was with his work. He was a remote man, though not unkind, and often let us sit in the big chair in his office and look through different types of lenses. My cousins and I would compete to see who could read the tiniest words on his eye charts, without magnification. I usually won, though possibly because I sneaked in to memorize the charts when no one was around.

Willi also joined us that night at the opera.

61

My grandmother preferred him over me because he was an enthusiastic participant in her political salons, while I would get bored and end up daydreaming under the chairs with Lebkuchen. Every other week she invited a select group of friends to discuss both literature and politics. When the Social Democratic Workers' Party was outlawed in the wake of the 1934 rebellion, she had been incensed. "What kind of future can there be for a country that doesn't allow pluralism?" she raged to my brother. "We're going to end up like Germany." She and Willi helped the Kultusgemeinde to settle German Jewish refugees in Vienna in 1935, after new German laws took away their citizenship. It was my grandmother's fault Willi was always threatening to join the resistance — any resistance group that talked of standing up to the regime, to Hitler. It frightened my mother.

When I tried to talk with my grandmother about things that mattered to me, like stories and animals, she grew impatient. "I don't have time for these frivolities," she'd say crossly. "You need to pay attention to the world. Important things are going on."

Fortunately, in our family opera was not considered frivolity.

Sitting between Willi and Anneliese, I was

overcome with contentment. Willi bent over his book — something in French I could not decipher — as we sat waiting. Anneliese and I leaned our heads together over the program. She always smelled like celery, as if she had just come from making soup. Almost everyone I needed was in this building. Only my father was missing, but that was often the case. When my mother was performing, he was also at work.

Slowly, the lights faded. The curtains drew apart, revealing the inner courtyard of a palace and the vicious, gossip-singing maids. The dissonance of the opening chords startled me, flooding my veins with fear. Notes and voices scraped at me, strummed my nerves. I pulled Ana's hand into my lap and pressed it between mine.

"Wo bleibt Elektra?" a servant began, her voice soaring over me. *Where is Elektra?* The others paused in their scrubbing of floors, their beating of laundry, to lacerate their mistress with song.

My mother sang Chrysothemis, Elektra's gentler, pragmatic sister. She was the only one in the opera whose heart did not bend to murder, my mother said.

"Ich kann nicht sitzen und ins Dunkel starren wie du." *I cannot sit and stare into the darkness like you,* sang my shimmering,

63

shivering mother to her Elektra. "Ich hab's wie Feuer in der Brust." *In my breast there is a burning fire.*

I had heard my mother's voice before, nearly every day of my life, but never like this. I had never heard it expand to fill a space so vast, soar to the highest of the balconies. Anneliese tugged her hand free of mine so she could lean forward into the sound. *That is my mother!* I wanted to stand up and cry to everyone around me.

"Eh' ich sterbe, will ich auch leben!" she sang. *Before I die, I also want to live!*

When the lights came up for the interval, I felt I had been blasted back into my seat. This opera was not so much music as a summoning. A calling forth of the fiercest of human emotions from the pit of my belly. I sat there, unmoving, until a line of opera-goers stood to our right, waiting for us to rise so they could get to the aisle. "Come, Peanut." Willi took my arm and hauled me to my feet. "You too, Ana. Clear the way!" Slowly, our bodies cramped from sitting, we joined the crowd.

My grandparents ran into friends in the lobby and stayed there to chat, while we headed to the bar for a snack. The café was at least half the reason I'd looked forward to going to the opera. Anneliese was unusually quiet, even when Willi braved the line to fetch us hot chocolate and a slice of Himbeerschnitten. We stood by the window of the salon, gazing out at the gilding of our city by the early evening sun, as we licked raspberries and cream from our forks. "Ana," said Willi, smiling at her, "has the opera put you into a trance?"

She shook her head. "It's just . . ." She looked away from us. "I wish my mother . . ."

I knew what she wanted to say. And I wanted to say to her then that I had often envied her for having a mother who was home every evening to tuck her into bed, who made her cakes in the afternoons, who never traveled outside of the city except to go to a lake in the summers. My parents worked all summer, performing and teaching at festivals across Germany and Austria. The Vienna Philharmonic closed for the summer because the concert hall was too hot. The windows could not be opened, as street noise interfered with the music. In the winter, it was often too cold, but the orchestra sent for soldiers to run around the place, panting and sweating in the Golden Hall until it warmed a degree or two.

But that night, I didn't envy Anneliese her

mother. So I said the next best thing.

"But Anneliese, your mother in Frie-denglückhasenland — our mother — she sings too." I passed her the fork we were sharing.

The shadow of a smile crept across Anneliese's face, but she didn't join in like she usually did. "You're so lucky, Orly," she said quietly. "You don't even know how lucky you are." She took a bite of torte and sucked on the tines of our fork.

"Oh, but we do!" Willi said gaily. "We have you, Anneliese, to tell us stories! We are the most fortunate people on earth." Among the many reasons I loved my brother Willi, his kindness to Anneliese ranked high.

"Kinder," said my grandmother, appearing by our table. "Enough talk." She wasn't the kind of woman one could ignore, standing inches taller than any other woman in the room. The way she wore her hair, swept into a shelf of wide curls on the top of her head, made her even more imposing. After a longing look at the last smears of cream on the plate, which we didn't dare to run our fingers through in front of her, we returned to our seats.

During the second half, I drew Anneliese's hand onto my lap and held it with both of mine. This time, she didn't pull away.

Even those who live are covered with blood, my mother sang. *And marked by many wounds.*

I was relieved she was one of the few to survive the opera's bloody ending, and proud that her words *Orestes! Orestes!* were the last the audience would hear that day. It was her voice that would linger in their ears as they filed out onto the street.

SEVEN

In July 1937, the Inspectorate of Concentration Camps opens the Buchenwald concentration camp in Germany.

After that first time, I heard my mother sing Sophie in *Der Rosenkavalier* and Tatyana in *Eugene Onegin.* I was there when she sang Elsa in *Lohengrin,* Constanza in *Abduction from the Seraglio,* and Liú in *Turandot.* But nothing ever equaled the first ringing notes of her Chrysothemis.

From then on, my grandparents or my aunt Thekla, my mother's older sister, often took me to see my mother perform. Thekla, short and round with glossy black curls, was my favorite aunt. She had been the first to move from Graz to Vienna. Once she had found jobs at both the radio station and in a dress shop, she had sent for my mother, introduced her to friends, and paid for her training. If not for her, my mother would never have become a singer.

Now, Thekla talked about books on Radio-Verkehrs-Aktiengesellschaft, and wrote short plays for the station. At least once a week she and her family ate dinner at our apartment. Afterward, she often sat on the edge of my bed and told me stories about the scandalous life of Alma Schindler.

"Once there was a very clever little girl," my aunt Thekla began, settling beside me on the bed. "Her mother was a singer, like yours. And her father was a painter. She loved to play the piano and to make up songs." Her fingers were light on my back, tracing designs through my nightdress.

"Like 'My Gorilla Has a Villa at the Zoo!' " This was a perennial favorite, especially when my mother or father sang it while waltzing about the room, arms swinging loosely from the shoulders and spine curved forward. It was the kind of song that I would like to have made up — jaunty and fizzing with mischief. My parents were not snobbish about popular music. My mother was as likely to sing me "Paddlin' Madelin' Home" as she was to sing me Lieder. Still, I don't think my mother would have told me these stories, at least not in such remarkable detail.

"I'm not sure Alma was terribly interested

in gorillas, but yes, perhaps. Her father approved of her passions for music and literature, when it was not at all fashionable for fathers to encourage their daughters' minds.

"But he died when she was only thirteen and her mother married someone else, which made her very cross. Alma continued to write music, but by the time she reached her teenage years, men were already distracting her. There was the painter Klimt, the first to steal a kiss, when she was only seventeen. Next was her music teacher Zemlinsky, who fell madly in love with her. It must have been very hard for her to focus on arranging musical notes when someone was trying to kiss her. Even worse if she wanted to kiss him back."

The idea of kissing anyone — but especially a boy — was nausea inducing. Stefi had told me that adults put their tongues in each other's mouths when they kissed, which struck me as both awkward and unsanitary. "Not my parents," I had insisted. "They would never do such a revolting thing."

"Oh yes, they would!" Stefi had laughed. (I never dared ask my parents if this were true, afraid of the answer.)

Aunt Thekla went on.

"Many of Austria's most brilliant men

ended up falling in love with Alma. Imagine trying to get work done with so many lovers! Klimt, Zemlinsky, and then Gustav Mahler.

"Mahler insisted that Alma give up writing her own music if she were to become his wife. So is it any wonder she was so unhappy? How he thought that an intelligent woman would be content to manage a household is a mystery to me."

I turned on my side and opened my eyes. "So why did she marry him?" I couldn't understand the appeal of a bossy husband. Mahler sounded like Anneliese's father.

Aunt Thekla considered this. "Because he was in a position of power. Because he wrote beautiful music. Because genius is alluring. Maybe all of these. I don't know. Gustav was a very important man, the director of the opera. Maybe she felt that was the closest she would ever get to fame."

"Couldn't she be famous by herself?" It seemed so unfair, to have to live on borrowed fame.

"An excellent question. And one perhaps we'll save for another night. Good night, sweet pea." Abruptly, and despite my protests, she stood. "Mahler did eventually agree to publish some of Alma's songs. But by then it was too late. She had forgotten

71

how to arrange the notes."

"Is that why she's married to Herr Werfel now?"

"So many questions! Maybe your dreams can answer them."

Alone in the dark, I kept myself awake trying to imagine why anyone would choose to marry fame rather than to be famous. I wished Aunt Thekla would come back. I wished she could tell me bedtime stories every night.

Many years later I realized that Thekla didn't tell me these stories because she admired Alma. On the contrary: they were cautionary tales.

My cousins Klara and Felix — Aunt Thekla's children — were older than I was, older even than my brother, and sometimes came along to the opera. Klara studied piano and voice and was always at the top of her grade at school. Unlike me, she was quiet and difficult to read. But she was kind. I admired her, though she didn't fill me with the unbridled joy that her wilder brother did. I adored Felix, who was never serious about anything. He and Willi liked to hold me upside down by my ankles and spin me in circles, or lie on their backs on the floor and balance me on the soles of their feet like a flying angel. Felix could tell riddles for hours without repeating himself. He and Willi took me swimming at the Gänsehäufel and taught me the butterfly.

He got his élan from his mother. His father, my uncle Tobias, managed a knitwear factory and was silent and dull. But I suppose every family must have one steady member, one predictable pair of shoulders to carry its weight. After all, Aunt Thekla would not have wanted to marry a famous man.

Watching my father perform was a less dramatic experience than watching my mother. While I was pleased to be allowed to sit beneath those hollow gold women on the walls, in my opera dress with my own program in my lap, my father at work just looked like my father. He wore the same black suit I always saw him in before he left the house for a concert, and played the same pieces I had heard him rehearse dozens of times in our living room.

It was somewhat entertaining to watch the frantic blur of white fists moving up and down the strings and buttons, and the way the men became one body when they played, but I missed the costumes and characters of the opera. I missed the women.

It took all of my self-control not to take a pencil from my pocket and doodle in the margins of the program.

But I was just as proud of my father as I was of my mother, though I struggled to distinguish the notes of his viola from the sea of sound produced by the orchestra. I preferred to hear my father at home, without the distraction of the other instruments. In the Golden Hall, he became a cog in its machinery, like all the other cogs. At the opera, audiences came to hear a specific singer, but in the Musikverein, no one came to hear the third viola from the right.

By the time I was nine, I was allowed to sit at concerts or the opera alone, or with Anneliese, whose parents rarely took her to hear music. We sat with our knees leaning together, tracing messages with our fingers on the soft insides of each other's forearms. Afterward, we waited in the lobby for my father or mother to take us home.

"That sounded like the national anthem of Friedenglückhasenland." Anneliese nudged my foot. We were at a café after a charity concert in May 1937, to hear Beethoven's Fifth Symphony and Strauss's Eine Alpensinfonie. *The Alpine Symphony.*

"Maybe it is the national anthem of Frie-denglückhasenland. Though it sounds different when rabbits perform it." I cupped both hands around my hot chocolate.

"The orchestra has a carrot section."

"And a celery section. They crunch to keep time."

"For the finale, they eat the instruments."

We started laughing, spraying crumbs across the table. A stout man with grey hair and a monocle frowned at us, making a clicking noise with his tongue. No one can do disapproval with the passion and precision of Austrians.

I have searched so many times for programs from the concerts I attended in the 1930s, but they are not so easy to find. I suspect it is because so many of the audience members who would have gone to those concerts, who would have treasured and tucked away those programs, have been erased.

On January 16, 1938, I took Anneliese to see my father perform Mahler's Ninth Symphony. I remember the applause; it sounded like a summer rain on a tin roof. We didn't know it then, but it was the last time Anneliese's parents would allow her to go outside of our building with me.

It was also the last time Mahler's music would be performed until the war was over. It was the last time that seven of my father's colleagues would be alive to play it.

EIGHT

On July 19, 1937, the Nazis open the Degenerate Art exhibit to condemn paintings and sculptures they find unacceptably un-German.

Though I wanted to learn to sing, my mother insisted I start with piano. I don't know if this was because she suspected my voice lacked potential, or if she simply wanted me to learn the notes on a more tangible instrument. I put up no resistance. Piano would at least differentiate me from my brother. Like my father, Willi played viola. Unlike my father, he was lazy about practicing. While Willi had an ear for music and could mimic any melody, he preferred to be at the pool or stretched out on the sofa with a book. My father didn't understand how anyone could demonstrate such an utter lack of respect for his talent. It was a constant source of tension.

Anneliese had begun piano lessons, too, and I couldn't bear the thought of her having a musical life that didn't involve me. Although Anneliese's parents had become stricter lately, no longer allowing her to stay for dinner or go with us to the Prater or the Vienna Woods, they permitted her to come over every afternoon to practice because there was no piano in her apartment. For my parents, a piano was as fundamental a furnishing as a bed or a kitchen table. My mother played to accompany her voice or my father's viola, while he played to entertain us or to stretch his fingers in new directions. They made it look so effortless, hands flickering across the keys like light, like shadows.

I was sure that as soon as I began lessons, I would be able to do that too.

Our teacher, Frau Milch, was quick to disillusion me. When she asked me if I knew what any of the keys were, the only one I could point to was middle C. Thus we began the laborious process of learning the location of each note as well as how it was written.

Learning piano, it dismayed me to discover, was very hard work. I had thought that my parents' skills would simply have been passed down in my blood, that as soon as I touched an instrument I would channel both their talent and their education. Not until I had been studying for more than a year was I able to pluck out short pieces and sense the joy that could come from playing. Anneliese, who had her lesson in our apartment after mine, picked up things more easily, but she too was lazy about practicing. It didn't help that we used up some of her practice time talking and planning games to play at school. As soon as her allotted hour was up, her mother would be hovering at our doorstep to fetch her, though she wouldn't come in. When I protested the new restrictions, Anneliese told me that her parents thought she needed to be more serious about her studies.

At least I had the consolation that those studies included piano.

On the night of our first recital, Anneliese and I stood in the shadowy wings of the auditorium. My heart was beating so fast I could feel it in my navel, in my palms. Inhaling deeply, I smelled sawdust and face powder. Anneliese found my hand in the dark and squeezed it. Frau Milch droned on about the music we'd chosen, while our parents rustled their programs and recrossed their legs. Anneliese was to go first, then a boy named Thomas, then me.

"Are you scared?" she whispered, her breath wafting chocolate across my face.

I shook my head. Then, realizing she couldn't see me, I whispered back. "No, but I'm glad you're first!"

She pulled me closer, and then swiftly, her hands were on my cheeks and her lips found mine. Her warm, soft lips, slightly sticky and sweet. For luck, she said.

". . . and first to play for you tonight will be Anneliese Meier, playing 'Kinderball.' " As our parents broke into polite applause, I gave Ana a push toward the lights. "Hals und Beinbruch!" *Break a leg!*

I watched as Anneliese approached the piano bench, smoothed her skirt beneath her, and lifted her hands to the keys. While her cheeks had flushed and strands of her dark hair stuck to her forehead, her hands did not tremble. As I listened, I became aware that someone was watching me. Turning my head, I saw the dim outline of Thomas lurking in a corner of the stage behind me. How long had he been there? I pushed the thought of him from my mind. Thomas was not important.

Anneliese played her piece with fierce near-perfection, fumbling only one note near the end, and then exited the other side of the stage. Thomas brushed by me. I was dismayed to hear that he had chosen "Unter Bäumen," the same piece I had chosen, though he played it with an unsuitably martial precision.

And then I was there, in the middle of the stage, a blaze of nerves and sweat under the lights. I dried my hands on my skirt as I tucked it under me. The piano keys were cool and familiar. I lifted my wrists.

I cannot remember a second of my performance, only the rising of my ribs as I played, a feeling that my fingers were propelled by pulses of electricity that shot from my heart down my arms. It was a simple little piece, but to me it was Mahler, Wagner, and Tchaikovsky.

"Much better than Thomas!" Anneliese hugged me.

As we started toward the door to find our parents, we passed Thomas, still shoving music into his bag backstage. He puckered his lips and made a kissing sound. "I saw you," he whispered.

"So?" Anneliese stared at him until he turned away. "What are you, the kissing police?" The way she said it made me laugh, my worry melting away. Everyone kissed people they loved, didn't they? No one thought it strange when I kissed Stefi good night.

Our parents met us in the street, by the stage door. My parents shook Anneliese's hand and kissed my cheeks. "Not terrible," my father said, smiling. "That was lovely, Orly," said my mother, drawing me into the curve of her arm. "Does Anneliese want to come with us for a cake?"

Anneliese looked pleadingly at her parents, who had greeted us formally, and refrained from commenting on my performance. When her mother shook my hand, her pale blue eyes gave me such a piercing look I felt she could see all the way down to my heart. That she could see the imprint of Anneliese's lips on mine.

"Perhaps another time," said her father, buttoning his fur-collared coat. "If there is one."

Anneliese's mother smiled without her teeth. "Oh, and I forgot to tell you, we've bought a piano! So there is no longer any need for Anneliese to trouble you."

NINE

On February 12, 1938, Austrian chancellor Kurt von Schuschnigg meets with Hitler in his mountain retreat in Berchtesgaden, hoping to find a way to avoid war with Germany.

My hands were full of shining things — buttons, ribbons, and rolls of orange crepe paper — as I leaned on Anneliese's doorbell. Every year, we made our costumes for Fasching together and today we planned to begin transforming ourselves into flowers. This was Anneliese's mother's idea; she could make exquisite blossoms out of crepe paper, peeling apart rows and rows of stiff petals. Anneliese said she'd rather be a grape vine so she could wear green and walk around holding bunches of her favorite fruit, but her mother thought grape vines too suggestive of wine and Bacchanalia. Last year, she had helped us to sew twin harlequin cos-

83

tumes, but this year we wanted to be something that reminded us of country holidays, of life outside the city. Anneliese's mother had become obsessed with nature. She made Anneliese eat a paste-like Bircher-müesli made of oats and hazel nuts and apples for supper and gave her lectures about the healing air of the mountains. She had even stopped eating meat, telling us that "flesh foods were damaging to spiritual health."

Anneliese was taking forever to answer the door. "Ana! I'm going to drop everything!"

I heard her footsteps, fast and then halting, arrested by her mother's voice, too low for me to hear the words. Ana's voice rose in protest, her mother's tone growing sharper, until I could discern a few phrases — *remember the danger . . . not an association . . . your friend* — but nothing that made sense.

Finally the lock on the door turned. "Thank goodness! Here, take some of this, it's all slipping and sliding." I held out my arms but Anneliese just stood there, her arms hanging limp at her sides. "Ana?"

"Now isn't a good time," she whispered, her brow creased and her eyes trying to say something to me that her mouth could not.

"But we planned —"

"I know what we planned. My mother, she says you can't come in."

I stared at her, crinkling the paper against my chest. A button fell and rolled down the stairs. We listened to it descend.

"Tomorrow then?"

She shook her head. "She says you can't come at all anymore. She's gone mad, Orly, she says it's too dangerous."

I couldn't move away from her door. Not at all? To the apartment I had freely entered for the entire decade of my life? I could smell frying dough, hear something sizzling in the kitchen. "She's making Faschingskrapfen?" My mouth watered. Every year her mother made doughnuts that oozed apricot jam and we ate them when our costumes were finished.

Anneliese reached for my hand. "I'll bring you one later. When she's not being so stupid. I'm sorry."

I nodded and turned before she could see my tears. As I ran back down the stairs to our apartment, I wondered if we would still go to the processions together. I had never celebrated Fasching without Anneliese. I didn't want to go without her.

Our apartment was silent. My parents were both at work and Willi was studying. I dropped my armful of materials on the dining-room table.

"Erdnuss, is that you?" Willi appeared in the doorway of his room. "I thought you were making your costumes? Oh no, what is it?"

I shook my head and tried to swallow my tears.

"Her mother —"

Willi wrapped his arms around me. I rubbed my forehead against the wool of his sweater. "What did she say, that cow? Here, come sit with me." He pulled me to the sofa in the parlor and held me on his lap, though I was too big for it.

He listened as I told him what she said, his forehead wrinkling. "That woman has some nerve. In our building!"

But I didn't want his anger. I didn't want to punish Anneliese's mother. All I wanted was to be let back in.

The morning of the processions, Willi came to my room, holding something behind his back. "Close your eyes." I sat up in bed, clutching Lebkuchen to my chest. Something heavy and smelling of glue descended over my head. Rough edges weighed down my shoulders. I opened my eyes to darkness and reached my hands up to feel it.

"Don't worry, Peanut, it's just a costume.

Look —" He adjusted the heaviness on me so that I could peer out small eyeholes and turned my shoulders so I could see myself in the dim mirror over my bureau. Willi had made me a giant bunny head out of papier-mâché. It was painted a light brown, with pink on the ears and nose. Its small mouth turned up at the corners.

"I was hoping you'd come with me to watch the parades. Mutti and Vati have already gone." My father was playing on a float with a group of musicians from the Philharmonic, and my mother was riding with them.

I stared at myself. It was a beautiful bunny head. But the smell and the heaviness overwhelmed me. I lifted it off. "I just need to breathe a little."

Willi sat down next to me. "You don't have to wear it. I'll wear it for you if you don't mind being seen with a giant rabbit."

"I'd rather be seen with a giant rabbit than any human I know." I smiled at him. "Maybe we can take turns."

He stayed with me the whole day, holding my hand as we watched the strange sights go by: the Old Viennese Ladies' Band, country girls with giant headdresses, a steam train replica, a demonstration of sausage making, and even a miniature Riesenrad. We waved to our parents as they passed, my father's elbow moving furiously up and down as he played and my mother blowing us kisses, looking elegant in a long violet dress with flowers on her hat. We added our voices to a group singing "I Want to Be in Grinzing Again." We mostly carried the bunny head, but having it with us made me feel both protected and part of things.

Anneliese had gone to the festivities with her parents. We didn't see them. When Willi and I came home, we found Anneliese had left two doughnuts on our doorstep with an apologetic note. "I didn't have a choice," she wrote. "You are my forever favorite flower."

I crumpled the note in my hand and carried the doughnuts into the kitchen and stuffed them in the trash.

Everything was different after that. No longer was Anneliese's door open to me every time I knocked. No longer did her mother send up little plum tarts on Fridays. No longer did her father take his hat off and give a little bow when he saw me in the hall. A hundred times a day my feet started for the stairs. A hundred times a day, I stopped them.

TEN

On February 24, 1938, Schuschnigg gives a speech urging his country to fight to maintain its independence.

My father tucked his viola into its case a few minutes before 8:00 P.M. on March 11, 1938, when Austrian chancellor Kurt von Schuschnigg would make his final speech. He and my mother had just played Brahms's "Sonata for Viola and Piano in F Minor, Op. 120 No. 1," distracting us until it was time to switch on the radio. My mother had said she didn't feel like singing, but her fingers were steady on the piano keys. My grandparents and our aunts and uncles had come for dinner. The adults were restless. My mother paced nervously from the kitchen to the table, reminding me of Willi. He had pushed his chair back from the table and was whispering with my grandmother. When I glanced down at the book in my lap, no one told me to stop reading. The music hadn't eased the tension; it sounded like Eurydice slipping back into the darkness of Hades. I set down my fork and knife and hoped someone would suggest dessert.

My parents had had high hopes for Schuschnigg, for the plebiscite that would determine our future. The whole country was to vote on whether to become part of Germany. How could we possibly lose? It was inconceivable that Austrians would vote to dissolve their own country. Only crazy Germans could voluntarily submit to someone like Hitler.

My grandmother, however, was not taking victory for granted. As soon as Schuschnigg had announced the plebiscite two days earlier, on March 9, she had swiftly drafted flyers in support of an independent Austria, sending out a cadre of her friends and acolytes to scatter them across the city and to paint the sidewalks red and white. Willi and his friends had festooned Vienna with pro-Austria slogans. We were not Germans.

My mother had been too anxious to eat. Stefi frowned when she came to clear the plates and saw the untouched soup. The radio crackled and the adults shifted their chairs closer to where it sat at the end of the table. Too far away to hear properly, I slid under the table with my book without anyone noticing and crept closer. My mother's wool skirt brushed my cheek. I wanted to press my face against it but didn't dare distract her.

Above me, my aunt Thekla and uncle Tobias, my aunt Klothilde, Klara, Felix, my grandparents, my parents, and Willi leaned their ears toward the sleek Zenith tombstone radio. My parents had debated whether they could afford such a fine radio, but ultimately, sound was too important to them. My mother had purchased the Zenith with her own savings.

I sat clutching Felix Salten's *Fünfzehn Hasen: Schicksale in Wald und Feld.* Fifteen Rabbits: Fate in Forest and Field — a book I'd read so many times I had most of it memorized — against my chest. Anneliese had given it to me for my seventh birthday. Its rabbit protagonists, Hops and Plana, bravely endured attacks by man and beast, dividing their energies between vigilance and love. The floor tiles pressed a chill into my bare thighs, but I didn't want to stir and call attention to myself. I glanced down at my book.

"You can breathe for once," Plana went on, "and feel yourself safe."

Hops grew thoughtful, held his head tilted abruptly upward, twitched his nose and said, "We can breathe all right. Oh, yes . . . but we rabbits can never feel safe . . . never! Don't ever forget that!"

The book was not helping. Gently, so as not to make any noise, I closed the covers.

The chancellor's voice sounded scared. He was resigning! The man we hoped would save us was saying good-bye. He wasn't saying it in that cheerful way people say good-bye when they know they will see each other again. He wasn't saying it in a hopeful way that suggested better times ahead. He was saying it in the voice of a ship's captain reluctantly abandoning his passengers to the mercy of Poseidon. (Not that I would have said or thought of it that way at the time, of course, never having been on a ship. I suppose it's only in retrospect I think of it like that. I'm at an age where I think mostly in retrospect.)

Willi's feet jerked from under the table as he jumped up.

"The coward!"

"Willi, shush."

"God protect Austria." Schuschnigg's final words. God protect Austria because he could not.

The plebiscite would never happen now. We would not have a say after all.

There was silence around the table above me. I sat frozen in place, waiting for someone to say something. When I heard not only my mother, but my father, my stoic father, begin to cry, I knew that all was lost.

There were 185,000 of us in Vienna then. And some 225,000 in Austria. Give or take. Mostly take.

ELEVEN

On March 12, 1938, German troops enter Austria.

On March 12, 1938, the day of the Anschluss, the day the German soldiers came, my mother begged my father to stay home. He had a rehearsal at two o'clock in the afternoon. "Please," my mother begged. "The streets won't be safe." But my father had not become a musician in order to be safe. He became a musician because there was no possible way that he could not be a musician. Thus, no matter what was going on in the world around him, my father would turn up for work. It wasn't something he considered optional.

It was late when he returned, long after midnight. Stefi had tucked me in bed and was asleep in her own little room off the kitchen. My mother sat up at the table, staring into a cup of coffee that had long ago lost its heat. I know this because I was not asleep. I needed to hear my father arrive safely home before I could rest. From my bed I listened to the cheering in the streets, the shouts of men. I had propped my door open just an inch, so my mother wouldn't notice, and lay in that slender strip of lamp-light.

At last I heard the tumble of the locks on the front door. I swung my legs to the side of the bed and sat up, listening.

"Jakob?" My mother's footsteps, almost running to the door. "Jakob!" I would have felt relief then had it not been for my mother's muffled sob. I ran to the door to look out.

"They're everywhere," my father said as he removed his hat and set it on his hook by the front door. "Already they are every-where. They're taking people, Julia. I'm sorry I was so long getting home. I wanted to stay out of their way."

"What do you mean 'they're taking people'? What does that even mean?" My mother's voice rose an octave.

"The men — they're arresting Jewish men."

"We need to go. Jakob, we can't —"

"We don't have visas. We need to organize ourselves." His voice was a deflated balloon.

"Have they been here? To this building?"

My mother must have shaken her head. "I would have heard. They would have been here. Everyone knows who we are."

Instead of going to sit in the kitchen as they usually did, they retreated to their bedroom, meaning I had to actually sneak out of my room in order to hear them, my feet going numb away from the warmth of my bed.

"And Arnold is leaving."

"Arnold?" My mother's voice was bewildered. "When? Where will he go?"

I could not hear my father's answer, just the creak of the bed as one of them sat down.

The door flew open before I could move or formulate an excuse for being up. "Orly!" my mother began, cross. Then she sighed. "Go back to bed, my love. Your father is home." She took my hand and walked me back to my room, waiting until I was under the covers before turning to go. "No more listening at doors. This is not for you to solve."

I lay awake for a very long time. Arnold must mean Arnold Rosé, the first violinist who had been concertmaster of the Philharmonic forever, longer than I had been alive. He was Catholic, but my father said he was born Jewish. He often played me a recording of a duet Arnold played with his daughter, Alma, Bach's Double Violin Concerto in D Minor. "It was recorded the year you were born," my father told me. "I always thought of it as your welcoming song."

It would be decades before I discovered how we were saved that night. Only after the war was over and I had become another person did I learn that Anneliese had been sitting on the front step when the Nazis arrived. Like me, she had been eavesdropping on her parents, whose conversations had an entirely different tenor from the ones I overheard. She had also crept out of bed, knowing she had to see the Nazis before her parents did. "I'm so pleased you've come," she said, standing to shake their hands. "My parents own this building and they think that the Jews are a scourge."

This, of course, was the opposite of the truth. My family had owned the building for generations. "We have only two tenants, an old lady and my cousins. But please come in."

"Step aside." She was a just child, though tall for her age. She may have passed for thirteen or fourteen.

"Of course. Though I heard you were

97

looking for Jews?" She turned the lock on the door and swung it open.

The two men glanced at each other. They had many other buildings to get to. "You have no Jewish men here? None at all?"

"I wish we did, so we could help you round them up. But my parents, they're very strict." She beamed up at them. "They would never allow a Jew to live in our building."

We woke the next day to rejoicing in the streets. Cheering, chanting, music. We could hear it from our apartment, from our beds. They were happy noises, celebratory noises. It didn't seem possible that our neighbors, our friends, could be celebrating the end of our country. That they could be welcoming the planes roaring overheard. There could not be so many Austrians who wanted to become German. I had to see it for myself.

Without waking my parents, I ran upstairs for Anneliese. It was unlike me to leave without telling anyone where I was going, but I needed Anneliese. Ever since Fasching she had been trying to make it up to me, though she still couldn't let me in her apartment. On school days she met me around the corner so we could walk to classes together and sometimes she came over after school if her parents were out.

I had already tapped our secret knock on the door when I remembered I was no longer welcome. Quickly, I started back down the stairs. But just as I hit the first landing, I heard her door swing open. "They're not here," she hissed. "Come."

Anneliese's parents had gone out early, she told me when I got inside. They had wanted her to go with them but she had pretended to be sick. "I was just going to come see you. Those traitors!" She shoved a stockinged leg into a leather boot. "Including my parents." Her face looked tight, her eyes as anxious as mine. I noted she wore a white sweater with a red skirt, the colors of the Austrian flag. "I'll get my coat." She didn't say out loud that she thought I was in more danger than she was. She didn't have to.

We wouldn't go far, I told myself as we clattered down the stairs. Just far enough to see what was going on. It couldn't be risky to look out our front door. This was still our city. This was still our own neighborhood. We pushed open the heavy door against a surge of jubilant noise coursing down our street. The crowds were all moving the same direction, away from Alsergrund, surging in the direction of the

Ringstrasse.

"They're having a parade?" Anneliese gripped my hand.

I stood silent for a moment, unwilling to understand. "What are they celebrating, Ana? How can they?"

She shook her head. "I don't know. I don't want to be German."

Our feet began moving, swept along in the current of people. "Where is everyone going?"

"My parents said Hitler's giving a speech in the Heldenplatz." She glanced at me. "Don't worry, we won't go there. I don't want to see that man."

Women in their hats, girls, men, everyone lined the streets, the surge of their bodies restrained by human chains of police officers. Jolly music played, a marching tune conveying the opposite of everything that was to come.

Foreboding paralyzed me. I recognized the flags our neighbors were waving as the Nazis proceeded down the street with their machinery, legal at last. Rolling, walking, and riding sleek, fat horses. A muddy river of brown flooding our city, spiders on their arms. I clutched Anneliese's hand as the crowd jostled and shoved us along, foolishly longing for the quieter carrotmobiles we had invented years ago, the tiny carts that dominated the streets of Friedenglückhasenland, powered by wind generated by the swish of Japanese fans.

The Nazis barreled noisily through our streets toward the Heldenplatz, and children scrabbled for the toy flags the soldiers tossed down as though they were sweets. Those swastikas were everywhere now, unfurling from balconies, falling down across the faces of our buildings like masks. Crawling across everything I loved.

"Juda Verrecke!" I heard a voice cry. "Perish the Jews!" our neighbors answered.

Except Anneliese.

Fear rose from my belly. Could people tell I was Jewish? Was there anything about my face that gave me away? The rust color of my hair? The green of my eyes? My hand in Anneliese's went limp and cold. Then suddenly, she was pushed forward, propelled by the rapturous, roaring crowd. My hand was empty.

"How dare you!" I heard her voice somewhere in the crowd before us. "You are not Austrians!" She would get herself killed.

"Anneliese!" I plunged after her. She had been to our house on the Friday evenings we lighted candles, had even spent a Pesach at our table. Yet Jewishness had never been

101

a topic of our conversation, just as we had never discussed the color of our skin or eyes. Religion wasn't something that had concerned me until recently.

My family wasn't particularly observant. Sometimes we lit candles on Shabbat, but only if my parents were not performing. It would have been impossible for an observant Jew to work as a musician in organizations that required them to play on the Sabbath. Yet their work created no inner discord for my parents; for them, singing or playing was a kind of prayer.

On Pesach, we gathered at my grandparents' apartment for Seder. We answered the four questions, we searched for the hidden matzoh. But there wasn't much else to differentiate us from our Christian neighbors. We listened to the same operas. Our parents sipped the same Einspänners and Franziskaners, took tiny bites of the same Apfelstrudels and Imperialtortes. We hiked in the Vienna Woods together on weekends. Anneliese took me with her to the Ostermarkt, where we marveled over the pyramids of colored and sugared eggs. It never even occurred to me that eggs were religious symbols. Surely eggs were eggs.

I struggled to catch up to Anneliese, but the crowd closed around her. I stopped to let them flow past me. She would turn around. She would come back for me.

Something struck my arm and I looked down to see a chubby, blond toddler grinning up at me. He was vigorously waving a red-and-black swastika flag. I stepped backward. I wanted to be home. Turning, I moved upstream through the jubilant sea of the raised arms of my neighbors and friends, a salute so synchronized it almost looked rehearsed. Ordinary people, turned into an army.

A tram swept by, its roof displaying a massive swastika. Across the street I could see a curly-haired girl who used to be in my class; my former math teacher; the waiter from the coffeehaus at the end of the block, their arms all flying upward. They threw flowers to the soldiers, blew kisses as they marched past, cheering the death of our country.

This was not how to greet an enemy. My neighbors — the butcher, the cellist, the lawyer, the hairdresser, the elderly woman who always sat in the park feeding pigeons, watching us play — celebrated the arrival of the men who had promised to wipe me and my family from the earth. Maybe they just didn't understand Hitler's plans, I told myself. They couldn't possibly want to hurt my merry brother, my elegant mother. They couldn't possibly want to hurt me.

"Orly!" My mother magically appeared in the crowd behind me. Turning toward her, tearful with relief, I reached for her hand. Yet just as my fingers closed around the fabric of her sleeve, Anneliese's mother, Frau Meier, materialized beside me. Had they come together, noticing Anneliese and I were both gone? This seemed unlikely. The moment I saw Frau Meier's face I felt afraid. This was the woman who had given me Lebkuchen — both the gingerbread cookies and the rabbit named after them. Who had wiped the tears from my eyes when I tripped over my own feet and fell up the stairs, my lower teeth puncturing my lip. Who had cooked for me countless times when my mother was traveling and while Anneliese and I told each other stories in the next room. Despite her recent distance, I couldn't believe the ten years we had known each other now meant nothing.

Yet Frau Meier was unrecognizable, disfigured by feverish emotion. Her face split into a delirious and unfamiliar smile, her glazed eyes slid over me. She was happy about this, about whatever was happening. And my mother, reaching to fold me to her side, was not.

As we turned to weave through the crowds

toward the relative safety of our home, I heard Ana's mother call after me. "Orly!" I looked back at her. "Where is she?"

I gestured into the crowds, mute. I hoped Anneliese hadn't gotten herself into trouble.

"Where is she, you little Jew! Where is my daughter?"

I stopped, my feet suddenly unable to move forward. I had been called a little Jew — and worse — by people on the street, but never by Anneliese's mother. It took my mother a minute to realize I was no longer by her side. As she turned back, Frau Meier stomped toward me. "Did you bring her out here to defend you, Orly? What have you done with her? You stay away —" She placed her meaty hands on my shoulders and began to shake me. "You stay away from my little girl, you dirty little — you little *pig*!" With that last word she shoved me with such vigor I lost my footing and fell back into the street, where the passing horses had left a steaming pile of excrement. It was still soft and warm. For a moment I lay still, feeling it soak through my stockings and skirt, the bottom of my blouse.

Anneliese reappeared through the crowd at that moment, her face transforming into a horrified question at the sight of me struggling to my knees in the street. She halted so suddenly she tripped up a surge of merry revelers, who cursed her as they moved around us. "Orly! Who — ?"

Moving faster than Anneliese, my mother stooped to lift me, stinking and dirtied, into her arms. I could not remember the last time she had carried me. Squeezing me to her chest, she made it all the way back to our building, hurling herself through the crowds, up the stairs to the apartment, and into the bathroom. My body began to tremble. With the bathroom door closed, she undressed us both, peeling off layers of clothing and piling them in the laundry basket. My legs folded under me and I sat huddled on the throw rug, pulling my knees to my chest. "I'll be right back." In the kitchen she heated the kettles of water, traveling back and forth as I sat paralyzed.

Go to Friedenglückhasenland, I told myself. You will be all right there. But for the first time, my mind refused to drift away. I was stuck here, in the present, in this bathroom, reeking of horseshit. Then my mother was lifting me again, settling me into the warm water, settling herself underneath me, wrapping her arms around my ribs.

"Why?" I finally asked.

It was the first of many questions she would be unable to answer.

■ ■ ■ ■

I waited for Anneliese to come, to explain to me that her mother had gone mad. I waited for her to tell me that she was sorry. I waited for her to tell me how things were different in Friedenglückhasenland.

I waited all day.

Her mother must have locked her inside. Her father must have beaten her so badly she couldn't move. Maybe she argued with the Nazis and they took her away. Maybe they had punished her for her friendship with me. I had no way to know.

Willi had also been out looking for me. When he came home and my mother told him what happened he put his fist through the kitchen window. "We don't have enough violence in this country?" my mother asked. "We need you to join them?" She stared at him, burning her fury through his skin, until he fetched a piece of cardboard and began fixing it to the window. His hands shook as he tried to slice the cardboard with a knife, as he unpeeled the tape. When he finished, he came and sat beside me in the sitting room on the blue velvet sofa. "What're you reading, Erdnuss?" I turned my book over to show him the cover. *Fünfzehn Hasen.*

"You're not bored with the rabbits yet?"

I glared at him and pulled the book to my chest. To me, the plight of the rabbits, stalked by two-legged murderers, felt more relevant than ever. Willi could be such a snob.

"You and your bunnies."

"Today, let her have the bunnies." My mother stood in the doorway to the kitchen, her face expressionless. "Though that one's banned now. It was banned in Germany ages ago. Burned or banned, or maybe both."

"You're joking. Those Saupiefken banned a book about rabbits?"

"Apparently they're a metaphor." Normally my mother chastised Willi when he used rude language, but today I had the feeling she didn't consider the word strong enough. She turned back toward the kitchen, lifted a lid over a pot. The flatulent smell of broccoli filled the air. My mother didn't cook very often, but Stefi was spending the day with her parents.

"Let me guess — we're the rabbits?"

"Well, somehow I doubt we're the predators," she replied drily. I heard the oven creak open and slam shut.

"Hard to believe the Third Reich is devoting time to reading children's books." He pulled me onto his lap. "Wait until they discover the secret Jewish conspiracy in *Bambi*." I didn't smile. "I know a better bunny story. Tell us, Erdnuss, tell us about Friedenglückhasenland. Tell us tales of a better world."

As soon as I thought of Friedenglück-hasenland, I thought of Anneliese, and my heart went cold. I couldn't tell the stories without Anneliese. Every word of them had been a collaboration. If she were lost to me, then so was our world. Our sitting room blurred around me.

"Willi?" I whispered. "Ana —"

"Hush," he said. "Mutti told me. But that isn't Anneliese, Peanut. I think I know her a little by now." He was quiet for a minute. "How I would like to wring that woman's neck."

For a moment, I agreed, before remembering that if we were to strangle Anneliese's mother, she would be left alone with her father. "Willi, don't."

He sighed. "How did those two ogres create that child? Tell me that."

"They used to be nice."

"Used to be doesn't count." Willi's smile slipped away.

I wriggled back into his arms, back into

his familiar smells of damp wool and tobacco. He had taken up smoking at my grandmother's meetings, although my mother wouldn't allow it in our home. I wanted to cheer him up. "Well. You would like Friedenglückhasenland, Willi, because it's full of silence. There's nothing to ruin your writing." Willi wrote lots of poems, though I didn't understand all of them.

"Do you think I could come to Friedenglückhasenland with you one day?" He sounded wistful. He pulled me closer, tucking his chin over my shoulder. His curls tickled my neck.

I shook my head. "You don't have the right passport."

"How do I get one?"

"They aren't issuing them anymore. You'd need a visa anyway."

He fell silent. "So it's like anywhere else then."

"It's not like *anywhere* else." I was indignant. "There is no money! People just give things to each other. And they drive around in carrots that are completely silent! It has the best cinnamon rolls in the world and there are hardly any boys at all!"

"A paradise indeed."

"I'm sorry for you," I told him as gently as I could. "I'm sorry for you that you don't

110

have a country of your own."

He turned my shoulders so that he could see my face. "Erdnuss," he said. "I'm not sure any of us do."

TWELVE

In March 1938, street violence against Jews escalates in Vienna.

The next afternoon they came for us. My father had gone out to work, or rather to discover whether he still had work, although my mother had pleaded with him to stay home. She had already been told not to bother coming to rehearsal. Stefi had not come. The streets were no longer safe for us, if they ever had been. Willi had gone out for a paper, defying maternal orders. But I, her youngest, was home. My mother was sitting over her third cup of coffee — we were no longer allowed in our cafés, she told me — not sipping it as she gazed into the middle distance. Kept home from school, I lay on the blue couch with a book, red-eyed and trying not to think about Anneliese. We listened to the German planes descend on our city. We listened to the end of Austria.

There wasn't anywhere left we could go. We could not go to the parks. We could not sit on public benches. We were banned from theater and opera and cinemas. We could not swim in public pools. We could do nothing but pace the streets or sit in our apartments like rats in a trap. Our world had shrunk so fast it made my head spin.

The knocking brought us both to our feet and the coffee cup crashing to the floor. "Don't answer it," my mother ordered, watching the milky coffee leak across the tiles. I tiptoed to her, slipping my hand into hers. It was ice cold.

Again, the knocking, followed by the shouting. "Aufmachen, Juden!"

I felt my mother trembling under her dress. *"Open or we will break down this door."*

"Go to your room, Orly. Go to your room and hide. Under your bed, somewhere." I didn't want to leave her side, but I obeyed her, running into my room and closing the door. A second later I heard them in the kitchen, their boots on our floors. "You're alone?"

"I am alone." There was no tremor in her voice. Her voice she knew how to control.

"You won't mind if we search the apartment then."

I glanced around my room. There was

113

nowhere they wouldn't find me. I could crawl under the bed or into my wardrobe, and those would be the first places they would look. Both of them were too big and too heavy to shift. All of our furniture in Vienna was heavy and immovable. Permanent. Or so we thought.

I was too big to try to flatten myself under the quilt. A humming had started up in my ears that made it hard for me to think. I had dropped to the floor to start under the bed when the door opened behind me. "Gut! On your knees already! Filthy girl, come with us." Two men stood in the doorway, their arms wrapped in swastikas, their guns as shiny and black as new toys. Two men with guns, I thought, to fetch a ten-year-old girl? Then I looked at them more closely. I knew the dark-haired young man; he was the older brother of one of my schoolmates. "Fritzl?" I said, astonished.

"Shut up, Jew!" He yanked my arm. "Where is your toothbrush?"

The demand confused me. Were we going overnight somewhere? Down the stairs they hauled us, jubilant with their success. My mind reeled with the discovery that Fritzl, who knew us, was a Nazi.

I wanted to say something to my mother, to apologize for my failure to hide, but these men did not need further provocation. Outside, they flung us to the pavement and shoved a bucket of cold, dirty liquid stinking of lye toward us. "Go on," they said. "Do a proper day's work for a change." The Schuschnigg plebiscite slogans we and our neighbors had painted on the pavements with such nationalistic passion only days before had become the means of our humiliation.

I slid to my knees close to my mother, trying to see her face. I wanted to lift her back to her feet, to tell her to sing, to show these men who she was. "Orly, don't argue," she whispered.

We did as we were told, crowds gathering around us as more and more of our neighbors came to watch or were forced to their knees beside us. *A proper day's work for a change.* The heat those words aroused.

My fury warmed me as I channeled the violence of my emotions into my tiny toothbrush. What would I use for my teeth tonight? My mind could focus only on the smallest problems. I had looked up to see elderly Herr Grunberg the tobacconist pushed to the ground in front of me, and been unable to bear seeing anything else. I looked only at the paint below my fingers, and my mother's wrist, red and raw, to my

115

left, to be sure of her.

By early evening, our ranks had swelled. My clothes were damp from spilled water, my fingers burning from the lye and my toes numb with cold. Our fellow Viennese stopped to laugh or to spit on us. I started humming to myself so as not to hear what they were saying, but it was hard to drown it out. I paused to switch hands, and my breath caught in my throat when the girl next to me put her hand on mine. The scent of celery and sage nearly made me sob with relief. But terror immediately followed. "Ana!" I whispered in disbelief. "Ana, you'll get in trouble."

"I am not the one in trouble." The ferocity of her scrubbing rivaled mine. She had covered her hair with a kerchief and her father's glasses disguised her face. Our neighbors had not recognized her yet.

"You will be." I looked up, to see if anyone had noticed. "Keep scrubbing, swine!" taunted a teenage boy who had seen me pause. Flushing, I bent back to the pavement. Ana kept her scarf on and her head down. With her brush she wore a hole in the word Schuschnigg. Had she brought her own? Surely a soldier hadn't dragged *her* from her home? I whispered still more quietly. "Ana, I'm serious. Your mother . . ."

"My *mother*," Anneliese spat.

"Ana." I was afraid of Anneliese's mother. I was afraid of what she would do to Anneliese almost as much as I was afraid of what the Nazis would do to her for talking to me.

"Orly, I will say this one more time and hope you believe me. What I am, you are. What you are, I am. Promise me you believe me."

I couldn't look at her, but I nodded at the ground. I no longer needed fury to keep me warm.

"Promise me, Orly!"

I risked a brief glance at her, though not a smile. "I promise. I promise you."

THIRTEEN

In late April 1938, the Gestapo rounds up some fifteen hundred Jews deemed "unwilling to work" and sends them to concentration camps.

I never went back to school after the Anschluss, although I knew some children did. My mother was afraid of what might happen to me on the streets. I worried I would never share a classroom with Anneliese again. Even if my mother were to let me out of her sight, I'd have to go to a Jewish school now. When Anneliese and I met in the hallway of our building, she told me that the crucifix at the front of the room had been replaced with Nazi flags. She and her classmates were expected to sing "Deutschland über alles." (*I swear I don't sing, Orly; I just mouth the words.*)

Against my parents' wishes, Willi insisted on going to a swim meet a week after the

Germans arrived. "Are you insane?" my father shouted at him. "Do you have a death wish?"

"The kids on my team are nice, Vati. They know me. And no one else is any good at the butterfly. They need me." My mischievous spark of a brother had always been popular in a way I never was. People sought his company — girls especially. He made them laugh with his imitations of cabaret and film stars, put them at ease with his lopsided smile. Everything about school came easily to him, though he was too lazy to achieve top marks, and he excelled in fencing and swimming. He could not imagine himself unloved.

"That doesn't matter anymore. Are you not paying attention?" My father's shoulders trembled with the effort of raising his voice. "Are you somehow missing that this city is now wallpapered with swastikas, as if Hitler has branded the entire city? Have you missed the flags from every building, from the trams, the light posts?"

"I'm *paying attention,* Vati. I was paying attention when you were still refusing to think about anything but music. But allow me to think I know who my friends are." With that, he turned and slammed out of the apartment.

By the time Willi got home that night it was dark and I was already in bed, though wide awake. My mother had not moved from the front window since 6:00 P.M., when she expected Willi home from the pool. When she heard his key in the door, she flew at him, ready with sharp words for making her worry. But after he closed the door and stepped into the light of the kitchen, she stopped midsentence. I crept to the door of my room and peered out.

I couldn't find my brother's face. Blood poured from a cut in his forehead and both eyes were swollen and purple. His shirtsleeves were torn and he had lost his jacket. He stood with his arms dangling as though they didn't belong to him, and did not speak.

"Sit," said my efficient mother, who was already readying a washbasin and cloth. Then, as she touched the damp cloth to his split skin, her composure slipped. "My beloved boy." She choked on the words. "Those beasts."

When I woke the following morning, the house was silent. Alarmed, I ran down the hall to my parents' room. Sun danced across the dirty glass of the windows and no birds sang. It was late. My father was a lump under the covers. I tried to think if I had ever seen my father lying still under the covers after dawn. Next to him my mother sat with a book on her lap, staring at the wall in front of her.

"Liebchen," she said, turning when she heard me. I bounded into bed beside her.

"Is daddy sick?" I lifted the scratchy wool blanket gingerly, trying to find his face.

She shook her head. The lump next to her did not stir. His face was closed, curled into his chest.

"Sweetheart, your father lost his job last night."

"What? Why? Did he forget his notes? Did they think he was bad?"

Again she shook her head. "I'm not sure your father could ever be bad."

"Then what?"

"It wasn't just your father. They got rid of all of the Jews. Some of them they sent away." All of the Jews. All of them.

"Who? Where?"

My mother swung her legs over the edge of the bed, her white nightgown twisted around her body. "I'm not sure. Viktor Robitsek, certainly. Max Starkmann. Arnold Rosé. Armin Tyroler. And he even received the Ring of Honor from the city of Vienna! This is the kind of person they want to disappear?"

"They want us to disappear? Why don't they want the Jews in the orchestra? Aren't Jews good at music?" Even as I asked this I knew it was a stupid question. Jews created at least half the music I knew.

My mother seemed to immediately regret her outburst. But really, what could she say? My mother wasn't a liar. "We're good at everything we want to be good at. Sometimes I think that's why they hate us."

"Really?"

She sighed. "No. I don't know. But some people think we make too much money, we write too many books, we sing too much. Maybe they think we don't leave enough room for them."

"I don't understand." I looked at my father, wanting him now to stay asleep.

"I'm glad," she said, and pulled me close to her side. "I'd be worried if you did."

I would make pancakes, I decided. My father loved pancakes. My mother and I often made pancakes on Sundays she was home. Today wasn't Sunday, but no one was going to work.

It was easy to find the right page in the cookbook; it was rumpled and stained, speckled with dried batter. In the silent kitchen, I cracked an egg against the bowl, stirred in flour and water, brushed a pan with oil. Carefully, I poured the batter into the pan and turned to look for the coffee.

When I returned to the stove, flames danced from the cookbook. I had propped it too close to the burner. Dropping the coffee on the floor, I reached for the measuring cup of water and dumped it on the pages. Too late; the book had turned to ash.

"I know that recipe by heart, my love," my mother murmured into my hair as I curled next to her in bed, disappointed tears rolling down into my ears. "I don't need the book. There will be no shortage of pancakes in our future."

I opened my eyes and tipped my head back to look at her, scanning her face for censure, but it was soft. Between us on the bed, long strands of my pale apricot hair mixed with her darker auburn curls. Combing them together with my fingertips, I admired the range of hues, the contrasting textures. "It looks like a fire. The colors of flames, our hair all together." I thought of the cookbook, the heat that devoured it.

My mother tilted her head slightly to see them. "No, my love, look again. Our hair together is a sunset."

A night long ago, when my mother had been cross with my father for staying out too late or working too long, she had said, half in jest, "Don't ever fall in love with a musician, Orly. You can't compete with his instrument."

"But you are a musician!" I protested. "And I am in love with you."

She hugged me when I said that, as tight as tight. "I'm in love with you, too, Liebling."

"As much as you are in love with Daddy?"

"The same amount. I love you and Willi and Daddy all the same."

"Do you love me more than singing?"

"I love you more than anyone has ever loved anything. More than Lebkuchen and Liszt."

"But more than singing?"

My mother sighed. "It's different. But if I were forced to choose whether to lose my voice or my child, I would never choose to lose you."

I never asked my father this question; I was afraid his answer would not be the same.

My father reached for his viola before he

got out of bed in the mornings, even before he reached for his wife. Each morning, I drifted up from sleep to the tremors of his strings and would sit up to listen. They were gentle, his morning songs, rough and slightly out of tune. They called me forward and up, into my day, my life. They also signaled permission for me to come to their bed, to pull up the sheet and slide in next to my mother's warm skin. Only once he had set the viola back in its case and headed for the kitchen did we need to stir. Before the Anschluss, all of our cues were musical.

For nineteen years my father had played with the Philharmonic. For nineteen years he had crossed the city swinging his viola case at his side. For nineteen years he believed that music was a common language.

Close to half of his colleagues eventually became Nazis. Whether this was a result of conviction or a desire to stay employed made little difference to us. There is no record of any musician in the orchestra ever protesting the expulsion of his Jewish colleagues. These men who had played alongside Jews for decades, who had tuned their instruments to those of Jews, who had created harmonies with Jews, these were the men now calling for their exile. For their deaths.

After my father finally awoke the morning after his last evening at the Philharmonic, he locked his viola into its case and placed it alongside the small cases we were already filling with our few valuables. He would not open it again in Vienna.

My mother's work had been declining since 1934, although she had still managed to be cast in a few operas each year. The range of allowable composers and works had dwindled to nothing. No more Meyerbeer. No more Schönberg. By 1938, no one even wanted to be in a room with a Jew.

My parents had another full-time job now: getting us out.

FOURTEEN

In April 1938, the Nazis require all Jews to register any assets worth more than five thousand Reichsmarks. These were then appropriated to "support the German economy."

Not long after the Germans arrived, I made a terrible mistake.

The moment the Anschluss was announced, swastika pins and badges of the Nazi Party sprouted on the shoulders of my former classmates, of shopkeepers, and of our neighbors. People who knew us. People we had spoken to almost every day of our lives, but who turned overnight into enemies. Anneliese's mother pinned a swastika to her daughter's dress every morning, but Anneliese swore she took it off as soon as she was out of her mother's sight.

The day of my mistake, we planned to sneak away to the movies while my parents

127

were out in search of visas. We couldn't be in danger in a cinema, I thought. There was no reason a Jew couldn't watch a movie in her own city.

"She'll kill me if she ever finds out I'm not wearing it," Anneliese said as we set off, showing me the swastika pin she'd slipped into her pocket. She turned to me, frowning. "Orly. Yesterday I saw Frau Cohen turned out of the baker's. They wouldn't even let her buy bread!"

Anneliese's astonishment made me impatient. Of course non-Jewish bakers didn't let us buy bread. Every day there were fewer people we could trust. The butcher wouldn't sell meat to us. He said, "Don't you people have one of your own?"

Anneliese and I continued walking in silence, past a giant billboard proclaiming Judentum ist Verbrechertum. *Judaism is criminality.* Leering over the words was the giant head of a long-nosed caricature of a Jew. These signs, these noses, were everywhere. Anneliese followed my eyes.

"Your nose is nothing like that." She took my hand. I didn't know how to explain that the noses didn't even rate in my hierarchy of fear. A shape-shifting unease had become part of us. We were steeped in it, sweating it from our pores. There was nothing our

128

parents could do to protect us from it because we absorbed it through the air.

I didn't know how to articulate this to Anneliese, to explain what it felt like to live in my skin. I shrugged.

"Look, wear this." She pulled another swastika pin from her pocket. "I have an extra one. At least that way they will leave you alone."

I stared at her. Put on a *swastika*? Betray my parents? Betray almost everyone we knew?

Anneliese shifted her weight impatiently. "If you don't wear it we can't get into the film."

"Ana, no, you don't under—"

At the same moment, a gang of teenage boys in Hitler Youth uniforms rounded the corner and started toward us. Anneliese pulled her own pin back out of her pocket and fastened it to her collar. Hurriedly, my cheeks flaming with heat and fear, I followed suit, accidentally sticking myself with the pin. I thought I might vomit.

The rampaging youths hurtled by, looking for an old man to torture, no doubt. As they passed they glanced at us, but only cursorily. They registered our badges and moved on.

"See? If we wear it to the theater, they'll let you in. Come on!" She tugged at my

129

hand. But suddenly I didn't feel like watching a movie. I didn't feel like walking the streets with Anneliese. I tore the pin from my coat, not even caring if I ripped the fabric.

I couldn't look at Anneliese's face. I didn't want to see pity in her eyes. I threw the pin into the sewer grate at my feet and turned my face from hers. "I need to go home."

My feet quickened on the pavement, but I did not feel them. I did not feel my body at all. I hovered somewhere above my skin, somewhere I couldn't be hurt.

"Orly, wait!" Anneliese's footsteps, coming after me. Breathing hard, she grabbed my hand. "Don't be a fool. You shouldn't be alone."

I whirled to face her. "I need you to protect me, do I?"

Tears started in her eyes. "Oh, Orly, I don't know what to do! Everything's gone mad." Her skin started to get red blotches like it did when she was upset.

I started walking again and she kept pace with me. "Orly, I —"

But I never heard the rest of her sentence.

"Look who's here," came a low voice behind us. "It's the Büchsenmasseuse. The Jewish Büchsenmasseuse."

I didn't even need to look at his fat, grin-

ning face to know that it was Heinrich Müller, our old tormentor, in a brand new
uniform. We were still two blocks from
home. The last time he had used that word
with us, we had slapped his face. But he
knew I couldn't hit him now. Even Anneliese didn't dare to slap him now. She took
my hand again.

"How touching. A Jew lover," he sneered.
Something jabbed the back of my thighs,
lifted my skirt. I spun around, yanking the
material down. I was in my body again now,
burning hot. I opened my mouth.

"Orly, don't." Anneliese pulled my hand,
this time with force, yanking me back.

We ran. We ran all the way to our building, Heinrich singing as he huffed along
behind us. I recognized the words of his
song. "Der Jud! Er ist überall auf der Erde
zuhaus und ist so verbreitet wie Wanze und
Laus. Der Jud!" *The Jew, he is at home all
over the world. And is as common as a bug or
a louse. The Jew!*

"Where are you going, little Jew? We were
just starting to have fun. Anneliese, does
your Daddy know who you're playing with?"

We fell against the wooden door, my hand
shaking as I fumbled with the doorknob.
Heinrich used his baton to lift my skirt
again. "Just wanted to see if it's true you

131

people have tails."

"Stop it, Heinrich, leave her alone." Anneliese tried to shove him away from the door but he forced his way past us.

"I think I need to have a chat with your parents about the company you're keeping."

We took the stairs two at a time, Heinrich easily keeping up. I prayed that Anneliese's parents were not home. As we passed my door, my steps faltered, but as Anneliese continued, I followed. I could not leave her. I could not lead Heinrich to my parents. But we were leading him to Anneliese's. We should not have come home. We should have gone anywhere but here. Then again, Heinrich had always known where we lived.

"Mutter! Open up, please open." Anneliese rarely had keys; her mother was usually home.

The door swung inward, and Anneliese stumbled into the doughy bulk of her mother. Heinrich was right behind me. I willed myself to look up at Frau Meier. "Let her in, Mutter, please." Anneliese had turned back for me.

Frau Meier's lips stretched toward her ears, but I couldn't call it a smile. I knew then I wouldn't go in even if she let me.

"Frau Meier." Heinrich swept his hat from his head. "I felt it my duty to let you know

132

the filth with whom your daughter has been consorting."

"Thank you, Heinrich, but I will deal with my daughter myself." She began to close the door. "I'll leave you to deal with the Jew."

I didn't wait for her to turn the lock. While Heinrich was still speaking I flew down the stairs and was already halfway to our apartment by the time he started after me. I slipped inside home and closed the door against him.

But I no longer had any illusion that I was safe.

The next morning I found a paper slipped under our door. Anneliese had written me a story of Friedenglückhasenland, of our rabbits, their planets and solar systems, their lakes and mountains and apples and music and friendships. Curled in a corner of our sofa I stared at it, the promises of our world feeling empty.

I tried to write my own back to her, but my imagination failed me. My bunnies failed to be adorable, failed to be peaceful. They betrayed each other, starved each other. In the end I crumpled up my story and dropped it in the trash.

FIFTEEN

In mid-June 1938, the Nazis arrest nine thousand alleged criminals, including at least a thousand Jews, and send them to concentration camps.

My father fought in the Great War. This was something I sensed he was proud of even though he wouldn't discuss it. Most Jews had fought for Austria in that war. The bayonet he had carried — that he had most likely used — hung on our wall over the fireplace, just above my reach. The blade still shone, bearing no mark of its grisly journeys. Even the two studs on its handle were kept carefully polished. Like the medal he kept in my mother's jewelry box, it was a symbol of love, of what he had done for Austria. What he was still willing to do. I didn't like to think about that bayonet. I thought of my father with only a stringed bow, committing music, not murder.

Austria, it turned out, was not as loyal to us as we had been to it.

I don't remember the precise date it happened but I remember the city was warming and the lilacs were in bloom. It must have been a Friday in May, as we had already placed the Shabbat candles on the table next to a small loaf of challah and a vase of purple blossoms. We had no excuse to skip lighting the candles anymore, now that neither of my parents could work. I was in the kitchen with my mother, cutting raw potatoes into pieces after she peeled them with a knife. Not only would no one sell us meat, but we could no longer afford it.

As the potatoes sizzled in oil, our apartment door blew open.

This time, no one had bothered to knock. They were all noise and aggression and self-importance as they shouted to my father from the hallway. Borderless fear shot through me.

But I recognized their voices. The voices of the people who had come to take our home away. These were not the voices of German soldiers. These were not the voices of Nazis. They were the voices of two people I'd known all my life. Our upstairs neighbors. Anneliese's parents.

They arrived accompanied by two police

135

officers wearing swastikas. My mother's hands froze when she heard them. The potato she was peeling slipped between her fingers and fell into the sink. I watched her to know how to feel. To know what to do.

But she did nothing.

Through the door to the living room I saw Willi standing on the threshold of his room. Surely he would have something to say? But he stayed silent, unmoving.

"We have put up with you Jews long enough. You will leave this house tonight," Herr Meier said to my father in the hall. "Go on and get your things."

Still, my mother did nothing! "Mutti," I whispered. She turned to me then and shook her head.

"Did you hear me? This is no longer your apartment. There are good Christians who need it."

Our home in Alsergrund, the home in which I was born, in which my mother was born, was not our home. I could not absorb that. How could there be life without our home? I wondered where Anneliese was. "You will go live with other people like you in Leopoldstadt."

There are no other people like us, I wanted to scream. There are no parents like mine. No one else could lift me up to touch the golden ladies of the Musikverein or bring me pieces of famous chandeliers.

Leopoldstadt was the second district, a Jewish neighborhood where we often went to have dinner with friends or to go to the theater. It was crowded and noisy. Anneliese and I took the tram there on Sundays, to ride the Riesenrad, the tallest Ferris wheel in the world. It spun above the Prater amusement park, where I hear it still spins today. From the top we could see the river, winding away from us to unknown lands. "Some day we'll drive a ship down that river," Anneliese told me. "Someday we'll take it all the way to Friedenglückhasenland."

Who in Leopoldstadt would take us in? It's almost laughable to me now that I imagined we would have to find someone with a spare bedroom. As if anyone had a spare bedroom. As if we would ever again be permitted to have any space of our own.

Even as I wondered all this, a more pressing question was throbbing in my mind. How would Anneliese find me?

My father finally spoke. His voice was low. I had to strain to hear him, my knife hovering over the cutting board. "We own this building. My wife was born in this apartment."

137

"Do you know, *Jew,* that if I denounce you, you are going to go straight to a camp?"

My mother and I turned as one, stepping quietly toward the door. My father was standing between the door and the hallway closet, where my mother's height had been scratched into the paint of the doorframe with a pencil each year of her girlhood. The marks were still there, next to marks for me and Willi. We were taller than she had been, every year.

No one was going to hurt my father. He was ours. Other fathers had already been taken, already stolen from their families and sent to the camps. They could not take mine. I would not let them. I curled my fingers around my knife. What did I think I was going to do? Go after Herr Meier with a potato knife? Stab Anneliese's father? Any one of his broad fingers could have flicked it easily from my hand. And then there were his two Nazi friends.

One of the police officers who had entered with the Meiers walked down the hall into our living room and looked around as if it were his already. When he saw my father's bayonet, he moved to lift it from the wall. Willi took a step into the room but my father shook his head at him.

"With that weapon I fought for my country, for Austria." My father's voice was clear and strong, though I saw his fingers twitching by his sides. "With that I defended her." Under the bayonet was his certificate of honorable discharge: *You are herewith assured of the Fatherland's gratitude.*

I knew Anneliese's father hadn't fought in the war. He had been too sickly, she said. Some kind of childhood lung infection.

My father picked up a silver-framed photo from the mantel over the fireplace, turned it toward the officer. I knew that photo well; it had always stood there. It showed my father young and round-faced, smart in his uniform, bayonet in his arms.

"I give this to you, to remind you who we are."

I didn't understand why my father would give them something so dear. That image was precious to me. I expected the man to smash it, to send it to the ground with the rest of our hopes. Instead, he tucked the photo of my father into his jacket.

He had known, before it dawned on the rest of us, that nothing in that apartment was ours anymore.

There ended my memories of my first home. With the blur of our departure. With the monsters at our heels. With the sound

of my knife, dropping useless to the kitchen
floor.

Sixteen

In July 1938, delegates from thirty-two countries meet in Evian, Switzerland, to discuss what to do with Jewish refugees. Nearly all refuse to relax their immigration quotas. Australia says it has no "racial problem" and is uninterested in importing one.

We moved first to 2 Czerinplatz, where we were crowded into a one-bedroom apartment — a forced communal apartment called a Sammelwohnung — with my Vienna grandparents, Aunt Thekla, Uncle Tobias, Aunt Klothilde, my cousins, and a dozen Jews from other families. My grandfather had lost his ophthalmology practice. My aunt Klothilde had been expelled from the Medical University of Vienna, along with the rest of the Jewish students. I remembered her telling us about the day a band of Nazis had lined up in front of the steps to her classroom building, to keep Jews from entering.

The apartment was filthy and stank of excrement. The toilet was always overflowing. We slept in our clothes on the floor, pressed tightly together. We had left almost everything behind — the piano, our books, Willi's soldiers, the green-and-white dress my mother had made me for my first piano recital. Stefi. I had no memory of life without Stefi. She had always been there, chastising me for ripping another skirt, insisting that I stay at the table until I finished my dinner. Yet there was hardly any time to say good-bye. She had been out buying bread when they came for us and returned just as the men were prodding us through the apartment with their guns, as we gathered the few things we could carry. She clutched the dark loaf of rye to her chest like a child. No one bothered to speak to her. She was not Jewish.

"Stefi!" I ran to her, squishing the bread between us. Her warm arms wrapped around me, brief reassurance that some good remained in Austria. I pressed my face into the rough cloth of her dress, breathed in the faint scent of perspiration and dishwashing soap. What would happen to her once we were gone? "Orlanthe," she said in a strangled voice. "The *Meiers*?"

"Not Ana!" I pulled back, anxious to defend her.

"Of course not Ana." Stefi set the bread on the counter, took a breath, then picked it up and handed it to me. "What else do you need?" With renewed purpose she pulled me into my room and yanked my dirndl off a hanger and pulled it over my head, on top of the plain green dress I had on. "Wear this, it's your favorite." She tied my apron and stuffed my pockets with clean underpants. "Wash them out every night. Comb your hair. Help your parents. Where is Lebkuchen?"

I had time only to tuck Lebkuchen into the waistband of my apron, wrap a coat around me, and extend my hand and for the briefest caress of the worn posts of my bed. The only bed I had ever known, the bed that had seemed the stable foundation of my life. Never again would I lie beside Anneliese as we fought off sleep with our stories. Never again would we jump up to touch the carved lion heads on either side of our front door, telling them hello and good-bye. Never again would I run through the halls to her apartment, taking the stairs two at a time in a hurry to be with her. Never again would my mother or Stefi pull our breakfast rolls from that oven. All of the loss happened so quickly it was impossible to absorb. Loss must be assimilated in increments.

As the men and the Meiers urged us over the threshold of our front door for the last time, Stefi watched from the kitchen. When the Meiers passed her, the last to go, I heard her unmistakable whisper. *"You should be ashamed."*

I hated the apartment on Czerinplatz. There was always someone climbing over me, always parents or uncles or grandparents or cousins or strangers quarreling. My grandmother, my powerful socialist grandmother who had been evicted shortly after we had, fell mute. My grandfather, who couldn't stand to stay inside, paced the streets despite the dangers. My father stared out the one window, absently patting his pocket for the pipe that he could no longer afford to smoke. The pipe he had sold months ago. No one was in the mood to entertain me, not even Aunt Thekla. No one was optimistic enough to offer me comfort. I could never go to the toilet without someone hammering on the door the entire time. Chronic embarrassment constipated me. I shared the bedroom with five other children and four adults. We put the littlest ones in the middle of the two beds, so they wouldn't fall out, and at least once a week one of them wet the bed. Those who couldn't claim a spot on the edge of a bed slept on the floor on mattresses or in nests made from blankets. I preferred to sleep with my parents on the floor. The other nine adults who couldn't fit in the bedroom slept on the floors and sofas of the living room and the kitchen. Every other day I washed out my underwear in the sink, as Stefi had instructed.

I tried not to complain to my parents. They were miserable enough. They were powerless enough. They didn't need to be reminded of my discomfort. What could they have done?

Because Willi was so much older and had often been out with his friends and activities, I had been accustomed to a tranquil home, with only Anneliese, Stefi, or my parents for company. I liked quiet, in which I could lie on my bed dreaming up new adventures from my old life in Friedenglückhasenland. I liked hearing nothing but the scratching of my school pencil on paper. Or when my parents were home, a stream of sonatas and fugues. But Leopoldstadt was full of people, and all their sounds. Perhaps because it was so loud, everyone shouted to be heard.

Now there was not even music.

At first the only place I dreamed of going was back home. Back to the scratched wooden surface of the kitchen table where I did my sums and read my schoolbooks while listening to the controlled tremor of my mother's voice. To those soaring notes that were the background of my life. I dreamed myself back into Stefi's comforting arms, to picking out songs on the piano with Anneliese, to racing with Willi through the paths in the Vienna Woods.

Yet eventually I was forced to dream forward instead of back. No longer could I dream of Friedenglückhasenland. I could not remember its contours or believe in its magic. I dreamed of escape to somewhere my mother could sing. A place where my mother would smile. It took too long for me to believe it, but it was becoming clear that this place was not in Austria.

Once we moved to Leopoldstadt, we spent much of our time standing in lines. My parents had to get official certificates from the Polizeikommissariat in order to apply for exit papers. They used their meager savings to pay the Reichsfluchtsteuer, the Reich Flight Tax assessed at 25 percent of our assets, to get permission to leave the country. Every single transaction required waiting for hours, sometimes an entire day, in a queue of equally frantic people. My mother pawned her jewelry for a sixteenth of its worth. She sold her gold wedding band, studded with small diamonds. "At this point I don't think I question your father's commitment," she said in response to my cry of dismay. It was the last piece of jewelry she owned. But it didn't bring in much. Not even enough for a single passage on a ship.

SEVENTEEN

On August 8, 1938, Nazis open the Mauthausen concentration camp near Linz.

Willi was already gone. He had left a couple months after we moved to Czerinplatz. Young men his age were supposed to be in the military; it was risky for him to be seen on the streets. It was something of a miracle that Willi, Felix, Uncle Tobias, and my father had escaped the initial roundups. My mother said maybe they were only taking Jews who had previous criminal convictions. Before we left home, the adults had gathered in our kitchen to figure out where Willi and Felix could hide. A former school friend of Willi's who was now an officer in the army urged him to flee. "If you present yourself to the army you will go straight to the camp. I've seen it. You must try to get away before they start looking for you."

He and my father sat up late with maps of

river and borders. Swimming had been a wise choice of sport, my father said. Swimming is going to be useful. Yet the plan they concocted meant Felix, a much weaker swimmer, would have to find another way.

Once we were evicted, it was clear Willi couldn't wait any longer. He said good-bye to us all, to the city, his friends, his life. My mother wrote down the address of her friend Violaine, a French singer in Paris, someone to whom he could send letters letting us know where he was. Someone my mother could contact with our whereabouts, should we be forced to move again. Once we found a way out for the rest of us, we would leave word with Violaine. Willi could join us wherever we landed.

I wanted to give him something he could take with him to remind him of me, but I had so little left. He refused my offer of Lebkuchen, much to my relief. So I sat down on the floor with my father's last pen and a scrap of carton I had found in the trash, and I drew Willi standing among forested mountains next to a lake, surrounded by rabbits. Over the top I wrote: *Valid from today until infinity.* It was a visa to Friedenglückhasenland.

When I gave it to him he turned his head away and when I pulled his face back to mine I could see he was crying. "Meet me there," he said. "Okay, little one? Promise you will meet me there."

And then I had no brother.

Everything happened abruptly. One minute you were forking noodles onto someone's dinner plate and the next second he was taken away. Children came home excitedly clutching a high mark on a school paper to find their parents gone, their homes echoing and empty.

So much worse happened after we left, so much that we didn't learn until after the war. So much that was unfathomable, incomprehensible. We were the fortunate ones.

We had no idea how fortunate.

We know what happened to Willi because he wrote to us, a letter that was left crumpled on the floor inside our front door. Delivered by someone whose face we would never know, who had brought it from Paris.

Willi's schoolfriend Jost, who was now in the SS (as was everyone who wasn't Jewish, it seemed), had bought him railroad tickets to a village near the Swiss border, just north of Lichtenstein. Willi waited on the banks of the Inn River until dark and then he swam to Switzerland. I was thankful that he crossed over in a warm month.

After the Anschluss, as thousands of us flooded the border, Switzerland began to insist we acquire consular visas before crossing over. But there had been no time for Willi to acquire a visa, there was no time for him to do anything but to run and to swim.

After August 19, 1938, Switzerland closed its borders to Jews, batting us back into the monsters' jaws. Only Denmark, alone in Europe, made any effort to rescue its Jews. Just that one cold island.

But in July 1938, Switzerland couldn't send Willi back — or so we thought. There was a rumor at the time that if you managed to get twenty kilometers inside Switzerland they had to let you stay. We heard stories of German Jewish families sent back over the border and promptly arrested. What happened to them after that we still didn't know, or refused to know.

When Willi had swum across the river he walked until morning. When he reached a village he stopped to ask a woman selling vegetables how far he was from the border. "More than twenty kilometers," she said, smiling. "You are safe." As if there were such a thing. As if there is.

But Willi could not rest. Switzerland had no intention of keeping refugees. It had declared itself to be a "transit-only" country for Jewish exiles. We could not settle in, set up professional lives, contribute to the economy, or contaminate their landscape with our offspring. Unemployment was high enough at the time, and its immigrant population already swelling. So they said.

Willi took shelter in a refugee camp financed by the Jews of Switzerland, and began his search for a country that would grant him sanctuary while he waited for us. My parents had had time to help him craft a way out of Austria, but neither the time nor the resources to help him find a path beyond the border. The next step he had to take alone.

EIGHTEEN

On August 17, 1938, all Jews are forced to adopt a Jewish middle name — either Israel or Sarah — to make them easier to identify.

Back in Leopoldstadt that July, we conducted our own, parallel search. There must be some country that would want us. There must be opera houses full of people clamoring to hear my mother sing. There must be orchestras in need of one Austrian violist. Surely somewhere no one would mind what god our ancestors worshipped.

Our choices were rapidly diminishing. The United States had established visa quotas for each country, including ours. While we had each registered for a number on the quota waiting list, we were unable to come up with the necessary affidavits of support. We had no relatives in the United States. We didn't know any U.S. citizens who might fill out the extensive paperwork on our behalf. We also needed proof that we had booked tickets on ships to the West. But how could we spend money on tickets when we were not sure of admission? The United States required recent tax returns and proof that there was money in our bank accounts. This made my mother laugh. "Have the Americans not heard what has become of our bank accounts? Don't they know that we are not allowed to leave the country with more than ten Reichsmarks in our pockets?"

My mother had taken over responsibility for all of our paperwork. My father was too slow, too methodical, and too likely to get distracted by the children crying from the corners of the squalid apartment, the adults bickering over food, or even a birdcall outside the window. My mother attacked our visa applications with the zealousness she once applied to a daunting aria. She wielded her fountain pen so fiercely she often punctured the papers upon which she wrote.

When the U.S. embassy turned us away, one or all three of us waited in lines at the embassies or consulates of France, Ireland, Latvia, Hungary, Brazil, Australia, Yugoslavia, Argentina, New Zealand, and Canada. We still thought we had a choice. My

154

parents still thought we might move some-where with symphonies and theaters.

None of these countries wanted Jews, particularly Jews who were guaranteed to arrive penniless. They didn't want musi-cians, actors, composers, singers, professors, writers, or intellectuals. They wanted people with practical skills who would earn a steady and taxable income. They wanted plumb-ers, undertakers, electricians, and carpen-ters. "Surely there is more to life than the fulfillment of basic needs for shelter and water," said my mother, flinging a stack of paperwork to the floor. "Surely there are souls in these countries who cry out for music. Why else live?"

"It is entirely possible, my love, that these countries have their own musicians and phi-losophers."

"Who don't want competition? Is that it? But I can't do anything else but sing!"

"I don't know." My father offered her a faint smile. "Your cooking isn't half bad."

We know now how lucky we were to be denied visas to the countries of Europe, but we did not feel lucky at the time. We were running out of options. It stopped matter-ing to us where we went — my parents no longer made any mention of their careers

155

— only that we be allowed to go somewhere.

Finally, there were just three countries left that might take us. We might be allowed into Japanese-occupied Shanghai, which didn't require visas. Or into the Dominican Republic, which had taken some distant cousins. And then, through the whisper network of those desperate to get out, came word that Bolivia was still taking Jews.

I had never heard of Bolivia. *Bolivien.* I rolled the word around in my mouth like a sweet. When my parents talked about going to Bolivia they used words like "primitive," "wild," and "tropics." My father had been on tour in South America (though not in Bolivia) with the Vienna Philharmonic in 1923, but when I pressed him, he would only say it was different from Europe. Later, I would find out that three members of the orchestra had died on that journey. Two contracted malaria and one committed suicide.

Left to my imagination, I envisioned living on a vast farm of some kind and riding horses across green fields, into lush forests, picking unfamiliar fruits from the trees as I rode along. In my mind Bolivia merged with Friedenglückhasenland until they were no longer distinguishable. They were my Eden, my promised land, my escape from fear. In

156

Bolivia we would have land and raise rabbits. In Bolivia there would always be sun. In Bolivia my parents could work again. In Bolivia when the sun set my mother would sing as she made Käsespätzle.

At the same time, I could not imagine a land without Anneliese. She had always been there. She was part of the architecture of my life. How could I venture into any world without her?

Dear Anneliese, I wrote on scraps of paper in the darkness of our room at night as the other children whimpered or slept. *Did you know there are sinkholes in Friedenglück-hasenland? Sometimes you fall into a hole in the street and fall and fall almost forever. You could stop halfway down, but then you have no way to get back up. It's best to just let yourself fall until you are on the other side of the world.*

I never sent the letter; my mother told me I might endanger Anneliese if I did. No one's letters were private anymore. This did not stop me from writing. I needed to speak to her, even if she never heard my words.

Getting visas for ourselves was difficult enough, but my parents also wanted to save their families. My mother had two younger sisters still in Graz, who remained reluctant

157

to leave Austria, unable to imagine a life elsewhere. The younger of those two had a husband, my uncle Marcel, and a daughter, my little cousin Violette. My Graz grandparents' bakery had been "Aryanized," meaning it had been stolen by the Nazis. "How will they eat? They cannot survive there," my mother fretted to Thekla. Yet things were hardly better in Vienna.

We needed fourteen visas. Not counting Willi, and not counting my uncle Franz, my father's brother, who lived in Berlin and refused to consider leaving.

I walked to the Bolivian consulate with my father, grateful to be out of the clamor and stench of the apartment. The consulate occupied the top floor of a cold and narrow house on Waaggasse, just two and a half blocks from the Naschmarkt, where we used to go on the occasional Sunday for lunch. My father liked to buy the Austrian pancakes called Palatschinken, while I helped my mother pick out cherries, Turkish honey, and fresh fish. Knowing we no longer had enough money to stop, I didn't slow my steps as we passed the market. Maybe they wouldn't even take our money anymore. Jewish vendors had been driven out, their wares stolen.

At last we caught sight of the Bolivian flag,

fluttering red, yellow, and green above Waaggasse. As we drew closer, my father pointed out the Bolivian coat of arms in its center. A long-necked animal stood beside a palm tree and a golden sheaf of wheat as the sun rose over a mountain in the distance. Above it all, a bird was poised for takeoff. This pleased me. A country with such a pretty picture on its flag could not be too scary. Not as scary as a country with flags like ours.

In a throng of other supplicants, we spiraled up the narrow stone staircase, pausing to catch our breath before the brass plaque announcing that we had arrived. We were not permitted to see the consul himself, but a diminutive, sepia-skinned woman let us in and — after we had waited with the others for nearly five hours — gave us the stack of documents we needed to complete in order to apply for visas. "You will need thirty-six dollars per family member to launch your life in Bolivia," she said crisply.

"We can't take that much out of the country," I whispered to my father.

"We'll worry about that later."

On the forms, we had to state how we intended to make a living in Bolivia. It would help our cause, the woman in the

159

consulate informed us, if we would agree to become agricultural laborers. My father stared at her as if she had asked him to join the circus. "Agricultural laborers?" he asked in wonderment. "But we are Viennese!"

"I am trying to help you, Herr Zingel." The woman was clearly offended. "If you want the very best chances of getting out of Austria, you will agree to become agricultural laborers."

"And if we don't?"

She shrugged. "You might get a visa, but I cannot guarantee."

It wasn't the Bolivians, however, who gave us the most trouble. I cannot complain about the Bolivians. Before we could leave we had to acquire a tax clearance certification from the new government — proof that we owed no money in taxes.

The SS used all of their sadistic bureaucratic might to toy with us. Every time we arrived with a signed document we were told it was the wrong one, that we needed to start again. Or that we had failed to provide an adequate photograph. Or that there was a fee we had neglected to pay.

In October, we again had to apply for new passports (after having already been forced to trade our Austrian passports for German ones) that identified us as Jewish, with a large red stamp. It says something about our state of mind that this did not even seem bizarre to us, given everything else that had happened.

"If they want us to leave, why do they insist on making it so damned impossible?" I had rarely heard my father curse. He was not an angry man.

My father and mother waited endlessly in lines while the Gestapo men shouted at them, kicked them, and, worst of all, laughed at them. This struck me hard. I could understand anger, could understand shouting, but that anyone could actually derive pleasure from — could laugh at — the misery of another person was an unpleasant revelation.

One late afternoon at our local police station, one of these black-booted men tripped my mother as she tried to leave, so that her papers (apparently filled out incorrectly, again) went flying in every direction and my mother collapsed onto her knees. Wincing, she pulled herself up from the marble floor, slick with tracked-in rainwater, and crawled after our documents. One of her hairpins fell from her hair, loosing a lock of it that dragged in through the slush. The men around us laughed uproariously. "Stupid, clumsy Jewish cow." I stared at the square face of the officer who had spoken. What had happened to our world to turn it so upside down? Men had once stood outside of my mother's dressing room with flowers. Men had once traveled from other cities to hear her sing. Men had once wept when she opened her mouth. Now, as angry tears streamed down my face, I couldn't help turning back. My mother's fingers dug into my arm, urging me forward. "My Mutti," I called to them as she dragged me away. "My Mutter is Arabella. She is Isidora and Liù and Eurydice and Ariadne and Salome and —" I tried to think of another. Just as my mother pulled me through the door I yelled, "My Mutter is a *nightingale.*"

I am guessing their surprise at my audacity is all that kept them from taking me from my mother to teach me a lesson. By the time they had registered my words and started toward the door, we were gone, my mother breaking into a run. "Don't you *ever,*" she said, stopping in a nearby alley to shake me by my shoulders so hard my back teeth rattled together, "do that again. They could take you away from us, Orly. They could hurt you. Oh, don't you ever, *ever* again!" And then sobbing, she pulled me into her arms in an embrace so tight it drove all of the air from my lungs.

■ ■ ■

We also required money to purchase passage on a ship, although we didn't want to buy tickets before we had visas in our hands. The Italian ships were less expensive than the English or Dutch, so it was an Italian ship on which we hung our hopes. There were several leaving from Genoa in the autumn, and we wanted to sail as soon as possible.

Every morning, my mother rang the Bolivian consulate from a neighbor's still-working phone to check on the status of our visa applications. At least once a week, I walked there with one of my parents, in the hope that the sight of our abject faces would move them to mercy. But all they saw all day were abject faces.

We could only wait.

We were running out of money. No longer could we buy fish or fresh fruit. Strudel was out of the question. I was always hungry. At night sometimes I woke to feel my mother's fingers tapping along my ribs, as if counting how many of them she could feel through my skin. I didn't want her to worry. I started rummaging in the dustbins in the streets and alleys around us, especially near food markets, to find the occasional half-eaten roll or rind of cheese. I brought back bits of bread or carrot for the smaller children when I could find them.

One night, sometime after the Anschluss but before the end of the year, we were listening to the radio over a dinner of soup without bread when Hermann Göring said, as if this were a rationale for it all, that the Jews had controlled art, theater, and everything else. In case his meaning was unclear, he added, "The Jew must clearly understand one thing at once, he must get out!"

So why was he making it so hard to leave?

NINETEEN

**On November 7, 1938, Herschel Grynsz-
pan, a German-born Polish Jew, assas-
sinates German diplomat Ernst vom
Rath in Paris. On November 9 and 10,
the Nazis use this pretext to burn down
or vandalize more than a thousand
synagogues, rob and destroy thousands of Jewish stores and businesses,
arrest approximately thirty thousand
Jewish men, and murder at least ninety-
one.**

I remember the sound of shattering glass.
Call it Kristallnacht if you want, but for us
it was Pogrom Night. Kristall is too pretty,
too glittering, too pacific. The word
"kristall" — for me — evokes the shimmer
of the Musikverein, of the opera, of the
eleven tons of glass suspended over our
heads. So I cannot call it Kristallnacht.

Two nights before the pogroms, the dark

erased the moon, hid her face from us, took away even her reflected light. An eclipse, my mother said.

Everything before that night has a dream-like quality to it now. As if my entire life until then had been a diorama I was observing from the far side of the glass, a pretty whirl of lights and music that disguised the festering hatreds all around us. The hatred we had been too caught up in our own world to see. I only woke up when the last vestiges of our world broke apart. My memories of that night are so sharp they could slice through skin.

As soon as we heard the first cries demanding Jewish blood, we locked ourselves in the apartment, although we knew even there we were not safe. I huddled close to the others and waited for someone to come murder us. On that filthy, overcrowded mattress, we listened to our fellow citizens calling for our death. We waited, listening to screaming from the street, the sounds of gunfire and beatings. I lay curled against my mother's warm back. "Why?" I kept asking her, as my father paced by the windows, keeping watch on the street. "Why are they doing this?"

My father started to explain about the Jewish boy who killed a German diplomat in Paris, but faltered. It was too flimsy an excuse for the enormity of what was happening. This had clearly been planned. All around us things shattered — things, and people.

Only the very youngest children were asleep; the rest sat up with the radio. We kept our lights out, not wanting to draw attention to our continued existence. And then they came. They banged on the door until it opened, locks splintering. My mother wrapped herself around me, pulled my head to her chest. In the dark of her embrace I listened to the boots trampling through the apartment, the bloodlust in the voices ordering us to turn over our money, our jewels. I heard my father's voice, explaining we had nothing left. I heard the voices of the other men, the other women, pleading for their wedding rings. The children next to us cried when their brothers and fathers were taken, while their mothers tried to keep them quiet. I heard my cousin Felix's voice above them all. "Don't wait for me, Mutti. Go when you can." But they didn't take my father. Perhaps they took one look at his spindly violist's body and could think of no possible use for him.

I heard Aunt Thekla's cries.

My mother began to sing to me. To all of

167

us, really, given that it was impossible to sing in that small room and not sing to us all. She sang in Italian, perhaps not wanting to sing in a tongue we shared with Nazis.

Perhaps the worst thing the Nazis did to me that night besides stealing my beloved cousin was fail to register my mother's song. Arms full of our coats and our last items of jewelry, they pounded back down the stairs, moving on to the next Jews. "Earn your own money!" I wanted to yell. "You sing *Elektra* five times a week!" Was this what they called "a proper day's work"? Taking our valuables? What lazy men, I thought as I lay there. Nothing but common thieves.

They were nothing but common murderers, too, of course. But I did not know that until the next day.

As the sounds from outside grew louder — I could hear the fracturing of the world, smell the smoke from the fires, hear their cries of Juda Verrecke! — her voice did, too, as if she thought she could hold up our walls around us with sound alone. I pressed my face against her skin, no longer scented with lilacs but with bitter sweat. I focused on the reassuring feel of her rib cage expanding under my fingers. Here she was, my mother. Breathing. Singing. If I could just narrow my world to that, I would be all right.

168

They took so many men that night. Broke into their homes, stole them from their wives and children. Some they beat to death before they even got to a camp. Some they tossed out of windows like refuse. Some they sent to the camps. Some they lined up in the street and shot in the head, one by one.

We never found out where they took Felix.

The next day, I slipped out of the apartment before anyone was awake. I wanted to see if there was anything left of our city. Someone had to see what they had done, I reasoned. I was small; I could easily hide. Besides, the Nazis were not after children, were they? They had only taken men.

Outside, the streets were silent, most people were finally sleeping or too terrified to emerge — or gone. I stared around me in shock. Splinters of glass crunched under my feet with every step. Anxiously, I scanned the sidewalks for remaining Nazis. I walked past shattered shop windows and spray-painted slurs. I stepped over the stiff body of a cat.

The window of Weiss's shop, where I used to take the Groschen my mother gave me to buy Küfferle Schokoschirmchen and chocolate-covered marzipan balls, was gone, just a few shards of glass left around the edges. Chocolates had been scraped from the shelves, barrels of shiny boiled sweets emptied on the floor, crushed beneath boots. Where was kind Mrs. Weiss, who always gave us an extra piece of marzipan, shaped like a tiny cherry or banana? I crouched down to retrieve a marzipan bunny from the pavement, where it had fallen from a thief's pocket or hand. One of its ears had been torn off. I wanted to burrow it into my own pocket, to place it somewhere safe. But I did not. Treading carefully, I stepped quickly through the glass and set the small rabbit back on a bottom shelf.

The department stores had been emptied, food shops robbed, flower shops reduced to a scattering of bruised petals. A few shopkeepers stood in the wreckage, looking around for something they could salvage. Scrawled on the walls, in ugly jagged letters: *Jud.* As if it were a curse word.

A charred shadow had replaced the nearest synagogue. Nothing remained but a field of cinders, a few still smoking. I saw a man on his knees, digging in the ash with his fingers, searching for something left. This is what they had been burning. Around the periphery, bodies lay scattered like broken dolls.

The orphanage in the next block was gone. Mobs of our delirious countrymen, I later heard, had hacked its contents to pieces and driven the children barefoot into the streets before setting it ablaze.

That was enough. I turned and ran all the way back to our room.

We heard the rest of the news on the radio. More than a thousand synagogues had been set on fire, not only in Vienna but across the whole of Austria and Germany. Sacred scrolls had vanished. Tombs were invaded. Even our dead were not safe.

We couldn't stay inside forever or we would starve. I often volunteered to look for food. I couldn't bear to stay in the crowded apartment for long. My mother didn't want me to go, but she was quickly learning the limits of her ability to protect me.

Some days I passed among the crowds unnoticed. Some days an arm would stretch out before me, barring passage. "Dance for us, little Jewess," someone would say.

And so I would do jumping jacks, my arms and legs opening and closing, opening and closing, as my braids danced across my back and my breath came in gasps. When my mother asked me why I came home

171

sweaty and disheveled, I told her I'd been racing other children in the park. It could have been worse. So much worse.

One of my few treasured possessions was the dirndl that had been my grandmother's when she was a girl. While my father's parents had always been city dwellers, my mother came from the countryside. The red of the dirndl's skirt had faded to pink and the blue of the apron had been washed to a pale grey, but to me it was as vibrant as ever. I loved its little puffed sleeves and laced bodice and that it felt like a kind of uniform. Even though city children sometimes teased me for dressing like a peasant, I loved it because it had always been ours. I loved it because it was Austrian, because I was Austrian. I had been wearing it the night we left home; it was one of the two dresses I still owned.

I kept forgetting we no longer were Austrian. And somehow my mother and I had missed the edict stating that Jews were no longer allowed to wear the national dress, including lederhosen, Styrian hats, and dirndls. Or maybe there was no edict. Maybe our Austrian neighbors did not need an excuse.

One afternoon while my parents were waiting in yet another line, I slipped out of

172

the apartment and made the long journey on foot back to Alsergrund, grateful I had done it before with Stefi and Anneliese on our way home from the Prater. I had been waiting for the chance to go back to our neighborhood. I needed to see Anneliese, to tell her where we were, to be sure of her. I wasn't going to go to our old building, I wasn't that stupid, but I thought perhaps if I waited in the Jewish cemetery on our street, I'd see her walking home from school. I was lucky no one stopped me on my way. No one looked at me at all.

But I had only just rounded the corner onto our old street when our former neighbors set upon me. My second-grade teacher saw me first. "Orly, you can't come back here."

"And you can't wear that anymore." Frau Floch stood in the doorway of her intact butcher shop. I paused, unsure if she was trying to be helpful or mocking me. As if to answer my unspoken question, she stepped forward and tugged on the strings of my apron. "These clothes, they are not for you," she said, like a stranger. "They're for Austrians."

By the time she tore the apron from my body, I was surrounded. A man yanked my right arm behind my back while another

173

used his pocketknife to slice away the strings of my bodice. "It was my grandmother's," I protested weakly, still believing logic might make some difference. "We're Austrian."

"No," said the man with the knife as he tore the skirt from my legs. "You're a Jew."

When I returned in the shredded remnants of the dress, my parents were furious. "What were you thinking?" my father yelled. "Do you not understand the danger you put us all in when you call attention to yourself? Do you really not understand?" My mother was almost more concerned about the fact that I now had only one dress left, a worn green frock already too tight. Part of me, some irrational, reptilian part of me, wanted my parents to go back to Alsergrund and fight for me, to go after the people who had stripped me, hurt me, made me sweat until I thought I'd faint. But they wanted to live. They wanted me to live.

TWENTY

On November 12, 1938, the Decree on the Elimination of the Jews from Economic Life bars Jews from operating any kind of business.

After Pogrom Night, my parents began to talk seriously about sending me to England with a large group of children, a rescue effort by the British government that was being organized by German Jewish organizations. Kindertransport. The first transport was just for German children, but there could soon be more.

Our visas had still not come through, and we did not know how much longer we could survive. My parents argued about whether to keep me by their sides, or send me to safety. It was urgent that they get me out of Austria, my father said. They could always meet me somewhere later. But we can still get her out with us, my mother cried. The visas could come any day. Haven't I already given up my son? She could not see any new life without me.

I didn't want to go on any transport. What child wanted to leave her parents? But then, what child was given a choice?

Unaccustomed to idleness, my parents paced the floors of the cramped apartment, beating out desperate rhythms on the bare floorboards with their feet, dodging arguing children and the elderly huddled on mattresses in the corners. My aunt Thekla and uncle Tobias, in contrast, were still. They stared out the window as if they hoped to catch a glimpse of their son passing by. Klara looked after them, scavenging with me for food, making her parents drink water. She had even gone to the police station to inquire about Felix but had been told no one knew where he was. In the early evenings, we all pressed close to the small radio someone had salvaged from home, trying to predict the future.

"Mutti, sing," I would say to my mother when she tucked me in with the other children or beside her on the floor. And she would only shake her head, folding her lips into her teeth. "I'll sing again when we are free," she whispered. "I will sing when we are safe."

It occurred to me only later that she never even asked if Bolivia had an opera.

"Is this what war is?" I asked my mother.

She looked away from me, toward the kitchen, her fingers pinching the fabric of her dress, sliding it back and forth. "No. Yes, in a way."

"Will we stay here?"

"No, my love. We will not stay here. I don't know where we will go yet, but we will not stay here. Here is already gone."

A caliginous autumn descended on Vienna as we waited for our visas, or what would come in their place. As we made what preparations we could make. Mist clung to our streets and the chill sank into our marrow. I missed going to school. Some people in the apartment had books, and I read them all. I played games with the older girls; I held the babies; I plotted ways to find my way back to Anneliese before we left. If we left.

Finally, when we had begun to consider various illegal ways to smuggle ourselves out of the country, a letter arrived from the Bolivian consulate saying our visas were ready. My father and I were pulling on our shoes before my mother had even finished reading it to us. "What if someone else gets there first?"

"They're our visas, Orly, they can't give them to anyone else." But he beat me to the door. I had to run to keep up with him all the way to the consulate, where we discovered there were visas for only the three of us.

"Regular visas?"

"Regular as visas go."

"I won't have to plant anything?"

"My understanding was that you didn't want the agricultural visas."

My father straightened. "Thank you."

"I hope you know how lucky you are. I don't know how many more of these there will be."

"I understand. Thank you. We are grateful."

Visas for the rest of our family, she said, would — perhaps — come later.

"But!" my grief-stricken father began.

"I said, we have three visas. Do you want these three or shall I give them to the gentleman in line behind you?" Her voice was weary rather than unkind. Our misery had numbed her.

My father closed his mouth and collected our visas. As we turned to go he remembered our last visit and stopped. "And if they agree to be agricultural laborers? My

178

parents?" I tried to imagine this, tried to imagine my stout grandfather planting rows of corn in his pin-striped suits, tried to see my militant grandmother pushing a plow.

"We will do our best, Herr Zingel."

My Vienna grandparents insisted they were relieved. "We're too old to travel so far from home," my grandfather announced. "We're better off somewhere nearby. France, Poland." He said this as if those countries were real possibilities. As if those countries were safe. My aunts and my Graz grandparents promised to keep trying to join us in Bolivia. Aunt Thekla and Uncle Tobias said they would not leave without Felix.

We needed now to find enough money for the ship and the landing fee demanded by Bolivia in return for accepting us. My grandfather gave us a little of it, bills he had hidden away in his office filing cabinets and carried with him in the lining of his jacket. We'll pay you back, my father told him. We'll send you money for your own tickets. But it wasn't close to enough. My mother went out early one morning and was gone for most of the day. When she returned, she had an envelope of bills in her girdle. "But where did you get it, Mutti?" All of our relatives were in our same situation. She gave me a thin smile. "Odiane and Ilse."

"Really?" I had forgotten Odiane and Ilse. I guess they were not Jewish. They could still work.

"Really. There are some good people left, Orly. Some very good ones."

When we had counted out just enough schillings to purchase our tickets, we walked to the Italian Line offices in the Opernring.

The queues sent my spirits plunging. Surely there would not be seats left on any ship for us. We waited all day, stamping our feet and clapping our hands to stay warm, but did not make it to the door. We began rising before dawn to join the throngs, with the hope that one day soon waiting would get us across the threshold. It felt hopeless. There were lines every day of desperate people willing to settle on any available vessel.

Yet a couple of weeks later, just before closing, we made it inside.

We can book passage from Italy for three people, the ticket agent told us, but not until April.

My father looked at him in despair. "We may be dead by April."

The ticket agent sighed. Always the same

story. "For the money you are willing to pay, I have April. If you can find more, I can get you on a ship in December."

My father bought the tickets for April. We could still try to find enough money to leave earlier, he said, but at least now we had something. There was an exit sign in our future. We had to survive four months more. Just four months.

TWENTY-ONE

On January 30, 1939, Hitler announces his desire to annihilate all the Jews of Europe.

On December 3, 1938, my parents' driving licenses become invalid. "Good thing we don't own a car," says my father.

On December 5, we are no longer allowed to sell our jewelry. "Good thing we have nothing left," says my mother.

On December 12, a new law is passed stating that we will not be allowed to leave the country with anything other than "items for personal use." I look at my parents with bewilderment when we hear this announced on the radio. "What else do we have?"

On the first day of Chanukah, I present my parents with a handwritten book of stories from Friedenglückhasenland, written on scraps of paper torn from food cartons and discarded wrappings and held together with a piece of string. I suggest we light candles — one of the other families has a menorah — but my mother just looks out the window and pretends she doesn't hear me.

In February, we walk past Fasching parades and celebrations. It seems a long time ago that I cared about Fasching, that I cared about anything as frivolous as a costume. We see a German man in a long-beaked stork mask handing a swaddled infant to a blond Austrian maiden. A group of children marches by in Roman costumes, followed by a pack of Amazon warriors. When a group of adults dressed as the blue-green Rhine begin acting out the rape of the Danube, my parents pull me away.

On February 23, *You Can't Take It with You* wins an Oscar for Outstanding Production. Had we registered this, we might have noted the appropriateness of its title.

On February 28, the Reich's transport minister announces Jews are banned from dining and sleeping cars on trains. Our anxiety increases. Surely we will be banned from regular cars next? I wonder if we could walk to Italy. I wonder if maybe we should start now.

We huddle in the apartment around the radio, awaiting a knock on the door.

Those four months stretched out over an eternity. When my father offered to sell his viola, my mother took it from him until he promised he wouldn't. "I married a violist," she said. I bit my lip to keep from reminding her that he had married a singer. Twice more we were moved to different and smaller apartments, where even more of us were crammed together in increasingly desperate conditions. My parents grew thinner, my bones pushed closer to skin, my aunt and uncle became strangers. We began taking our meals from the soup kitchen opened by the American Jewish Joint Distribution Committee — the same organization that would eventually play a large role in our new lives in Bolivia.

During all of this — the paperwork, the incessant trips to embassies, consulates, and police stations — the idea of leaving for a new country remained in the realm of fantasy for me. I was nearly eleven. I had never lived anywhere but Vienna. Everyone I had ever loved, every food I had ever tasted, every game I had ever played was here. I simply could not imagine inhabiting a different landscape. Nor could I imagine a journey on a ship. While I had often traveled on trains for summer holidays and to visit relatives, I had never seen the ocean. I am not sure I had even seen a photograph of an ocean liner.

All of my parents' preparations were happening, therefore, at a distance from me. Even in the final days I did not believe I would never again sit in the Golden Hall of the Musikverein, or climb the steps inside the opera house, passing beneath the sculptures of half-dressed children wielding instruments. I did not believe that the waiters at Sperl would never again set a silver tray in front of me bearing whipped-cream-bedecked hot chocolate and strudel. I could hardly entertain the thought that I would never play with Anneliese again. Anneliese was irrevocable.

While it's true I had already lost the domestic landscape of my home, lost my Stefi, whom I mourned nightly, lost my proximity to Anneliese, this city was the only context in which I could imagine myself. Its streets terrified me, teeming with the boisterous, shouting Nazis and the regular, ordinary people joining in their sadistic fun, but they were still my streets.

TWENTY-TWO

On March 15, 1939, Czechoslovakia ceases to exist.

A few weeks before we left Vienna, in early April 1939, I sneaked out of the apartment for the last time, in the darkest part of morning, before anyone else was awake. So that my parents wouldn't panic, I left a note saying I would soon return. They would worry anyway but it couldn't be helped. As I made my way through the dim streets, I pulled my coat around me and almost wished for the protection of that swastika pin. Almost, but not quite.

I walked fast with my head down and made it to the cemetery this time without anyone seeing me. When I was sure no one I knew was on the street, I walked the rest of the way back to the building where we had been happy and where we had been made miserable. Our stolen home. It was so cold my toes went numb in my thin leather shoes. I knew it was dangerous to walk alone where someone might recognize me, that it was dangerous to walk through Vienna's streets at all. Yet what other streets did we have to walk? My heart hurtled ahead of me, fearing the expression on Anneliese's face almost more than the dangers all around me.

I stood in a darkened doorway across the street from our old building. I listened for the church bells that would tell me Anneliese would soon be on her way to school. I stood there forever, freezing, petrified, waiting. Wondering if I would find her changed. Wondering if Frau Floch would emerge to slice off my last dress with her butcher's knife.

The bells had rung before she flew out of the house, late, her coat half on, skirt flying up around her, and her blouse untucked.

"Ana!" I took off after her at a sprint, but as she had stopped the second she heard my voice, I collided with her, knocking us both over. "Orly!" She dragged me to my feet and around the corner. "You're alive, you're alive! Come, farther away." We ran toward the Lichtenstein gardens, toward clusters of trees and bushes, toward obscuring greenery, and fell to the grass. Our breath coming fast, we lay on that frigid April lawn side by side, our hands clasped. *My Anneliese.* Her soft, thin arms, her bruised legs, her skin. "I'm leaving," I said. "Right away."

"How will I find you?" she asked. "How?"

"You can't. I will find you."

My mother had forbidden me to tell anyone where we were going. "Not even Anneliese," she had said. "Promise me, Orly." I had never kept a secret from Anneliese. How could I keep this one, this most important one? But then I thought of her father's belt, and what it might draw from her.

"I will write to you. You mustn't move, Anneliese. You must stay here. You must wait."

"But I need to write to you. How can I not write you?"

"I'll send you our address when I can. When this ends. Just don't move. Stay right here so I know where to find you. Promise me."

"I don't want to let you go. It's been horrid, Orly, I can't —"

We stayed there longer than we should have, until the sun rose in the sky and warmed the air, until we could hear people entering the park around us. Finally, I knew it was getting too late. I couldn't let my parents worry too long; I didn't want them to try to look for me. This fear drove me to my feet, pulling Anneliese up with me. Letting her go, I linked my thumbs and raised them over my head, my fingers fanned out on either side, like wings. The international sign language for "I am a citizen of Friedenglückhasenland. I come in peace."

Smiling, tears sliding down her cheeks, she linked her own thumbs above her head in response, her fingers fanned out on either side, her thin elbows forming a diamond around her head.

Then I turned and I ran.

TWENTY-THREE

On April 28, 1939, Hitler renounces Germany's nonaggression pact with Poland.

We walk all the way to the train station. We have four days to get to our ship in Genoa.

At the Südbahnhof, the SS holds each of our precious belongings aloft, displaying them to the entire station. My mother's spare dress. My father's top hat. The stuffed rabbit named Lebkuchen, who is everything I have.

"I don't think you'll be needing this in Bolivia." I watch as the man rips Lebkuchen apart, searching her stuffing for hidden wealth. He doesn't even give her remains back to me, though I salvage one small bit of fluff from the dirty floor as we're prodded forward. I refuse to cry in front of these men.

My father is — miraculously — allowed

to keep his viola.

The last thing we hear in Austria is the rhythm of the wheels on the tracks, beating out a song of exile.

to keep like viola.

The last thing we hear in Absalom is the rhythm of the wheels on the tracks. No one is speaking.

CAESURA

There is so much I do not remember. Things my mother and father remember, things the dead remember.

I do not remember the failures in Evian, where no asylum was offered. My mother never told me that it wasn't just Austria who abandoned us. My father never told me the world had given Hitler permission to do with us what he wanted.

I do not remember the five thousand disabled children cavalierly slaughtered, their tender young bodies stretched awkwardly upward by the faceless hands I saw in photos many years later.

I do not remember the roving bands of teenage boys urging each other to deeper hatred, greater crimes.

I do not remember when journalist Dorothy Thompson reminded the American public that eradicating the Jews had always been part of the Nazi platform. I never heard her too-lonesome voice reminding the world that the Nazis were doing *exactly what they had always said they would do.*

I do not remember the little girls with their dark braids, holding their mothers' hands as they were prodded into train cars.

I do not remember when the Wagner-Rogers Bill, the bill that might have saved twenty thousand children, was defeated.

I do not remember November 23, 1938, when the Nazis reminded the world that the Jews would be wiped out if no one evacuated them. Even though I was there. Even though I should have been listening.

I never saw the skeletal women. The skeletal men. The skeletal children, their eyes still absurdly hopeful. The children.

I do not remember the inside of the train cars bound for the camps.

I do not remember watching my family members murdered. Waiting for my turn.

I do not remember the mountains of shoes, hair, bones. I do not remember the bulldozing of the bodies, the obscene flapping of desiccated breasts and buttocks.

I do not remember the drawings of the children. The drawings that survived, the children who didn't. The thin-stemmed flowers, the black-capped soldier, the man with the drooping mustache. The crayon-sketched rainbow, insisting the world still contained beauty.

I don't remember because I was too young. Or I wasn't there.

My parents gave me that.

■ ■ ■ ■

SECOND MOVEMENT:
BETWEEN WORLDS

■ ■ ■ ■

TWENTY-FOUR

My mother, who had always had all of the answers, didn't have them anymore. She knew how to tie my shoes and how to make a frog with her fingers and how to plait hair. She knew songs in many languages; she knew when a piano was only slightly out of tune; she knew how to take a breath so deep it would last for an entire song.

Now, as we hurtled away from Austria, she didn't know anything. She didn't know where we would stay in Italy. She didn't know whether there were rabbits in Bolivia. She didn't know if Bolivians had toilets inside their houses. She became impatient with me when I asked.

Yet questions were all I had left. When I asked her if Willi would find us, if I would see Anneliese again, if we would ever return home, my mother only laced her fingers through mine and turned her face to the window.

I fell silent, rubbing the bit of Lebkuchen's dirty fluff between my fingers until it disintegrated.

When I travel from one city to another, I can't help but see connections between the two places. For me, Vienna and Genoa are irrevocably linked, not only by my presence in both cities in 1939, but by the scent of coffee and butter drifting from the doors of cafés, by the glazed Falstaffs in bakery windows, and by thick, warm chocolate. I saw faces on the streets in both places I was sure I recognized. The church bells rang in the same key.

Other than those things conjured by my own circumstances, the cities are utterly different. Genoans moved to a softer, more arrhythmic beat. In April, the sun had already gained the heat of spring. People looked at me, at my face, and smiled. Some of the older women paused to pat my cheek. Perhaps they did not know that I was Jewish. In Genoa, I was freer than I had been in years. I could taste things with every part of my body, my tongue, my fingers, my ears — the wind off the harbor, the clouds, the voices of the grocers calling to their customers.

I could almost convince myself we were

on holiday as I wandered through the pretty streets listening to the strains of opera drifting out of the open door of a café. I could almost convince myself we were on holiday — if I never looked at the faces of my parents.

We had to wait three days for our ship, the *Proteus*. But there were Jews in Genoa, Jews willing to feed us noodles in strange green sauces and put us to sleep in their attics.

Walking at last to the harbor, I took my parents' hands, remembering how they used to swing me between them when I was small. Ein, zwei, drei! And up I would sail, my feet reaching for the sky. I wished I were small again. I wished their arms were strong enough to hold me up.

When we emerged from the warren of little streets into open air and were confronted with the harbor, with the water itself, I ran forward, searching the horizon. But nothing was there. Just a flat, misty grey that stretched on forever, interrupted by the silhouettes of hundreds and thousands of boats of every conceivable shape and size. It was impossible to get a sense of the size of the ocean itself. I looked along the edge of the city, listening to the water flop against the concrete, searching for the sandy beaches I had read so much about, but they did not exist. The harbor was cluttered with buildings, noisy, and populated mostly by shouting men. The line of palm trees along the shore awed me with their exotic height, their feather-duster tops.

When I looked back up at the city behind us, I saw that it was surrounded by the greenest of mountains, a series of gentle peaks that held all of the city and port in their embrace. The appearance of those mountains lifted me as my parents arms once had, gave me hope for a peaceful life.

White-haired men sat out on the decks of small boats, their bare feet dangling over the water. I wondered where all of the boats were going, where they had all come from. It comforted me to know that we were not the only people on the move. That there were families taking to the sea even when they didn't have to go.

Beyond the seawalls, ocean stretched in every direction, rippling eternally outward. I had thought the sea would be blue or green or even teal, but it was a dull slate-grey. As if even it were weary. "Why can't you see what's on the other side from here?" I asked my parents. "Why can't we see Bolivia?"

"It's not on the coast, Orly. Also, it's a

very big sea," my father answered, gazing out at the horizon. "A very, very big sea."

I followed his gaze. "Will Willi find us there, Vati?"

He glanced at my mother and back to me. "I hope he will."

"If not," my mother said, "we will return for him."

My father fell silent and the three of us stood there for a long moment, faces to the wind.

Now, we walked all the way down to the Stazione Marittima, across from the beautiful Miramare Hotel. Long before we reached the ship, we could see it looming over the harbor, shrinking every other vessel in its vicinity. Its bulk dwarfed even the hills around us, its profile rising above them. It looked too big for the port, too big to be anywhere except in the middle of the ocean. The name *Proteus* was scrawled across its side. My father said he thought Proteus was the name of a sea god who could change shape at will. "Like the sea itself." I thought that was a good omen. That the god of the sea would be looking after us, keeping us safe. Conveniently, I forgot how temperamental the gods could be.

As we stood below the *Proteus* waiting to board, I felt a tightness in my lungs. It was cold by the water and the winds whipped my braids across my face. This monstrously oversized boat was going to take us away, to a place that was nothing more to me than an unanswered question. I watched my mother check her coat pockets for our tickets three times as we stood waiting to board, watched my father fold his arms around his viola case as though it were an infant needing to be soothed. I touched the packet of letters I had been writing to Anneliese on scraps of discarded newspaper and carton since we left home, tucked deep into my pocket.

Like Alice in Wonderland, I grew smaller and smaller. I felt myself dwindling to a speck, a bit of dirt being brushed off the sleeves of Europe. As if the sound of my mother's voice, my father's viola, had not made it more beautiful. As if we were the ones who had brought fear and hatred to the Continent.

"Orlanthe?" My mother looked back abruptly, as if she had lost track of me. "Come, Liebchen." I caught her arm, pressing it tightly against me as we stepped forward.

I had never been on a ship. I had hardly

202

traveled anywhere except to Graz and the Austrian countryside. Standing on the deck of the *Proteus* felt like a metaphor for everything. For the rocking of my world, the sway of solidity under me, the sickening churn of my insides. I probably didn't know the word "metaphor" back then, but I knew the feeling. "We are going to be safe," I reminded myself. "This ship will take us somewhere we will be safe."

My parents had told me that going on the ship would be an adventure. That's what my mother always told me anytime I faced something unpleasant or difficult. "Think of it as an adventure," she would say on trips to the dentist or on an exhaustingly long walk.

I didn't particularly feel the need for adventure. I had had no dearth of adventure. Yet I was still young, still resilient, and I still believed in the power of my parents to save me.

We didn't have any possessions to store in our dormitory room, and so the three of us stood leaning against the rails, looking back on land. With a roar, the engines shuddered to life beneath our feet and the whistle blew low and long. The few who had lingered on board to bid farewell to loved ones hurried tearfully back down the gangplank, clutching their hats to their heads against the wind. As we moved off our moorings into the water, I half expected to see battalions of brown-shirted men rushing to the seafront to stop us. Or to hear the crack of gunfire. But all I saw were a few handkerchiefs in the waving crowds, the jumble of pastel buildings, and a light mist covering our wake.

My fingers on the metal bars grew cold in the wind. My mother's arms encircled me from behind, her long, thin fingers next to mine on the railings. A crush of passengers filled the deck around us, but I felt protected in my mother's embrace. I felt her inhalation, her chest pressing against my back even through our worn wool coats, too warm for an Italian April. Then her voice at my ear, softly at first, her breath stirring my hair so it tickled. Like a lullaby. Leb' wohl mein Leben. *Farewell my life. My Austria, my Europe, my land.* Mein Sohn. Somewhere behind us was my brother. I knew she was thinking of Willi. She sang as though she were putting our old life to sleep until a distant day when it would be safe for it to awaken. Her voice grew stronger as we moved around the seawalls and oceanward, but the rumble of the ship was so loud I

don't think anyone but me could hear her.
Her voice soared upward and outward,
alone in the air, and I could feel her heart
go with it.

TWENTY-FIVE

Several lifetimes passed before we landed in Arica, Chile. Friendships were formed on board and lost in new ports. Books were devoured and traded away. I practiced my breaststroke when the pool wasn't too full. We borrowed a Spanish textbook to teach ourselves a few words. The waiters, evidently not intimidated by our numbers, told us they pitied the country that would take us in.

As we neared Chile, I stayed on the top deck, eager for the first glimpse of land. I wanted to absorb and touch all the things I had seen only in glimpses from various ports: palm trees, exotic fruits, Indians. On the ship we heard many rumors about Bolivia. "It's the most backward country on earth," my shipboard friend Volkmar's German mother told mine. "It's almost entirely Indians." Venezuela was much more advanced, she said. Every country in South

America was advanced compared with Bolivia.

"Perhaps we won't have to be there for long." My mother had looked worried, although no more so than she usually did these days.

I missed Volkmar, who had been a near-constant companion between Italy and La Guaira, Venezuela, where he and his mother had disembarked. Together we had collected books other passengers had already read, sprawled on the deck to turn their pages, and goaded each other to climb up a ladder on the outside of the ship to sneak into the cinema in First Class. Without him I was restless and bored. It had turned hot and the air clung to me.

A whole month we had been at sea. In my old life, a month flitted by. But the past month seemed as long as my previous eleven years. I had met hundreds of other refugees, eaten strange Italian food, and shared a bathroom with twelve women. I had washed out my underwear in the sink at least thirty times and cut my hair in frustration over the knots. It seemed impossible to me that I had ever skipped gaily to school with Anneliese, worried about a history test, or had a bathtub of my own. That Viennese girl had become a stranger. But what had replaced her? I would find out, I supposed, when we arrived in Bolivia.

We were waiting on deck when rocky bluffs emerged from the sea before us. The sky turned all to light. As we drew closer, I trembled with the anticipation of putting a foot down on a stable surface. I could already see a link between this world and the one we had departed a month ago: palm trees. I assumed that meant there would be plenty in Bolivia. Before us stretched an infinity of sand. At last, I was to step onto the beaches I had imagined, even if this wasn't yet Bolivia. The ship seethed with activity as the sailors prepared for arrival and we squinted into the relentless sun. I wondered if it would ever be winter here. If we would be able to both swim and ski, as we had done in Austria.

A moment later we were standing on the earth of a new continent.

Once ashore, we waited in clusters to be told where to go, feeling awkward and hot in our dresses, hats, and shoes in the middle of the beach. My mouth was dry, my lips cracked and sore. All around us men joked with each other in Spanish, laughing and hauling luggage. I looked longingly at the sea, wanting to throw myself fully dressed into the waves. To be clean again, of all of it. Sweat seeped through my dirty dress and torn stockings and made me itch.

At last a woman came to lead us to a nearby army barracks, where we were to sleep in a large hall lined with beds. An organization called La Sociedad de Protección a los Inmigrantes Israelitas, La Paz (SOPRO), funded by the American Jewish Joint Distribution Committee, had arranged for us and nearly a hundred other refugees to stay there until our train the next day. Feeling indulgent, my parents allowed me to strip off my stockings and run barefoot in the sand. I waded into the water, delirious with its caress, taking another step farther every time my parents looked away. I reached down to touch it with my hands, licking my fingers to taste the salt.

The village was small, with a church and clusters of low houses with curiously flat roofs. A woman at the barracks served us all bowls of soup and small bread rolls.

We had just one night in Arica before boarding the train for La Paz. "Don't eat too much on the way up," the army commander who ran the barracks told us. "It will be better for you if there is nothing in your stomach when you arrive."

It took more than two days for the locomotive to heave its way up the Andes with its load of refugees and Bolivians, all of us sharing wooden benches that bruised the bones of my bottom. At times, the train hardly seemed to be moving, inching its way up the arid slopes. The cliffs on either side were massive, steep, and bare. Many of our fellow passengers were various shades of brown. They smiled at me and said things in Spanish or another language I wish I understood. I could not remember ever having been on a train with so many smiling people. Nothing that the Nazis did with their mouths counted as a smile.

The train ground on, up and still farther up, until I wondered if we might actually pass through a cloud. I shivered in my winter coat. There was no heat on the train and it kept getting colder. I huddled close to my mother. The refugees around us began to get ill, some visibly and audibly, others quietly leaning their heads between their knees. None of us felt much like talking. I wasn't sick, but I felt very tired. I curled into my mother's lap and slept for much of the last day.

The following morning, pressing my nose flat into the dusty window of the train, I found myself — at last! — face-to-face with the Andes. I had expected them to be green, not this dark red and grey. I had expected the grass and wildflowers of the Alps. In an entirely new way, it struck me how very far we were from everything we knew. Far from the city. Far from the Alps. Far from Austria's scattered gentian and arnica, far from its chamois and stags. Far from the Vienna Woods, from the coffees, the canals, and the gardens. Far from Aunt Thekla and Anneliese. Far from Stefi, from the house where my mother and I were born. Far from a countryside and language we recognized. Far from the pavements scrawled with graffiti. Far from the Nazis. Far, most of all, from my brother.

We were nowhere I knew at all.

My breath became shallow and fast. When my parents spoke of Bolivia I had imagined something lush. I imagined wild horses and monkeys and alligators and llamas and parrots, as if these creatures could all coexist in the same place. Bolivia is home to all of these animals, but not all of them lived in the Altiplano — one of the highest plateaus in the world.

Still we were moving, up across a tabletop plain. It looked for an instant as if the train would plunge right off the edge of earth, into a vast emptiness and then —

211

La Paz. It appeared below us, a city of redbrick buildings and tin-roofed mud houses trickling down the sides of a bowl in the middle of the mountains. I stared and stared, my eyes going gritty and dry. These buildings were not grand or beautiful. This was not a city. Who had told us it was a city? This was a village. A large village in the middle of a valley on the moon.

There were no palm trees. There were hardly any trees at all. La Paz was not lush. It was dry and high and far from anything alive. As we had neared the plateau above the city, my nose began to bleed, the blood dripping through my fingers to stain my last dress. "I'm sorry, I'm sorry," I said to my mother, bending over so the blood fell to the floor of the train.

My father, who had turned the bluish white of skimmed milk, silently passed me his handkerchief.

"Don't be sorry," my mother said. "None of this is your fault. None of this is any of our faults."

As I watched the cluster of brick and mud that made up the city grow closer and closer, my mother vomited into her hat.

I could barely hear anything above the rattle and roar of the train. Again the ground was moving under my feet. Again I swayed above it. I wanted the earth to be still. I wanted something firm underneath me. I wanted an anchor.

Once we had rolled slowly to a stop, all three of us stumbled as we rose from our seats and started toward the doors. We had arrived somewhere after all. A few metal steps and then —

My feet touched the top of the world.

This could not be the same sky. This could not be the same earth.

My eyes burned. Never had I seen a sun so stark or felt such force. The sun back home had been a weak and benign presence that had to be coaxed out of the clouds. It touched us gently, stroked our hair, warmed our fingers. But the sun of La Paz was all naked aggression; I worried it would blind me. How could the sky be so bright when the air was so cold?

It took a moment for our eyes to take in the landscape — the city and the vast bowl that cradled it. There were jagged cliffs, deep canyons, and mountains in every direction. I could spend all day staring around and not absorb it all. What an odd place to build a city, in mountains so high, in air hardly thick enough to sustain life. It sprawled down the rough sides of a valley, as if a local deity had tripped on its way to more fertile ground and had spilled a bit of metropolis over the edge. I gazed across the crater of the city and up the range of naked peaks on the other side, to the snow-covered slopes of the most beautiful peak of all.

"What's its name?" I asked, pointing to it.

My mother shook her head, but a small, dark man who had been sitting across from us on the train followed the direction of my finger. "Illimani," he said. "Se llama Illimani."

"Ill-ih-mahni." I rolled the word across my tongue. So much faded in the shadow of that great peak; so much was restored.

The buildings were shabby in such majestic company. Among the mud-brick huts were scattered half-finished square houses of red brick and ugly, round-edged modern apartment buildings. These homely structures were huddled so close together that I could see the tiny roofs of nearly every building all at once. Vienna had to be absorbed piecemeal, one street, one building, one canal at a time. While the population of La Paz was only an eighth of Vienna's nearly two million, the mountains gave the city a gravitas and scale that even the mansions of the Ringstrasse failed to evoke.

My eyes remained on Illimani. Hers was a

214

savage kind of beauty, not the gentler, eroded beauty of our mountains. The mountains of La Paz had no need for admiration from us, mere ants clinging to the hems of their skirts.

If I had felt small gazing up at our ship in Italy, I felt a thousand times smaller now.

■ ■ ■ ■

THIRD MOVEMENT:
LA PAZ

■ ■ ■ ■

Twenty-Six

It makes sense that our Bolivian story began, like that of so many foreigners in the country, with food poisoning. After we emerged from the train in La Paz we stood on wobbling legs, gulping mouthfuls of thin air. I searched the crowds for my brother, Willi. Maybe he had arrived in Bolivia before us, because he left Austria first. Surely he had already gotten out of Switzerland. But the crowds before us were empty. A crown of pain tightened around my head. I wanted Willi. I wanted to lie down. I wanted water.

Across from the station was a woman like no woman I had ever seen. As round as an onion, she appeared to be wearing many bell-shaped skirts all at once. This woman — I can still picture her because she was the first Bolivian I saw after stepping off the train — wore a turquoise overskirt with tiered ruffles and a purple and turquoise shawl pinned at her collarbone with a gold brooch. Her shiny black hair hung in two long braids, like the hair of a fancy doll. On the middle of her head perched a small bowler hat, so precariously positioned it appeared in danger of flying off at any moment.

I wanted to touch her. "Sie sind hübsch," I said to this grown-up doll. *You are pretty.* None of us spoke more than a few words of Spanish. The round woman looked at me, her creased brown face breaking into a smile. She reached out her hands to take my small one between them. Her fingers were hard and smooth. "Que linda," she told my mother, "que linda su hijita." My travel-numbed parents just stared at her. Before her was a waist-high wooden cart and a stack of oranges. With a small glass juicer she had been squeezing half oranges into a pitcher before pouring the juice into cups.

Nothing had ever looked as tempting as that juice. Our mouths were parched and it seemed like hours since I had had anything to drink. Months. But when I looked imploringly at my parents my mother shook her head. "Wir haben kein Geld," she said, turning up her empty palms.

The man who had sat across from us on

the train, who was still fiddling with the straps of his suitcase, stepped forward and pressed a crumpled note into the woman's hand. "Jugo para toda la familia." My parents, who would normally have refused any kind of charity, didn't protest. They were as thirsty as I was.

That first taste of Bolivia. That sour sweetness. The sun warming our pale skin as the pulpy juice slid down our throats. The austere beauty of the mountains against the sky, forming a protective ring around us. Dusty children with uncombed hair stared at us. I smiled, the skin of my lips cracking.

"Do you think Willi is here yet?" I touched my mother's sleeve.

With her hand shielding her pale eyes from the sun, she scanned the city's silhouette, as if she could find him there. "Probably not." She and my father had repeatedly reminded me that they didn't know how long it would have taken him to get a visa and book passage. They didn't even know how long it had taken my mother's note containing news of our Bolivian visas to reach him. "We can see if anything has arrived from Violaine." My mother's friend had promised to send word from Paris via poste restante once she heard news.

If Willi were with us, he would be holding

my hand. He would already have made friends with the orange-juice lady and found a way to communicate with gestures. He would know what to do with our parents, small and stunned against these new mountains.

As we finished our juice and gave the doll-lady back her tin cups, a tall short-haired woman in a navy-blue dress and jacket hurried toward us. "Willkommen! I'm Chani from SOPRO. Austria, Germany, or Poland? Name? Oh yes, the Zingels. We were told to expect you. Is anyone else with you? We're expecting many more families. You must have all met on the ship. How are you doing with the altitude? Do you mind if we walk to Plaza Murillo — the main square? It's downhill, don't worry. I find it's more pleasant than the buses. But we can find another way if you don't think you can make it. That's where our offices are. We'll take you there and help you sort out your paperwork and fees, then to somewhere you can sleep until you're on your feet." She kept talking, hardly leaving room for us to reply, which was fortunate given my sudden, heavy exhaustion and the dryness of my mouth despite the juice. Like a shepherdess, she gathered a group of other refugees and herded us together. We followed her in a ragged line down Avenida de América. It was just as well we had so few possessions to carry. The buildings we passed looked dirty and half built, steel rods sticking out of the brick. I peered curiously into the few shops. Roasting chickens turned slowly on spits in the window of a narrow storefront called Café Restaurant Goliat. The smell made my mouth water.

The people on the streets stared openly at us as we passed. Many of the women were dressed similarly to the woman who had sold us the juice. Some men wore dark hats and suits, while others were draped in colorful blankets. I wondered what we looked like to them, if they found our clothing strange or wondered why we were here in their country or if they knew.

We turned down a street called Ingavi, where Chani pointed out the recently opened Museo Nacional de Etnografía y Folklore. "They have some beautiful textiles and some wild carnival masks. If you want to learn a bit about the country." Most of us didn't even look up from the pavement, too exhausted to contemplate tourism. A few minutes later, Chani stopped in front of a dingy metal door that apparently led to the offices of the SOPRO, where volunteers waited to break our fall into this new life.

While my parents talked with volunteers about our paperwork, I lingered in the doorway of the dim, cramped office. "Little girl." A white-haired lady beckoned me over to her desk. "I have something for you." From a drawer she pulled out a cloth doll with a hard plastic head. It wore a yellow dress with a blue apron — an Austrian dirndl — and had blue eyes that opened and shut.

I did not want the doll. I had never wanted dolls. But it would have been rude to say so. "Danke," I said, and took it in my arms.

That night we became ill, taking turns in the bathroom down the hall from the room we were sharing. Our hosts, another Jewish family from Austria, shook their heads in recognition. You have Bolivia belly, they said. It happens to all of us. You will get used to it.

Hanna Gruber, who was a little older than my mother, brewed us pots of a strange, grassy tea and made us drink it. "It will help," she promised.

"With what, precisely?" My mother looked skeptically into her cup.

"With everything."

She was right. The band of pain around

my head loosened and my stomach settled. My exhaustion was not quite so complete.

"The Indians here chew it, you'll see. They chew it all day long. Anything wrong with you, they say chew coca. It's their entire apotheke."

The Grubers shared their three-room home, their food, and their rudimentary bathroom with us and their twin toddler girls. They were also hosting a newly arrived young couple, who slept on the floor of the kitchen after we had all gone to bed. The Grubers were strangers and yet not, compared with the world beyond the walls of their home. They too spoke German with Viennese accents. They too had endured the long journey from sea level to the sky. They too ate strudel and challah, though it wasn't anything like it was at home. The first time I saw a flat, misshapen loaf of challah in Bolivia I nearly wept to see something so familiar. My parents asked about how to find an apartment of our own, but I wasn't sure I wanted a home separate from the other refugees. I liked sharing a bed with my parents, tucked securely between them where I could listen to the sighing of the wind outside and not feel lonesome. In Vienna, they had always sent me back to my bed after reassuring me that my nightmares were nothing but flimsy shadows of my fears. But here in Bolivia, they never sent me away. There were nights my mother's arms closed so tightly around me in sleep I had to pry them apart so I could breathe.

We were lucky. Hundreds of other refugees who couldn't be squeezed into private apartments had to sleep in SOPRO-leased houses that held as many as fifty beds. Chani from the SOPRO offices had told us that she didn't think La Paz could hold many more of us. More than four thousand European Jews had already arrived, and the local people were complaining of food shortages. Mauricio Hochschild, a rich Jewish man who owned more than a third of the mines in Bolivia, was working on a project to save more of us by starting a colony in the jungle, she said. Jews with agricultural visas would be sent there, once they found land. I was grateful for our regular visas. I didn't want to travel anymore.

Our third morning, when Frau Gruber returned from her errands with a sack of crusty white rolls, I discovered one link between La Paz and Vienna. These marraquetas that the Bolivian women sold on the streets in the morning were not so different from our Viennese rolls. I broke one apart and inhaled the yeasty warmth rising from the soft interior. The white fluffy insides melted on my tongue. After a few days, I could not remember the taste of Stefi's rolls.

Like us, the Bolivians liked to dip their rolls into a hot beverage. Though both the definition of "hot" and the definition of "breakfast beverage" were different here. Because of the high altitude, water boiled at a lower temperature, making it nearly impossible to brew either strong coffee or strong tea. I found this confusing; surely boiling temperature was boiling temperature? But then one morning I accidentally poured boiling water over my left hand and was surprised to discover that my skin did not even blister in protest.

Bolivian coffee, according to my mother, was an unacceptable substitute for the coffee of Vienna. While farmers here grew coffee, there were no cafetières, no espresso makers, no evidence at all that the Bolivians made coffee in a recognizable way. Rather, they made their morning cups by mixing a syrupy black coffee concentrate with hot water. Because the concentrate was usually cold, the coffee was never more than tepid. Aggravating my mother further, there was no fresh milk or cream. Powdered milk came in a tin and was called Klim (only years later, as I learned a bit of English, would I figure out that this was "milk" spelled backward). Before too long, I rarely remembered that milk had ever come in a glass bottle with cream on top.

In the evenings, when my mother kissed me and tucked the coarse woolen blanket more tightly around me before going back to talk with the adults, I still asked her for a song. Every night, I asked her for a song. And every night, she touched my cheek with her cold fingers and shook her head. I thought perhaps it was the presence of the other children in the room, the crowd of adults gathered in the kitchen next door. That perhaps she was shy to sing in front of strangers. But that wasn't it, she finally told me one night to make my questions stop. "Singers require two things: air and joy. Here I have not enough of either."

"But you sang on the boat," I protested. "You sang when we left. There was no joy then."

My mother's fingers dug into the muscles along my spine, releasing them all the way down. "There was air. There was relief. We had escaped. I still had hope," she finally said. "And a great need to communicate something to the world I was leaving. I had to say good-bye."

"Don't you still?" I rolled over and looked up at her. "Don't you still need to communicate?"

I wanted to ask, "Don't you still have hope?" but I was too afraid of her answer. Of course it was hard, of course we were still breathless, but we would adjust in time, wouldn't we? Everyone said we would adjust.

She stood up, slipping from my grasp, and turned out the light.

During the days, we walked up uneven cobbled streets to nearby apartment buildings to look at rooms. The floors were coated with grime and the hallways dim. What we could afford with the loan from SOPRO was smaller than my room at home. Many apartments lacked lights or water. "Dear God," said my mother. "It's like going back in *time.*" Her despair deepened with each apartment we saw. "Do they not have soap and water here? Do they not have paint?"

Walking the streets by her side, I saw pretty red and yellow electric trams carrying passengers up and down the sides of the city, their bells ringing out as they rounded a corner. I saw men in brightly colored blankets sitting on the steps of the church playing little wooden flutes. I saw women in flouncy skirts laughing as they strolled in pairs down wide avenues. I saw the grand government buildings clustered around Plaza Murillo. Above all, I saw the mountains. Every time we turned down a new street, I was delighted anew to see the mountains at the end of it. To be confronted with the majesty of snow-tipped Illimani and her companions as part of our everyday errands tinted our days with magic.

It frustrated me that my mother couldn't see the same things. That her eyes absorbed only dirt and disappointment. How could she fail to note that every place we saw looked better than the few filthy feet of floor space we had had in Leopoldstadt? I didn't care what our apartment looked like, as long as it was ours alone. As long as it meant we were safe.

Some refugees lived in boardinghouses, some in one-room apartments. In one of the buildings we considered, there were twelve families per floor, each with just one room. A single toilet served them all. My mother walked back down the stairs without speaking. "Vati?" I began tentatively, as we walked to the next building. "How long will the loan last for?"

"Until I can find work, I hope. We have a little extra your mother's friend Violaine sent us from Paris."

"Can Violaine send money to Willi where he is?"

"She has, sweetheart. At least to where we last knew he was. But she hasn't heard anything from him." He squeezed my fingers gently. "Maybe he's just on a ship."

My breathing relaxed. I was grateful that my mother had traveled, that she had friends in other countries — countries that allowed money to be sent to Jews.

Two weeks later, we found two rooms in a white stucco house on calle Genaro Gamarra in the neighborhood of Miraflores, a twenty-minute walk downhill from the central Plaza Murillo. Our apartment was adjacent to that of a German couple, Mathilde and Fredi, who were friends of the Grubers. We split the top floor, sharing a toilet and bath. Chani, who told us about this place, said the landlady had recently lost her husband and needed the extra income from boarders.

She and her children lived on the ground floor. The landlady, a diminutive, hazel-eyed woman we were introduced to as Señora Torres, met us and Chani by the front door.

"Bienvenidos!" She smiled, kissing my mother's cheek and offering my father her hand. As she continued speaking, my mother and father and I looked at each other in confusion. Chani stepped forward to translate.

"I see you don't have luggage. I'll bring you some towels and a cooking pot."

"Ah! Danke," said my father.

Señora Torres let us in to our rooms, gave us the keys, and apologized via Chani that she had to get back downstairs to fix dinner for her family.

As soon as they heard us in the hallway, Mathilde and Fredi emerged from their room. They were about the same age as my parents, and had arrived a few months before. Mathilde, fair and frail, wasn't much bigger than I was. "We brought you a few things," she said smiling. In one hand was a pitcher of water and in the other, a vase of roses. The sight of them brought tears to my mother's eyes. It had been a very long time since anyone had given her flowers.

"Danke," she whispered. I pushed open the door of our apartment and they all followed me in. The wood floors, painted a dull brown, were flaking and dusty. Olive green paint crumbled from the walls. Dust coated the sills of the two windows. Even the air looked dirty in the morning light. Mathilde set the water and roses on the floor and looked around. "We'll have to find you some mattresses." She spoke in German. "How are you doing with the altitude?" This is still the first question we ask new arrivals; only the altitude remains unaltered by time. Mathilde's wide blue eyes were gentle and kind. "Have you been ill?"

"Not since the first few days. I suppose one adjusts?" My mother glanced around her for something to clean with. Her whole body hummed with disorientation.

Mathilde shrugged. "Everyone is different. Some people never adjust and they have to move to Cochabamba or Coroico. But some don't even feel it."

"I don't feel it," I piped up, eager to prove my sturdiness.

"Good," said my mother, fixing her eyes on the dirty floors and windows as if they were a personal affront. "You can help clean."

"Oh, I'll help too! Everything gets so dirty between tenants. It's the dust, it's so dry here and everything comes in the windows. I'll get some rags." Mathilde ran into her apartment and returned with a handful of torn cloths and a bucket of soapy water.

"Here's a start."

The three of us wiped the walls, windows, and floorboards of our new rooms until they shone, although there wasn't much we could immediately do about the paint. Once I had finished the second window, I stood staring out at the mountains the dust had obscured, at snowy Illimani, sharp against the clear blue sky. Our Vienna apartment had been a place of luxury in comparison, but it didn't have a view like this.

The men wandered across the hall to Fredi and Mathilde's rooms, discussing the probability of war. Fredi and Mathilde, my father told me later, had recently arrived from Berlin, where they had both worked as journalists. Like us, they had left most of their families behind. They were just beginning to learn Spanish and to look for work.

Listening to my mother and Mathilde talk in German, with the murmur of the men's voices in the background, I could almost pretend that we were still at home. If I closed my eyes. And if I didn't notice the missing tenor.

That first night, the three of us made a nest from our coats and went to sleep on the floor. Mathilde and Fredi had given us one of their blankets to use until we could get one of our own. I wriggled in between my parents, still wanting them to stand guard between me and the world. We had kept our clothing on against the cold and my father's jacket was scratchy against my cheek. Despite my exhaustion, I found it difficult to sleep. I wanted my old bed. My Stefi. My Lebkuchen. My brother. I wanted to wake up in the morning and have hot chocolate and bread. I wanted to run upstairs after breakfast to fetch Anneliese for school. I even wanted school itself, a normal rhythm to my days.

The doll the lady in the SOPRO offices had given me sat in the corner, watching me. Even in the dark I felt the gaze of her false, unblinking eyes.

Once my parents were breathing evenly, I slid carefully out of their arms and walked to the window. It got cold quickly once the sun fell behind the mountains, and the glass was icy under my fingers. Our room looked out on a small patch of grass and a cluster of redbrick buildings and squat adobe huts. It was too dark to see even the silhouettes of the mountains now, but in every direction but down I could see the stars. In vain, I searched for the familiar constellations Willi taught me — Hydra, Hercules, my favorites, Ursa Major and Minor — but could find no recognizable patterns. Perhaps we were not merely in a different country, but on a new planet, in a new universe.

TWENTY-SEVEN

That first morning in our own rooms, I woke shivering with cold. Sunlight burned through the naked windows, waking me, while beside me my parents slept on, as if unwilling to open their eyes to our new Bolivian lives. I pressed an ear against my mother's back, listening to the air inflate her lungs, wishing I could feel her ribs vibrating with melody, the way they used to. She was so quiet.

At last, unable to go back to sleep, I climbed again from our nest of coats.

"There's fruit on the table," my mother murmured before turning over.

There wasn't fruit on the table. There wasn't even a table. The table she imagined was home, in Vienna, where a china bowl always overflowed with plums, cherries, and apples. In a corner of our floor was only tea, instant coffee, a can of powdered milk, and a flat loaf of bread Mathilde had made.

But I wasn't hungry. I didn't get hungry here like I did in Austria, with that ravenous empty feeling. My stomach felt constantly full, though often with air. In these mountains, we inflated like balloons.

I walked past Mathilde and Fredi's door, padded down the stairs, and stepped outside, shielding my eyes. In front of the house I saw a small boy with shaggy dark hair squatting in the rutted, empty street, tossing pebbles into the dust.

He looked up at me and grinned. "¿Eres una de los blanquitos que viven arriba, no?" I stared at him uncomprehendingly. While I had learned a few words and phrases of Spanish in my first couple of weeks, I still struggled to understand. He had a flat nose and a scar on his lower lip. His short-sleeved white shirt was carelessly buttoned, so that it hung unevenly over his dark trousers. "¿Cómo te llamas?" When I remained silent, he said. "¿No hablas español?" I shook my head. He sighed and tossed another pebble, striking a larger rock in front of him. "Mira," he commanded.

Not recognizing the word but knowing the tone all too well, I walked over and squatted in the dirt beside him. He dropped a dusty stone into my palm and pointed at the rocks laid out in front of us. It wasn't long before I caught on to the rules, and we played his nameless rock game until my mother finally woke and called me in for breakfast.

The boy stood to watch me disappear inside, looking disappointed. He was shorter than I was, with sturdy little legs and a wide torso. When I turned back to wave at him he brightened and grinned. "¡Chau kantutita!"

Kantutita, I echoed as I climbed the stairs to our rooms. What a pretty word.

The boy's name, I soon learned, was Miguel, and I was grateful he was willing to play with me, given that he had no shortage of playmates. In the three rooms downstairs, he lived with five siblings. His two older brothers, thirteen and fifteen, were in a different school from Miguel and not often around. His little sisters were two, three, and seven. Miguel was ten, nearly my age.

Our second morning, I sat on the front step waiting until Miguel emerged. When he and his younger sisters tumbled through their door, arguing about something I could not understand, I sprang to my feet. "¿Marraqueta?" My father had given me a coin to buy us breakfast. I wasn't sure how much it was worth or what it would buy.

Miguel looked at me. "¿Tienes hambre?" He turned to go back into his home, as if to get me some of his own food.

"No!" I extended my arm, showing him the coin. "I want to buy them." My words were German but the coin spoke for me.

"Ah. Momentito." He turned to his sisters, ordering them back into the house before waving an arm down the road. We walked in silence two blocks to the right and one to the left before I saw a woman sitting outside a small shop in front of a massive sack of rolls. Behind her, the mountains again. Everywhere the mountains.

"Miguel? How many?" I held the coin out. He took it from my palm and gave it to the woman.

"Siete, por favor."

Siete por favor, I whispered to myself.

The woman dug large, calloused hands into her bag and handed me seven rolls without speaking. Not having brought a basket of my own, I folded up the hem of my skirt to carry them.

"Gracias," said Miguel.

"Gracias," I echoed.

Walking back I was bursting with questions I could not voice. How much money was that coin worth? How did people here make money? Where was the school? Where could we find fruit? My ignorance made me ashamed.

"Miguel?" I pulled a roll from my bag and offered it to him. "Marraqueta? Marraqueta, gracias."

When he wasn't at school, Miguel flew from his door whenever I returned from a walk with my mother or father and invited me to play with him and his siblings. I didn't understand their words or games at first, but Miguel was patient with me, using chalk to scribble on bits of pavement, exaggerating his pronunciation until I said a word correctly. When I got something right he would brighten and say, "Bien hecho, kantuta!"

He and his sisters — Ema, Nina, and Celia — absorbed me into their games, asking no difficult questions. They never asked if I was a Jew. It was the first time in forever that someone treated me as an ordinary child.

"Salta!" Miguel would cry, leaping from the front step. "Corre!" he called as he sprinted down the road and back. "Para!" He jerked to a halt in front of me.

Their games were not so different from ours. They kicked balls. They raced toy cars they had fashioned out of empty Klim cans. They played something like hopscotch called thunka, which involved drawing squares on the streets with chalk and labeling them for the days of the week. On one foot, we hopped from Monday to Sunday, before kicking the stone out of the squares. We borrowed a neighbor's wheelbarrow to push each other around. Things I already knew how to do. Wheelbarrow in Spanish is carretilla and I loved the Spanish *r*'s, the way they skipped across my tongue. I loved the soft *yuh* of the double *ll*'s. I especially loved the eñe, that exceptional letter.

My parents' tongues rebelled against the Spanish *r*'s, their less flexible brains struggling to adapt. My mother often refused to speak anything other than German. It wasn't long before I took over our negotiations at the shops, learning the words for flour, potato, rice, and the invaluable sentence: "That's too expensive. We can't pay that much."

When I finally knew enough to grasp the essence of Miguel's questions, and he asked me why we came to Bolivia, I didn't know where to start. Sitting in the dust in front of our house, I sent a rock skittering across the road.

"Nowhere else would take us."

"But why did you have to leave where you are from?" He squatted in front of me, offering me another stone. We were playing thunka.

"We're Jewish." I tossed the rock on Tuesday.

Miguel frowned. "What is Jewish?"

"It's our religion." One hop, two.

"¿Entonces . . . ?" *And so?*

"So . . . most people don't like Jews over there." I handed him the rock. He turned it over in his hands.

"Why?"

I shrugged. I had no answer. "Isn't there anyone here people don't like?"

Miguel looked thoughtful. "I guess some people don't like Indians very much," he finally said.

"Indians?" Keeping one foot off the ground, I remembered the things people had said on the ship about Indians. That they were dirty and strange, maybe violent.

"You know, like the Aymara, the people from the highlands. From the lake. Or the Quechua. My father was Aymara, but he moved to Coroico to grow fruit and coca." Intrigued by the idea of highlands, I overlooked his use of the past tense when describing his father. There were people living higher than La Paz? Not possible.

"Why don't people like the Indians?"

He threw the rock and imitated my shrug.

243

"Because we Indians were here first?"

At the end of our second week in his house, Miguel took my mother and me to the market. Mathilde offered to take us, but I wanted to go with someone who would be able to explain things.

"Miguel will know what things should cost," I reasoned.

"How will he tell us?" My mother wasn't yet sure of Miguel. "I understand Mathilde."

"I understand him, Mutti. At least some of the time. He's nice." When the skin of her forehead did not relax, I continued. "Mutti. Would you want a French person to guide you around Austria?"

As Miguel and I walked together, chattering and waving our hands, my mother followed silently behind. I wished she could be like she always had been with Anneliese: inviting, interested. Why couldn't she at least try? I wanted her to be nice to my friend. I wanted her to try some Spanish words. For years she had been singing in Italian, French, and German. Spanish should have been easy.

We passed little stores with battered signs reading TIENDA ANA MARÍA or TIENDA MARISABEL. Like every store was named

244

after someone's aunt. At the side of the street I saw a pile of something that looked remarkably like human excrement. "Is that — ?"

Miguel shrugged.

I glanced back at my mother, hoping she would not see, that her views of Bolivia would not be made still darker. Yet I couldn't suppress my own revulsion. It was hard to believe I would ever adjust to the fecal stink of the open sewers that ran along some of the streets. Paving stones glistened with urine and gobs of greenish spit. Every time we took a walk we returned covered with dust. I shared my mother's horror at the lidless bin next to the toilet for discarded toilet paper. All that stained, festering paper sitting around in the open air. In Austria, bodily functions had been a private matter. But here, we were continually confronted with our animal reality.

A quarter of an hour after we set out, the Mercado Camacho opened before us. Row after row of woven blankets spread on the ground displayed vegetables, fruit, coca leaves, and maize as well as many things I didn't recognize. Selling these things were the people Miguel called Indians, who were mostly Aymara like his father. They included the cholitas, those many-skirted women with the long braids and bowler hats. Busily they stacked their earth-crusted potatoes and cucumbers for our inspection, babies strapped to their backs with brightly colored cloth Miguel called aguayo. The babies stared at me over their mothers' shoulders with round, brown eyes.

They had come from the semitropical Yungas Valley or from the plains around Lake Titicaca to sell their produce in La Paz. Their men wore thick woolen ponchos and hats with flaps that came down over their ears. In their hands they carried pouches of green coca leaves. Their calloused feet were nearly bare in sandals that appeared to be fashioned from automobile tires.

I stopped in front of a display of mangoes and other fruits, amazed to discover so many unfamiliar shapes. There were lumpy green fruits that Miguel called chirimoyas, little round guavas with pink flesh inside, like the ones I had seen in the port of La Guaira, Venezuela, where our ship had stopped on our way here, and gourd-shaped papayas. "Mutti, look!" I reached for a pearlike yellow fruit.

"Membrillo," Miguel told us. I shook my head. Not a word I recognized. "And here, maracuyás. Good, but sour." He pursed his lips so I would understand the word.

The vegetables were less exciting; carrots, peppers, tomatoes, and garlic were all familiar. I stopped again, however, when I saw the rough green skins of what I now know are avocados, looking to Miguel for explanation.

"Palta," he said. He spoke to the woman selling them and she cut one open for me to see. The inside was creamy and green. With her knife, the woman sliced a bit of the flesh for me to taste.

The buttery smoothness on my tongue was a revelation. After that initial encounter, I bought them every time we could afford them. My favorite lunch was an avocado with a spoon to scoop out its insides. I felt I could never again live anywhere that did not grow avocados.

"If we ever have a garden, I want to grow an avocado tree!"

Miguel laughed. "You think these grow in La Paz?" Almost all the palta, all of the fruit, came to La Paz from the hot, wet lowlands, he explained. Mostly from around Coroico, a village in Los Yungas. They came to La Paz on trucks, or on the backs of men. I wondered if I would ever see these distant jungles, mythical sources of water and oxygen.

My mother shopped cautiously, purchasing only fruit with peels that she scrubbed with vigor and rinsed with boiled water in the hope that any contamination would not seep inside. Allowing Miguel to negotiate her purchases, she carefully selected plátanos, which looked like bananas but were starchy and bland; tamarindos, which came in brown pods; tuna (cactus fruit with prickly skin); and mangoes, fruits that were either a luxury or unheard of in Vienna.

As we wandered through the market, we passed men sitting at street corners, playing music on sets of wooden pipes. The women, it seemed, did most of the selling.

I couldn't stop staring at their faces, so flat and alien. They stared back at me. What did I look like to them? I wondered. Was my pale face frightening or just strange? Was my orange hair ugly to them? Did they find the lack of color in our clothing a sign of dullness? I wanted to know.

Behind a table spread with potatoes was a girl with skin darker than Miguel's and black plaits hanging to her waist. Her eyes too were darker than Miguel's, so black I couldn't find the border of her pupils. She wore a fringed shawl of turquoise cloth around her shoulders. My mother ran her hands over the potatoes as if they were valuable gems. While we had always thought of potatoes as white, here they were yellow and blue and orange. I couldn't take my eyes off the girl.

"Soy Orly," I said, offering her my hand. She stared at me, arms by her sides. "¿Cómo te llamas?"

She looked uneasily at the older woman beside her. Her mother? "No mucho español," she finally said.

"Yo tampoco." Me neither. I smiled. "Estoy aprendiendo. ¿Qué idioma hablas?" I was mystified as to why this clearly Bolivian person did not speak Spanish. I still hadn't learned the history of this country, that Spanish was not its native tongue but that of its brutal conquerors. I looked around for Miguel, but he and my mother had walked on ahead.

The girl was silent.

Pressing both hands to my chest I tried again. "Soy Orly." She smiled shyly, and pressing her hands to her own chest, she answered, "Soy Nayra."

"Mucho gusto." I reached out to touch her hand, but she jerked back, fear in her eyes.

"Orly!" My mother called, realizing I hadn't followed her and Miguel to the poultry.

"Lo siento," I said, tilting my head to convey my apology. "Tengo que ir. Mi madre. Me voy! Hasta luego!" Across the market I flew until my mother caught my hand in hers, anchoring me to her side.

"Miguel, what language do the potato ladies speak?"

He laughed. I must have said it wrong. "Aymara."

"Do you know it?"

"Of course. From my father."

"Can you teach me?" I augmented my halting Spanish with gestures.

"Why?"

I shrugged. I wanted to explain more, but I just didn't have all the words yet.

We examined the chickens. A city girl, I was unaccustomed to watching animals be slaughtered. For me, meat had always come in bloody packages from the butcher. But at the Camacho Market, the food was still alive. Chickens and ducks fluffed their wings in cages, and fish swam in tanks. When Miguel bought a chicken for his family, a cholita sliced off its head right in front of us.

I closed my eyes to block out the squawking bird and absorbed the sounds of the market. The rustle of skirts, the voices of vendors, the clop of hooves, the wind. The

Spanish! I could not get enough of its melody. Those lilting words; I wanted them all for my own.

Before abandoning the market, Miguel stopped at one last stall that sold half-moons of pastry baked until they turned gold. "Salteñas," he said, offering one to my mother and dropping the other into my palm. It burned my skin and I waved it in the air until it was cool enough to bite. The crust was sweeter than I expected, and it was so juicy inside that broth ran down my chin. "It's like stew in a strudel," I said to my mother, who was eyeing her pastry with deep skepticism. "I think it's beef inside? And potatoes. Spicy!"

Miguel smiled. "Ají," he said. "It's a kind of chili."

My mother took a cautious nibble. And then another. I watched her lick the juice from her fingers and I smiled.

After we had left the market and were walking the mile or so downhill (at last) to our rooms, a herd of furry, long-necked animals rounded the corner in front of us, heading our way. There were dozens of them, with matted and dusty coats. I'd seem them before from the windows of our train, but not up close. I grabbed my mother's hand, unsure whether they were dangerous. We stared at the creatures. They didn't look hostile. In fact, on closer inspection they looked almost cuddly. Miguel laughed to see the expressions on our faces. "They are not dangerous," he assured us. "They're llamas."

My mother looked pale. "In — in the *city*?" For my mother, the city had been an escape from village life. A place far more refined and cultured. Herds of filthy animals did not wander down the Ringstrasse.

"They are going to market," Miguel said. "They are delicious."

While I felt sorry for the llamas, I was also curious. I wondered what llama meat tasted like. I wondered if we were allowed to eat it, or if it was forbidden, like pork. (Although we didn't keep kosher, we never ate pork.)

I reached out a hand to touch one of the animals as it went by, and it turned its head, drew back its lips, and spat at me. Shocked, I looked down at my blouse, where a glob of greenish llama spit hung from a button. Unprepared for this visceral reminder of home, I started to cry. I hadn't shed a tear since we left Genoa — not for Austria, not for Willi, not for Anneliese — but that llama spitting at me shoved me over a precipice I had not known I was approaching.

"Oh, Orly. You shouldn't have tried to touch one!" My mother looked vaguely repulsed.

Miguel gently pulled me to the side of the street. "We have a saying: If you kiss the llama it won't spit at you."

Kissing a llama didn't sound that much more attractive to me than being spit on by one.

I had expected Miguel to laugh at me, or to chastise me. But instead he used a sleeve of his shirt to carefully wipe the spit off my blouse. "The alpacas are much nicer. They don't spit as much," he said. "And they make nicer yarn. The vicuñas, too, but their wool is very expensive."

"Is it warm?" My mother was always cold here, so her interest in alpaca yarn was not mere politeness. After taking a trembling breath, I translated for Miguel, who confirmed that yes, it was warm, and that he knew someone who could knit us sweaters.

Talking with Miguel steadied me the way talking with Willi once had. I was embarrassed for crying in front of him. For crying about something as stupid as llama spit when Willi was still missing. When we began walking again, I muttered a quick prayer under my breath — to whom I am not sure — promising that I would bathe in llama spit if it would bring Willi to us.

So much of being in this new place was observation. I didn't know how anything in this world worked; I had to watch how Bolivians moved and talked and played so I could relearn everything. My mother and father and I were like children again, not understanding how to buy food, what it should cost, how to greet a stranger, or where to find soap. Here, my Austrian impulses were wrong. Every day I found myself in a culturally coded world without the key. While this could be overwhelming and confusing, it was also terribly exciting. Having to focus so much energy on navigating our new home distracted us from the fathomless fear and grief at our heels.

A few blocks from the market, Miguel took my hand. "Come. I have something to show you." With my silent mother struggling to keep up with us, we picked our way through the crowded streets to a woman sitting against a brick building, bunches of flowers arranged in clay vases in front of her on the ground. There were white roses, flame-colored begonias, and bunches of flowers I had never seen. After greeting the woman, Miguel reached his hand to a single bloom, a tubular flower that flared out at the end like a Spanish skirt. "Mira." Stroking the underside, he showed me how its color turned from yellow to orange to red. "Like your hair." He lifted one of my braids and held it close to the flower. "It's our national flower. It's called kantuta."

On the way home we stopped in one of the many small Bolivian shops that sold powdered milk, matches, and other odds and ends. "I want to buy a peli," Miguel explained. He showed me the slender bits of film containing frames from movies that you could see if you held them up to the sun. He and his friends collected them. "I love the cinema."

I touched the fragile scrap Miguel gave me, held it up to the sky. "I see a boy in a funny hat. And — is that an elephant?"

"That's from *Elephant Boy*. Have you seen it?"

I shook my head. "I've seen *The Tale of the Fox*," I offered. Willi had taken me and Anneliese one Saturday afternoon, had made us laugh imitating the animals.

"Never heard of it."

"It's German. It had animation."

Interest flickered in his eyes. "I've only ever seen one animated film. I saw *Snow White*. Do you know it?"

"Everyone knows it!"

"Not everyone here." A defensiveness had crept into his voice.

"My brother took me to see that one too." I said it to change the subject, to keep Miguel from being mad at me.

"You have a brother?"

"Didn't I tell you?"

He shook his head. Shame spread through me like hot poison. I could not have forgotten my brother. I could never forget my brother. I glanced at my mother, who was speaking quietly with Mathilde, whom she'd met in the shop. I was thankful she could not understand us. "My brother, Willi. He's still in Europe, in Switzerland. He's coming here."

"When? Why didn't he come with you?"

I shook my head and looked up the street. "Soon. He's coming soon."

TWENTY-EIGHT

"When will grandma and grandpa come?" I asked my mother one bright afternoon as we stood on the steps of the post office. "And Aunt Thekla? When will Klara and Felix be here?" My mother was studying a thin page of cramped writing with a hand over her eyes to protect them from the sun. The family members we had left behind were still trying to find a way out. Visas had dried up and the few letters we received were steeped in panic. My mother wrote to Bolivian officials, to Austrian officials, to distant relatives in other countries. She received no replies.

Today's letter was from my Viennese grandmother, who had been moved with my grandfather into yet another communal apartment.

"Felix is still missing. Thekla won't leave without him." My mother shook her head over the letter, her hand crushing the edge of the paper before handing it to my father. "There's going to be war. There's going to be war and then how will they get out?"

My father frowned over the paper. "I should have gotten them the agricultural visas. What a fool I am."

"You're not a fool, Vati."

"We are all fools, Orlita. Letting them walk right in." He slipped the letter into his pocket and stared grimly out at the mountains.

I fell silent. I thought about my aunts and uncles and my grandparents. I thought about Willi. "Is Klara still there? And Aunt Klothilde?"

My mother took my hand. "Everyone's alive, we think. But I doubt their situation is going to get better."

"And if there's war?"

"If there's war," said my father, "we'll know even less."

Over the first few weeks of our new life in La Paz, we pieced together a home from three straw mattresses, donated dishes, borrowed books, and a table and chairs crafted from packing crates. As soon as these set pieces were in place, my father sat down on a crate after dinner one night and took out his viola for the first time. He hadn't opened the case since we arrived, although he had often played with other musicians on the ship. Now, he ran his fingers over the instrument like he was relearning its surfaces. He tightened his bow and drew it across the D string. We both winced. But half an hour later, as I lay on the floor reading at his feet, a stroke of his arm drew forth the flight of notes that began Fantasia Cromatica.

My heart leapt after those notes, following them like butterflies up a path it knew well. It didn't matter that his fingers were stiff and weak, that they faltered at that speed. Listening to him play reminded me of times when I didn't know I was thirsty until I started drinking and then the whole glass went down. Home had been with us all along; it lived in the air shimmering around my father's strings.

"Well. There it is." He lifted his eyes from the viola and smiled a real smile, the first I could remember seeing since the Philharmonic expelled him. "So. What shall I play for you?"

I closed the book of fairy tales on my lap that I had borrowed from the Grubers. "Schumann's Märchenbilder! The fairy tale songs."

"Nothing simpler? I don't want to start panting and faint in the middle of it."

"You just did Fantasia Cromatica!" I sighed. "All right. A waltz, then: Strauss." I glanced over at my mother lying on a mattress, her eyes fixed on the ceiling. She did not stir.

My father pulled the viola from his chin and rested it on his knee. "No waltzes," he said. "I think I am finished with waltzes."

"Well, don't ask me then," I said irritably, turning back to my book. "Play whatever you like." I couldn't see the harm in playing a waltz. Hadn't we already given up enough of Austria? We had to give up Strauss now too?

A mild amusement tugged at my father's mouth. "Which Märchenbilder piece, then? I suppose you want 'Lebhaft'?"

"Lebhaft" — lively or spirited — was my favorite of the four. But I thought about how fast my father's fingers would have to move on the strings and how he had struggled with the Fantasia. "No, I'm in the mood for 'Langsam, mit melancholischem Ausdruck' tonight." This piece, "Slowly with a melancholy expression," was one he had played me in the evenings before bed, its gentle rhythms drawing me irresistibly into dreams. It seemed to describe the undercurrent of our life in La Paz, the way my mother drifted up and down its streets.

Slowly, with melancholy expression.

"A wise choice, kleiner Hase."

Tucking the viola back under his chin, my father lifted his bow and played me "Langsam, mit melancholischem Ausdruck." Within the first six notes, I was in Vienna. I was in my own bed, soft sheets drawn to my chin, Lebkuchen tucked in my arms. I had forgotten how swiftly music could transport me.

His fingers were still clumsy on the strings — even I could see it — and his rhythm staggered, but he played it all the way through. Then he started again.

Scooting across the floor to lean against one of the crates, I closed my eyes. As the vibrations of his strings stirred the air around me, the small muscles along my spine spasmed and then unclenched. My stomach relaxed into roundness. My hands fell to my lap. Fear that had secreted itself in my body crept away. I let the sounds move over me like warm hands. When I heard my father play, I began to believe in our life here.

A siren startled me one morning while I was outside kicking a football with Miguel. At first I thought it must be a fire truck, but I'd never seen a fire truck in La Paz. A few seconds later, Mathilde came hurrying from the house, pulling on her jacket as she came down the steps. "That means news!" she called as she passed us.

I kicked the ball to Miguel and ran after her. "What does?"

"Orlita!" Miguel sounded cross.

"I'll come back!"

"The siren, it's from the newspaper." Mathilde explained that whenever something important happened, the siren summoned people to the latest headlines scrawled on the blackboard in the windows of the newspaper office. "That way you don't have to wait for the paper." I remembered then Mathilde had been a journalist, one of the few women writing about politics in Berlin. I wondered if she wished she were still in Europe, covering the biggest story of our lives. But of course a Jew would not be allowed to interview anyone. Not now. She was here for a reason. Mathilde had become the story.

As we neared the street where the offices were, we saw other refugees hurrying in the same direction, their faces tight with fear. Had Hitler expanded his reach yet again? I felt an impulse to take Mathilde's hand, but resisted it.

Breathless by the time we reached the

small crowd gathering in front of the window, we threaded our way to the front. The message written on the chalkboard in the window was brief:

More than 900 refugees aboard SS St. Louis forced to return to Europe after denied entry by Cuba, the U.S., and Canada. Dozens threatened suicide.

I translated the Spanish for Mathilde. The language had made itself comfortable on my tongue. I was just young enough to absorb the whole of it, structure and vocabulary at once, without book study. Miguel and his many siblings were better than any book.

"Returned to Europe?" Mathilde repeated.

"Did you know anyone on it?"

Mathilde didn't answer. She just stood there with her arms hanging limply at her sides. "There's nowhere left," she said. "There's really nowhere left."

Twenty-Nine

While my mother was resolute in her decision to abandon singing, my father could not stop playing once he had begun again. Some days I felt it was an inconvenience for him to eat or to talk to us. He played as if, by drawing his bow across the strings enough times, he could erase history. As if he could lure his wife back to her voice and play his son home. As if he could erase everything but sound, and we could all live in that.

The following week he began to take on students. There was no La Paz Philharmonic. There was no opera house or ballet. If you wanted to make a living as a musician, you taught. Eager students are a reliable constant; music, it seems, is a universal craving.

At first he taught only the children of other refugee families, families that had been in La Paz long enough to start a business and save a little money. But unable to turn anyone away, he also taught recent arrivals for free. As word got around, a few of the Paceña families with money — the palest descendants of the Spanish invaders — asked if he would teach their children too. He began to earn a little, traveling from home to home or teaching from our bedroom. But it wasn't enough. We needed pots and pans, shoes, spoons, a comfortable chair. I was tired of balancing on crates and boxes during meals. We wanted to save something for a real apartment, a proper kitchen table.

I wanted to go to school, but my parents said I would have to work until we had enough money to survive on our own. Besides, we hadn't yet found a school. I wanted to go to the local Bolivian school with Miguel, but it was Catholic, and my parents said it wouldn't teach me enough; they wanted me to have classes in German or English as well as in Spanish. This did not alleviate the despondency I felt when Miguel abandoned our early morning games to head to school. He had other friends there, friends who didn't sound so stupid speaking Spanish.

The Grubers hired me to look after their toddlers some mornings. In the afternoons,

I often tended to the children of other refugees. Thus I was able to contribute a few bolivianos each week to our coffers. I didn't mind the work itself — there was something relaxing about being with smaller children, concerned with simple things like food and finding places to play — but I hated feeling I was falling behind in my studies.

My parents had never been especially good with money, their attention caught up in the perfection of sound rather than in the more pragmatic aspects of life. In Austria, their families had helped them when they ran into trouble. In particular, my Vienna grandfather had worried about our money. Here, we all had to.

Many Jewish entrepreneurs didn't do badly in Bolivia. They were able to start import businesses, textile companies, or restaurants. But my parents didn't have the right skills or minds. Nor had they any talent for self-promotion. Their talents had to sell themselves or go unused.

Once my father had enough students for us to pay for potatoes, onions, and the occasional pat of butter, he began meeting with three other refugee musicians in the evening to play Baroque music. Rarely had my father ever played the viola alone; he had always been a part of something larger. He was an arm severed from the body of the Vienna Philharmonic. He wanted to be grafted onto something else, anything else. He was, I realized only later, lonely, without even my mother's voice to accompany him. All my life, my parents' relationship had consisted of music. They sang phrases to each other, talked through their difficulties at work, hummed pieces of symphonies, sat down together by the piano. They inhabited the same world. Now, only my father lived in that world. My mother was still beside us, making us meals and reminding us to wash our faces, but there was no nightingale anywhere.

"Julia, why must you punish yourself? It was not music that did this. Not the sound of your voice. How can you let them take that too?" My father was confused, did not know how anyone lived in a world without music, least of all his wife. His wife who turned away from him, who did not answer.

After near-silent dinners, my father would come to life when one of the other musicians knocked on our door. "Julia, do you know," he said excitedly as he rose to let them in, "I am falling in love with music all over again. I can experiment now. I do not have to play the same repertoire year after year. I am free!"

My mother stacked plates and carried them to the washing basin. "Free? Yes, you are free — from the Philharmonic, from our parents, from your son. Me, I could live without such freedoms."

"Julia —"

But then Gregor was in the house, changing everything. "Frau Zingel! Guten Abend! So kind of you to tolerate us once more." He swiveled on his heels. "Jakob, an honor, as always."

I liked Gregor, a violinist, the best. He was the happiest, dancing as he played, his body bouncing forward and backward, rocking left to right, sometimes rising up on his toes as his eyebrows shot toward his hairline at a particularly emotional juncture. He came from Salzburg and was only twenty. Like my father, he took in students, but he also worked in a textile factory during the week. There were three textile factories in Bolivia, where workers spun cotton or wool into thread, dyed it, and wove it into cloth. Gregor was a dyer, and his hands were always stained with color. I liked to watch his sunset-streaked fingers dance across his strings.

The two of them were eventually joined by a Czech cellist and a German violinist, both Jews. One evening, Miguel and I were drawing with chalk in the street when they began playing, the notes cascading from our windows. Miguel stopped, squatting back on his heels. "Is that your parents?"

"My father. And his friends. My mother is a singer but she doesn't sing anymore."

He listened for a few minutes more, rapt. "This is what he did when you were in Austria?"

"It's what he does everywhere. What he has always done."

Miguel looked at me, the smooth skin of his forehead crinkling. "And they threw him *out*?"

THIRTY

Our social life in La Paz was far more casual than it had been in Vienna. None of us had telephones at first, so we had to venture out to find each other at home or meet up in Plaza Murillo, in the heart of the city. In the mornings, I liked to climb the mile or so up to the plaza with my mother and Mathilde, even though they always needed to stop and rest a dozen times along the way. In those early days we traveled regularly to the SOPRO offices on calle Junin, near the plaza, mostly to connect with each other, but also to pick up emergency cash, trade books, or offer to help a newer refugee with paperwork or a meal. When one of us had a few coins, we rode the Tranvías de La Paz electric trams all the way downhill to the pastoral neighborhood of Obrajes and back. The red streetcars had the nicest seats, but mostly we rode the yellow and green cars because they were cheaper. There wasn't much to Obrajes back then; it was countryside. But the descent was thrilling. I couldn't stop myself from the delicious torment of imagining a failure of brakes that would send us all sailing into the blue.

My mother sat with Mathilde or Hanna on the benches (we were allowed to sit on benches again!) across from the grand Presidential Palace and the Cathedral of La Paz, watching the trams disgorge passengers and the salteña vendors ply their juicy pastries while they exchanged news from home. More of us arrived every month, in varying states of shock, confusion, and grief. I chased the pigeons with newly arrived refugee children, careening around the statue of independence fighter Pedro Domingo Murillo and irritating the old women who were scattering corn for them. While I joined in games with the other children, I didn't make a friend like Anneliese. No one was exactly my age; no one could draw a map of Friedenglückhasenland; no one stroked my arms with tender fingers. I had only ever had one best friend. Besides, now I had Miguel, whose happy company usually felt like enough.

Once we were settled, it was our turn to host the new families. Like us, they arrived pale, nauseated, and panting for air. We were the experts now, thrusting cups of coca tea into their hands and instructing them to drink. We told the newcomers how long to boil the water and where to find the best textiles. We guided them up the uneven, twisting streets to the markets, to the textile factories, and to the paseo del Prado, a wide, grassy area of avenida 16 de julio, where you could watch couples parade in their fanciest clothes on Sunday afternoons. We took them to the refugee-owned Brückner & Krill, which sold European-style sausages, pastries, and other food they recognized. My mother liked to stop in there, more for the pleasure of running into other refugees and speaking German than to actually buy anything. Mathilde had told us there was a Viennese restaurant somewhere nearby, though we didn't yet have enough money to go.

Most of us grasped for the familiar, cooking Austrian and German food and speaking German. Many never became comfortable with Spanish. Many never considered Bolivia a permanent home, but merely a place to wait out the coming war.

Not everyone adapted. Some stayed ill, some never learned to sleep. But there were limited alternatives. While not all of Bolivia is close to the sky — there are jungles in the lowlands, cities close to sea level — these too had their hazards. As we would learn.

Some families moved to Cochabamba, a sunny little city closer to sea level, where they opened small hotels and bakeries. But most of the work was in La Paz. Most of our community was in La Paz. Travel was difficult, making it hard to move between cities.

Eventually, we formed clubs — the Maccabi Sports Club, the Austrian Club, and others — where we had meals, arranged concerts, and played tennis. The Austrian Club was often where we heard news — who had come down with amoebic dysentery, who had died in childbirth, and who had heard from relatives in Vienna. Our mothers exchanged dress patterns and suggestions for coping with altitude or food-borne illnesses.

On our first Sunday at the Austrian Club I was amazed to suddenly see so many of us, so many German speakers, so many Jews, in one place. It was as if we had abruptly been transported back home. The full name of the club was Federación de Austríacos Libres en Bolivia — Federation of Free Austrians in Bolivia. There, I almost felt like a free Austrian. We ran around playing games we had played in Vienna while our parents heaped their plates with potato salad and Schnitzel, talking not only about home and the coming war, but about books and films. I couldn't remember the last time I had heard adults talk about anything other than how to stay alive.

My father suggested I join the troupe of actors at the club. "You'll learn some Austrian plays. Maybe make a few friends." He was sitting on the end of my mattress on the floor, his knees poking up nearly as high as his head.

"I have Miguel." The other refugee children were not as interesting. Why did I need Austrian friends? No one but Miguel could tell me the names of the fruits and flowers. No refugee kid could tell me that the cholitas' hats were called borsalinos or that a grain called quinoa was one of the few crops that thrived at altitude. I didn't understand why so few of the other refugees made Bolivian friends. How else could we learn how to live?

"Wouldn't it be nice to have a girlfriend?"

A girlfriend. The word sent a dart of longing through my ribcage. Maybe I hadn't made a girlfriend among the refugee children because the comparisons with Anneliese were too obvious; it would feel too much like betrayal. Yet the idea of performing in a play, of being someone else, was attractive. When my father told me the next play was to be Johann Nestroy's *Der Talisman,* a comedy featuring a girl mocked for her red hair, I tried out for the part. Who but me could so naturally utter the line "Whoever has something against the red color knows not what is beautiful"?

I got the role.

After that, I split my nonworking time between theatrical activities at the Austrian Club and street games with Miguel. While I enjoyed rehearsing and running around with the other German-speaking children, I still found no special friend. The girls in our community already had best friends, or were not interested in things that interested me. None of them were as much fun as Miguel.

Gradually, my parents allowed Miguel to take me farther and farther from home to explore the city. Given the number of children his mother had to keep track of, she rarely even knew he was gone. Señora Torres was also starting her own business. While she made enough money from the rents we paid her to survive, she had begun designing knitted clothing that she sold in the markets. She worked when most of her children were in school, and after they were in bed. "She doesn't have to work so much," Miguel told me. "But she likes to design. Her father — my grandfather — he's a trader and he still helps us. A lot of tin was hidden in the Bolivian mountains. My abuelo found places to sell it."

One Saturday he took me to see the Paris movie theater in Plaza Murillo, walking so swiftly I struggled to keep up even though my legs were longer. Posters outside advertised *Union Pacific,* but neither of us had money. "This is where I saw *Elephant Boy.* Also *A Day at the Races* and *Wild West Days."* His face was wistful as we turned away. "I have pelis from all of them."

Lacking coins for the tram, we wandered down to the San Francisco church, which sat in San Francisco Plaza at the bottom of calle Sagárnaga. Standing outside, we gazed up at the arched windows, at the bells clamoring in and out of its tall stone tower. Though it was majestic, it couldn't compete with Illimani.

"Are you allowed to go in?" he said.

"Why wouldn't I be?"

"It's not your religion."

"Jews are allowed to go in anywhere we want." This was what I wanted to be true.

Miguel suddenly grinned. "Are you al-

276

lowed to practice witchcraft?"

I was caught off guard. *What?*

"Magia. Like making magical potions with herbs."

I considered this. "I don't know."

"Ven." He set off at a swift pace up the cobblestone street. We seemed always to be walking uphill, whether we were going or coming.

We left the iglesia de San Francisco and headed up the steep calle Sagárnaga. Several small burros passed us, laden with packages wrapped in striped blankets. I was continually amazed by the vibrancy of color everywhere. A woman in a green, fringed shawl and bowler hat crouched on the street to tie up a bundle more securely. Shopfronts were almost obscured by bright hanging fabrics — children's dresses, hats, tapestries of animals, and woolly ponchos. Two men in black hats and dark suits stared at me. I tilted my head up, wondering if people lived in the buildings above the shops, with the pretty wrought-iron balconies and red clay roofs. When we reached the narrow calle Linares, we turned right.

"Mira." Miguel swept an arm before us. "El Mercado de las Brujas." The Witches' Market.

Turning to examine the shops that lined

the cobblestone street, I saw what I first thought were toy animals, hanging in rows of furry bouquets over the fronts of shops and sitting atop tables on the street. Also on the tables were stacks of colorful boxes and tins, polished stones, handfuls of things that looked like bones.

I wondered if I should be nervous. "Are there really witches here?"

"Aymara witches. They are called yatiri."

I tasted these words, letting them roll around in my mouth. Yatiri sounded like a bird in flight. "What do they do?"

"They cure people."

"Of what?"

"Sometimes they cure bodies and sometimes they cure souls."

"Are they real?"

"Of course they're real!" He looked offended. "This is a serious place."

Chastened, I bit my lip. As we continued up the street I looked more closely at the animals dangling over our head. They looked dried out. "Are those — what *are* those?"

"Those are llama fetuses," Miguel explained cheerfully. "You have to bury them under every house, or the builders won't work."

I nodded as if this made sense. *They kill so*

many babies? They put them under their houses? He went on. "The fetuses are an offering for Pachamama, Mother Earth. They bring luck and health and they keep the builders safe. Builders are often dying."

I stopped walking. "Is there a llama fetus under our building?"

"Of course! All buildings."

"Even though you're just half Aymara."

"Mother Earth is home for all of us, no? Why should we not all make her offerings?"

I stared at the vacant eyes of the dangling llamas. "Why did your father leave Coroico?"

"He didn't."

"But you're here —"

Miguel kicked at a matted feather stuck to the cobblestones. "Do you want to look at the shops or not?"

I nodded without speaking, sorry I had upset him.

He ducked into the closest shop and greeted the woman behind the counter. I followed, careful not to touch anything on the crowded shelves. What if I accidentally set off some kind of spell? Under the watchful eyes of the yatiris, we looked at twigs, herbs, and powders with names that I didn't understand, presumably to cure various ailments. Miguel pointed out the array of coca

279

teas and creams for altitude sickness and pains in the body, powdered frogs, stone amulets to bring good health or good business, and dozens of compounds for virility and fertility. But I couldn't stop looking at the little llamas, in widely varying sizes and stages of development. They fascinated me.

"They must have to kill a lot of baby llamas."

"No, they don't kill them," said Miguel. "They are born dead. Or their mother dies and she is pregnant."

I felt slightly relieved, though I had no way of knowing if this was true. There were an awful lot of fetuses to be accounted for.

"Do you use these things?"

He shrugged. "If we need to."

"I thought you were Catholic." I didn't understand how these witches fit into Miguel's worldview.

"We are Catholic. But we also believe in witch doctors. And in kallawayas. Wandering healers. Why pick just one thing?" He did not understand why I found this confusing. "Do you believe in witches?"

"I don't think so. I'm not sure."

"Do your parents?"

"No." But I was uncertain. I didn't know what my parents believed in, other than music.

"Maybe we can take them here. Show them."

I looked around, trying to imagine my mother's reaction to the bouquets of dead baby llamas, the strange smells of the powders, the candles shaped like penises. "Maybe not yet."

After each outing with Miguel, I brought something home for my mother, like a cat presenting its owner with a dead mouse. I picked up a turquoise bead from the street; plucked a rose from a stranger's abundant garden; cradled a handful of tiny guavas given to me by a cholita at the market. I didn't know what might make my mother be herself again, so I tried everything. But after our trip to the Witches' Market, I returned with empty hands.

At dusk, as my parents rested beside me, I watched Illimani until darkness took it. The snow, it seemed, never melted from its summit. Each hour, each season, the color of the snow slightly altered, flickering from rose to gold in the mornings, fading from lavender to grey in the evenings. I found it difficult to read in our room during the day, with that imposing peak before me. Every time I saw it something in me swung upward. My faith in God might have been shaken in Vienna, but I believed in Illimani in her snowy robes. It made sense to me that the Bolivians worshipped Pachamama, surrounded in every direction as they were by the fierce force of her.

THIRTY-ONE

My father began going to synagogue at the Círculo Israelita, a community organization founded by eastern European Jews in 1935. "Think of it," he said the first Saturday he went, trying to convince my mother to go with him. "Do you think there's a higher synagogue anywhere in the world? Could we get any closer to God?"

I stared at him. My father had only rarely gone to synagogue in Vienna; he had never been given to talking about God. He reserved his reverential tone for Mahler. It had been my impression that he thought of religion as something for people who couldn't play an instrument.

"Was that why God couldn't hear us in Austria?" my mother asked, looking up from a volume of Rilke's poetry. "We weren't high enough?"

She returned to her reading.

My father pivoted to me. "Orlita?" While

my father's Spanish remained rudimentary, he had quickly adopted the Bolivian tendency to add a diminutive to the end of every other word.

"I want to stay with Mutti." I couldn't understand my father's sudden interest in the God who had taken away from him everything he loved. The God that had separated us from Willi.

He went alone.

Yet the following Friday evening, I helped him light the candles. We had taken to doing this nearly every week, more often than we ever had in Vienna. No matter what the state of my beliefs, the familiar light of the candles comforted me. We had to be careful to keep them out of drafts; they blew out easily in the thin air. Not enough fuel for the fire. (At least we don't have to worry about the house burning down, my father had commented after using seven matches to light one slender wick.)

My mother conceded to pour the wine into our small ceramic mugs. Nothing in our Bolivian home has ever been made of crystal. Nothing has ever been made of glass. Our bowls were crafted from heavy Bolivian clay and didn't break when you dropped them. Our cups too were ceramic or tin. When a visitor arrived with a pretty set of wine glasses, we gave them away. The sound of glass shattering was forever tied to the night we knew our lives in Vienna could never be put back together.

What my mother contributed was almost as precious to me as the candle flames with which my father tied us to our past: a loaf of braided bread, an extraordinary culinary feat at nearly four thousand meters above the sea. And so with candles and bread, we maintained a bridge to our past.

Every morning after making coca tea, my mother wrote letters. She wrote to her parents, to her sisters, to everyone we knew in Austria. She wrote often to her friend Violaine in Paris, hoping she would have heard something from Willi. Nearly every other day she walked all the way to the post office, to ask if there was any poste restante for Zingel.

"Why hasn't he written?" she asked my father on a Friday evening when he returned from the synagogue. We were chopping carrots on our one, all-purpose table. "Switzerland has a good postal service."

"Maybe he isn't in Switzerland?" My father sat down and snapped open his viola case.

My mother's face stilled. "Are you trying

to kill me, Jakob? What do you mean, not in Switzerland?" Her knife hovered over the carrots.

He looked up, the viola balanced on his knee. "Nothing, Julia, nothing. Just that he could have gotten a visa. He could be on a ship. Don't panic for nothing was all I meant."

"But he would have written to us before he left," she insisted. "He would have written."

"Maybe he has," said my father, lifting the instrument to his chin. "Maybe he did. It's a long journey for a letter." He drew his bow across the strings.

Scooping up my carrot slices and dumping them into the pan on the kerosene stove, I tried to imagine what Willi was doing, what was keeping him from us. I could see him leading the children in the Swiss refugee camp in a game of hide-and-seek. I could see him secretly printing anti-Fascist pamphlets for airplanes to set loose over Germany. I could even see him ending up on a ship to Shanghai instead of Bolivia. But I never let myself imagine him dead. Willi was not a dead kind of person.

I worried about my mother, about her inability to muster enthusiasm for any aspect of our life. I tried to think of what things made my mother happy in Vienna. She had loved the sound of the piano, singing me songs about monkeys and cactuses, and rehearsing a role. None of those things were useful to me now.

If only she could smile at me. If only she could sing. One evening she disappeared into the bathroom in the hallway for an unusually long time. "Go check on your mother, would you?" my father asked from the corner, where he sat turning the pegs to adjust the strings of his viola. "Mathilde and Fredi might need the bathroom. Make sure she hasn't drowned in there."

We bathed irregularly in the shared hallway bath, as we had to heat pan after pan of water on the small kerosene stove in order to fill it. Also, the water was often turned off in the evening, or at random times for no discernible reason. I had never appreciated water more than I did once I knew we could lose it at any moment. The things we learned to appreciate in Bolivia — oxygen, water, heat — were things that had hardly crossed our minds in Vienna. My mother kept large pans of boiled water on the floor next to the stove so that we could drink it and use it for cooking when the water to the house was shut off.

I knocked on the door. We were a modest family, afraid of catching each other naked, which made living in such close quarters particularly mortifying. "Mutti?" I called. When there was no answer I reluctantly turned the knob.

My mother lay on her back in the bath, her bare skin dotted with patches of soap bubbles. Staring up at the ceiling, she apparently hadn't noticed the ebbing of the water. She turned her head to me when I stepped into the room. The tiles of the floor were cold on the soles of my feet. "It all ran out," she said tonelessly. "All of the water ran away." Her skin was shriveled and grey, as if the color of her lips and cheeks had drained away with the water.

"I can see." I backed out of the room and ran down the hall. "*Vati!* Can you come?" My father stood, laid his viola gently in the case beside him, and walked to the bathroom without questioning me.

I heard my father's voice, soft and coaxing, as he got my mother out of the bath, dried her off, and wrapped her in a dressing gown before leading her back to our rooms. "You're going to scare Orly," I heard him say. I found it odd that he used the future tense, as if she had never scared me before.

They walked by as if they didn't see me

standing there, and sat on the edge of the mattress in the next room. My father pulled back the sheet and tucked my mother underneath it. He sat there next to her, silently stroking her hair, until her eyes finally closed.

In Vienna, music had propelled my mother through the day, through her own practice, her rehearsals, her performances, and her cooking. She was a warm, living radio, projecting melody as she moved. It was difficult to get her to sit down with us; she was always keeping time with some internal rhythm. Even when she was cross with us she would chastise us with a song. "Orlan-the Charloooootte!" she'd trill. "Have you finished all your maaaath?" or "Whose wet skaaaaates are these in the hallway, beloved son of mine?"

But in Bolivia, our house felt silent, despite the flights of my father's viola. My mother not only resisted adding her voice to his melody, but now left the room when he took out the instrument, as if his playing was painful for her. As if it were possible for her to avoid it, to remain in our two rooms without her ears filling with its sound.

When I came to bed that night, she was curled in a tight ball, facing away from the window. Often when she slept beside me I would shift to curl around her, but tonight something in the rigidity of her back kept me at bay. I rolled over toward the window, through which I could see the stars beginning to appear. Nowhere on earth had as many stars as Bolivia. Nowhere on earth was so close to them.

THIRTY-TWO

One morning I walked all the way to the German School. Miguel was at the nearby Catholic school during the afternoons and I was bored and impatient to return to my own studies. My mind was restless. I kept track of the months of classes I had missed in Vienna, the months I was already behind. I wondered what Anneliese had learned since I left. I wondered if I would ever be able to study in my own language again. My fingers itched to write things, to put words to paper. My stack of letters to Anneliese grew daily.

But that isn't why I went to look at the German School. I went because I had to see for myself if the rumors were true. The children I met in the Plaza Murillo, while our mothers exchanged news from home, had told me that it was a Nazi school. This should not have shocked me — naturally a German School would be run by the current German government, meaning Hitler — yet it did. How could the Nazis be here, so far from Germany, so far from Austria? Why had Bolivia let them in? A fear I thought I had left behind took hold of me. Were there Nazis in La Paz?

I had never seen the German School, nor had I met any children who went there. Refugee families knew to stay away. There was no Jewish school for kids our age yet, though there were plans to open one. Some families sent their children to Bolivian schools. The youngest ones could attend a day school the Joint Distribution Committee funded in Miraflores and many of the older children worked. I asked Miguel about the German School but he didn't know anything. It was the only question I ever asked him that he couldn't answer.

It was early, before breakfast. I left before my mother was up, stopping to buy a marraqueta to eat on the way. No one had told me I couldn't go out alone. The bread ladies were always up earlier than anyone, waiting at the corners of the streets with their sacks of hot rolls.

I wished Miguel were with me. "What if they are Nazis, and they come after me?" I said as we sat on our stairs sharing a marraqueta.

"Wait until later and I'll come with you."

"It will be closed by then."

He shrugged. "You're a pretty fast runner."

He was the only person I had told. He couldn't miss classes, so he couldn't accompany me. But he asked around for the address of the school and drew me a map. The school was uphill from us in Sopocachi, and though La Paz was relatively small, it was a farther and steeper walk than I had anticipated. I took several wrong turns and kept stopping to ask the way. My skin flamed with heat. My legs began to ache and my feet hurt in my old shoes. When I finally reached the street Miguel had circled, I saw mothers with children hurrying ahead of me toward a gated brick building. Feeling suddenly shy, I hung back so they wouldn't see me. The gates were not yet closed and locked, and mothers were still kissing the blond heads of their children and ushering them inside.

I waited until the street was quiet, then sneaked to the gate.

When I peered through the black bars, I saw the German children lined up in rows, arms rigid by their sides. A moment later, the Nazi flag slithered up the flagpole across the schoolyard. I saw the children's arms rise in unison, heard the Heil of their salutes, and the first few bars of "Deutschland über alles." For a moment disbelief froze me in place. Here? *Here?*

I turned and I ran.

My legs had new life as I sprinted downhill — thank God it was downhill — through the city. I didn't want to allow myself to think about what I had seen until I was safe in our rooms, but my mind raced. I thought we had left those flags and salutes behind when we boarded the boat in Italy. I slipped on a pile of rotting garbage and nearly fell. We had traveled so far! How could they possibly be here? I ran faster. I imagined what those children would do to me on the playground. I imagined who their parents were. Would they try to take control of Bolivia? They were taking everywhere else. We heard it on Fredi and Mathilde's radio. Hitler had taken Czechoslovakia. What was to stop him from taking over a small city named Peace?

When I finally reached the sanctuary of our rooms, I crept into my parents' bed. Pressing myself against my mother's back, I sobbed with fear. "Mutti, please. Please, sing." She made no reply but I felt her body tense against me. "Mutti. I need you to sing to me. *I need you.*" When she remained silent I whispered to her what I had seen.

Still, she didn't say a word. I wanted to shake her, to dig my fingernails into her shoulders until she turned back into my mother.

Yet watching her press her lips together, it occurred to me that perhaps she never would.

That was the first day I felt real fear in Bolivia.

The second was the day President Germán Busch died. It was August 23, 1939, the middle of Bolivian winter. The son of a German immigrant and a power-hungry authoritarian eager for German approval, Busch had nevertheless been our savior. Mauricio Hochschild, the German Jewish mining entrepreneur who had been working in Bolivia and elsewhere in South America for decades, building an empire from the extraction of tin, had convinced Busch that Jewish immigrants from Europe would help the country's economy. Now that Busch was gone, who would take his place, and would we still be wanted? While I was only eleven, I was acutely sensitive to talk of political change. Had we all worried a bit earlier in Vienna, had we all seen the danger Hitler posed to Austria, perhaps things might have turned out differently. Transfers of power did not fill me with optimism.

Busch can't have been optimistic either; he shot himself.

That's the official story anyway; Miguel told me with great confidence that Busch's death was a political execution. Beyond that, however, he could provide no details.

Bolivia was not politically stable. The leadership of the country, Fredi and Mathilde said, was more likely to be determined by a military coup than an election. Now another president was gone and a new military appointee was taking over. What if the country descended into chaos? Who would seize control? What if we were exiled once again? And where would we go? These worries chased each other in my head as I changed the diapers of the Grubers' twins, as I cut up pieces of apple for them to eat.

Miguel claimed that Busch's death was not a disaster. "We get new rulers all the time," he said. "It's not unusual. It doesn't mean anything."

But nothing he said could convince me.

THIRTY-THREE

On September 3, 1939, the newspaper sirens went crazy, waking me just as the sun was turning the snows of Illimani pink. I sat up and reached for my undershirt, my fingers stiff and cold as I struggled with the buttons of my dress and boots. My parents had not moved. I was amazed that they could sleep through the noise, this sign of changes afoot in the world. Europe had already been awake for hours, I thought. So much could already have happened there today.

I ran nearly all the way to the Plaza Murillo, meeting several of our refugee neighbors on the way. War, they said to each other, it must be war. The world could not keep letting Hitler carry on unchecked forever. Could it?

Panting from the climb, I finally had the blackboard in my sights.

Britain declares War! A crowd had already

formed around the message, was already abuzz with talk.

At last, I thought. At last, at last! Perhaps even in time to save my grandparents, my aunts and uncles, my brother. I swelled with hope. But then I remembered that all of those people I loved were now in countries under attack. Enemy countries. Not only were they vulnerable to the Nazis, British and French soldiers were now headed their way. How would they be able to tell that my family was prey and not predator?

As I stood there, my mind darting in several directions at once, I thought of the Dudeks and Zajacs, Polish families who had been so disappointed with life in La Paz that they had returned to Poland a month ago. My parents didn't spend time with the Polish refugees; they didn't speak the same language, clung to different cultures. But we met them in the SOPRO offices or on the streets. We knew who they were. What would happen to the Dudeks and Zajacs now?

I turned toward Illimani, comforted by its constancy above the city as I ran home, nearly colliding with Mathilde and Fredi on the way. "War!" I cried.

They looked grim. They were old enough to remember the last war. Silently, they clasped hands and turned to walk slowly down the slope of the city.

That morning, as we did every Sunday, we listened to the news in German broadcast from London on Mathilde and Fredi's radio. I thought of our Zenith radio at home in Vienna and wondered who was listening to it today. Aunt Thekla was no longer on the radio, so how was she surviving? It had been two months since my mother had heard from her. As Fredi fiddled with the knobs on the small wooden box, my body tensed in my chair. Perhaps we would hear something about Vienna, something that would tell us the fate of our relatives. For a moment, I longed for Lebkuchen. Then the radio crackled to life.

"It is the evil things that we shall be fighting against." Neville Chamberlain's pinched and nearly indecipherable voice picked its way through the static. *"Brute force, bad faith, injustice, oppression and persecution — and against them I am certain that the right will prevail."*

I did not understand the English words, but the broadcast translated the text of the speech. I had so many questions. Did this mean that Britain would be bombing Austria? Germany? Could they do this without hurting the Jews left there? Could bombs recognize Nazis? My parents could not answer these questions. There was so much my parents did not know. I wondered why Poland had been the breaking point, and not Czechoslvakia. Or Austria.

I was relieved when Bolivia joined the Allies a few years later and expelled many Germans, including the head of the German School.

But it did not expel them all.

THIRTY-FOUR

When I first heard about the *Orazio* I was standing on one foot in front of our apartment building, playing thunka with Miguel, Ema, and Nina. It was January, the peak of the Bolivian summer, which meant rain could interrupt our game at any moment. Rain and mothers. While I loved to stand outside in the torrents to feel the water on my scalp, my eyelids — I didn't remember rain falling so fast in Vienna — my mother was convinced that wet clothing was almost as dangerous as drinking orange juice on the street.

"Orly?" Mathilde appeared in the door of our building.

"There's no rain yet!" I worried Mathilde had been sent to fetch me inside. "And I'm only on Wednesday!" Wobbling on my right foot, I tossed the rock into the Thursday square.

"It's not about the rain. Orly, stop for a

moment?"

I looked up at her, not letting my foot touch the ground. Miguel sighed. He didn't like interruptions to our games. Ema and Nina, figuring it might be awhile before they got a turn, sat down on the ground to play a hand game that looked like pattycake.

"Where's your mother?" Mathilde's face looked funny, crumpled.

I shrugged. "Cooking?" I was still balancing, seeing how long I could last. If I put my other foot down I would lose.

"No. I looked in your house." *House.* Our two bare rooms.

"Then at the market I suppose. What is it?" Something must have happened. Could a telegram have arrived? News of Willi?

"A ship burned." The adults had given up trying to protect us from the relentless news of the war.

My second foot hovered above the earth. "What ship?"

"Orlita!" Miguel tossed his pebble at my foot. *"Kantuta!"*

"The *Orazio.*"

The *Orazio.* We had been waiting for the *Orazio.* Every time one of the families in our community expected someone on one of the ships, we all waited. Every family member was our family member. Every lost

302

friend or relative was our lost friend or relative. Despite our vast social, cultural, and educational differences, our refugee status bound us. We passed around every bit of good news — a daughter found alive in Shanghai, a father who made it to the Dominican Republic — as we shared our favorite novels, with generosity and passion.

I tried to remember who was expected on that ship. The Hirsches? The Rosenthals? The names scattered like dry leaves before my pursuit; I could not catch them.

"All of the ship burned?"

"It sank."

"¿Vas a jugar o simplemente estar allí como un flamenco?" *Are you going to play or just stay there like a flamingo?* Miguel and the others were growing impatient. Lowering my foot, I stepped out of the squares, away from their game. "Sorry, Miguel."

As Mathilde and I walked up the slope to the market I thought about who might have been lost. Could Willi have been on that ship? But he would have let us know to expect him. Mathilde didn't try to speak to me; she seemed far away, in her own mind.

The market wasn't crowded and it didn't take long to find my mother. She was standing in front of Nayra's vegetable stall, transfixed by a pile of blue potatoes. Since our first visit to the market, we had been loyal to Nayra and her potatoes. Often, I stayed behind to talk with her once my mother had moved on, though she was shy and reluctant to speak. Aymara people are private, Miguel said. They don't trust white people. And why should they?

"Hola Nayra, qué tal?" She nodded, a faint smile hovering on her lips. I touched my mother's sleeve. "Mutti?"

She turned toward me, her eyes still on the potatoes. "Do you think they are blue inside?" At the market, my mother spoke to everyone with her hands, preferring gestures to Spanish. When I went with her, everything went much faster.

"I don't know. Mutti, Mathilde says that the *O*—"

"What would they say back in Vienna if we made blue latkes for Chanukah?"

"They look good, Mutti, but —"

"Julia." Mathilde found her voice. "The *Orazio.*"

My mother's body rippled as if she'd felt an electric shock. Her eyes focused on Mathilde's face for the first time. "What happened?"

"It caught fire. There are still 104 missing."

"And who — ?"

"The Neufelds. Their son and daughter. And the Kahns were expecting her sister. I can't remember who else."

"Not Willi?" Now I knew why Mathilde had been so anxious to find my mother.

My mother shook her head. "He would have told us." She turned to Nayra.

"Fünf," my mother said, holding up all the fingers of her right hand. Nayra nodded, plucked a handful of dirt-crusted potatoes from the stack, and placed them gently in my mother's basket.

"Un boliviano." My mother held out a handful of money so that Nayra could pluck the correct coin from her palm.

Clutching her basket to her chest like an infant, she turned toward Mathilde and they began walking toward home. With a small wave to Nayra, I followed.

My mother and I were making pancakes. I beat together eggs and flour in a pewter bowl while my mother mixed up pitchers of Klim. I was quiet. Listening. I hadn't thought it possible for my mother to make Palatschinken without humming. She always hummed or even sang when we cooked together in Vienna. Now she moved around our small room with a silent, grim determination, slicing the apples as if they had insulted her personally.

She hadn't wanted to make the pancakes; it was my idea. I thought it would be a nice thing to make for the passengers of the *Orazio* — those who were left — when they finally arrived. After their injuries were treated in French and Italian hospitals, the survivors had been collected in Genoa once again and put onboard the *Augustus*. We expected them later today.

For weeks we'd been planning the welcome party, funded by the Maccabi Sports Club and the Jewish Community Organization. Mathilde had come to our rooms to ask what we could contribute. She would be helping to make the Schnitzel.

"I'd be happy to play," my father said. "If you think that would be appropriate?"

"Would you? Your quintet?"

"I'll ask."

"Julia?"

My mother gazed out the window as if she hadn't heard the question.

I tried to think of the most special thing that we could do, something we knew how to do together, and I remembered that once, in a faraway land, we had made pancakes.

"Mutti." I touched her sleeve. "Could we make Palatschinken for the survivors?"

My mother smiled faintly. "Here? It would be difficult." My mother had shown little interest in cooking beyond what was necessary.

"They're pancakes, how can they be difficult? Besides, the other women are making difficult things. Austrian things. I'll help. Please, Mutti?"

In the end she couldn't refuse to exert herself for a group of people whose suffering was greater than our own. Frau Gruber loaned us her widest frying pan and we rose early on the day of the party to start frying stacks and stacks of paper-thin pancakes over our kerosene burner.

Next to my mother, I sprinkled cinnamon and sugar over the apples, stirred them over the flames, and spooned the puree into each pancake. In some of the pancakes we tucked a savory filling of salty Bolivian cheese and spinach (the Bolivian spinach had a bitter aftertaste, but it wasn't bad if you mixed it with something else), and in the last batch we rolled a thick jam we made from tumbos and maracuyas.

I tore a strip from a pancake in this last heap and popped it in my mouth. Sour and sweet spread across my tongue along with the buttery taste of my childhood. "Mmmm.

Mutti, they're perfect. They taste like home."

My mother took the piece I offered her, chewed, and frowned. "No," she corrected me. "Not like home at all."

As we waited in the garden of the Finca Elma in Miraflores for our guests, I helped some of the other women with the food, turning the potatoes on the grill, tucking handmade sausages into rolls, and pouring beer. We brewed pot after pot of coca tea. My mother set out our plates of pancakes at the end of the table.

The arrival of refugees was ordinarily a kind of holiday for us, for new people meant new friends added to our small colony, more lives saved from an ever more inhospitable Europe, and the hope of news. It was only later, when the refugees got their bearings and found confidants among us, that the darkest stories from home would emerge. Sometimes I wished I could erase these stories from my memory so that I would not lie awake at night imagining they had happened to Willi or my aunt Thekla. I needed to stay here, in the present, in the sun.

The arrival of the survivors of the *Orazio* was different. Their hopes had already been stripped from them and shredded beyond

308

recognition. When they began to file into the garden, our usual bustle and chatter dipped and silenced. Compulsively, irrationally, and with a stubborn optimism, I searched the crowd of faces for my brother's curly head, listened for his familiar voice calling "Erdnuss!" Pale women passed me, clutching the hands of small children as if they were all that bound them to this earth. Men of all shapes and sizes limped forward. Our mothers, an army of determined hostesses, moved toward them, thrusting forward their trays of food and mugs of foaming beer. Still unsteady on their feet, the new people took the food and drink but many just stood there holding it. The children were the first to begin, sitting on the ground with their plates and poking their potatoes with their forks. Chairs were brought forward and the newcomers sank gratefully into them. "Not too much beer your first week," the mothers warned. "You'll need time."

My mother didn't bother to warn people about the beer. She had other concerns. With each plate she handed over, she had a question. "Have you come across someone named Willi Zingel? Have you heard anything at all?"

No one had.

■ ■ ■ ■

I looked around the garden. I had never seen so many of us in one place. Hundreds of refugees milled around me, talking and eating. A tall woman in a long, silk dress stood to read a poem of welcome, urging us all to forget the past and turn our thoughts toward the battles ahead. Some of the children I knew from the Austrian Club performed skits. My father's quintet began to play. I carried a plate of food to a black-haired girl who looked about my age. She was standing alone. Her right leg was noticeably thinner than her left. She smiled and carefully folded her legs underneath her on the grass before accepting the plate. The grass in La Paz was never comfortable. It was stiff and pokey, sticking into you through your clothing. It wasn't like Austrian grass, so pliant and soft it was easily subdued. I sat down beside her and told her my name.

"I'm Rachel," she offered, in a voice so soft I had to lean toward her to hear it over the music. At the other end of the garden a group of children had begun to sing German hiking songs. She set the plate before her and seemed to admire its composition.

"How old are you?"

"Twelve." My age. She didn't look twelve. She was shorter than I was, small and narrow with sharp edges. When she finally looked up at me I saw her eyes were dark brown with starbursts of gold around her pupils.

"Which ones are your parents?" Adults trampled the grass around us but no one obviously belonged to Rachel.

She just shook her head, looking down to her plate.

"I'm sorry." What was wrong with me? I knew better. It was just that there were so few appropriate questions to ask. I pinched the skin of my thighs until my nails broke through the skin. "Rachel, I'm so sorry. I wasn't thinking."

She tried to smile at her plate. "My mother dropped me into a lifeboat. It had started to move down the ship's side and it was the last one, and she just picked me up and she threw me over the railing. All that way. I nearly crushed a man."

"She *threw* you?" I tried to imagine my mother having the strength to toss me over the edge of a ship. I pictured Rachel falling, her bird bones failing to fly.

Rachel nodded.

"Were you hurt?"

She nodded. "I fractured a leg. And the arm of the man who broke my fall. But we were lucky. Our boat didn't sink. It almost capsized when we hit the water. The ocean got into it. Freezing ocean water. But we managed to steady it. Another boat got smashed against the side of the ship. There was nothing left of it at all."

Our own voyage suddenly seemed miraculously uneventful. I couldn't think of what to say. "Your mother must have been strong."

She thought about this. She looked past me. Her eyes were glassy. "I think she was just desperate."

"Was it that leg?" I gestured to the thinner one.

She nodded. "I just got the cast off, on the ship."

"Do you have somewhere to stay?"

She looked around. "A lady has been looking after me. Eloise. She's over there, with the hat." I looked where she was pointing and saw a statuesque woman in a beribboned straw hat talking with the food servers. "She's a friend of my mother's. Was. She's nice. I guess she'll find us somewhere."

"Were you coming here to join someone? Do you have family here?" Now that so many of us were in Bolivia, many of the arrivals were expected by someone. Not us. No one expected us. But we were expecting Willi. Any day now we were expecting Willi.

She shook her head. "It was just the only place that would take us."

"Us too." We smiled at each other, bound by our undesirability.

"Do you like it here? In La Paz?"

"I do." I was surprised by how readily my answer came. "You get used to it. The altitude, the food, everything. Have you been ill?"

She shook her head. "I'm fine. Just. Well. Compared to everyone else, I guess."

We ate in silence for a few minutes. "It gets better," I said.

"It can hardly get worse." She said it matter-of-factly, not like she was complaining.

"Yes. Though I hope the SS can't find us here." I thought of the children at the German School, wondered if their teachers were SS.

She startled, dropping her fork. "Let's hope not. Then there would be no point to anything."

Toward the end of the afternoon I went to fetch Rachel some of the Palatschinken and found my mother talking with Frau Gruber. "Julia, why did you never tell me you can make Palatschinken? This is better than anything you could get at Café Sperl."

My mother glanced at the empty plates. "Anyone can make Palatschinken, Hanna."

"Not like this. Listen, Julia, you know I just opened a café? It's very small, just somewhere we can go for drinkable coffee and a bite of something sweet. But I haven't much on the menu yet and I'd love it if you would make some of these for me. If you have time?"

My mother smiled, almost a real smile. "Time? Yes, time is one thing I have left."

THIRTY-FIVE

Two days after the welcoming party, I stood in Miguel's doorway, waiting for his mother to fetch him from the back room. On the hallway table was a stack of newspapers. Idly, I turned the top one toward me. It took me a minute to understand what it meant, but then it was unmistakable. On the front page of the paper was a drawing of two Jews — identifiable by their exaggerated noses — in fancy suits and hats, dragging a Bolivian to a cross.

I was still staring at it when Miguel appeared.

"Kantuta?"

"Is this what you think of us?" I turned the paper toward him.

Miguel glanced down at the cartoon. He was quiet for a moment. "Some people."

"You?"

"Not me. Not my family."

"But people you know. This is what they think?"

"I don't know what everyone thinks, Orly."

"What do they say about us?"

Miguel shifted from foot to foot, frowning.

"Look, I believe it's not what you think. I just need to know."

"They think there are too many of you, taking all of our jobs. That the government should stop you coming."

"Did my father take someone's job?"

"No . . ."

"Did my mother?"

"I don't think that Orly, I promise."

"But if other people do . . . You don't understand. This is how it starts."

Miguel stared miserably at the floor.

"Is that why your friend Hector doesn't come play anymore if I'm here?"

"Hector's probably busy."

I nodded, biting my lip.

Miguel flipped the paper over and looked up at me. "Orlita? Can't we forget about it? Whoever did that, they don't know you. They don't know your parents. And it's true that people don't have jobs. They're just worried, that's all."

"Most of us don't have jobs either."

"But it's not your country."

For a moment I forgot how to inhale. I stared at the floor, willing myself not to cry. I wanted to protest — where else did we have? — but it was true. "I guess nowhere is."

I looked up at Miguel. He wasn't my enemy. I didn't want to be mad at him. "Okay. Can we play something outside?"

When I returned to our apartment a few hours later, sweaty and panting, my father was home. He sat on a crate humming to himself as he made notes on a sheet of music. At the table, my mother kneaded dough in a bowl.

"Vati?" I began.

"Favorite daughter?" He smiled at me.

I smiled back. "Nothing."

THIRTY-SIX

Now that my mother had something to keep her busy, I worried less about leaving her to play with Miguel or to look after Lotte and Bettina, the Grubers' girls. Her Palatschinken were very popular with the customers of Frau Gruber's Riesenrad Café, who had long been deprived of anything so reminiscent of home. When she became bored with making pancakes, she experimented with other things, although other things, it turned out, were not so easy.

"I don't understand," she said, pulling gluey noodles from the pot on the kerosene burner. "It's always too hard or too soft." Meat took hours longer than it should have, and came out tough and chewy. Most of her breads were so dry they crumbled when she tried to slice them, or they inflated like balloons and collapsed in on themselves.

"It's the altitude," Frau Gruber told her. "Things cook differently." Everything needed longer in the oven and more liquid than a recipe demanded.

There were other challenges. A lack of refrigeration meant we had to shop for perishables every day. We had only the two kerosene burners and the small oven, all of which had to be pumped full of air to turn the liquid into a burnable gas.

My mother took the difficulty of producing edible food in her rudimentary La Paz kitchen as a challenge. Using the money Frau Gruber gave her to buy ingredients, she began baking even more impossible things, like Mohnstriezel, Austrian rolls filled with sweet poppy-seed paste. She had never even tried to make them in Vienna. Each morning for a week, my mother fiddled with the recipe, adding lemon or butter when she could find it, making them larger and softer until they could be sold at the café. The irregular availability of butter frustrated her. Twice a week (in good weather and barring accident), a train from Argentina delivered meat, butter, and other staples. But shortages were not uncommon.

In Bolivia, the women made everything: clothing, butter, bread, furniture. You couldn't buy furniture; you had to meet a carpenter and describe what you wanted. Or, in our case, you cut up your neighbors' leftover packing crates and hammered them into tables and chairs. I had a new and profound respect for the people who knew how to make all of these things themselves.

My mother's failures did not discourage her. What was a dust-dry bit of pastry compared with the ways the world had failed her? What was a lost tart compared with a lost country? A lost son? A lost voice? Cooking gave her something to push against. It was not that she derived true pleasure from the activity, but rather that she wanted to fight with something, something safe to battle.

If a dish turned out well, she recorded the recipe on a small scrap of paper and tucked it into a folder she kept underneath the silverware box. If it didn't turn out well, my father and I ate it anyway.

Even when she got the dish exactly right, when the Schnitzel was delicate and flaky, something was still missing. My father and I looked at each other in mutual understanding as we chewed each endless mouthful and swallowed it down.

We would rather she were singing.

THIRTY-SEVEN

Soon after the *Orazio* refugees landed, my parents enrolled me in the newly opened Escuela Boliviana-Israelita. It was in the same building as the synagogue, up on the paseo del Prado. All the Jewish children were planning to go there. I was relieved at the prospect of returning to a daily routine, some semblance of a normal life. Not only did we now have a school of our own, but I no longer had to work as a child minder. My mother had begun to make money cooking and my father had dozens of students. We could afford our modest life.

I had not been to school in more than a year. Though I read every book I could find in German (and, increasingly, in childish Spanish), I had not encountered mathematics, science, or history since we arrived. I knew I was terribly behind.

Anxious to begin, I was ready that first day before my parents awoke: I had pulled on the faded, mended dress I had been wearing since we arrived and a pair of woolen stockings that were already too small. Even if we had had extra money, we couldn't buy clothing. Here we had to buy cloth and sew the clothing ourselves, using patterns from the American catalogues circulating in our community — and sewing was not one of my mother's talents. I had accumulated two additional dresses from Austrian girls who had outgrown them, but neither fit me well. I also had one handknitted Bolivian sweater we bought from Miguel's mother. These items made up my entire wardrobe.

I splashed cold water on my face and cleaned my teeth before walking by myself to buy our breakfast rolls. The streets were mostly empty, save for the cholitas with their bread and fruit. "Buenos días!" I called gaily, grateful to be moving my body, grateful for the air around me. My heart beat too furiously for me to feel the cold. At last, school! I would be with other children all day. I would have new books to read. I felt the stones of the street through the holes in my shoes as I walked and didn't mind. I pretended I was getting a foot massage. Back at home, I set the rolls on our table and leaned over the bed to touch my mother's shoulder. "Mutti, school!"

"Wait, Orly wait, I have something for you." She rose with uncharacteristic swiftness. "I meant to be up earlier." Once she had pulled on her dress and washed her hands and face, she removed the lid from the cardboard box where she stored our clothes. Carefully, she lifted out a package wrapped in thin paper. "I made it."

I took the package and set it on our table, peeling back the layers of tissue. My mother had made something?

It was a dress. I lifted it from its papers and shook it out before me. Made from a dark blue wool, it had puffed sleeves and a fitted waist, the skirt falling in pleats.

"Mathilde helped me. We made it a little big," my mother said smiling. "So it would last."

"Mutti." I swallowed a lump in my throat. "When did you do this?"

"You've been spending an awful lot of time exploring and working, Schatzi. And I can't cook all the time."

Dropping the dress on my father's sleeping form, I ran to hug her. "You'll be late," she said, pushing me away. "Put it on! And there are stockings too."

Once my mother had buttoned up the dress and I had yanked on the stockings, I gazed down at myself. I looked grown-up. The dress was indeed long, hanging nearly to my ankles, some of the seams were slightly crooked, and the stockings kept sliding down my stomach, but there was not a single hole in anything. Not one single worn patch.

I spun around, watching the skirt flare out. "Mutti, you're a magician."

"That magic all came from Mathilde. Come, we'd better hurry."

By the time we walked out the door, my father was sitting up at the kitchen table with his viola, sending me off with a song. Just like he used to do.

In a small classroom not so different from the one I had left behind in Vienna, children of all ages stood talking in small groups. I looked around for someone I knew and saw Rachel sitting quietly by herself. I waved to her and she nodded. There were many other familiar faces, children I had met at the SOPRO or the Austrian Club. Children I had seen at the market, clinging to the hands of German-speaking parents. Our community was getting larger every day. By the time the war began there were thousands of us, not only from Austria and Germany but from all across Europe. By the time it ended at least ten thousand of us had arrived — perhaps twice that number, even — swelling the population of this city of some three hundred thousand people.

A thin, brown-haired woman I hadn't seen at first walked over to kiss my mother. "Guten tag, Julia. We will take good care of her." She wore a limp, fading dress the same cornflower blue as her eyes. Two combs scraped her hair back severely from her brow. She did not smile, but her eyes were gentle.

I thought I was quite old enough to take care of myself, but I shook her hand, trying to look as serious and independent as possible.

My deskmate was a freckled girl named Sarah from Leopoldstadt. "How strange that we have come so far to meet," she said in German. Perhaps we had once sat across a café from each other, or become dizzy on the same spin of the Riesenrad. Perhaps I had walked by her father's tobacco shop. She had come from Vienna with her mother and little sister. "They took my father," she said during that first conversation, as if to get it out of the way. "The night of the pogroms." Once again I was aware of my good fortune. There were so many lost fathers. "My brother is missing," I offered.

In Vienna, I had gone to school with the same children my entire life. I'd always had Anneliese. It felt strange to be in a classroom without her, with so many new people. While I knew many of the Austrian and German children, there were also children from Poland, Romania, and other eastern European countries.

Yet, in a way, we did know each other. I knew that, like us, my seventeen classmates had been cast out of their homes. Like us, they had been driven from their country. Like us, they had been afraid, cramped with cold, and stifled by heat on a ship. Like us, they had arrived here with nothing. Loss was assumed.

Perhaps that made us kinder to each other. No one teased the girls with worn and patched dresses, or the boys with too-short trousers. No one yelled *Your mother is a Tratschtante* — a gossipy blabbermouth — in the schoolyard, aware that too many mothers had met worse fates. I was not the only child missing a brother. We were reserved, careful not to cross each other's borders.

But while our exile bound us, stark differences remained. Some had given up God entirely while others clung more tightly than ever to the idea of divine intervention. We spoke different dialects and advocated different politics.

"*Niños,*" Frau Pichler interrupted our nervous chatter. "Take out a sheet of paper, please." I was surprised to hear her speak Spanish. She then repeated the phrase in German.

"Think of two people or objects or ideas or places that have nothing in common," she instructed. "Write them down." I was confused. I had expected a speech, a welcome, an introduction to our curriculum. But Frau Pichler, I was to learn, wasn't keen on small talk. After giving this instruction in Spanish and German, she sat down behind her small wooden desk.

I stared at my page. Two unconnected things. Every two things I thought of seemed connected. The Alps and the Andes. My old apartment and my new apartment. Willi and Anneliese. Coffee and tea. I began to feel I was connected to everything, between everything, the silk connecting strands of a spider's web.

"Two more minutes." I picked up my pencil. Two unconnected things! *Mahler,* I finally scribbled. *Nayra.*

"Bueno. Now, find a way to connect those two things and write that connection. What is between those things, what fills that space?"

It was a strange way to begin a class. I wasn't used to my teachers encouraging improvisation. Our Viennese teachers had valued memorization and neat handwriting and strict structures like fables, sonnets, or villanelles, not vague, unspecified forms. But the assignment had the effect of instantly distracting us from our individual tragedies and plunging us into our work.

I didn't know if I was any good at writing. I could not remember anything I had ever written in Austria, aside from my journals and the stories I created with Anneliese.

"She was a song of the earth," I began. *"The silence between notes of the melody."* For a moment I forgot whether I was writing about Nayra or Anneliese. Either. Both. My pen kept moving.

Sarah was still frowning over a line. "Are we writing in German?" she whispered, her breath yeasty like bread.

I looked down. I had started in Spanish. I glanced back at Sarah and shrugged. I was oddly free of the schoolwork anxiety that had plagued me in Vienna. There were worse things, I now knew, than getting an assignment wrong. Calm settled over me. I could write anything and life would still go on.

"That's time," said Frau Pichler. I looked up. I wanted more. Across the room, Rachel stared at an empty page.

When we read our pieces out loud, Frau Pichler smiled. "Do you see? You have started to write poems."

I had once written songs in my journals, I remembered. Music made of words. That was how an earlier teacher had once described poetry. Music made of words. Yet I had no proper education in poetic rhythm and form. No one had ever asked me to write a poem.

"It's often in the space between things we think are irreconcilably different that the most interesting connections are made. That space is where poems live."

I was happy at school, where I studied Bolivian history alongside grammar, writing, and mathematics. It confused me, however, that our Austrian geography teacher wanted us to study the rivers and cities of the Alps rather than those of the Andes. Of what possible use to me now was a detailed knowledge of European terrain? I wanted to learn more about where we actually lived.

Our music teacher taught us German folk songs, accompanying us on his accordion.

These classes steeped me in an uncomfortable nostalgia, longing rubbing up against revulsion. I missed the Austrian seasons, the forests of the Wienerwald. I missed my white skates with the blue pom-poms attached to the laces and the little pairs of wooden skis Anneliese and I would lug up the same hill over and over again. Yet even the ice and snow, even the trees, were tainted now with all that had happened in that landscape.

While our instruction was alternately in German and Spanish, depending on the nationality of our teacher, we mostly spoke German in the schoolyard as we lined up in the morning, or between classes. Yet my heart was turning away from my native tongue. I did not want to share a language with those children I had seen at the German School, blindly saluting. I tired of the way my fellow refugees began their sentences with "Back home in Austria . . ." We were not in Austria. Austria had spat us out. What was the point in talking about it all the time? Home was here. Apart from my memories of Anneliese, I didn't want to think about the past anymore; I wanted to live in the present. I wanted to live in Bolivia. I wanted to speak Spanish.

THIRTY-EIGHT

It started when I came in after recreo a couple weeks later, panting from our games in the schoolyard. I was hot and sticky, pulling my blouse away from my chest where it stuck to my skin. Normally I cooled down rapidly at altitude. But this day I didn't cool down at all.

Sitting at my desk I felt the beads of sweat run through the hair at the back and sides of my scalp and trickle down my spine. My face and hands burned and turned red with a raised rash. My eyes blurred; the fours in my math book became ones and then eights.

Frau Pichler noticed the angry red crawling across my skin and sent me home. When my mother saw me at the door, her face paled. She put me to bed, pulled my covers up to my chin, and made me sip as much lukewarm tea as I could manage.

All I wanted to do was sleep. For nearly a week I didn't get out of bed, except when my mother came to help me to the toilet. I didn't eat. I didn't want to drink, though my mother would trickle water through my teeth. What I know of this period is fuzzy around the edges.

A German doctor came to see me and gave me powders dissolved in a ceramic mug of water. European doctors could not legally practice medicine in Bolivia — the Bolivians did not want the competition — but many of them did anyway. We all went to them first, as our parents believed they provided superior care.

I did not get better.

The second week I was in bed, soaking through bedsheets already stiff with sweat, my mother grew desperate. We had heard of several refugees — the ones with agricultural visas who had been sent to work the land down below us — who had died of yellow fever, meningitis, or other kinds of fevers you could get in the tropics or semitropics. To travel to the lower altitudes, we were learning, was to risk an array of illnesses, often involving digestive problems, parasites, or amoebas. Things we had never encountered in Austria. In Bolivia, nature took over from the Nazis, though in a less organized fashion. I hadn't been to the tropics yet, but La Paz had its own fierce bacteria, like those we had encountered in our first glasses of orange juice.

"I've been to the Witches' Market with Miguel," my mother breathlessly told my father one afternoon when she returned from the market. "Do you remember Orly told us that Miguel knows healers up on calle Linares? We went up there to talk to them and I found a medicine woman who has walked the Inca trail and who can cure anything." Even in my feverish state, this made no sense. Why would this woman be walking through the Andes? How was that relevant?

Even more confusing was that this was my mother speaking. The fact that my mother would turn to Miguel and his healers for medical advice was the most worrying development thus far.

From my father I heard only murmurs of agreement. He had always left the care of sick children to my mother.

The healer came early the next morning. She was short like Nayra, but fat. A round little woman with long braids and smiling dark eyes. She stood over my bed, smiling down at me. There were gaps in her teeth and one of her upper front incisors was gold. I looked up at her. Speaking would have taken too much energy.

"Soy Wayra," she said. "Soy Kallawaya." The kallawayas, I had heard from Miguel and Nayra, were the roaming indigenous healers. The word comes from kolla-waya, which she says means "one who carries medicines on his shoulders." Or in this case, hers.

Most of the Indians didn't go to our doctors, but to medicine men. A few women worked as healers too. Women like Wayra. She put a dry hand on my forehead and murmured something in her bird language, which I later learned was a variant of Quechua. She touched my cheeks, my throat, looked in my eyes, and listened to my heartbeat in my wrists. "Abre," she instructed. I opened my mouth. After peering into my throat for several minutes she turned to my mother, gesturing for a piece of paper.

On the scrap of newspaper my father handed her, she scribbled in pencil: *amor seco, manzanilla, verbena.* More unfamiliar words. "Buy these plants," she told my mother, holding out the paper. "Boil them in water for two hours. Strain out the large bits, and give her the water as tea, one cup every two hours." When my mother just stared at her in bewilderment, the older woman shoved the paper into her hands.

334

"We need to get those things," my father translated. I opened my eyes, which had drifted shut. I hadn't realized my father knew enough Spanish to understand.

"Muchísimas gracias." My mother — who at least knew that much Spanish — thanked Wayra with uncustomary enthusiasm and filled her hand with coins.

When I woke several hours later the house smelled of a bitter soup. My mother was waiting at my bedside, mug in hand. It occurred to me, even in my delirious state, that we had no way of knowing what these plants would do. Maybe they were poisons, given to Jews to exterminate them. Maybe they were tired of so many of us coming to their country. My mother must have been desperate, to put my life into the hands of a stranger.

But she had. And I had always trusted my mother with my safety. I drank the tea. Later that night my mother bathed my entire body with a chamomile infusion, using a pan and a small towel so that I would not have to move from bed.

Twenty-four hours later I was out of bed. Two days later I was walking. And by the third day I had no fever.

When my mother made me stay home a few additional days as insurance against relapse, I discovered a pile of books Rachel had brought for me while I was sick. She was always collecting books other refugees discarded or left at the SOPRO offices for trading. My mother had stacked them next to my mattress. On the top was Vicki Baum's *Grand Hotel,* which I had already read. Beneath it were Rosa Mayreder's *A Survey of the Woman Problem,* Franz Werfel's *The Forty Days of Musa Dagh,* and a book I had never heard of called *The Scorpion,* by Anna Weirauch. I turned over Werfel's book in my hands, smiling as I remembered that he was one of the many men bewitched by Alma Schindler, star of my aunt Thekla's bedtime stories. But I wasn't sure that reading about the massacre of Armenians would hasten my recovery. I picked up *The Scorpion.*

The sun had sunk below the mountains and my parents were asleep by the time I turned the final page and lay back on my mattress in a kind of trance. So it was possible. It was right there in the pages. There were girls who felt about other girls the way I felt about Anneliese. There were women who lived together, who were everything to each other. Women who — and I flushed in the dark to think of it — lay in each other's arms. Whose bodies "seized each other as wild beasts seize and shake the bars of their

336

cages." Those words!

The book also, however, made it clear that this path was not free of trouble or adversity. On the contrary, it was a path strewn with suicides and drugs and other strange occurrences I didn't fully understand. Must love always face such punishment? I thought about Heinrich, about the names he had called me and Anneliese. Then I remembered Odiane, the mysterious tuxedoed woman I had met at the opera. She was like some of the women in this book. *There are all kinds of girls,* my mother had said.

I wanted to shake her awake and ask her a thousand questions, but something held me back. Just because my mother understood that there were women like this in the world did not mean she would want me to be one of them. I don't know how I knew this, how this message had been transmitted, but it was there, lurking in the underside of my psyche like a caution sign.

All night I lay awake, restless in my skin and unable to be still. Not until I saw the first light of morning did it occur to me to wonder if Rachel had read this book before she brought it to me.

After my miraculous recovery, Wayra was often in our house. In order to talk with her, my mother finally began to learn Spanish, although Quechua would have been more useful. While she continued to cook for the café, my mother became fascinated with herbal medicine and the plants of Bolivia, especially after Wayra said she knew almost one thousand species of medicinal plants. I almost think she would have tried to become a kallawaya had Wayra not told her that no white woman could become one. No outsider. No one whose ancestors had not passed on to her generations of knowledge and experiences. My mother said she just wanted the chance to study, to learn what Wayra knew about plants.

I watched them talking together and thought, it wasn't only me Wayra had saved.

Sometimes the two of them would send me to the market to ask for a certain plant that grew in the lowlands. Sometimes I knew why they wanted it, sometimes I didn't. The women in the shops of the Mercado de las Brujas wouldn't always have what my mother wanted, but often knew where to find it and would return with it the following week. My mother wanted to learn cures for everything: coughs, colds, rashes, aches, fingernail infections, and sore throats. Wayra was always obliging, though her instruction wasn't free. My mother paid her for each remedy, over my father's protests that we could not afford to cure anything else.

My mother just looked at him in that immovable way she now had. "We cannot afford not to."

When I was back at school, I spread a clean piece of paper on my desk as I waited for the lesson to start. *My Austrian mother,* I wrote at the top. *My Bolivian mother.* Slowly, I began to write the connection.

THIRTY-NINE

Miguel didn't like Rachel. Her Spanish was terrible, he said, and she didn't like games or sports.

"I guess you might not be fun if your parents were dead," I said. "I guess your Spanish might not be good if you weren't Bolivian." I was dismayed at Miguel's lack of enthusiasm for Rachel, especially given that she was one of my only friends who didn't tease me for spending time with him. I had always been tolerant of his school friends, even when they told me I couldn't play football with them because I was a girl. "Besides, you didn't seem to mind so much that my Spanish was terrible when you met me."

We were sitting on the steps outside the San Francisco church, watching the pigeons and eating puffed corn that Miguel called pasankallas. I didn't quite understand the appeal of this popular snack food, which tasted rubbery and stale. I was happy to let the pigeons have it.

"My father is dead." Miguel opened a sticky palm to drop the remaining puffs back into the bag. This immediately derailed my anger. It rarely occurred to me — though it should have — that Bolivians had their own tragedies.

In fact, Miguel had been telling me this in a dozen subtle ways for a very long time. I wondered why I hadn't questioned him about his father before. Perhaps it was the same reason he avoided asking me more about Willi. We were both afraid of touching a place of pain.

I was ashamed I had bragged so much about my own father. "What happened?"

"He had a farm in Los Yungas. He wanted to grow more things than he could grow by the lake. I was born there. Everyone but Ema was born there. My father is why I am so dark." It was true Miguel was darker than other Bolivians in our neighborhood, though not as dark as Nayra. His mother was paler than all her children and hazel-eyed, of Spanish descent. "He grew chirimoyas and guava, sometimes palta." Palta, that glorious green orb that had transformed my opinion of vegetables. "It was a good farm. Sometimes my father took the fruit to La Paz himself, on the new road. One day when he was driving back . . . Entonces, we call it Camino de la Muerte for this reason."

"I thought it was called that because so many people died making the road?" I had heard about the Camino de la Muerte. Paraguayan prisoners had carved the skinny shelf of a road into the sides of steep mountains about five years ago, during the Chaco War. Lots of prisoners died in the process, but exactly how many depended on whom you asked.

"They were the first to die, true. But the road has continued to earn its name."

I nodded, hoping he would go on.

"It was the only way to travel from Los Yungas to La Paz. Or to go the other way."

To get to the road, you had to first climb from the city another three thousand feet to La Cumbre before plunging down toward Coroico. The dirt road skirted the edge of the lush green mountains, arriving at last in the forests of Los Yungas. Looking away from the road for even a millisecond meant near-certain death for the driver and everyone else in the car, which would tumble through the thickening air to be buried in tangled vines. Hundreds of people had already died on this road, but the devastation represented by this statistic was not clear to me until I knew Miguel's father was among them.

"Did someone crash into him?" Parts of the road were only ten feet wide, Miguel had told me. If two vehicles approached one of these stretches at the same time, one of them would have to back down. And if staying on it going forward was difficult, staying on it going backward along the edge of a cliff required a feat of vehicular acrobatics.

He shrugged. "We don't know. Maybe he fell asleep? It was late. He had been working at the farm all day. It took them months to find his truck."

I shuddered at the image of Miguel's father's truck tumbling down through the air. If he had been asleep, I hoped he had not woken up before he hit the ground.

"When?"

He shrugged. "Three years ago? We moved in with my grandfather in La Paz after that." Miguel looked anxious to change the subject. "And last year we moved here. My point is that this doesn't keep me from being fun."

I nodded, to show him I understood. But he clarified anyway. "It's not me who's dead."

Things had begun to change between Miguel and me after Rachel came and I started classes. I now had a world without him. Rachel came over after school to do homework with me, leaving little time for thunka. Most of my classmates weren't comfortable with Spanish and I was reluctant to share Miguel with them. Few of my schoolmates had Bolivian friends, and no one even considered trying to make friends with the Indians. "They're too different," they said. Or, "I hear they don't wash their hands." When they saw me talking with Nayra in the market, they stared. Maybe they had already been forced into more contact with difference than they could handle. They hadn't asked to come here. They hadn't asked to be removed from the comfortable vernacular of their home. Refusing to adapt was one way to exert control over their lives.

I bristled at their prejudices, though perhaps I might have shared them had I not had the good fortune to live in Miguel's house. Had I not known him and his sisters. I wondered if we had come all this way, escaping a whole continent of people who saw no place for us in their vision of a single race, only to close ranks and turn on those who looked different from us. I did not want to remain an outsider, as we all so clearly were, forever. I wanted to belong here.

Most of my classmates assumed this was not a permanent move. Someday, when the Nazis were gone, the more forgiving planned to move back to Austria or Germany. The rest would find somewhere more hospitable, the United States, Canada, or the more developed countries of South America. Countries where it was easier to breathe. Sarah told me her mother couldn't wait to get back to Austria, "where there was culture." Here in Bolivia, Sarah said with a disdainful lift of her chin, there were no literary salons, symphony orchestras, operas, or theater. "It's just fiestas. All they have are fiestas. All these people do is dance in the street, chew coca, or drink." Although I knew she was parroting her mother's words — not so different from the words of my own mother — I couldn't help hating her for them.

Rachel was an exception. Rachel's only verb tense was present. She could never return to the life she had had in Austria. I never heard her say anything unkind. She didn't talk much at all.

My classmates were more accepting of Miguel than of Nayra, simply because he was paler — pale enough to be allowed to walk through Plaza Murillo, to go to school, and to accompany me to the movies. The Bolivians, I observed, sorted themselves by color and did not like to mix with people whose skin tone didn't match theirs. Maybe we did the same thing; I couldn't remember spending time in Vienna with people who didn't look like us.

While I didn't have as much time to spend with Miguel, we still went to the matinees at the Tesla most weekends, to see the westerns that were Miguel's favorite. Afterward, we would go to the store near our house where you could buy pelis. They didn't cost much; they were something that we could buy without further impoverishing our families. We held them to the light and competed to see who could be first to identify the film it came from. *Union Pacific. Drums Along the Mohawk. Destry Rides Again.* I never got the westerns right — all those men on horseback looked the same to me. We traded them and made up games to play. Miguel would stick a peli in his science textbook, and then his siblings and I would slip ours in, trying to get it between the same pages. If we succeeded in inserting our peli in the same place as his, we got to take his peli. If we slipped ours into an empty page, we lost it to him.

Miguel had more pelis than anyone.

■ ■ ■ ■

One evening Miguel took me to see *Rebecca.* We had seen it before, and I had been mesmerized by the housekeeper, Mrs. Danvers. The rigidity of her profile and the cruelty of her calculations reminded me of our Austrian neighbors when they became Germans.

Hitchcock had changed the ending. Rebecca dies in an accident rather than at the hands of her husband as she did in the book, which I had read on the ship. It interested me that even without actually killing anyone, Maxim de Winter remained menacing. His need to control and belittle the women in his life, his way of suffocating them, was as effective as bloodshed. As deserving — I thought — of punishment.

"Now I know what I don't want in a husband," I joked to Miguel after our first viewing. But he hadn't found Maxim evil. "It was Rebecca who caused it all," he insisted. "She was the wicked one." We argued about it for the entire afternoon, and agreed to see it again to bolster our respective cases.

That evening, the screen was already crackling to life as we slipped into our seats.

Every film at the Cine Teatro Tesla began with a newsreel, one more way we kept up with the atrocities going on across the ocean. We were a noisy audience, greeting every mention of the Allies with cheers, every mention of the Nazis with derogatory whistles. It felt good to cheer, it felt optimistic. As if we were actually urging the Allies on to victory.

Tonight, the newsreel announced Germany's invasion of Denmark. I tried to think of what countries might be left for Willi. I hoped he was still in Switzerland. Why wouldn't he come? Could anything but Nazis keep him from us? Miguel and I whistled furiously, and I was comforted by the whistles of others around us. But then, from a seat not too far back, came a familiar cry. "Heil Hitler!"

My skin went hot. Fear pinned me to the seat.

Miguel was instantly on his feet, searching the crowd in back of us. "Heil Hitler!" came the voice again. By then I had risen to my feet as well. The teenage boy who had uttered the hateful words leered at me. "Go home, Jews!"

He had said it in German, but Miguel had understood. He started up the aisle toward the Nazi boy and his friends, but a group of

Jewish boys beat him there. The one in front swung a fist at the Nazi. I stared. A Jew beating up a Nazi.

It was difficult to keep track after that. The audience was in uproar, watching the boys attack each other, cheering on both sides. Miguel joined in with enthusiasm, an act that won him newfound respect in our community. Despite the terror I felt hearing that Fascist echo of Austria, I was suffused with a giddy euphoria watching Jews defend themselves. I hoped there were not more Nazis waiting in the wings, rolling up in tanks outside the theater. But maybe here, we had a fighting chance.

FORTY

On weekends, I woke early and went alone to the market to see Nayra, though she was often too busy to talk. The Aymara were at least as reluctant to befriend foreigners as the foreigners were to befriend them. It took me weeks of persistent effort to get Nayra to look at me, weeks longer to get her to speak more than a few syllables. Aymara people are shy, Miguel reminded me. They won't want to be friends with you. When I pointed out that he was friends with me, he said, "Just half of me." And laughed.

It was difficult for me to understand why the majority of Bolivians — people native to the country like the Aymara and Quechua — would not have the same rights that the paler Spanish descendants had. The Indians were not even considered full citizens, Miguel told me. Despite my own experience with insensible divisions, this explicit segregation bewildered me.

So I met Nayra standing before dirty pyramids of yucca, potatoes, and cañahua.

There were different rules for the Indians. If they had Indian names, like Mamani or Quispe, they were simply not admitted to school. If the girls wore the traditional clothes of the cholas, they were not admitted to school. Once I asked Nayra to come to the movies with us and she said she was not allowed. "Your mother?" I asked. But she shook her head. "*Bolivia* does not allow us." And I thought, *Just as Austria did not allow me.* The connections were everywhere.

The Aymara, Quechua, and other native populations were not allowed in the front seats of the tram. Indian children were expected to work, not to study and learn to read. When you were walking on a sidewalk and an Indian was coming the other way, the Indian was expected to step down. I could not do this, could not force an Indian to yield to me. I was always stepping down no matter who was coming toward me and I cringed when I saw my fellow Jews allow this humiliation to occur. Had we forgotten how it felt?

Some Indians worked as maids for the richer Bolivians or the Europeans. Everyone wanted to work for the Europeans, Nayra told me. They paid better and did not whip their servants. "People whip their servants?" The thought of anyone laying a hand on Nayra fueled my outrage. An image of Anneliese's scars flashed through my mind. But Nayra just looked at me impatiently, as if I were an idiot younger sister. How could I understand so little of the world?

The richer white Bolivians all had servants, usually Indian girls. None of the Austrians did in those first few years. Still, hiring a maid cost almost nothing, sometimes just room and board. That's why so many immigrant families eventually hired empleadas. Once my father was teaching and my mother was consistently selling Austrian pastries, we had enough to pay the pittance that maids demanded. But my mother wanted no strangers in our home. She had had enough of strangers in her home.

One afternoon, I took Rachel to the market to meet Nayra. She wouldn't make fun of an Aymara girl. She never made fun of anyone. In that way, she reminded me of Anneliese. She gave a grave little curtsy when I introduced her to Nayra, who looked bewildered by the gesture. I don't think she was accustomed to foreigners being interested in her at all other than as a means to her vegetables. I also had the feeling that perhaps she was not as interested in me and Rachel as we were in her.

We wanted her to teach us Aymara so we could speak with her in her own tongue. Besides, it was pretty. Everything sounded like the names of flowers. She initially resisted the idea, being both busy and reserved, but our persistence wore her down. While her mother was chatting with customers, she beckoned us behind their vegetable towers and squatted with her hands spread out before her. *"Maya, paya, kimsa, pusi,"* she showed us, counting out the numbers on her fingers.

In return, she asked that we help her with her Spanish. "It would help my mother," she said.

"But you know Spanish." She almost always understood her customers' requests.

"Not so much for talking." What Nayra lacked was not the words themselves, but the confidence to speak them aloud.

We started with vegetables. The potatoes had so many different names I got confused. There were dozens and dozens of kinds! More kinds of potatoes than I had ever seen in my life. And each one was a different color and size and shape, with a different name. Some of them looked like fat fingers, some like radishes, some had strange roots trailing off them. I didn't know the Spanish names for all of them. I just called them papas.

"More," insisted Nayra.

I shook my head.

"In your language then, what are they?"

"Erdäpfel."

Nayra was silent, waiting for more words. "That's it," I said.

"For all of them?" she asked in astonishment. *"Every kind?"*

Our own language suddenly felt limited, insufficient for describing the subtleties of the world around us.

Nayra came from a village up near the lake. Lakes to me meant summer resorts and bathing, waterfront cafés and sandy beaches. But when I had asked Nayra if she swam, she had laughed. "It's not that kind of lake."

"You can't swim?"

"You can, if you are loca. Or a fish. But if you stay in more than a few minutes under the surface you will die of cold."

Some of my schoolmates had been up to the lake. When I asked Sarah and other girls about it, they confirmed Nayra's assessment. Too cold to swim. Too cold even to picnic beside it, though many families tried.

Some even rented boats to travel across to its islands. "It's as big as an ocean," my deskmate Sarah told me. "You can't see the other side. And sometimes you have to take a raft to get across parts of it."

I wanted to see it for myself, but it didn't seem likely that Nayra would invite me for a visit. The Indians never invited us to their homes. Besides, it was hours away. You had to take a truck or a bus or a donkey. Nayra stayed much of the time with family in the La Paz neighborhood of Chijini, uphill from us, so she could get to work.

There were so many kinds of Bolivians, each belonging to her own specific geography, jungles or high, cold lakes or semitropical hills. Every mountain, every curve of a river held a pocket of people said to be so entirely different from those on the other side that they didn't seem to be from the same country. I wondered if the people in all of the parts of Austria I had never seen were as different from each other. I might never find out.

"Can we have Nayra to dinner?" I asked my parents. My mother, who spent so much time with Wayra and who was always hospitable to my friends — even allowing Miguel to join us for meals when we had enough food — hesitated. She looked at my father,

355

whose head was bent over sheet music he'd found in a local shop. "Do you know what she eats?"

I shrugged. "Potatoes, I guess?"

My mother nodded in her newly vague way. "Potatoes I could do. But will she come?"

It was much harder to convince Nayra to come to our apartment than it was to convince my parents to have her. She shook her head every time I asked, for months. When I asked Miguel why she wouldn't come, he said that Indians never mixed with white people or foreigners, and we were both.

I didn't give up. Nayra's presence comforted me in a unique way. She never asked questions. She didn't force explanations from me. Unlike Miguel, she didn't even try to find out what Austria was like. Nothing about her reminded me of home. She had never heard of Austria. When I talked to Nayra we rarely said anything that would sound significant to a stranger. But oh, how significant it was to me to sit with someone who asked nothing of me. She didn't even ask for my friendship. I had to drag her into it.

When Nayra finally agreed to come to our

rooms — perhaps simply to stop my incessant invitations — my parents were kind. They gave her our best chair, the only one with a back, and offered her everything first. Nayra sat stiffly on the edge of her seat, keeping her eyes lowered as she whispered responses we could barely hear. When food was served, she bent over her fried potatoes, eating quickly. Only when my mother began asking her — using me to translate — what kinds of things her family grew on their land by the lake did she seem to forget her shyness.

"Only certain things grow there. It's cold and the soil is not so rich. We have potatoes and beans. Some others grow corn, but we are better at potatoes." She looked hungrily at her empty plate and my mother refilled it.

"How much land do you have?"

"We don't own the land."

My father leaned forward, curious. "Who owns the land?"

"A mestizo. A rich man."

"But you live on it?"

"We work it. My family does. Other families too. Campesinos can't own land." Her tone was matter-of-fact. This was how her world worked.

We sat in silence for a moment. I didn't

know how to address this newly discovered injustice.

My father changed the subject. "What does the lake look like?"

Nayra glanced toward him, then up at our stained ceiling. "It's a mirror of the sky, almost as big. Around it are the mountains, the highest ones with snow. It's where everything begins, the top of the earth." The islands in the lake gave birth to the sun, the moon, and the stars, she told us. The boats and buildings in some of the villages were made from rushes that float on the surface of the water. The water was full of tiny fish called karachi that her family fried for lunch.

"Mostly I am living in Chijini now," she concluded. "It's closer to the market. I go back to the lake only for holidays, for fiestas."

I listened, rapt. Lake Titicaca sounded mythical, a place where only gods could live.

My parents had also fallen silent.

"Where do you go to school?" my mother asked. Reluctantly, I translated. Didn't my mother know anything?

"I don't." Nayra swallowed and set down her mug. She had kept on her little hat, and I noticed a small tin animal was pinned to the brim. "I work."

"I see." My mother nodded. "And your

father? He works?"

"He's in the Colquiri mine." Many of the men we knew worked for the mining companies. Bolivia had immense mineral wealth, largely in tin, tungsten, and silver. But the mines were dangerous. In the labyrinths within Cerro Rico de Potosí, the legendary mountain once home to the world's largest veins of silver, miners were always dying in accidents or from lung diseases.

"Her father knows how to make boats too. Nayra says he made one with the head of a puma on it, with fangs."

"How clever!" My mother's smile looked strained.

Nayra continued to eat her potatoes. I was ashamed that I didn't even know what kind they were. I wanted to ask Nayra but was worried I would sound stupid. She was always astonished when I didn't know basic things like the names of the many magnificent peaks around us. How could I not be able to name the components of this world?

My father sipped at a cup of coca tea and hummed a bit of Mahler's "Erinnerung."

Nayra didn't ask what my parents did for work or what I did at school. Maybe she didn't consider those things important.

She had been surprised that I didn't have brothers or sisters living with us, so I

359

explained that my brother was missing. This didn't seem remarkable to her, that someone should be missing. I wondered how often people went missing up by the lake, what forces might take them away. The cold water, perhaps.

When she got up from the table, Nayra saw the doll sitting in the corner of the room. "Yours?"

"It was a gift." I picked up the doll and handed it to Nayra. She turned it over in her hands. Its dirndl was growing stiff and dusty.

"From your country?" She turned the doll backward to make her eyes close. "Ojos de lago." Lake eyes.

"Nayra, this is for you." My mother held out a small cake. Nayra set the doll back on the floor. "It's a recipe from Austria. For your family." Nayra looked at the cake in her hands. "It's not usually so flat," my mother added ruefully. "Es la altura."

"It's good," I reassured her. "It's Gugel-hupf. With almond and fruits."

Nayra smiled. While I had wanted Nayra to know my parents, had wanted to share our food and show her our room, I realized now that I preferred it when we were alone. I liked it better when Nayra was allowed to be quiet, or tell the stories she wanted to tell, when she didn't have to answer questions or entertain anyone.

The next time I saw Nayra, she handed me a tiny alpaca sweater, a rainbow of colors knitted together. "To help your doll dress for Bolivia," she said. "She will be cold."

FORTY-ONE

"Under the water of our lake, all the way under, there is a city," Nayra began in the mix of Spanish, Aymara, and gestures we used to communicate. Her voice was so quiet that it always sounded as if she were telling me a secret. We were sitting on the dusty street in early April, leaning against the wall of a building near the market, sipping tin cups of api morado, a warm drink made from purple corn and cinnamon.

"Like Atlantis!" I had discovered the story of Atlantis in one of Willi's books, though I embroidered it considerably. "In Atlantis, everyone played music. Writing poetry was as common as writing shopping lists and artists painted every wall before money was introduced. At first people scoffed at the gold coins brought by a visitor. But a few, entranced by their glittering novelty, traded their prized artworks for them. The greed for coins grew until it was all anyone thought about. They stopped writing poetry and only wrote shopping lists. Apollo, or whatever god of music reigned then, sent a wall of water to submerge the city forever."

Nayra's face glowed in recognition.

"Yes, similar. Only our whole city was made of gold. But it too was sunk when people became greedy. If you travel underwater in the lake you can hear the music of the quena still playing." I had heard the quena, the Andean pipe that made a shrill, lonesome sound. The kind of sound a drowned musician would make.

"Who is playing it?" I imagined Andean mermaids and wondered if they braided their hair and wore little black bowler hats.

She smiled. "No one knows. The spirits trapped there?"

As Nayra continued the story of the city under the lake, I noticed something odd. When she referred to something that had happened in the past, she gestured in front of her. When she spoke of the future, she gestured toward her back.

"Say, 'When I was a little girl, I swam in the lake.' " I interrupted her, and she looked up at me, confused.

"Say the sentence, I mean. In Aymara."

Still looking puzzled she said, "When I was a little girl, I swam in the lake." Her right hand stretched toward the horizon. "But I didn't! I don't know how to swim."

"I know. But when you talk about being a little girl you move your hands in front of you. Like your childhood is in front of you."

"But it is."

"No, your childhood is in the past. And the past is behind us."

She laughed. "The past is right in front of us, where we can see it. It's the future we can't see."

"But that's backward."

"It can't be any other way."

I was frustrated. Were we not walking away from our childhood with every step?

Yet later that night, as I lay in bed mulling this over, I had to concede that it was only the past I could see. I could see the scar on Anneliese's lip, Stefi sewing a tiny dress for my bunny Lebkuchen, the men in brown trampling my city. I could see the braided rug by the door of our Vienna flat and the imposing silhouette of the *Proteus*. I could see Miguel running up the aisle of the Cine Teatro Tesla. But I could not see tomorrow. I could not see who would win the war or when Willi would come home or where I would live when I grew up or what my children would look like. It made a kind of sense to refer to the future as belonging to the blind spot at our backs. Hadn't Orpheus been reaching for his future when he turned back toward Eurydice?

It startled me that the way I had always thought of the world could be wrong. Yet at the same time, it filled me with a breathless sense of freedom and possibility. Closing my eyes, I imagined with all of my might that my brother Willi was standing just behind me.

When I told Nayra our stories of Friedenglückhasenland, she didn't mock me or raise a skeptical eyebrow. Telling stories about rabbits did not strike her as odd. Like my stories, hers were focused on animals, but Bolivian animals, such as turtles, foxes, vizcachas, snakes, condors, vicuñas, and jaguars. It was a puma, Nayra told me, that she wore pinned to her hat. The puma was a symbol of prosperity, among other things. Nayra could not write, but she allowed me to transcribe her stories, to create a record.

Nayra was nothing like Anneliese, except for her love of stories. Anneliese was a wild talker, expressive and turbulent. Nayra was still and quiet. Yet when it came to stories, a channel of fire seemed to rise inside both girls. I had no trouble writing the connection between them.

With our stories, Nayra and I created a common ground.

"Tell me the one about the fox and the monkey," I begged, another afternoon at the market. Nayra's mother had let Nayra take a break to sit with me when I stopped by after school. Monkeys were still exotic to me. I knew there were monkeys in Bolivia, but they didn't live in La Paz. I dreamed of traveling to the jungle, where the monkeys would come down from the trees and ride on my shoulders.

"The fox and the monkey sneaked into a rich farmer's house one night, to eat from the pot of quinoa porridge left on the fire." Another connection between worlds was the greediness of foxes. The Aymara fables were much like Aesop's fables, those stories intended to instill the values of modesty and unselfishness. But while Aesop's fox was clever, the Andean monkey was cleverer.

Tucking my skirt underneath me, I settled on the dirt beside her to listen.

When she ended the story with the monkey tricking the fox into holding up a piece of the sky, I was reminded of Atlas. I had always wondered how one person could hold up the sky, how he could keep it from falling in folds around him like a tent. If the sky is being held aloft, then what is between the sky and earth? What do we call that space we breathe? Another poem suggested itself.

"Now, Tiwanaku? Please?" While I loved animal stories, I was even more ensorcelled by tales of the ancient city whose ruins still sprawled across a plain near the lake. Tiwanaku was patterned after the sky, Nayra said. Doorways were aligned with the passage of the sun. "The moon used to be brighter than the sun," Nayra said. "But the sun was jealous and threw ashes in her face."

Temples were constructed from earth and a blue-green gravel collected from the beds of mountain streams that fed their crops. I wondered if there had been poetry in Tiwanaku. There must have been, because there must have been music, at least reed pipes from the lake. Someone would have had the impulse to sing along.

Sometimes Nayra's stories frightened or repelled me.

"There was a mother with two sons," one began. "These sons were lazy and did not like work. One day the mother sent the sons off with the seed potatoes to plant in a distant field. But when the sons got there, one stretched out on the ground and put his hat over his face. 'You go ahead and plant them,' he said. 'I'm tired.' The other son lay down next to him. 'I'm tired, too,' he said, wrapping himself in a blanket to sleep. 'We can plant them later.'

"But when they woke they were hungry and they ate the seed potatoes. Satiated, they kicked around a rock like a football, until the lords of the underworld got angry about all the noise overhead. "Stop your games or you'll have to play a match against us down here." Frightened, they went home and told their mother they had planted the potatoes.

"The following spring the mother went to the field to dig up the potatoes she thought her sons had planted. But as she began hoeing the dirt, a neighboring farmer stopped her. 'Your sons did no planting,' he said. 'They slept, they ate your seed potatoes, they played games and went home.'

"At home, the mother said nothing to the sons. There was no food for dinner. There would be no food for the long, hard winter. While her sons were outside kicking rocks again, she cut a piece of her thigh off with a kitchen knife, fried it, and served it to her sons.

"The next morning she was dead. When the sons realized what had happened, they were horrified. But it was too late. They could not undo what was done. The gods came down and turned them into wind, rain, and hail."

I had many questions about this one. Where was the father? Why should a mother punish herself for her sons' crimes? Or was the moral that a decent mother must sacrifice for her children, no matter how undeserving the children, no matter how great the sacrifice?

It was a warning to sons, Nayra said. If they were lazy, it could kill their mother.

There were many stories about mothers being cooked and eaten. Or being fed to the condors. Even Pachamama got thrown into a cooking pot in one of her stories. But there were also many stories of the lake where the sun and the moon and the stars were all born. Where humanity itself was born.

Over time, we wove the threads of our stories together, so that it became harder to sort out which belonged to her and which belonged to me. The pages on which they were preserved, however, were mine. These lived in a stack beneath my bed. Someday, I thought, I could read them to Anneliese. Someday, I could read them to my own children. When stories were not shared, they withered and blew away. The world was so full of stories just blowing around.

FORTY-TWO

April 1940

It was just a matter of time before my mother realized she could combine her two newest passions. She began by making special fertility bread with powdered maca root. Then a soup to cure fever. Coca cookies to help newcomers with the altitude — and with everything else. But our kitchen was too small and ill equipped for her to cook much of anything. Demand was constant. Refugees preferred to buy food from my mother, knowing that it would be cooked or baked to the standards of home. It would not make them ill.

At the same time, I was longing for a room of my own. I was nearly thirteen. No longer did I need the safety of my parents' bed. I needed a bed where I could think about things I didn't want to share. Where I could be alone with Rachel. Where I could reread and reread *The Scorpion.* I still hadn't

371

worked up the courage to ask Rachel whether she had read it and how she felt about its contents. She had never brought up the books she left for me when I was sick, and I began to feel that the inclusion of that particular novel had been an accident.

It wouldn't be easy to find a new apartment, a place where my father could play music and teach his students, somewhere with plenty of space and unlikely to disturb neighbors. Yet we had just begun looking when we heard that another Austrian family wanted to rent out the top floor of their home on calle Colombia near Plaza Sucre, including a share of the small garden. It had three bedrooms, a separate kitchen, a parlor, and large bathtub.

"Three bedrooms?" I asked my mother as we wandered the apartment. I noted that none of the windows looked out on Illimani.

She turned to stare at me. "I have two children. Did you forget your brother?"

My breath caught and my face went hot, because, in fact, I had. Not forgotten him, for he lived in the dull ache in my chest, but I had stopped factoring him into our Bolivian lives.

"You don't think he should have his own room?"

"Of course I do but —" I stopped myself.

"But what? You don't think he's coming?" My mother's voice had gone hard.

"I do. I do think he's coming. I don't know what I was going to say. I'm sorry, Mutti. I just wasn't thinking." I didn't know how to express how much I longed for my brother, how much I needed him to be constant and laughing, things my mother no longer was. But I also wanted to tell her how hard it was to think of him, how fruitless it felt to touch that wound over and over. I could not climb into that pain and disappear completely.

Her eyes narrowed. "He will need a room. Your father can use it for his lessons until Willi comes."

I nodded. "Of course."

We stepped into the kitchen, large and light. My mother touched the wood countertops, the knobs of the oven, and she smiled. "This," she said. "This will change everything."

While I was excited about the prospect of space, I dreaded leaving Miguel's house. No longer would I run into him and his siblings leaving our apartment or coming home. No longer would it be so easy for us to fall in step.

He took the news stoically.

"I guess I won't see you then." He stared off up the street in front of the house.

"Of course you'll see me!" I couldn't imagine life in La Paz without Miguel. He was part of the architecture of our existence. My foundation.

He smiled and shook his head. "It won't be the same."

He was right, of course. As soon as we moved into our new apartment, we became even busier, cleaning and organizing our new rooms, finding odd bits of furniture to fill them, and figuring out new routes to markets and friends. My mother began selling her food from a newly installed counter at the front of the Grubers' Riesenrad Café. In my new room, my own room, I was relearning the pleasure of solitude. While I still met Miguel at the movies, I didn't run into him several times a day in the street in front of our apartment. We attended different schools. I couldn't race downstairs and knock on his door every time I had a question or news to share. He couldn't race up the stairs to fetch me for a game. We had to make plans to see each other, with an ever-increasing gap between meetings.

Dearest of Annelieses, I wrote on one of my paper scraps. *I have room for you now. You*

374

could run down to me, stay the night in my bed, sing me the lullabies of Katzenland. Writing to Anneliese was a bedtime ritual. The fact that I was not allowed to send these letters — my parents still believed it would endanger Anneliese to receive letters from a Jew — did not deter me. Someday I would be able to write to her, and I didn't want to forget anything. I could not picture her face clearly anymore, yet she was still so sharp in my heart. Even sharper now that I no longer had Miguel as my daily distraction.

Next to my room in our new home on calle Colombia was the slightly larger room my mother painted a dark green with white trim. "I wish we had something of his to put in it," she fretted, examining the bed she had made up with clean sheets and the simple set of drawers. It struck me as odd that the absent child should get the larger room, but I kept that thought to myself. I tried to think if I had anything left of Willi's. I ran back to my room, where I rummaged through the few things on my shelves and found *Fifteen Rabbits*. It wasn't my original copy, which I had left behind in Vienna, but one that had been passed around our community. It would do. I settled it on Willi's pillow. "Be a magnet," I instructed the dumb book. "Bring him here."

The best room of our new apartment was the kitchen. It was big enough for a dining table as well as a real oven with gas burners. In the corner stood an icebox — the height of luxury! — and in the back was a pantry lined with shelves. My mother began to collect tins, mostly cookie tins from other Europeans or from Austrian-owned shops. She lined them up on our shelves, labeled them, and filled them with flours, grains, and cookies. Many of the tins were decorated with holiday scenes, featuring Christmas trees and ice-skating. They reminded me of the holiday markets of Vienna with their marvelous piles of ginger Lebkuchen, fir cones, and mulled cider. Funny that Christmas tins could evoke such nostalgia in the heart of a Jew. I wanted to be at those markets. I even longed for the cold, for the icy winds, the snow under my feet. I learned not to examine the tins too closely, to stay on the edges of that emotional abyss.

My mother was standing over her new stovetop one day, strands of hair creeping from the knot of curls on the top of her head to stick to her cheeks, when from my bedroom window I saw Rachel running down the street. I was not sure I had ever seen Rachel run before. Thin and pale —

like so many of us — Rachel normally found walking any distance at all exhausting. I suppose she is finally getting used to the altitude, I thought. I heard her knock on the door and come in, without waiting for a response.

"Frau Zingel!" she called. "Frau Zingel! Orly!"

I was puzzled. Why would Rachel be calling my mother too? I ran to the top of the stairs, but my mother had gotten there first. She had been baking, and her hands were covered with flour. "Gruss Gott, Rachel!" she said, sounding pleased. "You're just in time for some poppy-seed rolls. They'll be out of the oven in three minutes."

Rachel's thin chest heaved with her efforts to catch her breath. "Telegram," she finally said. "From France."

My mother nearly ripped it out of Rachel's hands. We stood staring at her as she tore it open and read the few brief lines. When she looked up at me, her eyes were bright with tears. I was alarmed for all of five seconds before she swept me into her arms and spun me around the kitchen. "He's alive!" she cried. "Oh Orly, he's alive!"

"Willi?" I said. "Willi's alive? Oh Mutti, is he really alive?"

She waved the paper at me. "That's what Violaine has just written. She has had a letter from him. He didn't leave an address, but he said he was in France."

"In France? But why?" I felt dizzy with relief and vertigo.

"I don't know, I don't know, but Orly, isn't it *marvelous*? Alive and in France!" She suddenly remembered Rachel was still in the room. "And you, dear girl. You have made me happier than I have ever been. Ever since. Well. Thank you. Thank you for running."

Rachel smiled shyly. "It was delivered to the SOPRO offices, and Eloise and I were up there this morning, so she said I should take it straight to you."

I hugged my mother again and took the telegram from her hands. *Willi alive. Here in my country. Address unknown. Letter to arrive soon.* It was hard to believe it was true. For more than a year we had heard nothing, and now . . . ! I thought of the room my mother had prepared for him, and wondered if that was what had summoned him from the beyond.

"You'll stay to dinner, Rachel? Where is my husband? Orly, where has your father gone off to? Tonight we are celebrating!" My mother's hands moved in so many directions at once it looked as though she were dancing.

"Mutti?" Black smoke had started to trickle out of the oven.

"Oh, the rolls!" Grabbing an oven mitten she pulled open the oven door, to find a dozen blackened poppy-seed rolls burned to their pan. Her entire morning's work. She pulled the tray from the oven and looked at it. "To hell with the rolls!" she exclaimed. And with the spatula she scraped them right out our window into the alley below.

I was glad for the excuse to run to Miguel's. As soon as we'd finished dinner I walked Rachel home and then ran nearly the entire two kilometers to his house. Yet when Señora Torres answered the door, she told me that Miguel wasn't there. He had gone to football practice. Disappointment fell through me like a stone. "You're welcome to come in and say hello to the others." She held open the door, and I could smell something frying in oil.

"Gracias. But I had better get home before my parents start to worry. I just wanted to let him know something. We had some news today." I shifted from foot to foot, the thrill of it still coursing through me.

"From Europe?"

I nodded. And while I wanted to tell Miguel myself I couldn't stop. "My brother, he's alive!"

"Oh, Orlita, that's fantastic news." Señora Torres hugged me. "Your parents must be so relieved."

"I guess you can tell Miguel when he gets back."

"If you want to tell him yourself I won't say anything. That's just wonderful news. Maravilloso."

I considered this. Tomorrow was school for both of us, then I had homework with Rachel and theater rehearsal. I sighed. "You can tell him. I'll try to come back this weekend though."

"I'll let him know. I think he misses you."

I smiled and looked down at the scuffed doormat. "Yes, I miss him too."

An agonizing month passed before finally the letter arrived from Willi, sent months ago to Violaine, who forwarded it to us. My father was correct; it was a long journey for a letter. He brought it back one evening from the post office and we opened it together at the kitchen table. "You read it, Julia," said my father, pushing the pages to her. My mother started to object, her hands

380

shaking with emotion, but she could not keep herself from picking up those pages.

Dearest Mutti, Vati, and Erdnuss,

I hope this finds its way to you. I know you wish that it was I there before you rather than a few inadequate slips of paper full of words that don't say enough, and I hope you know that is my wish as well. But there are things I find I must do here. There are ways here, I have discovered, of helping the others. I am being purposefully vague, but know that I am doing work I feel certain you would approve of, that I know you would want me to continue. There are children who are in our situation or worse. I will say that. As long as there is the smallest chance I could make a difference I must remain. Even one child could mean saving an entire family's life. I am working in more than one country. I am trying to tell you all that I can without endangering our work or the children.

I cannot tell you how glad it makes me that you are so far from here. Knowing that you are safe keeps my heart easy, frees me to focus on helping the others. Violaine has given me your letters,

Mutti, and yours, Vati. Erdnuss, will you send along some stories? Something I could read to the children? I can hear your voice when you write me, you write just as you speak. I hope you are writing down all your bunny tales, or are you now too old for bunnies? I try to imagine you now, you must have grown a foot! I will have to find a way to come to you soon, so as to be around to help you fend off all of the young men sure to come courting. Please tell me they haven't already? You are my little Erdnuss and mustn't let them come near you until I can be there to make sure they are worthy.

Mutti, I am glad that you are finding things to do, though I am sure it must feel awful not to be singing. Don't be cross, but I find it hard to imagine you spending all day in the kitchen! How the war changes us. Vati, bravo for finding people to play with. Is a Bolivian symphony orchestra next? I am so longing to walk in that thin air with you and taste that coca tea that seems to have you all under a spell.

I am well. I am healthy. And I am very sorry, Vati, but I don't miss practicing the viola one bit.

When it is time for me to come, I will write to let you know. I love every hair on your heads.

Your Willi

Our Willi. We still had a Willi. I felt a release of tension from muscles I didn't know I had. As if longing for my brother had become part of my body. Miguel came with an armful of kantutas for my mother and we sat outside on the ground and drew stick figures on the pavement with chalk while I told him how Willi had made me puppets out of his old socks and musical instruments out of lentils and cardboard tubes.

My father whistled waltzes as he put his hat on and headed out to give a lesson. For a few weeks, my mother was nearly my mother again. She hugged me often and for no reason. There was energy in her step. Her lips remembered how to curve upward. There were a few times I almost thought I heard an operatic sound coming from her throat. But I must have been mistaken.

We had almost begun to allow ourselves hope when France fell to the Germans. My mother was inconsolable. "What did he mean when he said he was in more than one country? Do you think he has gone

383

back to Austria? He never even said if he had managed to get a visa for here!"

"Maybe he is doing something in Switzerland? Moving people from the camp to France?" My father drummed his fingertips on the table.

"But France is no longer safe."

"What children does he mean, Mutti? Jewish children? Why don't they have parents?"

None of us had answers. In a way, it had been better not to know anything about where he was than it was to know the certain danger he was facing.

Every night we imagined the infinite things that Willi could be doing. Perhaps he was shepherding children to England. Or teaching them to swim in the Swiss rivers. Or crafting fake passports to get them to Shanghai. I fell asleep to visions of him playing follow-the-leader through the forests.

Whatever it was, it was more important to Willi than finding his way to us. We pirouetted our minds away from this thought. Nothing further arrived from him after that one letter and we did not know if he was still in France or elsewhere. Paralyzed with fear, we listened on the radio to the account of the humiliation of the French in the forest of Compiègne, where the country had celebrated victory over the Germans less than two decades ago. Just like when the Nazis arrived in Austria, everything in France had gone so wrong so fast.

"Willi would have seen it coming." My father tried to reassure her. "He would have hidden somewhere."

"He wouldn't! You know your son, Jakob. Has self-preservation ever been his first priority?" Despite her tears, my mother said this with a kind of pride.

My father had no answer for that, and the two of them sat there in silence until the end of the broadcast. Then my mother got up and went to bed.

The bad news was relentless. Aunt Thekla wrote to say that she had returned to Graz to find their parents and two sisters had disappeared. The neighbors claimed not to know where they had gone. A Christian family had taken over their bakery. Thekla had been afraid to approach them, afraid where her questions might lead. My parents didn't need Thekla to tell them that my mother's family had probably been sent to one of the camps. The camps from which no one seemed to return.

After that, my mother retreated again. She stopped cooking, stopped stewing herbal remedies on our stovetop, and stopped talking unless it was strictly necessary. She lost interest in the few friends she had made in La Paz. When Mathilde or one of the others knocked on our door, my mother feigned sleep or a headache. My father and I put meals together as best we could, mostly from potatoes and chicken. I made my mother a chicken soup from the bones, adding quinoa and carrots to fill it out, and was relieved when she managed half a bowl.

It was hard to know how my father was doing. His exterior changed so little, unless he was playing. By now he knew most of the European musicians, and he played with them almost every evening when he was done with his students. They performed small concerts, in our homes and clubs and, as Willi had predicted, talked about one day forming an orchestra. As in Vienna, their loose group was entirely male. But here, there were not enough classically trained musicians, not enough instruments for a formal orchestra. Maybe someday, my father said.

He hadn't heard anything from his parents, his sister Klothilde, or his brother Franz since we left. He avoided talking about them. When my mother brought them up, to ask him if perhaps he had heard any news, he became angry. "Don't you think I would have told you if I had heard anything?"

None of our family members had succeeded in getting visas of any kind. By the end of 1939 many Bolivians had already been saying that the only way the country could keep refugees was if they left La Paz for the countryside.

I missed my lively aunt Thekla and her stories. I missed sneaking into my grandmother's Sunday salons to sit on my brother's lap and try to distract him from the proceedings. I even missed my grandmother's stern lectures on decorum and politics. I also missed my aunt Klothilde, though not with the ardor with which I missed the rest of them. Klothilde was an enigma to me. She was bookish and science-minded, like her father, and had been studying to become an internist. Children never interested her. Even music couldn't hold her attention. I wondered what she was doing now that she could no longer study. Now that she could no longer do anything.

I missed Stefi as much as I missed my family. Kind, plump, freckled Stefi had been with me as long as my parents had. She had braided my hair in the morning and told me stories about the clever chickens in her village in the country, chickens that untied her boots every time she went to feed them. (I was starting to suspect that a person's value to me had always depended largely on her ability to tell me stories.) I didn't know what happened to Stefi after we were moved to Leopoldstadt. We couldn't write to her for the same reason I couldn't write to Anneliese and because we didn't know where she had gone when we were moved. My only comfort was that at least Stefi, like Anneliese, was not Jewish.

I needed something else to think about; I envied my father the escape he found in his viola. Despite school, Rachel, and Nayra, something felt absent.

"Mutti, I want to learn how to sing." We sat at our table, neither of us reading the books in front of us. Just because she refused to sing didn't mean I couldn't. My piano lessons had ended with our flight from Vienna, but music still lived somewhere in me. It rose up when I heard my father and his friends play; it had always been part of the air I breathed.

I knew we could not afford an instrument. But the melodies spinning through my blood demanded some kind of expression. When my father wasn't around, I wanted to fill the silence my mother created. Singing seemed logical. It was inexpensive and required no instrument. I already sang as I walked to the market. I sang to myself in the bath. I sang with my father's music when he let me. Miguel and I sometimes listened to music on his mother's radio; he taught me all the lyrics to "Échale Salsita" and "Solamente una Vez." I knew I didn't have an exceptional voice, but maybe I just needed training.

"So sing." My mother continued to stare down at *Effi Briest,* which she'd been reading for at least a month.

"But can you teach me? To sing like you?"

"Orly." She looked up at me. "You know I don't sing anymore."

"But couldn't you teach me?"

She sighed. "I don't think so."

"But why?"

She couldn't — or wouldn't — explain. "Music is over for me, Orly."

I fell silent, but my feet kicked at the bars of my chair. "It's not over for me!" Frustration turned to anger. I wanted to hurt her. "Would you sing if Willi were here?"

Her face tightened. "You do not understand." Her voice was unfamiliar, hard. "Singing comes from a place that no longer exists." She shut her book, walked to the bedroom, and closed the door.

I didn't know any other singers in Bolivia. Surely many existed, but not in my limited social circle. I wondered if I might have better luck with an instrument, if I could borrow one. I wanted something different, something that would be mine. Not piano, not viola. I consulted Miguel. We had been to see the Mexican film *Viviré Otra Vez* — I Will Live Again — up at Cine Teatro Tesla, and were walking through Plaza Murillo. (It was more fashionable to go to the 6:00 P.M. showing on Sundays, which our parents called the Vermouth — perhaps because it began at the usual hour for cocktails — but Miguel and I preferred to go during quieter times.)

"You could play the Andean pipes," he suggested, "or the charango."

"The charango?" I had vague memories of seeing the instrument in the hands of a street musician. The Andean pipes I heard everywhere, but their sound was too thin, as lonesome as the wind.

"It's got strings. Like a little guitar. You must have seen one. Come! I'll show you." He increased his pace and took me even farther upward, where the streets were older and narrower. "Mira." He had stopped in front of the window of a shop. In the window were dozens of instruments, including several long-handled, figure-eight-shaped charangos.

Miguel pushed open the door. The man sitting in back by the cash register looked up from the charango he was holding. "Bienvenidos." He rose to his feet, setting the instrument gently on the counter.

"We're just looking. My friend might want to play the charango."

"Might?" The man laughed. "Has she heard charango?"

Miguel turned to me.

I gazed at the wall of instruments. So many kinds! Miguel was right, they looked like tiny guitars, with fat, outsize handles and ten strings. I reached out a finger to stroke the wood.

"No los toques, por favor," said the man immediately. Turning to Miguel, he said. "Por favor dile a la blanquita que no los toque." *Please tell the little white girl not to touch it.*

"La blanquita puede entender," Miguel told him, smiling. *The little white girl can understand.*

"Ah!" The man's face opened into a warm smile. "Hablas español! Do you want me to play one for you?"

I nodded, suddenly shy to speak Spanish to a stranger. "Which one would you like to hear?" He touched several of the charangos.

"El escamoso. Con las rayas." *The scaly one, with the stripes.* It reminded me of the church I saw in Genoa, made of black and white marble. Everything reminded me of something else, something far away. Poems came to me so often now I had to carry a small notebook everywhere to pin them down before they fluttered away over the mountains.

"Ah! El armadillo!" Gently, he lifted the one I had indicated down from the wall. "Toca," he invited. I stroked the back of the instrument, which felt hard, like a tortoise. You could still see the silhouette of the living armadillo, the skin of its head and even its tiny ears stretched over the belly of the instrument.

Pressing his fingers into the strings, the man played a few chords before beginning to pick out a tune. "Conoces 'El Condor Pasa'?" I shook my head. "This is 'El Condor Pasa'."

I listened. It was a melancholy piece. A piece to be played alone on the top of a mountain. Restless, Miguel paced the shop, hands behind his back.

"Now hear the difference," the man said,

abruptly stopping and hanging the armadillo-shelled instrument back on the wall. "This one is wood."

He played the same song, but it took on a warmer tone, not quite as desolate. "It's the wood," he explained. "It has more resonance than the armadillo."

Another connection clicked in my brain. *"Wood vibrates with music,"* I heard my father saying as he tapped the golden women of the Musikverein.

I knew now what I wanted.

Toward the end of the year, as Bolivia's rainy season Christmas celebrations began, Miguel came to meet me at the cinema one morning holding a lumpy object wrapped in one of his mother's scarves. He refused to let me see it before the film, making me wait until we were strolling along the paseo del Prado afterward, mingling with the crowds in their Sunday finery.

When we had at last found enough space around us to avoid passing elbows, I unwound the scarf to find a gleaming charango. It was the most beautiful thing I had ever seen, carved from a small piece of cedar and fitted with twenty nylon strings.

Forgetting even to thank him, I sank down at the foot of the monument to Simón Bolívar, my dry and cracked fingertips on the strings. I plucked a few bright notes. "It's the child of a harp and a guitar, don't you think?" I looked up at Miguel.

He shrugged. "I do not think. I cannot imagine the guitar making love to the harp."

My face felt hot. I could not remember hearing anyone speak about making love before, not out loud, not so casually, as if it were a natural phenomenon.

"Now a guitar and a mandolin I could imagine," Miguel continued, unaware of my discomfort. "Or even a mandolin and a lute."

"Did you get it from the store we went to?" I wondered where he could have gotten the money to pay for such a beautiful instrument.

"I made it." He smiled and looked away from me, uncustomarily shy.

"You made it?"

"Well, parts of it. I had help from a real instrument maker. I am still learning."

"It must have taken forever! Look how smooth it is!" I ran my fingertips over its face, its beautiful brown face.

He shrugged. "It took awhile." He had been working a couple of days a week after school in the instrument shop, where he had met the craftsman who made many of the charangos. "I traded work hours for the cedar and knowledge. I can tell you just how to adjust the tension of the strings and how to rub Brazil nut oil into the wood."

"It looks bigger than the one we saw in the shop."

"It's a chango." The chango — invented in Bolivia, Miguel said — was one of the larger charangos.

"Miguel." I wanted to embrace him, but I wasn't sure that would be appropriate. I cradled the instrument in my arms instead. "It's a work of art."

As the war raged on, I spent hours alone in my room plucking at the strings of my charango. Given that it was an instrument my father could not teach me how to play — the tuning was different from the tuning of a guitar, and it had double strings — I wondered where to find a teacher. I couldn't afford to pay one. So as I sat in my room, listening to my father play in the living room, I tried to match my notes to his. Slowly, dissonantly, I plucked my way toward a melody. Progress was slow.

FORTY-THREE

"What is your greatest desire?"

It was a strange question, coming from Nayra. She so rarely asked me anything. We were standing near her blanket of vegetables, during a lunchtime lull in January 1941, our second summery January. The relentless afternoon sun was making me sleepy. I thought I should probably be getting home to do schoolwork or to practice before the rain started again.

"My greatest desire?" I didn't need very much time to think. "For my brother Willi to be safe."

Her dark brows pulled together. "I don't know if that will work."

"But that is my greatest desire."

"Is there something else?"

I thought. We already had a new home. I already had a charango. I assumed I couldn't ask for a person since Willi wouldn't work. I could always use new books but I wasn't sure that would count as a Greatest Desire. "The end of the war?"

"Something real. Something you can touch."

"So I can't ask for the Nazis to die?"

Her face was still for a moment. "This might be possible. Come. I want to show you something." She set off down the street, leaving the vegetables behind with her mother, who squatted behind the blanket, watching. I quickly trotted after her. Passersby stared at us when we walked side by side, but most of the time the sidewalk was too narrow for us to walk together. I wondered what I would do if a Bolivian were to demand Nayra descend to the street to make way for him. Would I protest? Would she? I balled my hands into fists at my side, prepared for a fight. I wanted to be tested. But our journey was not long, despite the fact that we had to detour around the plazas Nayra was not supposed to enter. We remained unmolested, and I was not forced to choose between loyalty to my friend and obedience to local custom.

Nayra halted before a table in a thronged and sprawling market. It was heaped with what I presumed to be dollhouse furniture: tiny rocking chairs, tiny beds, tiny lamps, tiny houses. Each one was smaller than a thumb. "It's the first day of the festival of Alasitas. It lasts a month but the first day is the luckiest." Her face was animated, alight. "We make everything miniature. You buy what you want to acquire in the next year. If you want a baby, you buy a fingernail-size doll to take home. If you want to own a home, you buy a little house. Then Ekeko brings you what you want." It worked best, she added, if you bought the items for yourself and got them blessed by a yatiri. "Your faith will make it possible for it to become reality."

"You can't buy something for someone else?"

"Some people do. It helps if you know the person's strongest desire. My aunt once bought her friend Nina a divorce."

"Did it work?"

"Nina has a new husband now."

So much about this market filled me with wonder. I felt I had stumbled into a kind of fairyland. I picked up a tiny radio. Everything about it looked real. "Who is Ekeko?"

"The Aymara god of plenty." Looking around the market, I began to see his diminutive figure everywhere. Grinning on top of the tables and surrounded by offerings of coca leaves and cigarettes, the mustachioed Ekeko was supposedly working to provide his hosts with their hearts' fondest desires. His mouth was always open to accommodate a cigarette and he was laden with packages. Some families had Ekeko statues in their home, Nayra said. After you bought the miniature of your heart's desire, you could place it near Ekeko with coca leaves.

We wandered through the rows of tables, all of them overflowing with mounds of colorful miniatures. Nayra had not exaggerated. There were miniature cars, typewriters, babies, houses, bags of cement, tool kits, chairs, beer cans, suitcases, tables, trains, fruit, diplomas, and certificates.

I was fascinated by the craftsmanship. The little houses had doorbells and gardens. The postage-stamp-size typewriters had letters on every tiny key.

When we came to one of the tables selling certificates, Nayra asked the woman behind the table something I didn't understand. The woman nodded and rummaged around in the stacks of certificates. "Mira," she said to me, offering a tiny piece of paper.

Holding it carefully by its edges, I read, Certificado de Defunción. *Death Certificate.* The name and date of death were blank. "You fill it in and the person will die."

I stared at the paper in my hands.

"You could write Nazis on it." Nayra waited.

Bile rose to the back of my throat. Though I had asked for that kind of power, I found now I did not want it. I could not turn myself into an instrument of death. I dropped the paper back onto the table.

Nayra looked at me. "No?"

"No money." I wiped my hands on my skirt, as if trying to brush off a fatal contagion. "What do you ask for?"

"We ask for good vegetables, a good harvest. We buy tiny beans and sacks of potatoes. We get good vegetables."

"Just vegetables? Every year?" The modesty of her request intrigued me. That she wouldn't wish for money, a way to escape work. A new skirt. Perhaps wanting things was Austrian. She nodded. "Without vegetables, we have nothing."

I nodded slowly. "But besides the vegetables. What about you? What do *you* want?" She didn't hesitate then — there was a difference, clearly, between what she asked for every year and what she wanted. For the first time, she took my hand and pulled me through the market. Her hand was warmer than mine, with soft skin over her knuckles. My hands were always rough and dry, my cuticles peeling away and bleeding. Sometimes a finger would get infected and swell like a sausage for a month, until one of my mother's remedies finally fought it off.

If Nayra hadn't been holding on to me, I might have been lost among the families pushing past me down rows of stalls that all looked alike. We walked by women frying bread in oil and roasting corn on a grill. Women pressing oranges into juice. My dry mouth watered.

At the end of the market, Nayra stopped at a woodworker's stall. In the corner of the table was a tiny wooden loom made of two sticks with strings connecting them, complete with a shuttle the size of a grain of rice. "It's a backstrap loom," Nayra told me. "You can move it more easily than the other kind." She showed me how one stick could be tied to a tree or a pole and the other attached to the weaver's belt. "Like my grandmother's loom. She is teaching me." On the loom was a half-completed tapestry woven from woolen threads of red and black. Alpaca, perhaps, or vicuña. I thought I could make out birds, or tiny human figures. I reached for it, felt the softness of the fibers. "I have no time to weave now," Nayra said. "What I want is some day to have time. To make my own designs."

We stood there for a while, admiring it. "I want to weave the stars," Nayra continued. "There are women who can weave designs that show the Great Road in the sky and the Grandfather Star."

"You can weave the stars?"

"You must first see them from a special place, a pukara, at a special time, then you can learn to weave them. We do this in October, sowing time. The time that the earth and the sky are talking the most."

"Does the sky look different then?"

"It's the best time to see the Goat-kids, and the Eyes of the Llama. Haven't you ever watched the stars move?"

I tried to remember the skies over Vienna. "You mean shooting stars?"

She didn't answer. "When the mountains breathe out the stars. The stars tell us the best time to do things. When it is time to mate the llamas, or to plant seeds. There must also be a full moon." She sighed, weary of my questions. "There is too much for me to explain."

"Bueno." It was becoming clear to me that I knew astonishingly little about the world. "Maybe someday you can tell me more."

"Maybe someday. Today I have to go back to work."

■ ■ ■ ■

I walked home with tiny llamas trotting around my brain. I couldn't believe such a magical festival existed. It was exactly the kind of thing that would exist in Friedenglückhasenland. I loved to imagine the Black Llama in the sky and a Grandfather Star. It all seemed dreamed up, as if Nayra had created a world as enchanting and mysterious as Friedenglückhasenland.

New stories were rising in me.

At home that night, I tried to write down these new stories, but my German was starting to sound stiff and unnatural. We still spoke German at home, and within our community, but I was beginning to prefer the softer sounds of Spanish. Were it not for my need to maintain a sturdy bridge to my parents, who never quite became themselves in their new tongue, I might have given up the corset of German entirely.

It occurred to me that Spanish could give me the freedom to write whatever I wanted. Neither of my parents could read Spanish well. They didn't help me with my homework. And while they understood enough Spanish now to do the shopping and greet acquaintances, they didn't bother learning to write it. To whom would they write in Spanish? All of their letters went to Austria.

I began to scratch out my thoughts in a journal. It was a relief, to put everything there, on the pages. Thinking I should start from the beginning, I began with Anneliese. I began with our imagined world and its sensible laws, its generous inhabitants. For weeks I wrote our stories, every scrap of them I could remember — in Spanish. Anneliese's face came back to me, its sternness when I once accidentally referred to our land of bunnies as imaginary. "There is no point in even talking about it with you if you don't really believe," she said.

So I did.

I wandered the streets of the Alasitas markets in January 1941 every chance I could, after school and on the weekends, alone or with Rachel, Miguel, or Nayra, admiring the tiny things. For Rachel I bought little colored books. Rachel was easy.

My own desire was most difficult. One day I stopped again at a table covered with stacks of miniature documents. The stout woman behind the table sat impassively as I thumbed through the piles of marriage certificates, birth certificates, and diplomas.

"Do you have a certificate for being alive?" I asked her. "For surviving the war?"

She shook her head. As I turned to go, she said, "We have visas! Visas for Argentina, Brazil, visas for the U.S. . . ."

I turned back. "Visas for Bolivia?"

She looked confused. "You have no visa for Bolivia?"

"No — I mean, yes, I do. But for my brother."

She shook her head. "No one here needs a visa for Bolivia."

"He's not here." I realized I sounded absurd. I didn't know how to explain.

She just shook her head.

"No, gracias." What good were visas to anywhere else? Willi would never find us if we moved again. All I wanted was for him to be here.

Miguel came with me one day after school. "Why don't you buy a health certificate for Willi? If he's healthy then he is alive, no?"

I don't know why I hadn't thought of this. I had seen the health certificates without registering their import. Using a few of the coins I earned from occasional child minding after school, I bought Willi a tiny health certificate. Squatting on the ground near the table, I took a pencil from my schoolbag and filled out the certificate with his name. The lines for the yatiri's blessing, the ch'alla, were long, but we waited. We watched as he waved smoke over the certificate, sprinkled it with bright orange flower petals.

With the health certificate tucked into my schoolbooks, I wound my way back through the tables until I found a woman selling tiny looms. Most of the objects were inexpensive, less than a boliviano. I bought one for Nayra, along with several balls of colored wool. Miguel trailed behind me, stopping to examine university certificates and wheelbarrows that came with tiny bags of cement. "Most people want building materials."

"Do you?" This did not seem a very romantic desire, but I supposed it was quite practical. If you had building materials you could make a home.

"We have a house. I would like some land, I think."

I wanted to get him something that might express what he was to me. I didn't want to give him the obvious things everyone bought for each other, the little brown suitcases of money, the parcels of miniature tools. At a woodworker's stall I fingered tiny carvings of llamas, people, the sun, and the moon. The sun was painted yellow and orange, with lightning-jagged rays of wood sticking out in all directions, reminding me of Miguel's tousled hair first thing in the morning when I found him outside. When he was distracted, I paid with a coin and slipped it into my pocket.

I brought the health certificate home to show my parents. "It might work better if we have an Ekeko." When I explained about the god and the offerings, my father agreed to go back to the market with me. "Maybe they have little Stradivariuses." The workmanship of the tiny objects entranced my father, who turned them over in his hands in wonder. He liked the pocket-size newspapers, with their satirical stories, the best.

"Nayra says they ask for good health and vegetables, and they almost always have good health and vegetables." I wanted to believe in something. Anything at all. After we had wandered among the tables for an hour, my father went back to a stall near the entrance and bought an Ekeko who fit into my hand. His grinning mouth was open, awaiting the offering of tobacco, and he wore a belt of tiny bolivianos.

"Danke, Vati!"

"Don't get your hopes up," he said. "It's just a doll." I was indignant. I was too old for dolls.

"The Bolivians say he's a god."

"It seems odd that we should have to pay for a god." But he smiled at me.

On the way back I collected whole coca leaves from the streets where the careless had dropped them — they weren't difficult to find. All of the builders and laborers we passed in the streets carried small bags of the leaves, which they chewed as they worked. I stood Ekeko on my windowsill, slipped Willi's health certificate underneath him, and spread seven coca leaves at his feet. Seven seemed like a magical number.

When I brought the little loom and yarn to Nayra, she flushed and tucked it hurriedly away under her table without thanking me. But I think she was pleased.

I couldn't find the right time to give the little sun to Miguel. I worried it was the wrong thing. He had plenty of sun, after all. Why should I want to give him more? I hadn't thought of that at the market, I had thought only that it resembled Miguel, or what he was to me. Maybe I should wait to give it to him on another holiday, when it could mean something different.

A week later I visited Rachel where she lived with Eloise, though she usually preferred to come to our place. She and Eloise shared a room in a house with several other families. It wasn't that she was ashamed of where she lived; our circumstances were not so different. I think she simply liked to be around a family — and my mother's baking.

In a corner of the room, alongside Rachel's mattress, I spotted a cluster of tiny furniture behind her stacks of books. Some of it I recognized from the Alasitas market. "Oh, there's the little lamp you bought! Can I look at these?"

She nodded. "Don't move anything, okay?"

I knelt on her mattress to better see the miniatures. They had been carefully arranged. Along the wall was a little wooden bed covered by a scrap of blanket and a blueberry-size pillow. Next to it on the floor a hand-carved dog sat on a red-and-orange braided rug. There was a rocking chair, a bookcase, and a little doll. "It's my room in Vienna," she said softly.

"It's so beautiful." I stroked the little dog.

"I don't think I believe in Ekeko but it seemed worth trying. Everything bad that has ever happened to me happened after I left that room."

FORTY-FOUR

One afternoon as I sat on my bed plucking the strings of my charango, my father knocked at my door. My mother never knocked. She didn't acknowledge borders between us. "Sí, Vati?" He stepped into the room, squinting against the light pouring in from the window behind me. In the glare I could see every small line of his face and the increasing gaps between the strands of his white hair. His forehead and cheeks had grown speckled with brown spots, the skin papery and dry. The climate was not kind to our faces.

Although my father was busy with students, I saw him more in La Paz than I had in Vienna. Recently, however, he had begun performing more often with other musicians. They played on a show on the local refugee radio station and talked constantly about starting an orchestra. They played together whenever and wherever they could.

No one had enough space at home, so they often practiced in our school after we went home, or in a room at the Austrian Club. He had been returning to the apartment late, when I was asleep. I tried to stay awake until he came home, to tell him about something that had happened at school, or to read him a new poem. But I could rarely keep my eyes open past 9:00 P.M.

He sat beside me on the bed, his weight tilting the mattress, forcing me to shift to keep from toppling into him. "May I try it?"

"But you don't know how to play. It's not tuned like a viola, or a guitar."

"I know." The charango looked tiny in his arms, a toy. He ran a hand along its gleaming curves before plucking each string in turn, tightening or loosening them until they rang true. "Better," he said. His fingers were long and thin, nimble viola-player's hands. He strummed a thumb across the strings, releasing a shimmering arc of sound. I leaned against the wall as he began to pick out a melody. The instrument sounded entirely different in his hands. Alive.

"How did you learn that?"

"My students are also teachers." He looked up from the instrument. "One student has taught me just a little charango in return for teaching him viola. But it will never be my instrument. I just wanted a sense of it, a sense of his teaching. I asked him if he would give you the lessons instead."

I didn't expect that. "Do you mean it?"

"I wasn't sure if you'd rather keep wrestling with it on your own or —"

"No!" It was clear to me I wouldn't get far on my own. "I didn't ask because I didn't think we could afford it."

"We can if I pay with my teaching." He rested his fingers on the strings. "My fingernails are too short to do this properly. Yours are probably better."

I took the instrument back, cradling it against my rib cage. My fingernails were not much longer, brittle and jagged. My father pressed my fingers on the strings. "C major," he showed me. I strummed a chord with my right hand. He moved my left fingers once again, resettling them on the strings. "D major. And that's about all I know. Someone else will have to teach you its particularities. Someone who knows this instrument from birth." He smiled at me, the familiar lines crinkling at his eyes. I couldn't remember the last time my father had smiled like that.

"Orly, there are sounds here I have never heard before. I have Bolivian students who can't read music but whose fingers are nimbler than mine, who play songs of their own like virtuosos. I don't know how to explain it, but the notes feel more connected to the world, to life. They are not something reserved for concert halls."

This was a long speech for my father, who had no particular affinity for words.

"I'm glad, Vati." I plucked a few strings.

"Your charango, it makes me happy. This sound, these sounds, will connect you to so many things."

Did this mean my father felt connected to this place?

"Maybe we should make Mutti learn something? The quena?"

His smile faded. "I don't think we can make your Mutti do anything."

The following Monday afternoon a man knocked at the door. He wore his long black hair tied back in a ponytail and carried a small black case. "Soy Vico," he explained. "¿Te gustaría aprender a tocar el charango?"

413

FORTY-FIVE

April 1941

One day as Rachel and I sprawled across my mattress, our schoolbooks spread before us, she arched her back in discomfort. "Ouch, what's this?" Reaching behind her, she pulled *The Scorpion* out from under my pillow. I had kept it there for the better part of a year, rereading certain passages in the privacy of night. *Their bodies seized each other as wild beasts seize and shake the bars of their cages.*

Afraid to breathe, I watched her face closely. "You gave that to me." I said it softly, as if trying to coax a kitten out from under a chair. "I always wondered if you had read it."

Patches of pink flamed in her cheeks, answering for her. She bent her head over the book so that curtains of dark hair closed off her face.

"I meant to ask you before. And wondered

what you thought because —"

She looked up at me, a glimmer of something — her hope, or mine reflected? — in her eyes. "Because what?"

I thought about how to put it. "Because I hadn't known other girls felt that way."

Rachel was silent then, but her face did not tighten with disapproval.

"There was a girlfriend of mine in Vienna, but we were so young that I don't know. . . ." I had never told anyone about Anneliese. Not in this way.

I wasn't sure Rachel heard. Her eyes had gone far away. "My aunt was that way."

I looked at her in surprise.

"She's the one who gave me the book. Not this copy, but the first one that I lost when we left. I think to try to explain to me. She lived with someone, a woman named Harriet."

"Like Odiane and Ilse!"

"Who?"

"Friends of my mother's in Austria." There was so much I wanted to ask. "Were your aunt and Harriet happy? How long were they together?"

"Forever. At least since I was born. I don't know where she is now. We haven't heard from her."

Rachel looked at me. We both sat up cross-

415

legged now, arms dangling over knees, our fingertips almost touching, the book between us.

"The women in the book are always so unhappy." They drank too much, they longed for death, they tortured themselves over their love affairs.

Rachel nodded. "But it doesn't have to be that way."

Not long after that afternoon, it was my turn to suggest a play for our refugee theater group to perform. I thought about the plays I knew, the stories I knew. I thought about Elektra and Schnitzler's *Professor Bernhardi* and the farces of Nestroy, but none of them inspired me.

"What about Ovid's *Iphis and Ianthe*?" I asked the group on impulse. I was thinking of Anneliese, of my mother saying we reminded her of those two. It was painful to think of doing it without her, but forgetting would have hurt more.

"Is it written as a play?" My classmate Sarah was one of the best actresses among us. A dozen of us were sitting at a table in the Austrian Club just after a Sunday lunch. I folded and refolded a red cloth napkin.

"We could write it." It wasn't a difficult story, after all.

"Why don't you write it, Orly, and then we'll see?" It was Sarah's suggestion — she who watched me scribble poems in the margins of my schoolwork every day — but not even the older girls found a reason to disagree. I began work at home that evening.

Rachel was the first to read my draft. Not a natural performer, she had been reluctant to join the group. Yet stubbornly, I wanted to involve her in one of my worlds, draw her out of her isolation and into our community. Out of her perpetual sorrow and into the joy of artifice and impersonation. "It's not you onstage," I told her. "It's someone not like you at all."

She wasn't shy at all when it came to criticism. She went through my first draft of *Iphis and Ianthe* with a heavy hand, crossing out lines of speech and scribbling notes in the margin. *Wouldn't Ianthe notice if she suddenly had a beard at their wedding?* she wrote. *Why doesn't Ianthe sound as smart as Iphis when she talks? Doesn't Iphis feel worried that she is in love with a girl?*

These were good questions, and I struggled to answer them, using as many of Ovid's own words as I could remember. By the time I had created something Rachel found acceptable, I had written seven drafts.

Talking about the play gave us a way to speak to each other about what concerned us, though we studiously avoided allowing our arms or fingers to brush against each other.

Our group loved it, immediately launching into arguments over who would play the roles. While I initially proposed Rachel for Ianthe, our collective wisely outvoted me, assigning her the relatively minor yet critical role of the goddess Isis. Sarah secured the role of Ianthe to my Iphis. I believed myself to be an adequate rather than brilliant actor, but the group had elected me, perhaps as a reward for my work on the script.

It was a relief when Sarah pressed her lips to mine and I felt nothing. No twisting inside, no electrical currents. It wasn't that I loved girls, after all. It was that I loved Anneliese. (And perhaps Rachel? These thoughts were still parenthetical, although now that I was thirteen they were more persistent than ever.)

Our initial rehearsals were not inspiring. Rachel struggled to move with confidence and to speak audibly, leading our director Lotte to suggest that she might be better off as a stagehand. I agreed to meet with Rachel before the next rehearsal, to see if I could help.

"Rachelita. You are a goddess." I squeezed both of her hands in mine, as if I could press divinity through her skin. We stood in the emptiness of the Austrian Club dining room, which still retained the odors of frying lamb and garlic. A cook clattered pots in the kitchen behind us. "Goddesses have no human emotions such as humility or shyness. They don't have worries. They are never embarrassed. They never question themselves. Forget that you are Rachel and all that that involves."

She nodded miserably. "I'll try."

"No, don't *try.*" Her relentless melancholy began to irritate me. "Just *be* her."

Rachel's shoulders slumped even further. I had a sudden inspiration. "You are not Rachel the Jewish refugee who is mourning her parents and a lost home. This is your chance to not be that. Just for a little while. If you can do that, well, I'll give you all of my books."

Her spine straightened. Her sharp chin lifted. "All of them?" Rachel spent every penny Eloise gave her at Osmaru, the German library that rented out used books for a small fee, or at La América, the only bookstore that stocked a few German books.

"Every one." I had only a dozen or so, but books were a precious commodity. "Except

419

Fifteen Rabbits. But my father just found me an almost-new copy of *Metamorphoses.*"

It was a matinee performance, as there was a ball scheduled for the evening. While we changed into our costumes in the washroom and painted our lips and cheeks with our mothers' lipsticks, decorators, prop people, and waiters raced about the dining room setting tables in the back and hanging things on the walls. Two of the oldest girls, Ruth and Emmi, hung the sheet that was to be our curtain, separating us from the lines of chairs where our parents would sit. Lotte, our director, paced around the room chewing the ends of her dark braids. So preoccupied was I with going over my lines in my head that I didn't pay much attention to what else was going on in the club.

Rachel sat quietly as lights were darkened and the murmur of voices grew louder on the other side of the curtain. I put a hand on her shoulder. "Hals und Beinbruch." *Break a leg.* Slowly, she turned her head to look at me, and then stood to face me. For the first time, I noticed she was slightly taller than me. "Mortal," she said regally, gently. "You dare to touch me?"

I smiled at her in the dark. Maybe I didn't need to worry.

Metamorphoses was an appropriate prize for Rachel's performance. When she first appeared to Telethusa in a dream, she seemed to have grown several feet. Her arms lifted with authority. Her voice, while thin at moments, was assured. When she promised to protect Iphis — me — from all harm, I believed her.

I got through my own part without any serious mistakes, although in one scene I tripped over my long robe as I ran to the Temple of Isis, falling at the feet of the goddess more dramatically than planned. Even that didn't throw Rachel, who had smiled benevolently and added, "Rise, mortal" before her line.

When it was all over, when we had taken our bows and dropped the sheet that served as our curtain, Rachel turned to me, her cheeks flushed. "You were right," she said, taking my hands. "I never want to be Rachel again."

When we emerged from the washroom in our everyday dresses, Rachel ran to Eloise while I searched the room for my parents. Something felt odd. It took me a few seconds to figure out what the difference was. Everyone was dressed identically. Those trousers. Those skirts. The men were wearing lederhosen. The women were wearing dirndls. I experienced a jolt of dislocation, a memory of my shredded apron. My voice, *I am an Austrian.* The voice of that leering man, *No, you're a Jew.*

As I stood there spinning into the past, my mother appeared before me, her eyes unnaturally bright. Was I dreaming? My mother, in a dirndl? My father beside her, in a Styrian hat?

"We borrowed them," my father said somewhat apologetically. "It's a Dirndl & Lederhosen ball after all."

I stared at them. I had never told them what happened to mine. "Where did they all come from?"

"Some people got out earlier, they were able to take things. Mathilde and Fredi had a few. Some people sewed their own. Not me, mind you!" My father bent to pull up a sagging wool sock. The lederhosen were loose on his skinny legs.

"We have one for you. We thought it might be a nice surprise." My mother reached into the basket she was carrying.

"No, thanks." I was already backing away.

"Are you sure?" My mother held out a folded green dress, a red apron tied around it. "It would be so pretty on you."

"I'm sure. I —"

422

"Oh, I'm sorry we didn't even say! You were a wonderful Iphis, Orly. You always loved that story." My mother looked critically at my faded dress. "Are you sure you don't want to go change?"

I shook my head. "I've got to go find Rachel. I promised her I — I just have to go. I'll see you at home." I turned and fled to the entrance hall. The other girls were busy with their families or still in the dining room packing up pieces of our sets.

By then it had settled into place in my head. The words I couldn't say to my parents. It wasn't only what had happened to me in Vienna; I was no longer sure I wanted to be an Austrian.

I didn't wait for Rachel or anyone else, but started down the road toward our home. I couldn't stay in the Austrian Club a minute longer. Before I reached the first corner, I heard footsteps hurrying behind me. "Orly, wait."

I paused, but didn't turn around. I was afraid to speak.

"Where are you going?" She stopped beside me. "Aren't you staying for the ball?"

I shook my head and resumed my pace.

"Are you angry with me? Was I terrible?"

"Oh, Rachel! Of course not!" I turned to her. "You were absolutely literally divine. I swear it. It's just, the dirndls . . ."

"Oh." She didn't seem to require further explanation.

"Not to do with you at all."

"No."

I glanced at her. "You don't want to stay for the ball either?"

"My family's all city people. *Were* all city people."

We walked the rest of the way home in silence.

At our building, Rachel followed me inside and up the stairs to my room. She hadn't asked if she could come home with me. Maybe she knew she didn't have to. We sat on the edge of my mattress.

When I turned to look at her, dread and desire competing in my pulse, a passage from *The Scorpion* came unbidden to my lips. "It was a longing without name or object. It was a longing for distant lands, a longing for affection." Rachel leaned her head slowly toward mine until our foreheads touched. Her quiet voice joined my own as I continued, "It was a longing for glittering fame, for heroic deeds, and a longing, too, for grandmother's quiet garden, for the meadow over which the bees hummed."

Her breath was soft on my cheek. I listened as it quickened.

"I guess you've read it more than once too."

She smiled, a pale ghost in the dark. "I guess I have."

She leaned closer.

Rachel's theatrical debut at the Austrian Club, it turned out, was also her farewell performance. Her guardian Eloise would soon be moving to the jungles, to an agricultural colony at the other end of the Camino de la Muerte. Eloise had married a man who — like most recent arrivals — had come over on an agricultural visa, so they had no choice. She was excited about moving to the jungle, Rachel said. Eloise had always struggled with the altitude and was looking forward to thicker air.

"But I've heard of lots of people who came on agricultural visas who are still in La Paz," I protested, panic closing in on my ribs. We were sitting in my mother's kitchen, raiding a tin of her crescent-shaped Kipferl pastries, our schoolbooks spread out on the table. "They only took the visas because there was no other way. Viennese people don't know how to farm." No one could get regular visas anymore. It was only because Mr. Hochschild had said the Jewish refugees would work the land that they let in any more of us at all.

"I know. But Wenzel is worried they won't let him stay if he doesn't go. He wants to follow the rules. And Eloise *wants* to go." She took a sip of her coffee.

"What will you be growing?"

I meant to say: *Stay here with me.*

Rachel shrugged miserably. "Pineapple, I think. Coffee. Mandarins."

"You'll be able to eat all the fruit you want!"

I meant to say: *I can't lose anyone else.*

I had become stupid with sorrow.

Fruit didn't impress her anyway. Rachel had never been terribly interested in food. "I don't want to move again."

While I understood this too well, I hoped she had at least one more reason to wish to remain.

A semitropical plantation sounded romantic in theory. There would be monkeys down in the lowlands. A profusion of palms. Lush forests. I didn't mention to Rachel the other things I had heard about Los Yungas from Miguel: the dangers of the road, the clouds of mosquitoes, the suffocating humidity, the venomous snakes threading themselves through the forests. It wouldn't have changed anything. It's possible that she had heard stories of these and other dangers from the foreign engineers and adventurers who had passed through La Paz after working in the area clearing roads or shipping goods down the Coroico or Mapiri rivers, but I didn't ask.

"Does Wenzel know anything about farming?"

"He was a lawyer."

"So how —"

"There's some kind of society that is supposed to give us equipment and seeds."

"And someone to show you how to plant them?"

"I guess. I don't know." She wiped her lips with a cloth napkin, leaving traces of confectioners' sugar.

I pushed the pastry tin toward her. "You better have a few more."

Rachel looked at me pleadingly, as if there were something I could do to stop this.

"What if there are no books? What if I have nothing to read?"

"You can take all your books, can't you?" I was glad I had given her my small collection. "Will you have *time* to read? Will you have to be picking bananas or something? Do you have to work too or just Eloise and Wenzel?"

Her small, sharp face crinkled with anxiety. "I don't know how to grow anything. I

427

never even had a plant!"

I couldn't bear to think of her so unhappy and so far from us. Yet I was powerless to keep her. "You're lucky," I said unconvincingly. "It will be warm. And they say there are avocados."

"But where will I go to school? I don't even know if there are schools there."

"Maybe it won't be forever?"

"I hope not. There won't be any cinemas. Or libraries."

"But there are hardly any libraries here either."

Books didn't seem to be as important to the Bolivians we knew as they were to us.

"Will you write? Will letters get there?" I asked.

She shrugged.

"I'll ask Miguel. He must know people who go down there."

She reached across our schoolbooks to wrap her fingers around my forearms. "Don't let me go, Orly. Don't let them take me."

But I have never been able to save the people I loved.

When I asked my parents if Rachel could stay behind with us, my father set down his viola to look at me.

428

"Eloise is her guardian. We just can't save everyone."

"We never save *anyone*! For once, can't we do something? Can't I be allowed to keep just *one person*?"

"Orly —"

"It's not *fair,* Vati! It's not *fair!*" I had never raised my voice to my parents before. My mother's shoulders stiffened over the sink, but she didn't turn around. Shadows flickered in my father's eyes.

"Which part of our journey together, my daughter, has given you the idea that life is fair?"

Once again, there was little time for good-byes. The Sociedad Colonizadora de Bolivia La Paz, which worked with Mr. Hochschild to resettle refugees in the hope of proving they were not a burden to the country, announced that Rachel, Eloise, and Wenzel would be joining other Jewish families in an agricultural colony called Buena Tierra — Good Land — the following week.

On the day they left, we joined the crowds gathered to see them off. Parents already standing in the back of the truck pulled their small children up over the sides and settled them on large sacks of goods, flour or sugar bound for Los Yungas. About a dozen families crowded into the back of the vehicle. Eloise stood aboard next to Wenzel, shielding her eyes from the sun with a hand, making sure Rachel was following.

Rachel shook off Wenzel's proffered arm and leapt onto the side of the truck bed, dragging a small case after her. I wondered if she had packed any clothes or only books. She turned her face toward the crowd, her eyes finding mine.

"¡Vamonos!" The driver slammed his door and started the engine.

Pushing past the families in front of me, I climbed onto the side of the back tire near where Rachel stood, gripping the cold metal with my fingers.

"Come back. Please say you'll come back."

"Orly." She reached for me with the arm not gripping the side of the truck, cupped the sweating nape of my neck.

"Everywhere life had angles and edges, points and sharp corners." My voice trembled but I continued. "Wherever one groped among the rosy, shimmering clouds that so beautifully enveloped them, one was struck and hurt. One had to be a cobblestone or a diamond not to be shattered by their hardness." I stood on my toes to lean into her, to press my cheek against hers, cold and dry.

"I don't remember that one."

"Remember that one. Remember that one, Rachel, when you fall through those shimmering clouds. Be a cobblestone." As if someone so soft could be made so hard.

The truck started to move, belching a black cloud of exhaust.

I leapt to the ground and raced after it as it pulled away.

"Why not a diamond?" she cried back to me. *Why not a diamond?*

We were never suited for the tropics. Lacking the natural immunities of the Bolivians, European refugees in Los Yungas contracted tropical diseases as unfamiliar to them as plowing a field. The Andes, the jungles of Coroico, the salt flats of Uyuni, they made it plain to us that we were fools to think we had any power over the world around us. We did not dominate nature here in Bolivia; we were bent by its will.

It was nature whose pests infected the Jewish colony in Los Yungas with malaria. Nature whose caiman eyed us warily. Nature who sent its bacterial emissaries into our blood.

In such a landscape, Rachel didn't stand a chance.

431

Her first letter — carried by hand by one of the farmers traveling to La Paz to sell produce and dropped at the offices of the SOPRO — strained for optimism. "I've never seen so much green, so many plants. And you were right about the monkeys! Though they are noisy in the night and stole the first letter I started to you. Everything is noisy in the night." It was a brief letter, probably written after a long day of work. "Also, the mosquitoes are ferocious. And the other bugs that bite. There are so many bugs that bite! If you saw me, you would think I had the measles. I itch all night long. Some people don't get bitten as much, but I guess I am delicious."

I knew she was.

When I opened her second letter, several large, dark grains fell out. "Look, cocoa!" she wrote. "We are planning to grow it here but it already grows in the wild. Did you know that chocolate was wild? One of the women from here, she showed me how to roast the wild beans over the fire and peel the skins off. Then we put them through a grinder until they were paste, which we mixed with sugar and canned milk to make

432

cocoa. It doesn't change my feelings about being here, but I never had better chocolate in Vienna."

I hadn't even imagined that chocolate came from a plant. Where did I think it came from, Weiss's candy shop? I envied Rachel that wild Bolivian chocolate, that sweet taste of home.

In her last letter, in 1943, Rachel wrote that many of her fellow colonists were ill. Strange fevers, rashes, and uncontrollable diarrhea were common. Later, we would learn the names of some of these diseases: leishmaniasis, hepatitis A, malaria, Chagas disease, typhoid, and cholera. Few of them had cures, even when properly diagnosed. There is a doctor in residence at the colony, Rachel wrote, but his Austrian education has not prepared him for the diseases of the tropics. She was afraid to drink the water, afraid to eat the fruit.

It was a combination of fever and self-starvation that killed her in the end, Eloise wrote to us. She had slowly stopped eating, and her weakened state had made her more vulnerable to illness. "We tried very hard to save her," Eloise wrote. "But we did not know how."

FORTY-SIX

The first song I ever wrote for my charango was for Rachel. In my helpless grief I practiced for hours every day, to prevent myself from being washed away. Like Orpheus, I played to survive, though without nearly as much skill. Rachel would want words, not just the simple series of chords I had learned. Music was never enough for her. I picked up my pencil. Vico could help me to arrange the chords, but the words I wrote alone.

I still reflexively started by thinking of two seemingly unconnected things, and then imagining a connection. At the top of a page I wrote *Rachel.* Across from it I wrote *Jungle.* By then I had learned other ways to write poems, but this particular exercise never failed to be useful in the generative stage. Yet today, the magic was failing me. I sat in my room on my bed, staring at the empty page. I decided to try something different. I wrote: Dropped. Broken. Lost. Small. Alive. Book hungry. Isis. Delicious. Scorpion. Cocoa. Bitten. Dreams. Lost. Lost. Lost.

I wondered what Rachel was like before she had climbed up the gangway of the *Orazio.* Perhaps she had once been plump and rosy, with a weakness for marzipan and caramels. Perhaps she clutched her mother as I had clutched mine walking up into the *Proteus.* Perhaps she had made dozens of friends on the ship, organizing games and races on deck. Perhaps she had made a friend like Volkmar, who shared books with her.

I started again. "If there is something after this," I wrote. "I hope you have something to read."

As I copied my final draft into a notebook, the rhythms of the words summoned a melody. I wasn't sure if I had invented this melody or if it was an echo of something I had once heard. There was no way to check. I had studied music theory as a child, but so much of it had faded. I wasn't sure how to move the melody Vico and I had woven onto the page. "Vati!" I called.

My father had possibly been waiting for this moment his entire life. The moment he could share this part of his knowledge, this part of his soul. Sitting down next to me, he drew the five-line staff, using a wooden ruler to keep the lines straight. "Now," he said, looking up at me expectantly. "Sing a few bars of it."

We held Rachel's memorial in the synagogue. Everyone came, even our schoolmates who had never spoken to her. Eloise couldn't get back to La Paz, but she sent a letter that my father read aloud. It spoke about the girl she had loved as a daughter, the girl who had seemed to mend the broken bones of her leg by sheer force of will. Her heart, she continued, was not as easy to mend. "At least now, that broken heart is easy." I was less sure about this. I saw no reason to believe that life beyond the grave would be any more charitable than this one.

My father had spent several weeks arranging Mahler's *Kindertotenlieder* for the twelve musicians he had been able to corral. When I got up in the night to use the bathroom, I often found him at the kitchen table, absently nibbling on my mother's pancakes meant for the café as he marked up a score.

Although Mahler originally scored these songs for voice and orchestra, my father knew better than to try to convince my mother to sing. He rewrote the part of the voice for a viola. He even managed to find a bass clarinet, an oboe, and a bassoon, although he was still short several of the brass instruments. I would hazard a guess that this was not one of the better interpretations of these particular Lieder.

"Jakob, those Lieder are twenty-five minutes long." My mother didn't think the length appropriate for the service.

My father looked up from the score he was annotating. "I couldn't find anything to cut, Julia. I couldn't bring myself to take away the right to grief in full. You can't rush through grief."

My mother could not argue with that.

I never liked those songs. The music was eerie enough, sounding as though it came from somewhere far beyond the grave, but the lyrics were untenable. The father waiting for his family to come through the door, his glance falling not on his wife but on the empty space where his daughter's face should be:

when you bright with joy,
would enter, too,
as you used to, my little daughter

437

FOURTH MOVEMENT:
AFTER THE WAR

FORTY-SEVEN

When Germany surrendered and the end to war in Europe was announced on May 8, 1945, I was confused. La Paz, La Paz! our neighbors shouted in the streets. La Paz! For a moment, I mistook the words as a celebration of our city.

When Mathilde ran up our stairs with the news, my father was out rehearsing and my mother was at the Riesenrad. I leapt up from my books to hug her. "Maybe he'll come now," she said. "Now it will be easier. I'll go find your mother. Meet us in half an hour at the club?"

When the bells began to ring, I ran outside. I was surprised there were not bigger crowds on the streets. There didn't seem to be any marching bands playing victory songs or unfettered dances of joy and relief. The faces of the women in the market were stoic, immovable as they counted out change and handed over earth-dusted pep-

441

pers. As if it were any ordinary day. I wished for Rachel. I wished for Anneliese. Someone who would understand.

I ran over to Miguel's house and he and his three sisters all ran out to hug me. They at least knew what this meant for us. "I thought everyone in the city would be celebrating," I said to Miguel as we stood in his doorway looking into the street. "Isn't the end of the war kind of major news?"

"It's far away for us."

"Still."

"And I think people are afraid."

"Afraid? Of peace?"

"Of Villarroel. He represses everything that moves."

"Represses?"

"Like, accidentally pushes off a cliff."

"Oh."

Villarroel was the latest military leader to take over the country. Some people said he'd been rooting for the Nazis.

"So I think people don't want to do anything to draw attention to themselves."

Celebrating the end of violence didn't seem particularly controversial to me, but there was much I still did not understand.

When I finally got to the Austrian Club, the atmosphere was considerably more festive.

442

Ecstatic arms waved Austrian and Bolivian flags. There was music. There was dancing. So many colors and sounds flooded through me as I stood in the throngs of sweating, happy Europeans, holding the hands of my dazed-looking parents — though at seventeen I was too old now to need this comfort — that I was dizzy. Peace! our friends and neighbors cried. Church bells were still ringing. I could smell meat roasting in the club kitchen, feel the music throb against my ears. On every side of me were perspiring bodies, whirling skirts.

Shoved and jostled by revelers, I felt no ease of tension in my body. My mind had registered the news as good, as wonderful, as the end of the slaughter in Vienna, in all of Europe, yet how could we celebrate when we didn't know if Willi remained? My grandparents? My aunts and uncles and cousins? My Anneliese? Yes, the Germans were defeated. Yes, Hitler was dead. But then, so were we.

My father was smiling. He dropped my hand to shake hands with everyone we passed. My father was happy. My mother's lips curved slightly upward at the corners, but only slightly. I squeezed her fingers even tighter. "Will we hear from Willi now?"

She didn't answer, but her fingers returned my pressure.

Of course I was glad the war was over. Of course the news had lightened my heart. But should we not all be sitting shiva for the millions of us who were gone? I glared at a man who stumbled against me, reeking of singani. At the same time, I wanted to drink something that would numb me, that would remove me from all of this sorrow, all of this joy and noise. I had tasted that liquor and knew its obliterating fire.

"Mutti," I said, suddenly a child again. "Mutti, take me home."

Leaving my father behind, we found our way to the door, we put our feet one in front of the other until we were at the house where we lived. I walked straight up the stairs, down the hallway, and into Willi's green room. Pulling back the covers from his bed — those pristine covers that had never been lifted — I crawled beneath them and pulled my knees to my chest. I heard my mother inhale, heard the start of a word, and then nothing. Nothing until she bent to remove her shoes, and climbed in beside me.

The surge of details from Europe threatened to drown us. We knew of the camps, of course — we knew before anyone, or before anyone would acknowledge them. But the details. The individuals. The photos of the liberated skeletons. The names. The relentlessness of the names.

By August 15, 1945, our relief at the end of violence in Europe was paralyzed by the news of the bombs. TERMINÓ LA GUERRA EN EL MUNDO, EL JAPÓN SE RINDIÓ INCONDICIONALMENTE blazed the day's headline.

Now all of the wars were over. But something else had begun, something new and terrifying. "Julia," my father said as we listened to a frenzy of North American celebration on our radio while my mother roasted a chicken. "Julia." He shook the newspaper in her direction. "They say that to be under that bomb was like being shot into the heart of the sun."

My mother turned off the oven and came to stand behind my father, resting her hands on his shoulders. He twisted to look up at her.

"Julia, every time a new weapon is invented it ends up being used on us. Someday it will be used on us." He didn't sound at all like my father. It was my mother's job to worry.

When the worst photos finally emerged in

the newspapers we passed around, they made us mute. The cloud they called a mushroom, the skulls left behind. The living body of a child, eyes brimming with terror, gazing up from the ruined ground. Just one of the many thousands. They said there had been no other way to end it. I was not convinced. We needed to murder children to stop the murder of children? None of it made any sense. None of it ever will.

The news insisted on arriving. My grandparents, both pairs, had vanished. With them, my grandmother's political salons, the haze of cigarette smoke in her parlor, the books scattered around her rooms. The gaze commanding obedience. That intimidating shelf of curls. With my grandfather went his research on the formation of eyeballs. The eye charts he held before us as we sat in his wide, soft chair. My cousins were gone. Klara would no longer conjure fugues on the piano keys, Felix would never tell me another riddle. With my Graz grandparents, whose faces I struggled to recall, went the bakery, their recipes for Palatschinken and strudel, the smell of cinnamon in the morning. I had hardly known my Graz aunts, slighter versions of their mother. My little Graz cousins.

My aunts and uncles, all gone but one. Thekla wrote to us from her hospital bed in Poland about the rest of our family, her letters scattered and nearly unrecognizable. "Thekla's alive," my mother had cried with joy when she recognized her sister's handwriting on the envelope. Before she had read its devastating contents.

Then came that final name.

We had gone to the post office as we did daily — always the three of us now, together — hoping to hear the date of Thekla's arrival. Having no one left to go to, she was coming to us.

Yet there was nothing from Thekla. Instead, there was a slim envelope bearing a French postmark and addressed in an unfamiliar hand. We knew Violaine had been searching for Willi in France for months, questioning the police, importuning the Red Cross, visiting other charitable organizations that may have heard something. But the letter was not from Violaine.

Without speaking, we carried the letter outside with us, sank down onto the steps of the post office. Between me and my father, my mother smoothed it on her lap, stared at it for a moment, then picked it up and tore it open.

"It's in French," she said, still staring at it. "I don't know if I —" Her shaking hand rattled the paper. My parents had both learned French in school, but it had been a long time since they had spoken — or sung — a word of it. My father and I peered over her shoulders.

Nous regrettons de vous informer de la mort de Willi Zingel. . . .

It was not difficult French. My parents understood. Even I understood. Yet the three of us sat staring at it as if we could resist the knowledge it contained. It was from the police, who we knew had been wrong before. Who had never been on our side.

"How do they know?" I said finally. "How do they know that it is him?" It could not have been him. It could not. My father made a strangled, guttural sound. He believed it.

My mother's calm was almost more terrifying than tears would have been. "They say it took them more than a year to figure out whom to notify. His death was recorded alongside the deaths of the children — the children of Izieu." Her voice shook.

The children of Izieu. I had heard the story. By then we had all heard the story, from our friends, from our neighbors, from

448

letters and telegrams. Not, by and large, from the radio or newspapers. There were forty-four children, accompanied by seven adults. We knew these statistics by heart. Together they had lived in a beautiful house in a small village in a remote part of France, where their parents had hidden them. Some had been orphaned when their parents were deported. Some had parents with no other means of keeping them safe. They were all between the ages of four and seventeen when the Lyon Gestapo sent them to Auschwitz to die.

"Willi was in Izieu?" I couldn't put the pieces together.

"They think he may have been working with OSE." Oeuvre de Secours aux Enfants, we knew, worked to help deprived Jewish children. During the war the OSE worked across Europe, saving more than five thousand refugee children from certain death. I remembered Willi had mentioned children in his letter.

In a swift motion my mother tore the pages in two and crushed them in her fists, dropped the pieces to the step and stomped on them with both feet. "Verdammt, die Franzosen in die Hölle! Verdammt, verdammt! Mein Sohn . . ." *Damn, the French can go to hell! Damn it, damn it! My son . . .*

My father and I stood, tempests of grief raging in our chests. We closed ourselves around her, arms overlapping, cheeks against her neck.

"Let's go home," my father finally said.

"There is no home," my mother cried. "There will never be a home again."

They began their halting progress down the stairs, entwined so it was hard to see which one of them supported the other. I bent to retrieve the scraps of paper, dusted them off, and folded them into my damp palm. I needed to know everything.

But this, it became clear, was impossible. The OSE had no answers for us when we wrote. They didn't have any record of a Willi Zingel. They didn't know where or how his death had been recorded. The police did not reply at all. We had no way to know why Willi never got on a ship to South America. Why he was in France. What he was doing in Izieu.

It took so long to find out where Willi had been, what he had been doing. Longer than we ever could have imagined.

FORTY-EIGHT

"Will we go back?" It was the end of October 1945. My mother and I stood pinching the edges of dumplings in the kitchen. She was fighting her way through pain with a rolling pin, flour, and butter. I tried to keep mine at a bearable distance with pencil and charango, escaping more and more into words and music.

A choking heat seized my throat as I asked. I could not imagine waking up without these mountains around me. I could not imagine surviving a flat landscape, pressed in that nowhere land between sky and earth.

The end of the war had triggered a flurry of planning. Now we were allegedly free; we could move to Argentina, Brazil, or Chile — cleaner places with oxygen and more reliable electricity — or move onward to the newly accommodating United States or to Palestine. We could return to what was left of Austria.

This sudden change in our status, these new openings in our horizons, had been causing me great anxiety. It seemed ungrateful, somehow, to abandon the country that had saved us. To seek an easier life. Was it really any easier to start over, again? I couldn't bear the thought of replanting myself in yet another landscape. Acclimating myself to different air, a new language.

And while I longed to go back for Anneliese I could not imagine returning to a Vienna without my brother, without my grandparents. I dreamed of sledding down Jesuitenwiese after the winter's first snow. Skating along the Alte Donau. Opera. Music. If we returned to Austria now I could start university there. And yet. Those things were very far away for me now. They were like dreams. Only now, I dreamed in Spanish.

I don't know what the others were dreaming. Many in our community were already planning their departures. Among them were those who had never adjusted to the altitude. Those who never learned the language. Those whose expectations of the world remained European. Those who could afford to leave — the entrepreneurs who had built import-export businesses or made money in textiles.

The Andes had not captured them; Bolivia had only been a place to weather the storms of war. And life here wasn't easy or free of conflict. Peace may have fallen on the rest of the world, but Bolivia had its own unresolved domestic tumult. In the summer of 1946, the country rose up against General Gualberto Villarroel. After a seething crowd tossed him from the balcony of the Presidential Palace, he and two other men were hanged in the plaza by their necks, their bodies left suspended there. I did not go to look. I already knew the message they sent. Peace or not, there was no safe place in the world.

We didn't actually have a choice. While my father's teaching income, along with the small amount my mother earned selling her food, was enough for us to live on, it wasn't anything close to the amount we would need to journey back to Austria. To restart our interrupted lives. It seemed impossible that there were any jobs in Bolivia my parents could do that would pay enough to buy passage back.

My mother's fingernails left deep grooves in the edges of dough she was shaping. She had stopped talking about Vienna, about what she had lost. During the war she had occasionally dreamed aloud of returning to Vienna. But now she spoke only in the present tense.

"To what?" she said. "Go back to what?"

I watched her for a while. Her face was closed to me. Why was her face so closed? "Mutti?" I finally ventured. "If you don't want to go back, could you try to be here?"

She didn't look up.

That night when my father came home, my mother and I were listening to the news of Rudolf Hess's forthcoming trial crackling through the radio. A reporter described his earlier suicide attempts as well as his recent efforts to convince the courts that he suffered from amnesia. I thought I could hear the skepticism in the reporter's voice.

"I don't know why they don't let him kill himself." My mother opened the oven to slide in a tray of rolls. "Is he such a great loss?"

My father set down his viola in the hallway and hung his hat on a hook by the door. With his coat still on, he walked over to the radio on the table and spun the dial. It took him a few minutes to find something that came in clearly, but he settled on Brazilian guitar music. "Ah, *Panqueca,*" he said.

I looked at him, curious.

"Heitor Villa-Lobos. 1900."

"Since when are you such an expert on Brazilian musicians?" My mother set her oven mitts down on the table and reached for the radio.

"Ah, see, even you knew he was Brazilian! Julia, no —" He put a hand on her wrist.

"We were listening to the news."

"We've had enough news."

"It's important! Hess is —"

"This enriches our lives how?"

"You think we shouldn't pay attention to what's going on?"

"Julia, I am tired of paying attention."

She reached for the knob again.

"Julia!" I startled in my chair, unaccustomed to my father raising his voice. *"Basta!"*

My father never spoke to my mother in Spanish but it was clear she understood the word.

Enough.

FORTY-NINE

My aunt Thekla, the only member of our family we knew to be alive, was among the first wave of survivors to come to Bolivia, arriving just a couple months after the war ended. It was October 31, 1945, and the Bolivians were getting ready to celebrate día de Todos Santos, cleaning and repairing their family tombs. Before the Spanish came, the Bolivians often removed the moldering corpses from their graves to dance with them before tucking them back into the ground. When something at all unusual happened during this time — a flash of lightning or even an ant crawling over a favorite food — it was taken as a sign that the dead person had arrived for her twelve-hour visit. When I caught sight of my aunt getting off the train, my first thought was that she was among the visiting dead. Her once-lively face was gaunt, her eyes flat and vacant as they scanned the crowds at the station.

I wondered whether she would recognize me. It had been seven years. I had grown tall, bony, and graceless. While my breasts had filled out, my hips remained narrow like a boy's. Almost half of my life was Bolivian, the half I remembered best. Spanish words came to me before German, despite the language of my schooling and my home. I was anxious to see my aunt. We had lived without any relatives for so long. It seemed a miracle there was one left alive. I was curious but also scared. I wanted to know what had happened in Europe, what had happened to her, but at the same time I didn't want to know. I wanted to fill my ears with Andean sounds to drown out unbearable news.

We were waiting on the platform where we had disembarked nearly seven years earlier. Strange to think we had missed seven years of Austria. Looking at Thekla's face, at the faces of the other survivors who arrived with her, I began to understand what we had escaped.

When she saw us, she didn't smile. She lifted one frail hand to her hat, as if to tip it to us, then let it fall by her side. Limp and weary with travel, she wore a navy-blue skirt and jacket and a dirty white hat. As she

457

stepped down from the train, she didn't look around. She didn't look up at the new sky, at our Illimani, at the red earth. As if it took the full force of her concentration, she set one foot on the ground in front of the other, walking on an invisible tightrope toward us.

"Thekla," my mother said, pulling her sister into her arms. She held her like that for several minutes. It frightened me to see how my aunt's formerly lively body sagged against my mother. Silently, my father embraced her next. At last, Thekla held out a thin hand to me. "Orlanthe."

I couldn't remember the last time someone had spoken my whole German name. "Auntie." I kissed her awkwardly and then hung back, suddenly shy. I had never seen my aunt Thekla without my cousins, Klara and Felix. Without her husband, my uncle Tobias. She had always been a whirl of activity, fixing Klara's hair, fretting over the state of Felix's trousers. I hadn't truly realized that my cousins were gone, actually gone, until that moment.

My mother took her hand and pulled her close again, twined their arms together. "Thekla."

I followed my mother and her sister like a dog all the way home. Not once did my aunt turn to look at me. I tried to remember what we used to talk about.

Once we reached our apartment, my aunt went into her room and shut the door. She didn't come out for dinner, despite my father's tentative knock on her door. Nor did she emerge before I left for work the next morning. Now that I had finished school I was clerking at a small bookstore near the Plaza Murillo called Arbres Morts.

Thekla stirred her food around but ate only the things she didn't need to chew. Soup. Tea. Soft fruits. My mother sneaked spoonful after spoonful of sugar into her tea, something to keep her upright. She arrived with just a few tufts of soft hair left on her skull under her hat and skin hanging loose from her thin arms, flapping when she moved them. "Don't have survived for nothing," my mother said. "You didn't come this far to starve."

My aunt stared at her. "For what did I come this far?"

FIFTY

My mother had prepared Willi's room for my aunt but Thekla insisted that I take it. "What do I need with so much space? Orly would surely find better use for it. If she wouldn't mind, I would much prefer her room."

I sat now in Willi's room, on the sheets my mother had spent years washing once a week in preparation for his arrival. I ran my palm across the cold pillow that never cradled my brother's head. An alpaca blanket lay folded at the foot of the bed. My books were stacked on top of the dresser. My mother's cookie tins filled a corner next to a music stand because we had run out of space everywhere else. I had always come here, to this room that contained no trace of Willi, when I most missed him. It had become my shul. This bed that should have been his was where I practiced the charango, where I wrote my letters, and where

460

I sat staring out at the blank windows of the neighboring building and imagining my brother in the Alps.

On my lap, I held a stack of letters to Anneliese. "I don't know whether to send them," I said aloud to my ghost brother. "I don't know if she could still be my Anneliese." The survivors' stories pouring from Europe were rife with tales of both self-sacrifice and betrayal, in near-equal measures. Just when we thought we could not bear to hear of one more death, one more shred of inhumanity, another would come. Our capacity to absorb trauma stretched like an overfilled balloon. Some days I thought it would all explode through my skin and shower a chemical rain on everyone around me.

I spread the seven years of letters out before me on the bed. There were stories of our adjustment, my illnesses, my school. There were stories of the city beneath the lake and the Andean animals. There was the story of Rachel. Would Anneliese remember who I was? Even as I asked that, I could hear my brother scoff. *Anneliese? Forget you? It sounds like it is you who have forgotten Anneliese.* It shamed me that my absent and now imaginary brother had more faith than I did. Shouldn't I trust her, our connection, our history? Yet my capacity for trust was irrevocably shattered.

In autumn of 1945 the war was over, but nothing else was. Not the loss that would resonate through generations, not the inhumanity of those who had fled justice, and not our displacement. Our family had a black hole in it, a bottomless magnetic absence that sometimes threatened to absorb us all. What remained was my longing for my brother, for my joking, teasing, singing brother. If only I had known how much I would miss being called Peanut.

I had stopped seeking connections between this home and that old world, the one now hollowed out of our people. I had begun to seek out difference, to welcome anything that separated us from the people who had destroyed so much.

I wouldn't send the letters yet, I thought, and risk them disappearing into the void. I would send instead a brief note to make sure that she had stayed, that she was where we had left her. I first had to know there was a safe house for these scrapings of my psyche. My heart stuttered when I thought of it, my new freedom to write to her. There was no way to sum up anything, so my note was as brief as possible. "My Dearest Anneliese — are you still my Anneliese? Tell me you haven't left for Friedenglückhasenland without me. Love, your Orly." My father gave me a stamp and his blessing and we walked to the post office together. At the last moment, when my father turned away to speak to the clerk, I quickly kissed the envelope before letting it fall through the slot, where it slipped into the stacks of paper-thin hope.

My aunt Thekla had arrived with one outfit, one pair of shoes, and a copy of the Torah. Unrecognizable as the aunt who had once taught me how to polka and told me gay bedtime stories about the scandalous Alma Mahler, she unnerved me. She never smiled, never asked questions. She sat at the table and stared at us. She was like a child, needing to be led from room to room and told what to do. Any sort of volition had vanished. Or rather, had been erased.

Aunt Thekla had lost her two children, her husband, and her parents. She had survived only because she had been given a job to do in Auschwitz, my mother said. I was afraid of learning more.

At night I sometimes heard her crying in her room. It wasn't energetic, crisis-related crying, a cathartic crying. It was the low moan of a hopelessness without limits.

When I heard that sound I wound my scarf around my head to muffle the noise. That noise peeled the membranes from my nerves, left me vibrating with borrowed pain. Atmospheric pain, weaving the web in which we all were caught.

Sometimes I heard my mother creep down the hall to Thekla's room, and found them curled together in the sheets in the morning. Sometimes I heard their voices in the night, my mother's steady and calm, Thekla's wild. As I lay there, listening, I couldn't help wondering why my mother had never comforted me like that.

One afternoon I was in my room, tugging the sweater over the head of the doll I had received my first day in Bolivia. Though I had never played with her, she had always lived in a corner of my room, her blue eyes staring vacantly at the walls. I don't know why I kept her. I could have given her to one of the children I had looked after, I could have thrown her out. But she had been a gift, and for that reason she stayed.

When I moved into Willi's room I set her on top of my mother's tins. The colors of the sweater Nayra made her looked faded in the morning sun streaming in through the window.

I dropped the small sweater on the bed.

"It's almost summer," I told her. "You'll be too hot." Underneath she still wore the dusty Austrian dress in which she had arrived. A pink apron, a blue bodice. If I washed the clothes, I could give the doll to one of the younger children.

As I tore the dress from her body, I heard the shuffling footsteps of my aunt approach my door and stop abruptly. One bony hand clutching my doorframe, she swayed as she stared at the doll in my hands. A look of horror had frozen on her face. I dropped the doll on the bed and went to her. "Aunt Thekla? Are you all right?" But she didn't say a word. Staring at the doll, she stepped backward, one tiny step at a time. "It's just a doll," I said. "I'm going to give her to one of the new children." My aunt didn't look like she had heard. She turned before I could say anything else, and fled down the hallway to her room.

I picked up the doll and found my mother standing at the kitchen counter, writing out a recipe. "Mutti, something odd just happened."

As I described my aunt's behavior, the vertical line between her eyes deepened. "Oh, what's the use of trying to protect you?" she said finally. "You'll know anyway. You'll know more than you ever wanted to

465

know about our inhuman species."

She sat down on a kitchen chair and looked up at me. Her face was thinner, her eyes darker. Her hair had gone flat and lusterless, though I'm not sure she cared. I was too nervous to move. "You know your aunt was in one of those camps."

I nodded. Of course I did. Everybody knew. It was obvious.

"Susse. Mein Schatz. At that camp. . . ." My mother swallowed. She looked down at her lap and would not find my eyes. She cleared her throat and began again. "At that camp it was her job to undress the babies and the smallest children before the showers."

I stared at her uncomprehendingly. "For the showers? What do you mean? What showers?"

Her jaw tightened. "The showers that were not showers. The showers that were death."

My body didn't feel like it belonged to me. It had gone rigid where I stood in the middle of the room. My mind had floated out of it. Away from this conversation. But my mouth continued to form words. "How did they die? Did they all die?"

My mother reached out and pulled me into her, so I collapsed into her lap, though

I was far too large for it. "They died different ways. In the showers they sent in a gas that killed them."

"Did it hurt?" I set the doll on the table before us and we looked down at her unblinking eyes.

"I don't know. No, I feel sure that it didn't hurt."

"But they must have been so afraid."

"Yes." My mother turned her head to the window.

"Aunt Thekla helped them? To send the babies there?"

"She didn't have a choice. If she hadn't done what they told her to do, they would have killed her."

Grabbing the doll, I stood and moved away from my mother. "She sent children in to die?"

"The children were going to die whether or not she undressed them."

"What if everyone refused to do it? Everyone?"

"Would you be that brave?"

I was silent.

My mother sighed. "You and I can never understand what happened there, my dove. What Thekla has endured is worse than we can imagine. We cannot know what we would do facing what she faced."

I tightened my arms around the doll, rocking on the soles of my feet. I wondered if Thekla had thought about choosing death. She must have.

My mother didn't say any more. I walked back to my room, put all the clothing back on my doll, and tucked her under the covers of my bed.

FIFTY-ONE

Violinist Viktor Robitsek's expulsion from the Vienna Philharmonic after the Anschluss had begun the exodus. Thirteen Jewish musicians lost their jobs. Five of those men were murdered: Violinist Moriz Glattauer died in Theresienstadt, and his wife, Anna, was gassed in Auschwitz; Robitsek and his wife, Elsa, died in Lodz; violinist/violist Max Starkmann and his wife, Elsa, were killed near Minsk/Maly Trostinec; concertmaster and violinist Julius Stwertka and his wife, Rosa, were deported to the Jewish ghetto in Theresienstadt. Rosa died in Auschwitz but the date of her death and the fate of her body are unknown. Oboist Armin Tyroler and his wife, Rudolfine, were deported to Auschwitz.

Two more, Paul Fischer and Anton

Weiss, died as a result of evictions and resulting illnesses. Even today we don't know their whole stories.

Only their deaths are recorded, little of their lives, their personhood, their disappointments and hopes, the people who depended on them, whose hearts they held, whose hearts they broke.

Nine of the expelled musicians were lucky enough to escape. Only two ever returned to Austria, and none to the Vienna Philharmonic.

There was nothing gold in the Teatro Municipal. Nothing gilded, nothing of lofty Viennese elegance. Except for my father, who looked uncommonly elegant in a black suit a Bolivian tailor had sewn for him. My mother had trimmed his greying hair, so it no longer drifted wildly around his head, dry and staticky. He was smiling as he took his seat and picked up his viola, tucked it against him. The drone of tuning instruments swelled to fill the small room.

The theater had only a few hundred seats and acoustics that would challenge a world-class orchestra. As my mother and I took seats in one of the middle rows, I wondered if she was also thinking of the last time we had seen my father perform. The height of that ceiling, the vibration of the wood. It must have been just before the Anschluss, when the men who sat beside my father, who lifted their bows with his, who tuned their strings to his, who had played Mahler without protest, were longing for his death. For the first time, I wondered what it had been like for my father to show up at work every day knowing that so many of the men around him were Nazis. Every time he walked through the door he took a seat among men whose vision of the future included his destruction. But my father believed in music; I wonder if he had been waiting for Mahler to convince them.

Every few minutes we stood up to say hello to a friend or to allow someone into our row. There were very few strangers. But Thekla had stayed at home. I waved to Miguel, who arrived with his mother and his sisters Celia, Ema, and Nina. I had hardly seen him lately, busy with work, looking after my aunt, and meeting Nayra in the market. But the sight of his face was like a glimpse of home. I had invited Nayra, but she had said she wouldn't be in La Paz. Perhaps she worried she wouldn't feel welcome in the crowd of white faces. Or

471

perhaps she had to work. Maybe both.

This ramshackle orchestra had drawn itself together as news of my father's former colleagues finally reached us. The handful of musicians who had escaped to Canada and the United States wrote to my father about the others. The Vienna Philharmonic had always prided itself on its strict standards. One must not be late for rehearsal. One must play in the tuning pitch of $A=443$ Hz. One must use vibrato only sparingly. One must not be female. One must not have dark skin.

It was never against the rules, however, to join the Nazi Party. It was never against the rules to send the musicians who had played beside you for decades to their deaths. Even now, even after the war, Nazis remained in the Vienna Philharmonic, which seemed to suffer very few pangs of conscience. The end of war had apparently not meant the end of the hatred that had caused it.

I took my mother's hand, thin and cold, and looked up at the ceiling. There was no chandelier. I wondered if the building could even support the weight of a chandelier; the weathered ceiling looked too derelict to withstand the vibration of the music. The walls were too hard. Music could not sound right here. It would rebound upon itself, find our ears too soon or too late. Anxiety hummed in my sternum.

Conductor Erich Eisner lifted his baton. The circle of musicians who once gathered in our rooms had grown, eventually including Eisner, a Czech pianist who had escaped from Dachau before the war. He had apprenticed under Bruno Walter, which immediately gave him and my father common ground. It was Eisner who had led this group of men, nearly all Jews from Austria, Czechoslovakia, Poland, and Germany, to form this orchestra. These men had all once been paid a salary for their work, which they now gave away for free.

Their gazes met at Eisner's baton before dropping to their individual music stands. They began.

Afterward, my father seemed unable to get up from his chair. As the other musicians rose to file out, he struggled to get to his feet, pale and sweating. As Gregor passed close to him, he paused, gently lifting my father with an arm around his ribs. Without glancing out at us, they continued slowly through the door in the side of the room.

"Is Vati all right?" My father had never been ill, never suffered from the altitude.

My stomach burned with fear. I reached for my mother, who was standing already, her right hand pinching the skin at her sternum.

"Let's go see him, shall we?"

But when we got to the door, the woman guarding the back rooms where the men had prepared for their performance told us we would need to wait in the foyer. Mathilde waved from across the room and we joined her and Fredi outside. "It's good to see Jakob in action," she said to my mother.

"He is always in action," I replied distractedly. "He never stops." My father's absorption in his music was so consistent there were moments I wondered if our change in circumstances had even touched him.

"Well," she said, with a short laugh. "I just meant onstage."

"Of course." My mother patted Mathilde as if she could brush off my rudeness. "How are you, Tildy?" Her Spanish not fluent enough to allow her to continue her career as a journalist, Mathilde had opened a dress shop, making clothing to order from American patterns she imported. Fredi had risen to the position of supervisor in one of the textile factories. They had been trying to have a child since they moved to La Paz, but Mathilde had suffered seven miscarriages, the last one at six months. "I can't try anymore," I had heard her tell my mother over tea when they didn't think I was listening. "I cannot take one more loss."

"We're doing well, Julia. We're still here, aren't we?" She smiled. "And we got to hear Jakob."

Other refugees came to congratulate us. None of us pretended it was the best concert we had ever attended. None of us declared the performance the definitive interpretation of Mendelssohn's Scottish Symphony or Beethoven's Third. Instead we talked about it as a "significant start" or a "wonderful effort." I looked for Miguel in the crowd, wanting to hear what he thought. But he and his family had vanished.

"Orly!" Sarah pounced on me, both hands around my arm. "Your Vati is wonderful."

"Isn't he?" I allowed her to embrace me, but I was having trouble focusing. Where was my father? Seven years earlier, he would have sprung from the back rooms to be with us by now, high on adrenaline, steering us all toward a café. "Nothing replenishes the soul after a performance like Palatschinken," he would say, taking my hand. He liked the thin pancakes rolled with apricot jam, especially as a reward for performing.

"Are you missing your golden ladies?" His

voice arrived, warm and low in my ear.

"Vati!" I threw my arms around him. His shirt was damp with sweat, nearly transparent. "Vati, you'll get cold."

His face was still pale, but his hands trembled only slightly. "Is that all you have to say to your father, who has provided such a marvelous sound track to your afternoon?"

"Oh, Vati, you know you were brilliant."

"I must confess, performing up here in the sky is harder than I had imagined." He pulled a handkerchief from his pocket and dabbed at his neck.

My mother abandoned Mathilde to take his arm. "You're all right?"

"It has been a little while since I had such a workout in front of an audience. Every time I think I might have adjusted to the altitude, something reminds me of the lowlands from which I come."

"I'm not sure the Alps can be considered lowlands."

"Ah, my charming wife, but it is your side of the family who come from the Styrian mountains. My relatives have always been city folk." He paused, perhaps reflecting that he no longer had relatives from anywhere, as far as he was aware. "Well. What do you think, Julia, are pancakes even a possibility?"

476

FIFTY-TWO

The room was small with a curved ceiling, cavelike, all the illumination provided by candles on the wooden tables. My father touched my elbow. "See, Orlita, birthday candles! They knew you were coming."

I hadn't had birthday candles since we moved to La Paz. When I was small, my mother would light the candles on a wooden wreath that sat on our kitchen table before I was awake. The tiny flames would burn all day. But since we moved to Bolivia, birthdays had been only minimally acknowledged, with a viola serenade and a kiss on the cheek. Festivity hadn't felt appropriate during the war, although we continued to celebrate Passover and Chanukah every year with Mathilde and Fredi and the Grubers.

Today, I was eighteen.

I hadn't expected much from the day other than one of my mother's Sacher tortes, which I had requested. But after dinner, my father had told me to change into my best dress and put on my shoes. "You too, Julia." My mother and I, exchanging arched eyebrows, obeyed. Aunt Thekla did not emerge from her room.

The three of us walked up to the café on calle Jaén, my father swinging his viola case and carrying a lumpy bundle wrapped in a pillowcase. I was mystified.

Now the three of us sat in the dancing light, waiting. Several of the other tables were occupied, mostly by Bolivians. My father ordered three singanis.

"Wait — make that four." He had just spotted Vico weaving through the tables toward us, carrying his charango case.

I stood to kiss his cheek. "What are you doing here?"

"A better question would be, what will you be doing here?"

I glanced at my father, puzzled, but he only smiled and lifted his palms.

Vico walked over to the low stage, where he stood chatting with one of the waiters. After a few minutes, he was joined by another man, carrying a guitar case.

I sipped my singani, sweet and smooth. I looked around at the walls, painted with murals of mountains and brightly colored houses. My mother shifted uncomfortably in her chair. She was usually asleep by now. It had been months since my father and I had listened to live music together; my mother had never before come to a Bolivian café to hear music with us.

Vico eased his charango from its case and cradled it in his arms as his friend tuned his guitar strings. Vico looked over at us. "Ready, Jakob?"

My father stood and picked up his viola case. My father played with Vico? I hadn't even known there was music for both viola and charango. And guitar, apparently.

The men continued to tune their instruments as several more people found seats. Mathilde and Fredi came over to kiss us, then the Grubers and my deskmate Sarah.

"¡Feliz cumpleaños!" The voice came from behind my left shoulder. I twisted in my seat. "Miguel!"

"Kantutita. Felicidades." He bent to kiss my cheek, smelling of an unfamiliar aftershave, and pulled a chair over to our table.

"Gracias."

"Did my father invite you all here?"

"I've been sworn to secrecy." He grinned at me, his teeth white in the dim light.

My father's bow drew across the strings. They began with "Rosita de Pica," Vico's fingers a blur on his strings before launching into Telemann's Viola Concerto in G Major, which I had never imagined could incorporate a charango. My feet stirred under my chair and Miguel's fingers tapped the side of his leg nearest me.

After their third song, my father stood up. "Thank you all for coming," he began in his formal-sounding Spanish. "I've been performing my whole life, but this is my first time performing with these particular instruments —" He gestured to the guitar and charango. "And with these particular musicians! So I thank you for your tolerance.

"And I beg of you one more favor. My daughter, Orly, some of you may know her —" Miguel elbowed me in the ribs and I heard Sarah's laugh. "It's her eighteenth birthday tonight. She has been studying charango for a while now, and I thought she might like the chance to play with some fellow musicians. And her papá." He held out his hand to me as Vico began plucking out the chords to "Cumpleaños Felices" on his charango.

My face flushed in the dark. As Vico began to sing "Happy Birthday," my father retrieved the bulky pillowcase from underneath his chair and pulled out a familiar instrument. "You may want this."

I took the charango from him and stumbled to the stage. I shouldn't have had that singani. Vico strummed a final chord and stood up, offering me his chair. I sank down and turned my attention to tuning my strings. "Just pretend it's a lesson," Vico whispered. "It's all practicing."

My father looked at me. "What shall we play?"

Vico spoke first. "Dos Palomitos?"

I shook my head. The fingerwork was very fast.

"Let's do La Cocinerita." The Argentinian folk song about a cook wasn't my favorite tune, but it was simple.

I looked out at my friends, only barely visible in the hazy light of the café. "This is for my mother, who is herself a cocinerita."

FIFTY-THREE

In early 1946, several months after my aunt arrived, something happened that changed everything for all of us. It was a late afternoon, near 5:00 P.M. My aunt and I sat on a wooden bench just inside my mother's tiny storefront adjacent to the Riesenrad Café. Children raced around in the park outside, chasing pigeons. We had bought a few vegetables at the market to take home for dinner and stopped to share one of my mother's poppy-seed rolls.

Now that Thekla had begun to notice her surroundings, now that she was willing to eat a bit of marraqueta with her tea, she didn't need constant supervision. When I wasn't practicing charango or shelving books, I walked Thekla to the plaza and through the open door of the café. Today, we watched people approach my mother at the counter and ask her questions about her food. I was proud that she was able to manage on her own, speaking Spanish. I didn't help her anymore. I sat in the corner, letting her struggle.

So I wasn't looking at my aunt when I saw our roll tumble to the floor and heard her strangled gasp. She was staring ahead of her at a man standing at the counter near the register, a tall, blond man cradling a bowl in one hand and shoveling large spoonfuls of soup into his mouth with the other. He looked uncommonly healthy, his complexion clear and his cheeks pink. Yet I would not have noted him were it not for his unusual height and for the fingernails suddenly deep in the flesh of my forearm. *"That's him,"* she whispered. *"Knochenmus."*

Knochenmus. I recognized the name. My aunt didn't talk about her time at the camp but certain details leaked out of her in unguarded moments.

"From the camp?" I whispered, knowing the answer and yet unable to believe it.

She nodded faintly. I would have said she went pale, but it was not possible for her to grow any paler.

I could feel her body trembling against mine. I wrapped my arm around her waist and helped her up, my heart racing. I wanted to run to the man, to beat him senseless with my fists, to shove the rest of my roll down his throat. But even as these murderous thoughts flashed through my mind, I knew I couldn't do it. I couldn't risk our safety. There might be more of them, more than we knew, more than we could count. They might be all around us.

"Come." I didn't want to leave my mother in her store, didn't want to leave her near that man, but I had to get Thekla away. I heard the man laugh loudly and say something in German to his companion. The German speakers we knew were fellow refugees, but we had all heard rumors of Nazi spies in the Círculo Israelita and the reports that Nazis were arriving now on the same ships as the survivors of their plans. But we had never met one who had been there.

Half dragging my trembling aunt, I waved to catch my mother's eye. Immediately, she knew something was wrong. Once she had rung up the last customers and ushered them to the street, she hurriedly locked the store and caught up with us as we pushed our way through the crowds toward home. "Thekla?" she said, touching her sister's arm. When I explained who we had seen in her store, my mother's face went still and hard. There was no surprise in her eyes. She turned and looked back toward the square, where the man now sprawled open-legged on a bench, pausing as if committing his features to memory. Stop looking at him, I wanted to say. Stop acknowledging his existence.

Seeing Knochenmus evaporated any progress my aunt had made toward wellness. She refused to dress or to leave the apartment. She wouldn't eat unless my mother spooned something into her mouth. She could not stop trembling.

Fury took root in my belly. But it was nothing compared with the fury that took over my mother.

It hadn't occurred to us that the Nazis would need to flee as we once had. It hadn't occurred to us that they could choose the same route we had, to the same country.

They walked with their heads high — how could their heads still be high? — striding casually through our markets, our communities. Bolivia, our savior and protector, had let them in. If the Bolivians had allowed the Germans refuge, did that mean they would also allow them to exterminate us?

We could not dismiss this worry as mere paranoia.

Those of us who had relaxed our defenses,

who had finally accepted the relative peace of this place, drew up our drawbridges again. We huddled together, sharing information on these men, monitoring their movements. When my parents took me to a dance at the Austrian Club, I viewed everyone with suspicion. The small mustachioed man holding a pale beer at the bar — was he one? The fat man shoveling Schnitzel down his throat? Fatness in and of itself was suspect. We were mistrustful of the new Germans and Austrians, unless they had come from the camps. We doubted anyone whose face wasn't haunted, who didn't keep looking over his shoulder. Anyone who had survived intact.

My mother, who for years — since our arrival — had allowed me to wander the streets alone or with my friends, suddenly didn't want to let me out of the house. I was eighteen, practically an adult. Despite the relative spaciousness of our three-bedroom apartment, the thought of being cooped up there, away from my friends, was untenable. Besides, I had to work.

"I'll go out with Miguel," I offered. I hadn't actually seen Miguel in months. Sarah told me she had seen him with a girlfriend. This gave me a curious feeling in my stomach, even though I had never wanted to touch him the way I touched Rachel, had never considered kissing his scarred lip. Had I seen Miguel recently, I would not have wanted to tell him about the men who had followed us here; he might be tempted to fight them. I wanted Austrian troubles to stay across the sea, far from Miguel, far from all that had saved me.

"Miguel doesn't understand."

"He does as much as anyone here does! Do you think he would let them hurt me?" Despite the widening space between us, I trusted in his friendship.

"These are Nazis, Liebchen. Did you forget?"

"You think I would forget? You really think I would *forget*?"

I loved my mother, but we had basic philosophical differences. I needed to connect with people, to weave myself into a cobweb of friends and in that way strengthen my own perch. I needed people. My mother was so solitary it worried me. "I have my customers," she said. "I have your father."

"And he has his viola," I was tempted to add.

When it came to the Nazis, however, I temporarily relented and agreed to avoid walking alone when I left the apartment.

The situation surely couldn't last. Surely the Nazis wouldn't stay here long. Surely there were people looking for them, people who would come take them away to justice. Surely the world would not allow them to remain free.

I began writing letters to Bolivian presidents. We had three that year: Gualberto Villarroel, Néstor Guillén, and Tomás Monje Gutierréz. The first two were not really presidents, but chairmen of a provisional government. Perhaps unsurprisingly, I received no replies.

After work, I spent more time with my mother in the kitchen, although she brushed me aside at first. "You've got work of your own, Orly. Apply to universities. Practice your charango."

My father had initially suggested I consider going abroad to study, if not to the United States, then to Argentina or Chile. "The universities here aren't worth anything," my mother agreed. "What good would such a degree do you?" I refrained from pointing out that we didn't have the money to travel to a foreign university, let alone tuition fees. I refrained from asking her what good her Austrian music degree was doing her. I refrained from pointing out that if I planned to stay in Bolivia, a Boliv-

ian degree would not be completely ir-
relevant.

Fifty-Four

At breakfast one morning my mother was oddly cheerful. When I came into the kitchen I was surprised to find her awake before me, sitting at the table sifting through pages of her handwritten recipes. "Guten Morgen!" She smiled at me and pushed over a plate of rolls still warm from the oven. "Do you have plans this morning?"

I lowered myself onto a chair and rubbed my eyes. "You're up early. Just practicing, I think. Though I'm working in the afternoon." I liked working at Arbres Morts, talking with customers about books, reading bits of poems. Writing bits of poems.

"Is there any chance you could go ask Miguel how to get ahold of Wayra? I seem to have lost track of her."

There was something too casual in my mother's speech. We hadn't seen Wayra in years, not since she had finished my mother's unofficial tutorial in Bolivian herbal medicine.

"Mutti, that was a long time ago. I'm sure Miguel doesn't know. And doesn't Wayra travel?" I picked up one of the rolls and tore it open.

"We have to start somewhere. Can you go?"

I took a bite of soft dough and looked at her with suspicion. "Are you sick?"

She shook her head.

"Is Vati sick?"

"No one is sick. But it's important. It's just in case."

"You can't explain to me why?"

My mother sighed, a whisper of impatience. "I can't explain to you why."

Whatever it was, it seemed to have renewed my mother's sense of purpose. For weeks after seeing Knochenmus she had been possessed by a wild fury, kneading dough so hard it flattened and refused to rise.

I got up from the table. "I'll go now, but don't get your hopes up."

"Tell him to tell her I'll pay," my mother called after me. "I'll pay whatever she wants."

It seemed pointless to go to Miguel when there was so little chance he would have any information, but I stopped at his house. He wasn't home, and his mother said he wasn't expected until late. I was relieved; I would have felt awkward asking him for a favor when it had been so long since we'd spoken. Alone, I walked the familiar route up calle Sagárnaga to calle Linares. My mother had apparently forgotten her own precaution. In this more populated part of town the stores opened earlier. I began in the first shop Miguel had shown me, asking if anyone knew Wayra's whereabouts. Many of the women in the shops recognized me now, as I sometimes came on errands for my mother, looking for a specific herb or powder. None of them knew where Wayra was, but promised to ask around. I returned to the stores each morning until the following Thursday when one of the shop owners told me Wayra would arrive in La Paz that weekend. I left our new address, as we hadn't seen her since the move.

Saturday morning my father and I took Thekla with us to the market. When we returned, my mother and Wayra were stirring things on the stove. Thekla headed straight to her room to rest. Shrugging to each other, my father and I retreated to our respective rooms, our respective instruments, relieved that my mother had something to do.

The following Wednesday I helped my mother carry things to her store and arrange the food on her shelves and cases. Once she opened the shop, I sat on a crate behind the counter with a book. I often spent weekend mornings like this, watching over my mother while exploring the world from my stool.

"Here you are, sir." Something in my mother's voice made me look up. My mother's customer was fair-haired and tall. "Danke schön," he said, taking the plate with one hand and offering my mother a crumpled note with the other.

Shock took hold of my tongue and kept it still. I watched him walk across the street to the park and squat down to eat. My mind reeled. My mother said, My mother said, My mother said, never never never talk. Not to them.

"Mutti." I watched my mother place a cloth back over the plate of Schnitzel and tuck it under the counter. "Why did you give food to *him*?"

My mother — my furious, exacting mother — seemed uncharacteristically unconcerned. "He was hungry. He had money. It's hard to be sure after all. What should I say when they ask?"

"But . . ." I didn't know where to start. Or end. Or what to say in the middle. My mother would never — but did I know my mother after all? "Mutti, you know . . ."

"I know."

"You would take money from *him*?" The earth and sky had somehow switched places and I found I had never understood the world at all.

My mother turned her opaque eyes to me. I used to know how to read them. "I took it last time. Is it better that he have it?"

I stared across the market at the man, filling his Aryan mouth with my mother's Schnitzel. My mother's, my mother's food. Into the *mouths of monsters.*

"You're feeding an evil, a fiend! Thekla . . ."

"This fiend probably won't bite the hand that feeds him. Trust me, Orly, I know what I'm doing. I am protecting us." My mother smiling, relaxed. Something was off.

"If Thekla finds out you —"

"She won't. And you won't tell her. Why don't you go home and get something to eat? You must be hungry."

Distracted, I shook my head. I didn't want to leave my mother alone. "I'll just eat something here." I pulled the small tray out from under the table and lifted the cloth. It smelled good. I pinched a bit of the meat between my fingers.

"Stop that!" Before my hands had fully closed on the Schnitzel, my mother had knocked it from my fingers. But she didn't look angry. She looked scared.

"Mutti?" I wiped the grease from the food on my skirt. "I'm sorry?"

My mother next to me, squatting, serious. "I'm sorry, too, sweetheart. I didn't mean to shout at you. But that plate is reserved for our customers. I'll fix you something else."

Silent, I nodded. My stomach hurt.

"There's another pan of it in the basket behind you. I'll make you something from that. It's fresher."

I examined her face. Her eyes were clear and steady. "I think maybe I'll go home."

My mother touched my forehead. "Are you all right? You haven't eaten anything all day, have you?"

"No." I stared at my mother. She stared back at me.

My mother had fed that man something bad, I was sure of it. Some kind of poison that Wayra had taught her how to brew. Puzzle pieces slid into place. I needed space to think. "I'll see you at home."

Numb, I hardly felt my feet on the stones.

There had been more of that Schnitzel she fed Knochenmus. I wiped my fingers repeatedly on my skirt. She would have told me if I needed to wash my hands, wouldn't she? I would wash them anyway. My thoughts erupted. Who else was she planning to feed? If too many died at once, wouldn't people guess? Would my mother be arrested? But surely she had planned carefully. My mother was meticulous. Her food would not be the only thing Knochenmus ate today.

I shook my head to clear it. No one had died. Not yet. And what if Knochenmus did keel over? Would anyone mourn? It was hard to resist the euphoria, the feeling of triumph and justice served that swept through me at the thought of my aunt's torturer brought down. That man who had been able to look into the newly minted eyes of an infant and see something deserving of extermination. My steps grew faster as I thought of it. Who else was coming after them? I didn't see the Americans or the Europeans arresting Nazis in South America. Justice had very short arms.

But not my mother. My mother, unlike the rest of the world, was *doing something.*

A week later, we found out that Knochenmus was dead. We heard about it from Mathilde, when we saw her at the Austrian

Club over the weekend. Thekla was not, of course, the only one who had recognized him.

Everyone assumed it was something Bolivian that killed him. It could have been dysentery or a heart problem caused by the altitude. The possibilities were nearly endless. Death was not so uncommon. Only if there were clear evidence of homicide would a death be investigated. And in the case of Knochenmus, there was no such evidence.

The confirmation of Knochenmus's death shook me. I had known, I had expected it, and yet now new fears took hold. *My mother was a murderer.* I did not want her to have anything in common with those men. Yet now she did. Though I had longed for Knochenmus's death, I hadn't anticipated the anxiety I suddenly felt for my mother's soul. "Soul" is the wrong word for someone as secular as I am, and yet I can find no other word for the part of her I wanted to preserve. And — this was all occurring to me in a landslide — mine as well. My father, I was sure, did not know. Thekla did not know. I didn't think anyone knew but me. If I did not tell anyone, I was complicit.

If my mother had thought Knochenmus's death would bring some relief to my aunt, she was mistaken. Thekla had not even smiled when we told her, just listened in silence and left the kitchen.

I followed her to her room and stood in the doorway. "Aren't you glad, Auntie?"

She turned from the window. Her eyes looked vacant, as if the person behind them had wandered off, leaving her body behind. "Glad?"

"That he's gone."

She considered me for a moment, partially returning to the space behind her eyes. "What good does his death do now?"

I was mute. She sighed and dismissed me, turning back to the window.

My feet still stood on her floor. I could not pick them up. "But at least now he cannot harm anyone else," I said.

She did not move. She did not register my words with a gesture or sigh. I was speaking to the air.

FIFTY-FIVE

Some people can live with the memories and some cannot. Three days after Knochenmus died, my aunt Thekla used my father's straight razor to pry open the doors to death that lived in her veins.

My mother found her. She was in the bath. Apparently she was worried that her wrists would not be enough; she sliced open the skin along both ankles, and the soft flesh of her inner thighs. My aunt Thekla was taking no chances. She wanted never to remember again.

Yet she had failed to consider the memories she would leave with us. For me, the memory of running in search of my mother, whom I heard screaming somewhere in the apartment. The memory of following the sound to the bathroom, to the tub full of sloshing scarlet, the color of the Easter egg dye Anneliese used to make from beetroot. My mother shaking with rage and grief, pulling Thekla's arms from the water to press the violated skin with her palms.

"Get a doctor," she ordered without turning around.

The doctor, as was usual in Bolivia, arrived too late.

A few weeks after Thekla left us, I woke in the dark. An elephant, or something its size, had settled on my heart. An animal that had nothing to do with Bolivia or the altitude. I felt it physically, its weight, the crushing of my lungs. If I stayed in bed, surely I would suffocate. On my feet, the feeling remained. Perhaps movement would shake this elephant, dislodge it from my chest. The worse I felt, the more I needed to move. As quickly and quietly as I could, I pulled on wool socks, a long skirt, a sweater. Searched for my hat. Collected all of the pages of our stories.

Outside, the sun arrived suddenly and brightly, like a surprise party on the horizon. Like stupid optimism. Always sun, every morning. It still amazed me. No matter how much rain we had during the day, a few hours later it was as though nothing damp had ever happened to this city. Its earth was resilient, resistant to dark forces, lighting up again and again.

I walked without thinking, always uphill. But in my heart, I knew where I was going.

Nayra was still unraveling potatoes from sacks of bright cloth, spreading them before her on the stones. She looked up and smiled, but her hands didn't stop. I squatted next to her, reaching into the sack to help. I had done this before, so she let me. Nayra didn't ask me about work or my other friends or my parents. It relaxed me, to be free of these bits of etiquette. There are so few people who allow you to be quiet.

Only after the first sack was empty did we stop and crouch against a stone wall to sip some tea. "Do you remember my aunt Thekla?" I began.

Nayra did not interrupt me. She asked nothing. Although her Spanish was no longer hesitant, she remained a quiet person. When her tea was gone, she untied the mouth of the second sack of potatoes. Her hands continued to move, sorting potatoes by color and size, nestling them together in pyramids on her mat. When she was finished, when I was finished, she sat back on her heels and looked up at me. "Would you like to come back to the lake with me tonight?"

At the end of the market day I returned home to fetch a change of clothing and tell my parents where I was going. My mother was lying on her bed fully dressed, with the lights off. "Mutti?" I reached for the lamp by her bedside. "Are you all right?"

She rolled onto her side to look at me, her hairpins coming loose so that her auburn curls fell in lopsided clumps from her head. Her hair had grown darker in recent months, its glossiness worn away. Silently, she took in the bag in my hand and my air of impatience. "Where are you going?"

I almost changed my mind when I saw my mother's white face, her shock that I would leave her. Never had I traveled outside of La Paz alone, spent a night away. I understood her fear. But Thekla — my old aunt Thekla, the one in Austria — would not have wanted her death to turn me into a prisoner. I cannot imagine she would have wanted that.

I couldn't follow my mother any further into the dark. "Vati is here. He is just in the next room." My father, I thought, might not even notice I was gone. He chose his viola over my mother more often now, slipping out of bed to practice while my mother wept into her pillow. I understood. I too felt myself straining against the confines of her bottomless grief. We were still alive.

"But those trucks, Orly, they are not safe."

She sat up, her eyes wide.

"It's all right. Nayra knows the driver." I rarely lied to my parents, but sometimes my mother seemed bewildered to discover I was not one of her limbs. That I moved autonomously. It never occurred to her that I was older now than she was when she married. When she had Willi. "Mutti, I'll be back day after tomorrow."

She sighed, an uncommon concession, perhaps at last abandoning the idea that she could protect those she loved. "Take some water. There's some on the stove. And some of the cookies." The night Thekla died, after the doctor had gone and the bathroom was clean and the stained bathmat crushed down into the garbage, my mother had baked five dozen ginger cookies. My father and I had not even been surprised.

When she finished speaking, she lay back down on her bed and turned her face to the wall, returning to the unreachable country where she lived.

If I didn't leave quickly, I wouldn't leave at all.

Nayra was waiting for me on a corner close to the market, next to an idling truck much like the one that had carried Rachel away. We added our cloth sacks to the heap in the back and climbed among the crowds, squeezing against each other in the middle. Other refugees had been to the lake, had talked about eating grilled fish on its shores, but I had never gone. I had never wanted to leave my mother and she had never been persuaded to leave the city.

Nayra had been born in Carabuco, an ancient village near the shores of the lake. But we were not going to her family home now, she told me. "There is not much to see in the village except my family and our church, which is famous because of the cross. I want to take you somewhere else. Somewhere I also have family." She had told me stories about the old wooden cross that had been buried or tossed in a lake but rose to the surface. There were many conflicting legends involving Spanish invaders and the Aymara and that cross, and I could never keep them straight.

It was a long and freezing drive to Lake Titicaca, bumping over uneven roads. I shivered despite my layers of clothing, and watched a woman across from us tear apart a roasted chicken in her lap, sucking each bone carefully before discarding it in a pile at her side.

Nayra went to sleep, her black head bent over her sack. She had told me only that we would disembark in Copacabana, but we would not be staying there.

I closed my eyes. The elephant clung to my chest like a fretful child.

When I opened my eyes again, the world stayed dark. It took me a minute to realize that night had fallen. The man next to me was snoring.

Nayra was sitting up, staring out at the sky, her breath puffs of mist in the air. "We'll be there soon."

The truck drove down the main street of a town and left us near the water, the driver getting out to toss our cloth bags down from the back. Behind us was a row of hotels and restaurants. Behind us was sound — music drifting from a restaurant, laughter, the hum of motors. Before us spread a vast darkness. Before us was silence, broken only by the lapping water at the shore.

"Wait here," said Nayra and she hurried down to a small shack next to a dock. A man emerged, and they appeared to negotiate something.

She turned and waved me toward her. Uncertainly, I picked my way over the dirt and rocks to the dock. "I found us a boat." She swept her arm toward something that looked like a canoe. It didn't look very stable.

"Shouldn't we wait until morning, when it is light?" I couldn't imagine finding anything in the vast black of the lake before us.

"I know the lake."

We climbed into the boat with a man who took up an oar. It was too dark to make out his features. He was a friend of a cousin of an aunt, Nayra explained. He nodded to me but did not speak as he dipped his paddle into the water.

It was a long way across that frigid expanse, the black water flat as ice. I was too cold to speak, too tired. I crouched in the damp bottom of the canoe, the fear of toppling over the side keeping me upright. Beside me squatted Nayra, expertly balanced on her sandals, her cloth bag between her knees.

As the lights of Copacabana faded and the darkness of earth was complete, I gazed with wonder above us. The stars, which I perceived in my numbness as a spray of glittering ice chips, were not only above us but all around, cascading toward the mountains on every side. I had never seen so many; I hadn't known there were so many. How could my aunt Thekla have removed herself from a world like this? She would never see these stars. She would never see this lake. I was furious with her for rejecting our planet, for succeeding where the Nazis had failed. I might have cried then, if my tears had not frozen on the rims of my eyes before they could fall.

"We call this Isla del Sol," Nayra said as our rower pulled close enough to the shore to allow us to leap to the grass and scramble up the steep slope. I could see nothing before me, but followed Nayra, occasionally reaching out to touch her top skirt to be sure of her presence. The cluster of houses appeared before me abruptly as we reached the top of a path, the starlight just bright enough to define their borders. Nayra knocked on the door of the third small hut. A dark shape answered the door and, after a whispered conversation with Nayra, admitted us. The room stank of animal and rancid oil. Her grandmother prodded us silently toward a corner of the floor, where we made a nest of the blankets we had with us. Grateful for the shelter, made slightly warmer than the night air by the bodies within it, I slept.

I woke striped with sun, which streamed from between the cracks in the thatched roof. Nayra had already risen and was outside; I could hear her murmuring to the woman we'd met last night. I stretched, my back slightly sore, unaccustomed to the ground. Yet I had slept deeply, dreamlessly. In the light, I could see that the hut had been built from bricks of mud and manure, like many I had seen outside La Paz. Our host's sleeping mat had been rolled up and tucked in a corner. Other than that, furnishings were minimal. A chair, a small table, a chest for storage.

I rifled in my bag for the thermos of boiled water I had brought. It was nearly empty. Picking it up, I pushed open the front door. This morning, the Isla del Sol seemed aptly named. I could not remember having seen a sun this yellow, this clarifying. The waters of the lake, rippling in the breeze, reflected the sky, making islands of clouds. Across the lake there were flatter channels that almost looked like paths. A memory of ice-skating across an Austrian lake darted through my mind. Around us, the green hills were terraced for farming.

I stood outside the door, staring, until Nayra called to me from the firepit to the right of the hut. "The sun god was born here," she said.

"I can see." I walked toward her, blinking in the blaze of light.

"I will show you his footprints. This is my grandmother." She indicated the older woman crouched next to her by the fire.

"Mucho gusto." I was unsure if she spoke Spanish. She nodded and smiled, revealing nearly toothless gums, before turning back to watch the tiny fish she was roasting over the flames. We had come ashore near the village of Yumani, she explained. Her grandmother lived on the fringes of the settlement.

We set off just after breakfast, our bags tied around our shoulders cholita style. Nayra smiled as she watched me imitate the knot she tied at her collarbone. We would walk a circular route, first traveling down the spine of the island, she said, stopping to see the sacred sites. "There were people here long before the Inca," she told me. "Our people."

The narrow dirt path we followed wound through tiny settlements and past fields planted with amaranth and potatoes. Baby pigs tried out their trotters alongside the path and I squatted down to touch their skin. There were no roads. No cars. No exhaust fumes. No noise. I had the feeling I had traveled back to the time of the pre-Incan settlers. Along the edges of the island grew familiar white and yellow daisies, as well as exotic fluffy red-orange flowers that grew as tall as my shoulders.

The villages tapered off as we climbed up to the island's backbone, walking a long, straight line toward what Nayra called the Sacred Rock, dwelling place of the sun. That same Sun, not an entirely benevolent deity, burned the skin of my cheeks as we walked, and I was glad I had brought a wide-brimmed hat. We walked mostly in silence, broken only by Nayra's occasional explanations or a story. Despite her disdain for the Incas, many of her tales were Incan tales. They had left so many of these relics. As I looked out at the sea — I mean the lake, which felt so much like a sea because I could not see how far it stretched — I noticed that its colors shifted constantly. In the shallow coves, the slate-grey of the deeper waters turned aquamarine. I felt I could sit and watch it all day.

The Sacred Rock disappointed me. I had expected something spectacular, carved, interestingly shaped. But it was merely a weathered grey mass plopped at the end of the island like a discarded heap of soggy muesli. Nayra said it resembled a puma, but try as I might, I could not find anything in it resembling that wildcat. I rested my hand on its warm side, hoping a divine energy would infuse me with some kind of peace. But all that happened was that my hand became warm.

Nearby were the Sun's footprints, odd oblongs carved into the stone. "The Huellas del Sol," Nayra said. They were large, though not as large as you might imagine a god's footprints to be. The strength of the Sun would surely burn holes in the earth far bigger than these two prints. Oh, how hard it is to instill belief — any belief at all — in the heart of someone who no longer believed in anything.

"And there is the table, where the Incas murdered their children." She gestured at a stone table surrounded by little square stones. The arrangement looked so unexpectedly modern that I wondered how long the stones had actually been in those positions.

Nearby was Chincana, the ruined labyrinth. As we wandered through the roofless rooms, up and down the maze, Nayra took my hand, though she dropped it as soon as we passed a man walking down. "There isn't much left," she said apologetically, as if it had been she personally who had let it fall to ruin. "Everything was stolen."

"Like what?"

"Gold and silver. Bowls, drinking cups.

Everything. All we have left are doorways."

There were many of those. If you stood at the top of the labyrinth looking down toward the lake, you could look through several doorways at once, all lined up. I realized suddenly how little I knew of this country. How much I wanted to know. This day, this island, would be a start.

From my vantage point, atop this small island in the vast lake, Europe felt impossible. War inconceivable. Everything but the elements fell away. There was only earth, sun, and water. People had always lived here, on this isolated piece of rock, since there were people at all. They grew things to eat. They fished. They played pipes and they danced. I tried to imagine this being enough, this life without books, cinema, or symphonies. The idea both tempted and terrified me, making my lungs constrict. What would I be like had I never experienced these things? Reading had ruined me for a life without books. Mahler ruined me for a life without orchestration. Yet, oddly, Vienna did not ruin me for a life in La Paz. It had only ruined my mother.

Stepping forward, I walked through a doorway.

"Did people live here, or was it only a place of worship?" I imagined roofs over these rooms, children hiding from each other.

"It is a mystery what was here." Nayra didn't mind mystery as much as I did, didn't have the same desire to tie up every loose end of every story.

Around noon we stopped in the home of a woman who cooked for passersby, and sitting on the green verge of her lawn we ate salted potatoes and fried karachi. After lunch we walked slowly along the jagged coast, Nayra spilling stories in her wake. In the village of Ch'allapampa, Nayra told me, tiny gold and silver figures had washed up on shore, gifts from the city beneath the water. "People have taken them," she said with a shrug. "The Incas, the Spanish." We wandered as close to the water as we dared, but I saw no metallic glints beneath the surface.

We could go back to stay with her grandmother, Nayra said, or we could stay on the beach. I thought of the stars, of sleeping with them above me, and chose the beach of Challa, forgetting that the stars' brightness would bring no heat. As soon as we stopped moving, the chill began to permeate my skin. It was even colder here than in La Paz, with the wind across the water whipping strands of hair in our faces.

Neither of us was very hungry, so we sat on the sand and nibbled on the packet of Lebkuchen I had brought from home. As the sun slid down, the surface of the water turned silvery, like snakeskin. From where we sat we could look across to the much smaller Isla de la Luna. How I would love to listen to Holst's *Planets* sitting here, letting the music of Jupiter and Neptune wash over me with the sounds of the water. I wanted Nayra to hear it with me. But I didn't have the words to explain my desire.

"Women used to live there." Nayra gestured across the water. "Holy women."

"Nuns?"

"Something like that. Virgins."

Like me. Unlike the girls at school, I had never fallen prey to romantic crushes on boys. A few times I had given in to various boys who had pursued me, going to the cinema or out for tea. But their attempts to press their lips to mine aroused only a mild revulsion. It wasn't boys I thought about when I was alone in the dark.

"Were they sent there by their families?"

Nayra shrugged. "Maybe they just had had enough of their men?" We smiled at each other, and something familiar twisted in me.

The dark descended fast. We each put on all of the clothing we had with us and unrolled our blankets. I could still feel the cold in my bones, in the heart of me. I could not remember what it felt like to be warm. Without thinking, I inched closer to Nayra, wanting to draw myself into her warmth. She had always been physically distant. Now here was her hair, her thick black hair, resting against my cheek, mixing its strands with mine. In the night, they were the same color. We had midnight hair. I could smell her smoky bread smell.

"Tell me a story," I said, inching slightly away.

She laughed as she turned onto her back to see the sky. "For your book?"

"For our book." I had dozens of stories by now, rewritten dozens of times.

"And you'll read it to me once you put it down, to be sure you get it right?"

"I always read them to you."

"But you're always changing them."

"That's true." I thought for a while. "Isn't that what happens when they are passed down from your grandmother to your mother? The words can't be the same."

"Maybe."

"I'll change them again if you want."

"We will see."

"Entonces . . . ?"

She sighed. "Do you see that star, the brightest one there? That is the Grandfather Star I told you about, Achach Warawara. It's the first one that appears and you are supposed to watch it with your grandmother or grandfather. Someone old. You have to find that one before you can look for all of the baby stars . . ."

I began to drift, and was nearly asleep when I heard her tone shift.

"Do you remember I said you had to watch the stars at a certain time of year? So that we know when to begin things?"

"I remember."

"For weaving, too, we need the stars. To be sure our animals have the right color wool, we place weavings over the backs of llamas and alpacas. A black weaving for black babies. For white babies we do not cover the llamas, so starlight can get into them."

I stared above us, trying to see colors in the stars.

"These patterns, I want to weave."

The stars were starting to grow restless, quivering in their places. "Is there a way to weave a story?"

"Many weavings tell stories."

"Like the one where the monkey sends

the fox away to find fire from the stars and he burns his tail on the moon?"

"It's possible."

I tried to imagine these celestial tapestries. "I would like to see those stories in a weaving."

When there was no reply, I turned my head to try to see her face but it was too dark. I heard her breath, quiet and regular.

Looking back at the stars, I thought about her stories, our stories, my stories, Anneliese's stories. I thought about the poems I had written for Ana, Willi, my mother. The poem I wanted to write for my aunt Thekla. I wondered why some things came out in stories and some in poems or songs, and marveled how clear it often was which thoughts belonged in which kind of writing. My stories were all imagined. They were about worlds far from this one, animals, fantastic landscapes.

But the poems, they told the truth.

I lay on my back staring up at the shivering stars until the Sun god stepped out of the lake and into the sky.

FIFTY-SIX

The day I began university, in February 1947, another Nazi died. I was spreading butter across a marraqueta for breakfast when Mathilde, panting from the stairs, knocked at the door of our apartment with the news. She and Fredi had also moved, but were just a dozen blocks away. It was always Mathilde — Mathilde with her journalist's obsessive attention to both world and local events — bringing us news.

This Nazi was older, in his forties or fifties. He had been a guard at Auschwitz. It was his heart, Mathilde told us, accepting a cup of tea.

"His heart?" said my father. My mother studied the inside of her teacup.

"That's what the doctor said." A Bolivian doctor who either didn't know who he was or didn't care had examined him and passed on the information to our German doctor.

"Nazis have hearts?" My mother's voice

was flat.

"Scorpions have hearts. Cobras have hearts. Though I imagine theirs don't do much more than push blood around the body. And in this case, that is what it failed to do." Mathilde sipped her tea. "For which I am grateful."

My father frowned as he stood up from the table. "I am not grateful for death in any form. Death is not something I can celebrate." Leaving an unfinished marraqueta on his plate, he walked down the hall to his viola.

I stared at my mother, willing her to look at me. I hadn't thought she would do it again, after Thekla's death. But she kept her face turned to Mathilde.

I scraped back my chair, swept the crumbs from the table into my hand, and carried my plate to the sink. Thekla had not been grateful for the death of Nazis. Their crimes were not something that death could reverse. Couldn't my mother see that?

Yet I, too, was enraged that these men were sharing our streets, our ordinary lives. When I thought too long about this my blood boiled so hot it seared my skin. I had to seal away that part of me in order to go on with my schoolwork, play my charango, or write a verse. Like I sealed away memories of Willi. Like I sealed off everything I felt for Rachel and Anneliese.

Perhaps that is what the Nazis did, sealed off in a locked part of their brain what they had done, how generations would suffer because of it. I could not even begin to imagine living with the memories that must cling to them. If Thekla couldn't live with what she had done, how could they?

"Mutti, I need to go. I'll be late." I grabbed my notebooks from the table and pulled the strap of my cloth bag over my head. She rose from her seat to kiss me good-bye. "Be good," she said. "Be careful."

When I returned from the lake trip with Nayra, I had informed my parents that I would begin university the following term, and begin it here. Only Bolivians, I tried to explain to my parents, could teach me what I wanted to know.

I registered at the Universidad Mayor de San Andrés, a fifteen-minute walk from our apartment, though the secretary who registered me warned that I would be one of the only women. I felt hungry for books and conversation, as though I had been fasting and abruptly regained my appetite. I wanted to keep moving forward as quickly as possible, to keep ahead of the pain. Away from thoughts of the empty places in me, in our family.

I was grateful for the walk to school. It warmed my fingers and toes, sent my blood dashing around delivering oxygen. As I moved, the sediment stirred up inside me settled down into compartments I could close. I would talk with my mother later. I would ask her to stop. Two deaths were enough on anyone's conscience. How many more had she planned? Did she have a list?

This was not what I wanted to be pondering on my first day of university.

It was not a beautiful campus, but then there were very few buildings in La Paz that strived for beauty. I glanced up at Illimani, that reliable friend, before climbing the stairs to the blocky orange building. "Wish me luck."

In the halls, groups of young men jostled me as they passed, talking and laughing, papers in hand as they searched for the correct classrooms. I stopped to pull my own registration sheet from my purse. Room 407. Introduction to South American Literature. After that I had English, which I hoped would allow me to read more broadly. Joining the throngs on the stairs, I started up. What staircase was Anneliese ascending now? I wondered. Was she also starting university? What would she be studying? I had received nothing but silence in reply to my note. It was possible that she had died. It was possible that she had moved, forgetting her promise to me. I had no way to know.

I was enrolled in the Humanities Department, in the hope of studying poetry. There was no music conservatory then, so I continued to study charango with Vico and music itself with my father when he had time. I enjoyed our frequent café concerts. But I also looked forward to studying the literature of this country, of this continent, literature my parents had never introduced to me.

No one else from our school had come here. They had gone abroad to study, or their families had left Bolivia after the war, or they had gotten married and begun families of their own. Some had taken jobs in the textile factories. Few refugees saw the point of enrolling in a Bolivian university, even if their Spanish was good enough.

The degree was not the point. The point was to dive into *here.* At the top of the stairs, I walked down the echoing hallway until I found my classroom, and pushed open the door.

Every day after that I told myself I would talk to my mother. Every day I put it off, telling myself she was done now.

Perhaps a part of me did not want her to stop.

A month into my studies, I was humming as I turned my key in the lock and stepped into the kitchen. It smelled yeasty and warm, like baking. "Hola!" I called, dropping my book bag by the door. "Home from the knowledge mines!" My mother wasn't in the kitchen, but the kerosene was on and a small pot was simmering. In a dish on the table sat a small round of dough. I picked up the bowl to sniff it.

"Put that down!" My mother's voice startled me so much I nearly dropped the bowl. She hurried from the bedroom, ripping the bowl from my arms. "Why are you here? I thought you were going out to the movies after classes?"

I stared at her, at her bloodshot eyes, her flour-speckled curls. "I was. But I decided to come home. I have an essay to write. And I wanted to tell you —" My mother's face was pink and damp. "Mutti, what's going on? Are you all right?"

"Orly, you didn't eat anything, did you?

Not even a taste?" She held tightly on to the bowl, as if I might try to take it back.

"Of course not." I looked at the pestle and mortar on the table. At the opened jars of unfamiliar herbs. Dizzy, I saw Knochenmus with the Schnitzel. I saw an elderly man accepting an apple strudel from my mother's hands. My mother's hands.

"Mutti." My knees were trembling so badly I had to sit down. I wanted something solid underneath me. At that moment, thoughts of my schoolwork evaporated in the steam of that kitchen.

"Mutti. I think you need to tell me." My hands gripped the seat of the chair.

My mother studied my face for a moment. Wondering, I thought, if there was any use in lying. "Are you sure?"

I nodded, eyes stinging. "You could have poisoned me. Just now. You owe me at least the truth."

"Once I tell you it can't be taken back. You will always know."

I lifted my chin. "You really think I don't already?"

With a deep breath, she sank into the chair across from me. "Well, I think we can skip the *why*."

She told me all of it then. The idea that had

524

crystallized with the appearance of Knochenmus. The dark secrets Wayra had taught her. The slow-acting poisons in near-tasteless herbs. The careful pacing of deaths, no more than every few months — or even longer.

No one else was doing anything about him, were they? No one else was doing anything about any of them.

"Usually I cook everything fresh in the morning. I'm nervous about having any of the German food in the house overnight. That's what I always call it to myself: German food.

"I have a metal box with a lock. My cookie tin. Do you remember this cookie tin?" She picked it up from the table between us and turned it over in her hands. Shaped like a Christmas tree and painted with baubles. "You were with me when we bought it up in El Alto at the market. Once I began making the German food, I closed it with a padlock. To avoid any accidents. Only I had the key."

I found my voice. "I thought you did that to keep Vati out of the pancakes."

"I *do* do it to keep him out of the pancakes. As you know. There are many locked tins. But only this one ever has the German food." She paused, picked a bit of dough out from under a fingernail with shaking hands. When she looked up, her eyes were dark.

"Orly, I had to *do* something. It's changed everything for me, having a purpose. Taking action. I'm so tired of being hunted. All those men who went to war against the Nazis, they got to do something. They didn't just run away."

"Mutti —"

"No, let me finish or I'll never be able to say it all. This is my war, Orly. I'm fighting it a little later than the rest of the world, but it is my war."

She paused. "Don't think I haven't thought this through. I am not killing mere murderers. I am killing the men whose career of torture and genocide cast a vast shadow over my own small deeds." My mother's voice had so rarely had this unwavering certainty. She was not given to lengthy speeches. She was not given much to conversation at all. Not since I was ten.

"Tell me these men should not pay. Tell me the world is not a better place. Tell me whatever you like but it will not change the decisions I made."

She leaned back in her chair, like a lawyer who has finished presenting a case.

My mind scrambled for a foothold on her logic.

She leaned forward again. "I was careful, Liebling. I kept no records. Nothing on paper. But I marked on the wall with a pencil — just as I recorded your height as a child — the dates and initials, faint in the grey paint of the doorway to the pantry, where it was easy to explain away."

She smiled, maybe thinking of that distant doorway.

Then. "It is lucky also that Germans will go to any lengths for a taste of home."

For a long while we were silent. My mother leaned across the table and took my cold hands into hers. "Please don't hate me, Orlita. I cannot bring myself to believe you have a heart hard enough to hate me, even now. Your heart was always so elastic, so strong. Your heart that was formed here, that was made for this place. It is stronger than mine."

Nothing about me felt strong. Even the tiles beneath my chair tilted under me, like they could slide me off into air. I could no longer refuse to make a moral decision.

I tried to find words for what was coursing through me. My mother, whose voice had brought thousands of people to the edge of their seats, a murderer several times over. Searching for a persuasive argument, I stumbled upon an image. My mother, on her knees beside Elektra. I pressed her hands. "Mutti, remember Chrysothemis?"

"What?" It took her a minute to follow me so many years back.

"Can't you remember? How you explained her to me?"

"Chrysothemis." She said it softly, as if it were a foreign word.

"She was the only one to live, in the end. She was the only one to stay sane."

My mother looked at me, her face twisting unrecognizably. *"I am envious of your common sense, but I hate your cowardice."*

"That's *Elektra*. That's not who you were, who you are. You always said it was a story about the meaninglessness of vengeance."

She was still, head bowed, but only for a moment. "They killed us for nothing. I have reason to exterminate them."

Exterminate. That word they used for us. That word decided me.

I could have said: Why not simply report him and bring him to justice? But I knew the answer to that one. Report him to whom? We could not assume the Bolivians would care. Nor could we trust the international community. Those same countries that stood by clutching their borders closed around themselves, letting us die? Justice was slow when it came at all. And my mother had never been a particularly patient person.

So this was not the argument I made. There was one argument, and only one, that had a chance of working.

"Mutti. You must promise me to stop. Stop now and I will never breathe a word. I will take this to the grave." I took a breath. "Promise me, or I will tell my father."

FIFTH MOVEMENT:
OLD FRIENDS

Fifty-Seven

One afternoon at the movies, I caught sight of a familiar, stout figure with a bent nose and a scar on his lower lip. He was frowning into his palm, counting change onto the glass counter of the snack stand.

"Miguel!" I abandoned my two university friends to thread my way through the crowd toward him. Only after he had picked up his paper bag of puffed corn and turned toward the sound of his name did I realize that he wasn't alone. My step faltered. But of course he wasn't alone! I chided myself. No one went to the movies alone here. With him was a girl whose long hair hung loose about her waist, which I thought very daring and beautiful. Miguel's face opened when he saw me. He waved, spilling puffed corn out of his other hand. "Kantutita!" When he smiled, it sent a sharp-edged memory through me of my first days on this soil. His smile was the first life preserver thrown to me.

When we found our way to each other in the crowd, he introduced the woman. "Carla is in my department at university." Another female student! We were a distinct minority. She smiled and nodded, her hands too full of puffed corn to take mine.

"Mucho gusto."

"Your hair is different. Darker," he observed. "Like burned pumpkin."

"I feel like a burned pumpkin sometimes." When my skin had too much sun, I did indeed resemble a roasted vegetable. "Where are you at university?"

"San Andrés."

"I'm there, too!" This was hardly surprising, given the dearth of universities in La Paz. I had considered universities in Sucre or Cochabamba, but I worried about leaving my mother for so long. Love and guilt had tethered me to La Paz.

I hadn't even known Miguel was at university; I had hardly seen him since my eighteenth birthday. Our lives had diverged as we became involved with work and friends who lived closer, who were a natural part of our distinct communities. Seeing his face now, I thought how rarely I was this happy to see someone. He had just started classes, he said, studying physics and mathematics.

The lights flickered and the crowds surged past us. "We had better get to our seats," Miguel said, touching Carla's shoulder.

"Could we meet some afternoon?" I asked, suddenly unwilling to let him go, not caring if Carla found me forward or inappropriate. "Could we have coffee?"

"Why not?" He shrugged, as if it didn't really matter to him one way or another. I tried not to look hurt. "Come find me. I'm still living in the same place."

As he and Carla were pushed forward into the theater, I scanned the crowd for my friends. They had already gone in, but had saved a seat between them. "Where were you?"

"I found someone." I squeezed myself into the chair. "An old friend."

A few weeks later, Miguel and I found ourselves seated in front of tiny glasses of singani in the cavelike bar on calle Jaén where I had spent my eighteenth birthday. It was fitting, I thought, to be meeting my oldest friend in the oldest street in the city. I loved calle Jaén. It was prettier here than down where we lived, where new buildings seemed perpetually under construction. The ceiling of the bar arced low over our heads, its walls now painted with murals of angels and devils, of deadly sins. They were always changing.

"It's the foundation of life itself," he was saying about his studies in mathematics and physics. "The forces that propel us and explain the planets." At the word "propel" his exuberance got the better of him and he pushed one of the glasses too hard and fast across the table — an impromptu lesson in friction — spilling its sticky contents. I wasn't even sure he noticed. His face was incandescent as he spoke of his studies, of numbers and stars.

"Explain the planets," I echoed, dabbing at the spill with my napkin. "Sounds like a job for poets."

I hadn't imagined Miguel as a scholar of the skies. I hadn't imagined him as a scholar at all, I realized to my shame, though I never doubted his intelligence. Hadn't he taught me everything I knew about this country? He had worked in textiles all through secondary school, spending long hours in the factory to earn his university fees.

"Are you suggesting you could do it better?" He grinned at me and I flushed.

"I wouldn't say I'm a poet. Not yet, anyway. I'm not even sure I want to be one." It seemed a too-lofty claim. But I couldn't imagine a life without writing them, just as

I couldn't imagine a life without music, without plucking tunes from the thin air. Poems, it occurred to me, could easily become songs.

"And there is the inconvenient fact that you have never lived on another planet."

I laughed. I had forgotten how easy it was with him. "Which makes it rather hard for me to describe one."

He took a sip from one of the four glasses between us and made a face. "I'm not sure this one is my favorite." He passed me the glass of greenish liquid. The bar made its own singani, as well as absinthe and coca liqueur.

"I thought you liked coca."

"Not sweet like that. Just in tea or to chew."

I sipped it and made a similar face. "Home distilled or not home distilled, this is horrible. Like something my mother gives me for a cough." I set it down and took a sip of the clear singani. I had always liked singani, the smooth grape liquor with only a hint of sweetness. It was better straight than in the chuflays — singani with ginger ale — many of the bars and hotels offered. "This is nice."

"Entonces, how is your family? Your mother still cooking for her shop?" My body tightened. But no, of course he couldn't know.

I nodded. "I think she'd crumble without it."

"Good. I always loved that apple thing she made, with the flat pastry."

"Strudel."

"Strudel." He laughed at the way the word emerged from his mouth, twisted toward Spanish. He finished the singani. "I'll get another. Your dad is still playing in the new orchestra, no?"

"Almost all the time, though he plays with Vico and Daniel too. And me! And he still takes students. The orchestra doesn't earn anyone any money." I sipped at the absinthe, rolled its anise around my tongue. "He's just happy to be playing with other musicians again." My father could have taken on more students, could have started a school, could have done so much more had he considered financial gain a goal. But he preferred to reserve as many hours of the day as possible for playing music with his friends, for rehearsing with me and Vico, or just listening as I plucked my charango.

"Does he want to go back to Austria? I assume that is possible now?"

I shook my head. "I don't think Austria is possible for any of us." When I looked up at him, there was understanding in his eyes. "Austria is like another planet now."

He smiled, gently, faintly. "So there, you have been to one then."

Later that night, after we left the bar and had begun to stumble down the cobblestone street toward our homes, he took my hand. I stopped walking. And in the thinnest air of the oldest street in the highest city, my arms trembling with the cold or something stranger, I kissed him.

I had never dreamed about boys. I had tried not to dream at all, afraid of what my unconstrained self might do with girls in the small hours of the morning. Though it wasn't girls in general that lured me out of myself, just two of them. Just as Miguel was the only boy. My school friends had fallen in love regularly and almost indiscriminately. I found it alternately amusing and somewhat horrifying to observe the ways in which they tied themselves in knots for lesser beings. I was relieved to have avoided the absurdity of falling in love.

Yet now that something inside me was beginning to uncurl, I felt a sense of peace rather than anxiety. Miguel, to me, was more home than man.

The next morning the peaceful feeling had

faded. Maybe I was ruining things with Miguel. I didn't know if kissing meant he was my boyfriend, or if it was the singani. I didn't know if I wanted a boyfriend. I got up, put on a dress and shoes, and ran all the way to Miguel's house. He didn't play thunka near his doorstep anymore. He didn't kick balls up the street. I knocked and his sister Celia answered the door. "Orlita!" she said, smiling. "It's been a long time." Then, calling back into the apartment, "Miguel! Orlita está aqui!" He came to the door still tucking a shirt into his trousers. "Did something happen?" His face creased with worry.

I felt stupid. "No. Yes. I . . . Come outside?"

"Let me get my shoes."

Together we walked toward Plaza Sucre. I had forgotten a hat and the sun burned the part in my hair. "I don't know what I want to say. I only want to know that it was all right. That we did the right thing last night. I've never —"

Miguel laughed, a gentle, kind, delighted laugh that offered reassurance even before he spoke. "Do you know how long I've been waiting for you to kiss me, Orlita?" Stopping, he turned and took my hands. To my enormous relief, I found that I wanted to kiss him again.

"But you have Carla and —"

"Carla's a friend. I can talk with her about science. She's not my girlfriend."

"Really not?" I felt eleven years old, as if I had once again arrived in a new country.

"Really not. I had a girlfriend named Angela, but we broke up a few months ago."

Still something hummed in me, something anxious and high. "So what happens now?"

"Whatever we want to happen."

"But. Bueno. Pero . . ."

"What is it?"

"I've never had a novio."

"Never?"

"Never. So I don't really know how —"

"Kantuta! You don't know how to be with me? The same way you have always been with me."

"Don't laugh at me."

"I promise I'm not." But his eyes were mirthful. "If you want rules, here are some rules. First, we should go to the cinema together. Then we should go for a walk down the paseo del Prado. Then perhaps you will invite me home to meet your parents."

"Miguel! You're laughing at me!" I whacked him on the shoulder.

"There is the Orly I know. Come on, let's

get an api and llaucha. I just woke up and I'm starving."

Now it was Miguel who came to our house to do homework with me, although he spent just as much time studying with students in his department. What surprised me the most was how ordinary everything felt, how ordinary he felt. That he had slid into a space that had been reserved for him all along.

At the same time, we were so young. I wasn't ready for too much. For me, this was all a beginning.

Partly to escape the claustrophobia of our homes, partly because sitting in a bar wasn't much less claustrophobic, Miguel and I began to walk. Long walks, from one end of the city to the other. Walks that would take us from lunch to supper on Sundays. Or from dawn until the start of our first classes. Walks that took us farther and farther past the edges of the city, to where the houses thinned and the land opened. We walked past where the tram ended in Obrajes. We walked all the way up to El Alto. We walked up the dirt roads that led toward La Cumbre, the highest point before the road descended to Coroico.

Sometimes we talked and sometimes we

walked in silence. Miguel talked about his
sisters, what he wanted for them. Nice
husbands, steady work. He told me about
his father. It astonished me how little I knew
about his family after living in the same
house for so many years. But then, we had
spent so much time in the present. The two
youngest, Ema and Nina, were going to
dance in Carnival this year. In our first
years, we had gathered to watch the Bolivians dance through the streets, but I did not
like the crowds. There were too many delirious bodies falling toward me, too many
unrecognizable faces. I didn't like the
oversize, garishly painted eyes of the masks,
their unchanging expressions. I didn't like
to get wet when the celebrants splashed
each other with water. Parades and crowds
reminded me of other parades in other
countries. Now during Carnival, I stayed
home.

Celia, the oldest and Miguel's favorite,
wanted to move to Coroico to grow coffee.
They still had relatives there. She preferred
the semitropical jungles to La Paz. But his
mother didn't like the thought of her traveling on the road that had killed their father.
She didn't like the thought of her daughter
falling in love and settling down there.

"How did your parents ever meet?" Given

543

the divisions between the worlds of the Spanish descendants and the Indians, it was an unlikely pairing.

"My father moved from Achacachi, near the lake, to Coroico when he was young, taking his parents and grandparents with him. They had bad crops for many seasons and my father thought the land was cursed, that they should start again. There were already Aymara near Coroico.

"My grandfather — my mother's father — was a businessman, a trader. He grew up in La Paz and traveled to Coroico to find produce to sell. He wasn't in the tin business yet. My father sold him fruit. Sometimes he came to La Paz himself to make deliveries. That's where he met my mother. My mother was still very young when she met my father."

We were walking along the river toward a rocky canyon below the city, a fantastical labyrinth of twisty stone spires that was one of Miguel's favorite places. The day was dry and hot, our feet kicking up clouds of dust. I kept my hat pulled low on my forehead.

"How old was she?"

"You know we don't keep track of years like you do. Maybe fifteen, maybe older." Younger than we were.

"My grandfather was furious. He didn't

544

want her to marry an Indian. When she ran away to marry my father my grandfather stopped speaking to her for a while." He stopped to run his fingertips over the quills of a cactus. They were the only vegetation around.

"And then you came back to La Paz when your father died."

He nodded, resuming his brisk pace. "And we needed money — even traders don't make very much here — and so we took you in."

"And Mathilde and Fredi."

"Yes. We found the Europeans were good about paying on time."

"Did my parents always pay on time?"

"I think so, after the first couple of months when your parents didn't have work yet."

"But you don't have boarders now." Miguel had moved into our old rooms, and Celia, Nina, and Ema shared Mathilde and Fredi's room. His two older brothers had moved to the growing city of El Alto and were working in construction.

"I still have some work at the textile factory, it doesn't pay badly. Watch your step here."

We reached the entrance to the maze of paths, and I marveled anew at the jagged pillars all around us, like the dripped turrets of a child's sandcastle.

"What made these things?" I brushed my fingers against the crumbling towers.

"Water. Wind. A lot of time." He reached back a hand to help me up a rocky section. "And the rock is soft. A mixture of rock and clay."

"It's like another country. The surface of another planet. Or the moon."

"That's why I like it. I would like to spend time on other planets." He glanced up at the sky, as if to see if the planets were listening. All we could see above us was uninterrupted blue.

"I guess we're closer to them than most people."

"I can almost touch Mars from the window of my laboratory."

I smiled, placing my feet in the wider prints his made in the dust. "That must be alarming for the Martians."

"Oh no, we're friends now. They shoot me down notes through an enormous straw. Terrible handwriting. Curious people; they always want to know more about our food."

"They don't have quinoa?" I had developed an affection for the grain, which grew little tails when you cooked it. Sometimes my mother made a pudding of it with cinnamon, sugar, milk, and cut-up apples.

"Nada de quinoa, nada de api, nada de singani. It's a terrible life. I feel sad for them."

"Do you shoot them notes back?"

"When I have time. Mostly I shoot them seeds to plant. Amaranth, quinoa, rice." We paused at a high point in the path to gaze around us at the vast field of rocky needles pointing toward the cosmos.

"How generous of you."

"I am a generous man."

"What if they don't grow on Martian soil?"

"I'll invite them down to live with us. We have a long history of opening our homes to immigrants."

Fifty-Eight

Miguel and I had been together for more than a year when I found the book. It was June 21, 1948, almost closing time, and I was the last person in the shop. I was tired. It was the first day of the winter solstice and the Aymara New Year, and Miguel and I had met before dawn to greet the first rays of the sun from the cliffs above the city. Dawn was my favorite time, the mountains around us glowing rosy and gold. The light promising that everything was still before us.

When we stood to walk back down to the city, I slipped a hand into the small leather pouch I had brought with me and curled my fingers around a pointy wooden object. "I've been waiting for the right time." When Miguel looked at me, I extended my hand, the tiny painted sun balanced on my palm. He paused in the road to take it from me and turn it in his hands. "Look," he said, gesturing to the rising orb we had just greeted. "It's already working."

The memory of his face that morning kept me warm as I worked. Several crates of books had arrived from Europe and I was shelving them by language. Most of the books in Arbres Morts were in Spanish, but we had a small collection of books in German and English. I always felt anxious opening the German books, afraid of the stories I would find. Wondering what kind of Austrians or Germans had written them, what new horrors the histories and memoirs might hold.

This day, I was hurrying to shelve the last few books so I could lock up the store and meet Miguel for a walk before dinner when I found it at the bottom of the crate. Gold embossed letters on the brown leather cover: *Geschichten von Friedenglückhasenland.* Stories of Friedenglückhasenland. I closed my eyes and read it again. It was still there. It still said the same thing, just above the image of a little gold rabbit. My hands shaking, I reached for the book, my legs folding underneath me. Sitting there on the floor, I examined the cover more closely. There it was, her name in small letters below the title. Anneliese Meier. She was alive. She had the same name. She had written our stories. With thick and clumsy fingers I fumbled to open the book and turn its pages. My thoughts raced around my skull like frantic mice, skittering into each other. The book fell open on my lap to the dedication: *For Orlanthe, cocreator of this land and coauthor of its stories. She lives there with me always.*

For a long time I could not move. Then I lay down on my back on the hard wood floor and let the tears run through me. She hadn't forgotten me. She hadn't forgotten me. I sat up again then, so abruptly I was dizzy, and searched through the pages for something about her. Something that might tell me where she was. There it was, at the very end. *Anneliese Meier makes her home in the South of France. This is her first book.*

France! She was in France! Where Willi was. She had probably never received my letter. I wondered when she left Austria, why she was in France. The two people I loved had both ended up there. Had they known of each other's presence in the country? Could they even have met? No, then she would know I was alive, know where I was. She can't have met him.

The bell on the door tinkled. "Kantuta?" Miguel stepped into the shop and closed the door behind him.

I had a strange feeling in my stomach, as if I had been caught doing something illicit.

"Miguelito," I said weakly. "Sit down with me. I have a story for you."

"Is it happy or sad?"

"It's both." I patted the floorboard next to me.

While I had mentioned Anneliese before, I now unfolded our friendship from the beginning, all the way through her mother shoving me into the street, and our final meeting just before I left. "I wrote to her after the war but I never heard anything. I have stacks of letters for her in my room. She never wrote."

Miguel sat leaning against the bookcase, his shoulder against mine, his legs stretched out in front of him, ankles crossed. He was quiet, listening without interrupting me until my words stuttered to a stop. "There is a reason you are telling me this story now?"

"Look what I just found." I held out the book, gold letters up. He took it between his hands and stared at it for a moment. Then it registered. "Orlita, your friend's alive! This is fantastic. Querida, I'm so glad." He set the book down to kiss me and then picked it up again, turned the pages. "What kind of book is it? This is German?"

I nodded and ran a fingertip over the title. "Stories of our country, the one we created."

"Does that mean she is still in Austria?"

"The book says she lives in the South of France, not even the name of her village."

"Will you write to her?"

"How?" I was still too giddy to put my thoughts in order.

He studied the first few pages. "Is this the name of the publisher? Can you write to her there?"

That night I took the book home and read every page before sleeping. I didn't tell my parents. I didn't want to share it yet. Nearly all of the stories were familiar, but a few she must have dreamed up after me. She had set them all in a frame, the story of a little red-haired Jewish girl frightened by the Nazis who begs her parents for stories to distract her from the terror and monotony of their lives in hiding. The parents take turns telling the stories, and in the end the little girl and her parents escape abroad. I recognized our bunnies, my Lebkuchen and her Marmalade. I recognized Krokodilland and Katzenland. I recognized the Carrot-mobiles. I recognized the generosity and spirit of my Ana.

My Ana. Could I still claim her? Was I still

hers? I wondered if we could belong to each other again, and if I could still belong to Miguel. I wondered if a heart could beat for several people at once.

When I had turned the final page, I tucked the book under my pillow and lay awake until all the baby stars over Illimani disappeared.

The next day after classes I hurried home to pick up my stack of letters, scraps of paper containing nearly a decade of my life, and sealed them into a large envelope. For a moment, I sat on Willi's bed, my bed, holding them on my lap. Here were my stories of arrival and disorientation, of thunka with Miguel, of Rachel's illness and Nayra's lake. Here were my stories of Alasitas and my father's orchestra and my mother's grief. Here was — almost — everything. I had lived with them for so long it tore at me to send them away. These were my whole Bolivian life. I counted out coins for postage; it would be the most expensive letter I had ever sent. In my neatest hand, I printed the address of the publisher, copying it from the title page of the book. It interested me that her publisher was Austrian although she lived in France. Maybe she wrote only in German.

I carried the letters up to the post office myself, and kissed the bundle before handing it to the clerk.

FIFTY-NINE

A letter from Anneliese arrived just two months later. *Forgive me if these pages are still damp,* she wrote. *I cannot write you without crying. When my publisher forwarded me your letters — all of your lovely, Orly-like letters! — I didn't sleep for days. I couldn't stop reading, could not tear myself away from your life. Your life! Your dear life. I don't think I have ever been as grateful for anything as I was for those letters. For your continued existence. I never let myself imagine that you were dead, but I had imagined that you had forgotten. Forgive me! It was my own weakness and not any suspicion of your character that is to blame. There is so much I will never get it all down. The only way for us to say all we need to is to see each other. I will not believe your hands, your face, your hair survived until I touch them. Can you understand? From everything you wrote, I don't think you want to return to Vienna. Nor do I. Austria does not deserve you. But I wonder if you might come to France? Though France's hands are bloody too. No, I think it is better that I come to you. You have done too much traveling already. I will come to you, Orly! I am impatient, but it can't be soon, as I will need to save. Now that I know what I need the money for I will become the most penny-pinching woman in all of France! For I must see your dear face once more.*

That was the beginning. Once I received that letter I wrote her nearly every week. She wrote me as often, always promising to come soon. But money was elusive. The country was still reeling. Passage to South America cost more than her writing could earn, and her small village offered few opportunities to supplement her writing income. A friend with a gallery had offered her some work writing exhibit copy. Still, the salary was paltry. Had I had enough money of my own, I might have been tempted to travel to France, as much to see where Willi died, to imagine his life, as to see Anneliese. I should have liked to know where to imagine him.

But in my family, we had never worked for the sole purpose of making money. We worked to create what it could not buy.

SIXTY

I thought of Nayra and her weaving as Miguel and I strolled the aisles of Alasitas after a summer rain. Nayra and her tiny loom, her dreams of threading constellations into cloth. It had been hard to see her during the past year, preoccupied as I was with school and Miguel. Yet in a way she was responsible for both of these things. On holidays and weekends when Miguel was busy in the observatory or on the football field, I sat with her at the market. She had a loom of her own, one of the backstrap looms like her miniature (gracias, Ekeko), and during slow times she would work. I just watched her, admiring the dexterity of her fingers. She was still frustrated with the shapes and patterns that emerged, though to me they seemed miraculous. They even looked a little bit like stars, with their dozen points. Someday I will weave one of our stories, she had promised me. Someday.

We walked past an array of tiny loaves of bread and pea-size pastries. My heart skipped. It had been a couple of years since my mother had made her promise. There were moments I almost told Miguel about it, told him all that she had done. I had no one else to tell; I wanted help carrying her secret. That secret also made me doubt Miguel's expressions of affection. Could genuine love be possible without knowledge, without accepting the dark I harbored? But I could not do it, could not place that guilt on his blameless shoulders. Nor had I ever told him the entire truth about Anneliese, about Rachel. Some truths are not worth the cost of telling.

I dropped Miguel's hand to examine the tiny boxes of oats, pasta, the little bags of flour. I never got tired of Alasitas, of admiring the craftsmanship of these tiny things. I bought a newspaper the size of my palm for my father, wondering what my mother might desire in the coming year. No, I knew what she desired. I knew I would never bring her anything approaching it. Besides, she had always rejected the premise of Alasitas as superstition and fruitless yearning. I would not buy her a gift.

Strange that some part of me still believed in the magic of Alasitas, despite the failure of Ekeko to give me back my brother.

"Mi kantuta." Miguel reappeared and took my arm.

"Would you like a set of tools? A new typewriter? A suitcase full of money?" The tiny notes were so real looking.

"I'd like to discover a new planet and have it named after me. You?"

I picked up a tiny motorbike. "I already have a charango. I almost have a university degree. I'm not sure what else I need. I don't suppose I could purchase a poetic voice?"

"Is there really nothing else?" There was a strange note of urgency in his voice. "Orlita —"

"Sí?" I imagined how a motorbike would fare on the Bolivian roads.

He thrust his hand into his front pocket as if to retrieve something, but hesitated.

"Nothing. Forget it."

I set down the motorbike. We walked on. The rain began again.

"It's just, what do you want out of your life? What do you want it to be?" He said it so earnestly that I couldn't respond with a joke.

"Haven't we already discussed this for forever?"

"Not quite for forever. And people change

559

their minds. I don't assume you will stay the same."

"Gracias."

"De nada."

"I don't want to work in someone else's store forever. I love the shop but — I would like to sing poems with my charango. Maybe finish the stories I wrote with Nayra. Maybe turn them into songs." I stopped and turned to face him, raindrops running through my hair and down the collar of my dress. "It doesn't matter where. At home or sitting outside in the mountains or onstage . . ." That was a new thought. But I enjoyed my occasional performances with Vico and my father. "I realize I will have to find something else to do to make money." I had another idea, something that had never occurred to me. "I could open my own bookstore."

"And what else?"

"That's not enough? I suppose I would eventually like a place to live on my own."

"On your own?" Miguel sounded surprised. In Bolivia everyone lived with their parents until they were married.

"I just want to see what it's like."

"Why?"

I shrugged. "Curiosity? Maybe to see if I can do it. Come on, I'm getting soaked."

We picked our way across the muddy ground to one of the food booths. Sitting at one of the round tables with small cups of coffee, we spread out our purchases before us. Miguel had bought a little black telescope, a model of the planets, and a tiny six-pack of beer. I had bought only a tiny music stand.

"You need to ask Ekeko for beer?" I smiled at Miguel. "I'll buy you the beer. Save your wishing for something bigger. And are you hoping that all the planets are actually going to land on your doorstep?"

Miguel laughed, tipping back in his chair. "Wouldn't that be something to see though? Jupiter balanced on the top of the Andes?"

"All nine of them, all around us."

"Pretty. But we'd probably get tired of them blocking the view."

I nodded. "It's not like these mountains need decorating." I took a sip of my Nescafé. (I was not as discriminating as my mother about coffee. I had left Austria too young.) "What do you want your life to be?"

Miguel looked down at the table and picked up my hand. "I want to be near my mother and my sisters, always. I want to understand the sky better. Maybe someday, if I keep going to school, I could teach physics. Or astronomy."

"And what else?"

He began fiddling with something in his pocket again. "I realize I shouldn't have bought it before talking to you, but you don't have to accept it." He drew his hand out of his pocket, clutching a miniature and quite crumpled document. Carefully, he spread it out before me, turning it around so I could read it.

Across the top, in careful calligraphy, were the words "Certificado de Matrimonio."

My breath got caught in my lungs. I looked up at him. "Miguel, I —"

He nodded sadly. "I know. You want to live alone."

"Yes, but that isn't what I was going to say."

He waited.

"Miguel, I'm Jewish."

"And?"

"And I am not going to convert to Catholicism. I am not a religious Jew, but I am still a Jew." I felt far surer about the things I did not believe than about the things I did.

He nodded. "Okay."

"Okay what?"

"You can stay a Jew. I'm only really half Catholic after all, remember?" He smiled. "I'm also half witch."

"I don't mind whatever you are, as long

as I can be what I am."

"Here I was, worrying that you would say you didn't love me, and your objection is my religion. I feel strangely relieved."

"It's not insignificant. My religion got me sent into exile. My religion lost me most of my family. My religion landed me here."

"For that last, I am thankful. I love any religion that brought you to me. But what does that mean for our children?"

I was not accustomed to this earnestness from Miguel.

"We're already having children? We just started this conversation!"

He laughed. "Orlita, I've been having it in my head for years. Though it wasn't as interesting without you."

"Well, just to keep things interesting, our children would be Jewish, according to Jewish law."

"They would?" He thought for a moment. "And you obey these laws even when you are not religious?"

"I don't know. It hasn't ever come up. Not this particular law. I guess I am not sure what it would mean for me to raise Jewish children. I need to think about it." I imagined a miniature Miguel in a yarmulke and smiled. "I would want them to know their history. I would want them to light candles sometimes."

"I always thought your Shabbat was a very rational way to spend a Friday night."

I thought for a moment. "Miguel, what are your actual beliefs?"

He leaned back in his chair again and looked up at the sky beyond the canopy of the food stall. "I believe there is a God. I believe in Mother Nature. I believe in gravity and orbits and mysteries. I believe God is in many places."

I drew a deep breath. Marrying Miguel would mean closing the door to Anneliese before she even got here. Closing the door to possibility. I did not want to be rushed. "It's not that I doubt my feelings for you. But I want to talk about this for longer."

"About the children part, or the marrying me part?"

"Both."

Miguel put the certificate back in his pocket.

"That wasn't a no," I clarified. "That was a not yet."

"I know," he said. "But you can't have it until you're sure."

I waited two years for Anneliese. For a brief period, I thought it might be possible to have everything I ever wanted. But I did

564

not think it through. How she might have changed. How my feelings for her might have changed. Whether she could be happy here. Whether I could ever return to Europe. Whether I could give up the hope of a child. Eventually, I realized that Anneliese might never arrive. That she might not actually want to arrive or be able to make the journey. That I might not like who she had become. I could no longer put my life on hold for an insubstantial dream. This fantasy of a life with a woman. With this particular woman. It was also becoming impossible to imagine life without Miguel.

I lived alone for two years, during my last year of university and the year afterward, writing and working on plans for the book-store, plans that blazed brightly once conceived. Miguel visited often, to spend the evening studying at my kitchen table while I wrote or played music or tried to figure out how to craft a business plan. I realized quickly that I actually didn't want to do bookkeeping or accounts. I really just wanted to talk with people about books. At some point I would have to find a partner. And a location. And money. The bookstore was a very long-term plan.

As was Miguel.

But he was growing restless. I told myself

to be content with the knowledge that Anneliese was alive. That she loved me still. That is more than most people I knew ever had.

We married in December — a lucky month for weddings, Miguel said — under a chuppah in my parents' garden. To keep rain away, we placed eggs in each corner of the flower beds. It was 1951. I was only twenty-three, yet I had already lived two whole lives.

We poured drops of singani into the earth of my parents' garden, a tribute to Pachamama. To the shock of both Señora Torres and my parents, we included a priest, who offered a marriage prayer, and a rabbi, who blessed our cup of wine. We also included an amauta, who spoke prayers to Pachamama in Aymara. (Any other god we ought to cover? Miguel commented as we reviewed the plans.) My father played with his string quintet; my mother made the cake (with my close supervision). I wore a white cotton dress with a wide green sash. Together, Miguel and I crushed the napkin-wrapped glass under our feet. I had thought for a long time about the wisdom of including this element. The breaking of glass carried weight for my family, carried pain. "But with this act, you can transform that sound for yourself, into something joyful," said my father, who knew more about sound and its meanings than anyone. While Miguel had been willing to crush the glass alone, I felt strongly that a Jewish foot should participate, even if it was female. As the cries of "Mazel Tov" and "Felicidades" broke out around us and I lifted my foot from the shards of crystal, I looked over at my parents. Tears ran down my mother's cheeks, but my father nodded at me, and smiled.

As a wedding gift, my parents had bought us a week at a hotel in Cochabamba, where I had never been. While it was still high, it was not nearly as high as La Paz, and I marveled at the softness of the air, at how easy it was to stroll the relatively level streets of the city. On our wedding night, we were gentle with each other at first. We took our time learning the geography of each other's bodies, despite our growing impatience. We had known each other so long, but there were still so many mysteries. The sex itself did not hurt; on the contrary, I wanted to start again as soon as it was over. How had we waited this long? Miguel eventually drifted off, exhausted, but I felt too alive to ever sleep again. When my thrashing legs accidentally kicked him, he woke and put a hand on my hip. "Are you all right? Can I help?"

"Yes," I said. "You could sing to me."

And Miguel opened his mouth and he sang. He sang a low, summoning song with words I did not know. An Aymara song. A song that drew before my eyes the landscape of the Andes, a song that summoned the sun or put it to bed. I had never heard Miguel sing. His voice was rough and kind. His voice held me. Before he reached the end, I was asleep.

We fought our way through those first few years, each of us clearing a place for ourselves in the marriage. Staking our ground. I hated cooking and Miguel did not know how to cook. I liked to be up early and he slept late. I didn't know how to make the right foods. He didn't know how to wash his clothing. He had had a mother who kept a tidy house; I left dishes in the basin for an entire day if I was in the middle of a poem or reading a good book. These domestic details required adjustment for both of us, required concessions and compromise. As they do for us all. Complicating matters was the fact that Miguel wanted a child right away, while I wanted to wait, to settle into ourselves and our lives. A child would bring further reshufflings and negotiations. I wanted there to be space between changes.

Yet it never occurred to us to part. This fighting was simply a process to be gotten through in order to figure out how to live and change together. A way for us to sort out what was important to us, what we could live with. A way to make our boundaries and priorities clear.

When Isidora was eventually born, her existence drew everything else into place.

SIXTY-ONE

I hadn't only married Miguel, I had married all of it — the mountains, the chaos, the waves of political unrest. We had barely set our feet over the threshold of our new apartment on calle Nicaragua in Miraflores when rumors of revolution reached our ears.

I sat tearing apart a marraqueta in early April, puzzling over the day's edition of *El Diario.*

"Don't expect to gain any clarity in those pages," said Miguel.

I sighed, and closed the paper. "I want to understand."

"I know. You understand a little already. You know that most Aymara, most Bolivians, do not have the right to vote. Most do not own the land they work. Something like six percent of the landowners own ninety-two percent of the land. Ninety-two percent! Did you know that? All the mines. Most of the farms. What have they left for the remaining ninety-four percent of us? Outside of the city, almost no one owns the land. They work all their lives to have nothing. Their land was stolen."

I nodded slowly, thinking about Nayra. Thinking about what I knew about losing land, losing a country.

"The MNR wants to change that, to give that land back to the people. To take the mines away from foreign hands." Miguel supported the Movimiento Nacionalista Revolucionario, the political party whose candidate, Víctor Paz Estenssoro, had won the presidential election in 1951 while in exile in Argentina, but was prevented from taking office by a military junta. "We want to give the vote to everyone."

"I don't know how anyone can argue against that."

"But they do. There is going to be violence, Orlita, but we are going to own this country again."

His predictions came true on April 9, 1952, when the revolutionaries surged from across the country. The church bells warned us first. They were always ringing, to announce the demise of a government, the rise of a new one. They rang to say it was time to pay taxes to a different man, to march in a new army, to fall in step with a new ruling party. The Bolivian government was overthrown with alarming regularity. Every time I heard those bells, my skin tingled with fear.

The previous government had given power to the military rather than cede it to MNR. Now, MNR revolutionaries marched to wrest control from the military. They blocked the roads; they fired rifles and ignited sticks of dynamite. They carried their dead home on their backs. There were explosions and gunshots in the streets. For three days they fought; for three days I kept the doors and windows locked.

Miguel had wanted to join the fighting. "I need to be part of this, Orlita. It's my country."

"You cannot be part of it if you are dead. How many people do I have left, Miguel? You want to take one more away?" A terrified fury rose in me. "I didn't marry you to endure one more heartbreak. I didn't marry you to grieve again. I married you because you gave me hope for happiness. You give me hope, Miguel. Does that mean nothing?" To underscore my final word, I threw the iron pan in which I had cooked his eggs across the kitchen floor, narrowly missing his feet.

When Juan Lechín Oquendo, leader of the

federation of tin miners' unions and Hernán Siles Suazo, vice-presidential running mate of Paz Estenssoro, led the revolutionaries to victory, Miguel stayed home. Even he was amazed by reports of the strength of the crowds, swollen by miners, campesinos, and government soldiers who changed sides, indicating their change of heart by reversing the hats on their heads.

When it was all over and thousands had died, the man the revolutionaries chose to install as president was Paz Estenssoro, who had won the vote the year before. A few months later, Bolivia had universal suffrage. Workers gained the right to organize. A few years after that, amazingly, nearly half of rural families owned the land they worked. The mines were nationalized, a significant step in Bolivia's quest to free itself from foreign marauders, although this triumph was complicated by the fact that much of the technical expertise needed in the mines left with the foreign engineers. Still, Bolivians were at least free to make their own mistakes.

Things would change again, I knew. Political tides in the Andes turned with the moon. But this was significant; this was a start. Nayra would be able to wander her city freely. She could cast a vote. Her government might even someday treat her like a human being.

SIXTY-TWO

My mother and I walked to the movies one Sunday morning in April 1953. It was a long walk for my mother, but she didn't complain. We went once or twice a month now, often with Miguel and my father. Miguel had a new teaching job at the university and I continued to work at Arbres Morts. We could afford the movies.

My mother was cross because a new law had been passed banning hats in the theaters, so that no one had to struggle to see over them. Having been regularly stuck behind extravagant millinery confections, I thought this was a marvelous law, but my mother hated to be bareheaded.

This particular Sunday we were watching *Othello.* "Demand me nothing," spat Iago. "What you know, you know. / From this time forth I never will speak word." As Orson Welles gathered himself to respond, my mother happened to glance back toward the door. I heard her inhale, felt her hand on my forearm, her nails in my skin. She looked back again, causing her hat to slide from her knees to the floor. "Orly," she whispered. "Get up." I knew better than to argue. Dismayed at having to miss the rest of the film, I reluctantly followed her up the aisle.

Outside she turned to me in the blaze of light. "Did you see who that was behind us? Did you see that man?"

"What man?" I put my hands up to shield my eyes. My eyeballs burned if I stayed out too long or forgot my hat. Outside, hats were useful.

"Behind us. He was behind us. The short man, with the scar on his right cheek." My mother's hand trembled on my arm.

I shook my head. I hadn't noticed anyone. We had arrived after the theater had darkened and slid into the only free seats on an aisle.

"Do you know who that man was?"

I shook my head again.

"That was Klaus Barbie, Orly. *Klaus Barbie.*"

Fear crept up my spine. We all knew who Klaus Barbie was. We knew all the facts and infinite rumors. We knew that although France had sentenced him to death, he remained free, living under an assumed name in Bolivia. We had heard he was working with the Americans. We had heard he was assisting the Bolivian military with interrogations. We heard constant claims of sightings. Someone had seen him buying a carpet at the market, someone had seen him entering the Ministry of Foreign Affairs.

"Isn't he in Coroico?"

"That's what I heard. He could just be visiting."

How was it possible that the man said to have tortured French Resistance leader Jean Moulin and ordered the murder of the children of Izieu could be sitting behind us in a movie theater in La Paz?

Yet I believed my mother. So many Nazis had already been made welcome in Bolivia. Why not one of the worst?

My mother pulled me down the street with her, my shoes catching on the stones. I would have fallen were she not holding me so tightly.

"Are you sure?" My skin prickled with sweat in the midday sun.

"His photo has been in the papers. I think I would recognize someone who murdered so many thousands of us."

"Why is he allowed to walk around?" Always we had the same questions. I wanted to go back into the movie theater and strangle him with my bare hands and I wanted to run as fast and as far as I could, all at the same time.

"I don't know." My mother slowed her pace. "Because Bolivia leaves everyone alone, I guess. Like it did with us. Like it has done with the others here." Her voice was bitter. "How can more still be coming? How many more will they take?"

A shot of alarm ran through me. "Don't even think about it, Mutti. You promised."

She didn't look at me, her lips pressed tightly together.

"You can't."

"*Barbie,* Orlita. Who was running the Gestapo in Lyon, near Izieu. Where your brother —"

"I know." I did want him gone. I wanted all of them gone. And no matter how I might resist her methods, I could not wish my mother's victims back to life.

I looked over at her, her face disfigured by rage. "I'm not changing my mind."

We learned more about what he was doing in Bolivia only decades later, in bits and pieces. Using the name Klaus Altmann, Barbie ran shipping and lumber businesses with a Jewish partner and was made a lieutenant colonel. In the service of more than one Bolivian regime, he tortured and inter-rogated alleged Communists, traded arms, and mingled with drug lords. He had friends in high places. Which is another piece of information I can never absorb. Why, how, could anyone befriend such a man? Bolivia had been at war with him, with his country. How little regard must a person have for his soul — let alone anyone else's — to take this demon into his employ.

It wasn't only Bolivia, of course. The U.S. intelligence services had also recruited him.

These governments knew about the children of Izieu. They knew of his relentless hunt for Jean Moulin, hero of the French Resistance. They knew of his torture and murder of more than twenty-five thousand of us. *They knew.* And *they let him live.*

■ ■ ■ ■ ■

SIXTH MOVEMENT: NEW LIFE

■ ■ ■ ■ ■

SIXTY-THREE

January 1963

Isidora and I were in the front garden watering the roses when she came. It was just before sunset, the air already cool. Carefully, Isidora had tipped the wine bottle we kept on the front steps for just this purpose, drenching the roots of each plant. She was five then, obsessed with saving the lives of plants and small animals everywhere. It was a never-ending job. The shelves of her room were lined with glass jars of insects, potted herbs, piles of odd-shaped stones, and a few fish darting around a glass bowl. These two roses were hers, a gift for her last birthday. I had never been very good at growing things, but Miguel made flowers stand upright and bloom just by looking at them.

A small Bolivian girl stopped in the street to watch her, clutching the hand of an older boy. She looked curiously at Isidora, at the bottle in her chubby fist. "Do you always feed them wine?"

"Yes," said Isidora solemnly. "They are *very* fancy roses." I wondered for a moment if she thought this was true, if I had neglected to explain to her that I refilled the wine bottle with water each morning. But then she turned to me and grinned, mischief darting in her eyes.

The girl's brother tugged her hand, but she resisted, wanting to know more about our fancy flowers. As he pulled her along, she began to cry. "Las flores, las flores!"

That's when an older girl paused in front of our house. She wore jeans and a thick green sweater, her dark hair pulled back in a ponytail. Her skin was very pale, her thick brows drawn together in the middle of her forehead, her eyes somehow familiar. She looked like a tourist, but this wasn't that kind of neighborhood. Miguel and I had moved farther downhill, to the bucolic neighborhood of Obrajes. There was more air here, more space for Isidora to stretch her legs. Travelers usually stayed up in the city, where all of the cheap hotels were. Our neighborhood was almost exclusively residential. After unbuckling a waist strap, she shrugged off an oversized backpack and set it on the street in front of her. "Frau Zingel?"

The German word, even spoken with an odd French accent, sent a bolt of electric surprise humming through me. And something like fear. But surely there was nothing to fear from this small girl? I shook my head to clear it of suspicion. "Sí?"

"I'm sorry," she began in English. "I don't know too much Spanish. Do you speak French?"

"Only a little. Do you speak German?"

"A little. Maybe English is best?"

"Sí, English." We had all wanted to learn English in secondary school, just in case someday we won a coveted visa to North America. In university, I had studied it to read Anglophone poets.

"I am sorry to come without warning. But what I have to tell you I need to tell you from my mouth."

I nodded, my pulse accelerating. Isidora had finished with the roses and stood staring, the wine bottle still clutched in her hand. I hoped our visitor wouldn't think she had just polished off a crisp sauvignon blanc before naptime. "Won't you come in?"

With relief, she nodded and leaned toward her pack. I stepped toward her. "I will carry that for you. When did you arrive?" If she had just arrived at this altitude, she should not be carrying anything this size. I hefted the pack onto my shoulders.

"Now? This morning?" She sounded un-sure, reminding me of the haze of my own first days. She followed me up the stone path and into our home, where she stood blinking in the darkness of the hallway.

"You are not sick?"

"From the height? No. Just I have a pain in my head, that is all."

"Come in." I left her pack in the hallway and settled her on the white sofa in our living room. She closed her eyes for a moment, clearly relieved to be sitting.

"Izzy, bring the lady a glass of water." I hovered at her side, waiting. When Isidora returned with the ceramic mug, she set it on the table in front of the girl and stood staring at her.

"Señorita, ¿de dónde es?" she asked.

"France." That much I had guessed. And she had understood Isidora; her Spanish must not be too bad.

"Paris?" It was the only city Isidora had heard of in France.

The girl shook her head. "Farther south. Chambéry. It is very near the mountains, the Alps." She sighed, carefully taking a deep breath before continuing. I understood the difficulty. I too struggled to weave together breath and speech whenever we returned from somewhere closer to sea level — from a weekend in Cochabamba or Tarija, a week's swimming in Santa Cruz.

Her curiosity temporarily sated, Isidora started upstairs to her room, no doubt to check on her collections.

I lowered myself to the armchair across from the girl, trying to think of any connection I might have with Chambéry, but I was not familiar with the city.

"My father, he died this year. In February."

"I am very sorry." This wasn't what I had expected to hear.

"But now, now I find out that he is not my father."

"Not your father?"

"Not biologically. He is the only father I have ever known. But a month after he died, my mother told me that there was another man she had loved, many years ago. Twenty, to be precise."

I did the math. She was born in early 1943. I suddenly wished Miguel were with me, but he was high above Sopocachi, at work in the San Calixto Observatory.

"This other man, he was your father?"

"My mother says it could not be anyone else."

"But she stayed with your father?"

She nodded. "This other man, he was a Jew." She took another breath and looked into my eyes. "His name was Willi."

It took a long time for her to get the entire story out. She was exhausted, and I knew I should let her rest, but I couldn't offer her a bed until I found out everything. I made her coca tea and kept her prisoner on my sofa.

Willi had left Switzerland not long after we had left Austria, walking through the forests across the border to France. This was before the war, when it was easier. When we didn't yet have reason to fear France. He had acquired a Bolivian visa in Switzerland and hoped to book passage on a French ship to South America.

In Chambéry, he had met the girl's mother through a Swiss contact from the OSE. She had been working for the organization, finding homes for Jewish children who had escaped Germany or Austria. "Your brother, he helped to move some of the children to safe houses. My mother said he was very good with the children."

I nodded, my voice gone. Yes, Willi had been very good with children.

"When he realized that the OSE needed help, that there was something he could do to help Jewish children, to resist Germany, he didn't feel that he could leave. He felt an obligation to do something. It was a way for him to fight the war without fighting the war. At least, this is how my mother said it.

"There was a passage through the Risoux forest between France and Switzerland. Willi collected the children from homes in France and guided them through this forest to Switzerland. Some stayed there while others were sent abroad. No one trusted him at first, because of his German accent. His French was not the most perfect, my mother says. But because of his passport, which proved he was a Jew, people believed him. And because the Resistance needed people.

"After a few years, once my mother knew him, he also helped escort children to homes in France. There were group homes operated by OSE as well as Christian homes that took in a child or two.

"Maybe it didn't feel so dangerous then, in Chambéry. He and my mother, working together, they became close. They fell in love. But she was married. To my father." The girl stopped, her eyes filling.

"Your mother was Jewish?"

She shook her head. "She was a good person. She loved children, all children. She had never been able to have her own child. Maybe that is why things went wrong with my father."

"But —" I stopped, confused.

"She never got pregnant. After seven years, she stopped trying."

"Until Willi?"

"Until Willi. Though I don't think she was trying. When she realized she was pregnant, it was a disaster. It could not have been my father's child, do you see? My mother had moved into a separate bedroom. Worse, the child — me — had a Jewish father. What if someone discovered this?

"The only thing my mother could do to save me, to save herself, was to fall back in love with her husband. At first she says it was a charade, something she had to do to save us. But things changed with them. Pregnancy made her happy, and happiness made her generous. With her body, with her heart. My father never even suspected that I was not his."

"And Willi?" My head spun with a dizziness I had not felt since 1939.

"She couldn't see him anymore. It was too dangerous. He continued to work for OSE, and then he stopped that day in Izieu, to take some toys, some stuffed animals to the children."

"That's why he was in Izieu?"

"We think so. That's what my mother said. She said he had done it several times before, so that must have been why he was there."

"That's why he died."

"He was deported with the rest of them and killed."

We sat for a moment in silence.

"Do you want to know more? My mother, she investigated for a long time. Or is it too — ?"

"I want to know every detail you have."

The home in Izieu, the girl continued, was run by Sabine Zlatin, a Jewish nurse. On April 3, 1944, Sabine traveled alone to Montpellier to seek a new hiding place for the children. She had heard of recent raids on other children's refuges and worried her charges would be discovered.

While she was away, four trucks arrived in Izieu on the morning of April 6, 1944. Soldiers seized the children and their minders — Willi must have been among them, though no one knew his real name — slinging them like sacks of flour into the backs of these trucks.

"The first person to run to the house after hearing of the raid found half-finished bowls of hot chocolate on the breakfast table." She stopped for a moment to take a breath.

That detail, those abandoned bowls of cooling chocolate, diverted my attention from Willi to the dozens of small, gaily breakfasting children. My hands began to tremble in my lap. Those bowls, still sticky from their lips.

"The villagers said that when the trucks drove away, the children in the back started singing, so loud the villagers could hear. 'Vous n'aurez pas l'Alsace et la Lorraine!' " *You will not have Alsace and Lorraine!*

I wanted to tell her to stop. That I couldn't absorb more details like that.

Then I thought of all the details I had the luxury of not knowing.

All the children and adults were inter-rogated in jail in Lyon before they were taken to Drancy to be loaded onto trains to Auschwitz.

The first train, with thirty-four children and three adults, arrived in Auschwitz on April 15. The remaining ten children and three adults arrived in later convoys.

Léa Feldblum, who had looked after and loved the children, was taken from their arms just before they were gassed to death. She was the sole survivor. She told the children's story.

But not Willi's.

Perhaps she was upstairs with the children

when he stopped with the toys. Perhaps she was in the kitchen. The intersection of their paths is not recorded.

As the strange girl told these stories, I saw my brother in the shape of her brown eyes, the length of her lashes. I saw Willi in the curve of her jaw.

At last she fell silent, her face white with exhaustion.

We sat there, unmoving.

"Mamá?" Izzy came running down the stairs. "My beetle is on its back and it can't turn over. It's waving its legs like it wants to be crawling but I don't know how to flip it!"

I stood, vertigo clouding my vision. "I'm coming, Iz." I turned back to the girl. "You must be tired. You will stay with us, of course. I can make up the bed in the guest room."

"My mother sent a letter." She unbuckled her pack, rummaged around inside. "It is for you and your parents."

I took the thin letter but tucked it in a pocket. I did not want to read it alone.

As I started upstairs with her pack, I turned back. "Your name," I said. "I never asked your name."

"Oh! I am sorry. My name is Julia."

■ ■ ■ ■

I wanted to run to see my parents, run to them with this news. We didn't yet have a phone, there was no way to send a message. It would be better, I eventually decided, to take Julia to them in person. A phone call, a message, would create in them an unbearable anticipation. Better that Julia tell them herself. We would go the next day, once she was rested.

The next morning I was reading *The Magic Flute* to Isidora as she ate mango and chirimoya in our breakfast room when Julia came downstairs. We had put her to bed before dinner, before Miguel arrived home, and she had not emerged before we had gone to sleep ourselves — very late. Miguel had been wary, wanting to be sure that Julia was who she said she was before we told my parents, before we risked breaking their hearts again. "All you need to do is look at her," I said. "She is Willi's child." For the millionth time I remembered with a pang that Miguel had never known Willi, had never even seen a photograph.

The letter still lay unopened on my nightstand. I told myself I wanted to wait for my parents before reading it. But I also wanted

594

to delay reading the last letter we would ever receive about my brother. I wanted to savor the mere fact that it existed.

Isidora was anxious to see Julia again. She loved guests, always believing they had come especially to see her. This morning I had found her sitting outside Julia's room, trying to see through the crack in the door.

Now here she was at last, dressed neatly in skirt and cardigan.

"Good morning!" I rose, offering her my place beside Isidora. "Did you sleep?" Julia was still pale, but her eyes were clear and alert.

She nodded, sliding obediently into the chair. "What time is it? I must have slept for ages!"

"Seven." The sun was already blazing through the windows. "Are you hungry?"

"I don't know."

"I'll make you tea." While I boiled the water and poured it over coca leaves, Isidora showed her our book.

"I don't speak Spanish," Julia apologized.

"Te voy a enseñar. Mira." *I will teach you. Look.* She lifted her plate. "Fruta."

Julia laughed. "Fruta."

I set the teapot and a cup on the table before her. "I could cut you up some fruit, too, if you'd like. And there's marraqueta

— bread rolls — that Isidora and I bought this morning."

"All right. Thank you."

She was visibly more relaxed, having relieved herself of the burden of her story. As she ate a few bites of fruit and drank her tea she allowed Isidora to teach her Spanish words, repeating after her.

By the time Miguel came downstairs, showered and dressed, they were fast friends. Isidora ran to him, and he scooped her up into his arms. "Buenos días, conejita," he said, kissing her cheeks.

"Papá, I am teaching Julia Spanish."

Julia stood up, looking uncertain.

"I'm sure she's thrilled." Miguel smiled at Julia. Ignoring her offered hand, he bent and kissed her cheeks. "Bienvenida, sobrinita." *Welcome, little niece.*

"I am sorry to come without warning you. My mother thought it would be better if I explained in person."

"That was wise of her. Besides, you don't have a lot of competition for that guest room." Miguel picked up a marraqueta and sat across from her. He never wanted anything but Nescafé and a roll in the morning.

"Thank you." She sank back into her chair.

I stood, hovering over the table. "We think you should stay as long as you want. It will take you a few days to feel normal at this altitude anyway, and we'd like to show you more of the city." I found myself unable to behave normally or appropriately, whatever that was, and instead babbled at her as if she were a tourist passing through. "At the weekend we could even take you outside of the city. Down to the jungle or up to the lake."

Miguel rescued me. "But before any of this, Orly will take you to meet your grandparents."

"Yes. Oh, Julia, I'm sorry I am all upside down. Forgive me."

"Of course." Julia explained that she had tried to find them first, but had been unable to discover their address. The publisher of my one slim volume of poetry had directed her to our house. It occurred to me that I owed some significant moments to book publishers.

"We'll go see them once Izzy is off to school." For the first time in my life here, I had something — someone — I knew would give my mother joy.

"Ven, hijita." Miguel stood, brushing crumbs from his trousers. "Guardería."

"She still needs to clean her teeth. Go, Izzy."

"Only if Julia comes." Isidora wrapped her arms around the girl's neck.

"It's okay, I don't mind," Julia said quickly. She followed Isidora up the stairs.

"Isidora seems to like her." Miguel sat down on the stairs to tie his shoes.

"Isidora likes everyone."

"True. How did we raise such an undiscriminating person?"

"Mira, Mamá, mira!" Isidora ran down the stairs, nearly knocking her father off the bottom step, clutching a hardbound book. "Look what Julia gave me!" I caught a flash of a rabbit on the cover before Isidora sat down in the middle of the hallway and began turning pages.

"I forgot I brought presents for her. For all of you. I'm sorry but some are in French. I wasn't sure if you read French. There are a few others, in German and Spanish. I'll get them." She ran upstairs and returned with an armful of books she dumped on the table. I picked them up one at a time, examining the titles.

"You couldn't have brought us anything better," I said. "Books in German! We get so few."

Isidora got up and pushed the book into

my lap. "Read it to me?"

"Later, Izzy. You have to get to guardería."

"But Mamá, it's bunnies!"

I took the book from her chubby hands to see the cover more clearly. I had thought it looked familiar. Sure enough, it was an old friend: Felix Salten's *Fifteen Rabbits.*

My heart was jumping in my rib cage as I walked with Julia up the steps to my parents' new home. They were still in Sopocachi, but now in a small house of their own. The whole way there I wanted to keep my arm in Julia's, to make sure she was real. To keep her from vanishing, this girl who returned to us pieces of our lives.

My mother came to the door in her apron. "Orly! Come in, come in. I've got something in the oven." She reached a hand out to the girl beside me. "Mucho gusto," she said. "I'm Julia."

Julia looked at my mother, at the face subsiding into creases, her grandmother's bright eyes, and burst into tears. "Me too," she sobbed. "I'm Julia too."

My mother looked bewildered. "Come in, child. Come sit down. What is it?" She guided Julia into the front room and sat her down on a sofa. "Stay there. Let me fetch you something to drink."

"Mutti, can you make her coca tea? She just arrived yesterday. Where's Vati?"

"In his practice room." My mother asked no questions, but disappeared into the kitchen.

"I'm sorry," Julia said, her face in her hands. "I knew I was named for her, but seeing her . . ."

I touched the back of her head, stroked the dark hair. "Do you want me to tell her?"

She shook her head. "No, I should."

I left Julia sitting there while I went to find my father. He was at work, making notes on a sheet of music, his viola at rest on his lap. There was a single bed in the corner of the room; he had taken to sleeping here, with his music. He looked up, impatient at the interruption.

"Orlita. I need to finish this."

"Vati," I said. "It's important." Something in my voice prevented further protest.

In the doorway of the living room he stopped, staring at Julia as if he recognized her from somewhere. His white hair stood up in tufts from his head and his shirt was creased, as if he had slept in it. My mother reappeared, setting the teapot and a small plate of strudel in front of Julia. "Jakob," she said, "we have a guest." She sat on the sofa and folded her hands in her lap, smiling like a child awaiting a puppet show. I nudged my father into the room, but he remained standing.

"Frau Zingel," Julia began. "Herr Zingel. My mother lives near Chambéry."

"My parents speak French," I interrupted. "You can speak French." My parents understood French better than English.

I watched their faces as Julia told her story, watched the polite expressions fall away, the shock replaced by sorrow, the sorrow replaced by the first glimmer of joy. Like mine, my mother's hands trembled in her lap. "Willi loved someone," she murmured, dismissing as unimportant the circumstances of that love.

My father's face remained still, as he sank to the sofa beside my mother. "I knew when I saw you," he finally said, looking up at Julia. None of them seemed to know how to proceed from here, what to do with this new knowledge.

Julia rose and knelt by my mother's feet, picked up her thin hands. "I am named for you," she said. "Willi named me. He managed to see me a few times before he was deported, but it was very dangerous for him, and for my mother."

"You're all grown up." There was melancholy in my mother's words. She had missed

Julia's childhood, her adolescence, her entire life.

"Would you like me to stay?" There was hope in Julia's voice. "I can stay for a while."

My mother gave a half nod, turning her face from us, swallowing hard. Unsteadily, she rose. "I'll make lunch."

After lunch, we read the letter. Julia perched on a chair across from us as I squeezed between my parents on the sofa, flattening the pages on my lap. They were thin as onionskin and creased.

July 1963

Dear Julia, Jakob, and Orlanthe,

    I write in the hope that you can somehow forgive me, although I don't deserve it. I should have sent her to you long ago. It has been selfish of me to keep Julia all to myself, for all of these years. But to tell her while my husband was still alive would have destroyed them both. I didn't want to ask her to keep secrets for me, to keep secrets from the man she believed to be her father.

    Yet in doing what I have, I have withheld from you a member of your family, a granddaughter who belongs to you as much as she belongs to my parents. You have lost so much already, how could I keep from you perhaps the only relative you have left in Europe? And I have no answer for that.

Willi would have been — and was, for that first year — a different kind of father from my husband. More a playmate than a ruler. For him, becoming a parent was more than an honor, a sacred trust. It was a delight. It was seeing him with children that first drew me to him. He used to sit down with them on the ground and just with his imagination turn pebbles into mice or rabbits, pine cones into cars.

Had he lived, had the world not been as the world was, had France not been rotting from the inside out, the end of the war would have heralded the end of my marriage. Willi could have raised her with me, taken her for walks in the mountains behind our home, sung her to sleep.

But had I left home when it happened, in 1942, Julia may not have survived the war. Living with Willi, it would be impossible to conceal her parentage. You must know this. And so I appeal to your own parental love and ask you to forgive me for my cowardice.

There is more, but it is hard to put it all in a letter. I would like to meet you one day if you are willing.

I will let Julia say the rest.

Yours faithfully,
Arielle

I left Julia with my parents when I went to fetch Isidora from guardería. It was the hottest hour, when I would normally be inside if I didn't have to pick up Isidora. The guardería was at the home of a young Bolivian woman named Estefania, a twenty-minute walk from our house. She had three children of her own and was pregnant with a fourth. When I rang the bell she came to the garden gate to kiss me. "She's in the back, with the conejitos," she said, waving her hand toward a wooden hutch where she kept two enormously fat rabbits. Isidora liked to feed them, poking sticks of celery and handfuls of parsley through the openings in their cage.

"Mira, Mamá," she called when she saw me. "Look at them chew!"

"I see. Adorable. Vamos a casa?"

Reluctantly she turned away from the rabbits, catching sight of the book in my arms. "Where is Julia?" she demanded. "Why hasn't she come to fetch me?"

I caught her hand and we walked toward Estefania to say good-bye. "She's with your grandma and grandpa, Izzy. I'm going to explain to you about Julia as we walk home."

At the gate we met my friend María Teresa, rushing to pick up her son, Gael. María Teresa had been my first friend in this rural part of town, and remained my closest. "I'll be at the store in an hour," she said, kissing me quickly. "I'm dashing to get Gael to my parents."

A single mother, María Teresa relied on her parents for child care. She was the managerial and financial mastermind behind the bookstore I had finally saved enough money to open. It was a tiny storefront, but we had installed floor-to-ceiling shelves along the walls and a narrow bookcase dividing two aisles. On the wall behind the cash register hung a small woven tapestry in which a red fox gazed at the moon's reflection in a dark lake, while a monkey swung overhead from a branch, an opening-day gift from Nayra.

Most of our books were in Spanish, but we also carried bookcases of German and French literature and a few slim volumes of Aymara and Quechua fables. If anyone wanted a book in English, which was rare, we would special-order it. At the back of the store there was just room enough for two smallish armchairs. Isidora had helped to paint the wooden sign bearing the name of the shop: *La Esquina de Rachel.* Rachel's Corner.

We started up the hill, Isidora taking three steps for every one of mine. "So Julia," I began, "is actually your cousin."

Julia stayed, dividing her time between our house and my parents'. As her Spanish got better, she helped me out a bit in the shop, or with Isidora. When Miguel and I were both working, she helped my mother in the bakery. My mother didn't have a mere storefront anymore, but a proper bakery on a corner in Sopocachi. "Julia has a much lighter touch with the cakes than you ever did," my mother told me, delighted.

Julia's arrival cheered my mother more than anything had since we arrived. The sadness in her, the dark behind her eyes, would never leave her, but she carried it more easily. I felt guilty on the days Julia came to us, knowing that we were depriving my mother of her company. But Isidora was devoted to Julia, the first relative she had ever met on my side. I didn't want to deprive her either.

Suddenly we were all studying languages. I took up my French with renewed passion, taking children's books home from the store at night to read. At night, Isidora patiently corrected Julia's pronunciation as she stumbled through children's stories in Spanish. My mother instructed Julia in the finer points of altitude cooking in very rusty French. As for Isidora, she was demanding to learn not only French but English, because that is what she heard us speak most often with her cousin. Miguel spoke passable German, having endured many hours in the company of my family and other refugees, and had studied English at university. "And there I stop," he said. "Otherwise there will be no room for meteors and black holes."

"Black holes take up space?"

Miguel smiled. "How much time do you have to listen to the answer to that question?"

"Why can't Julia read to me?" Isidora asked me one spring night in late September. "The books she gave me?"

For a few weeks she had forgotten about all her new books, swept up in the excitement of entertaining a guest.

"But Julia reads in French, mi corazón."

"I know French now!" This was an exaggeration. But I had no desire to discourage her ambitions.

"If you really want then, Julia can read them to you. I'm sure she wouldn't mind."

"In French?"

"If you like."

"I like, I like, I like! In fact, I just happen to love French." She sang the words. How did I manage to raise such a joyful daughter? How did such happiness emerge from a heritage of darkness? Ah, I thought. Miguel's genes. He was a constitutionally happy person. He loved his work, he loved us, he wasn't yearning for anything far away. Once I asked him where he would live if he could live anywhere on earth, and he looked at me with surprise. "Here," he said. "Of course here." Yet he and his family had also suffered. Where did they live, these cells that determined our resilience? I wondered. Which cells enable us to survive horror while others jump from their rooftops or cut open their bodies to let the life out?

So Julia read one of her books aloud in French, sitting on the edge of Isidora's bed, while I stretched out on the floor beside them in the dark, my head resting on a stuffed rabbit. When Julia finished a book,

Isidora pretended to read to her in German from Anneliese's book, one of her favorites. Though she turned the pages, she knew all the stories by heart.

When I closed my eyes and let the girls drift away, I could hear Anneliese's voice in our parlor on Seegasse, see us on the carpet with our rabbits.

"All of the treasures of the country —"

"Like its recipes for strudel and photographs of sunrises and the smell of cloves —"

"Are kept in wooden chests —"

"With magical locks —"

"Around each treasure chest is a silvery light. To unlock it, you need to move your head into the light and pick up the pen attached to the chest."

"Yes! And then holding that pen, you trace the password on the trunk of the chest. Mint leaf apfelsaft."

"How long do you usually let her read for?"

So far had I drifted it took me a minute to hear Julia's question. How long had Isidora been reading? It could have been minutes, it could have been hours.

"Oh!" I rolled to my side and sat up, the room settling into place around me. "Ten minutes? Fifteen? It depends."

"We'll stop there then, ma puce. We can continue tomorrow." Julia took the book from her and set it on the bedside table.

"Mamá!"

"You can read more tomorrow."

"That's so far away!" She frowned at me, then turned to Julia. "What does 'puce' mean?"

Julia laughed. "It means flea. I called you my little flea."

Isidora looked cross again. "Do I make you itch? In what way am I like a flea? I am not so little!"

"In France, fleas are considered a sacred bug. We call only our most adored people fleas." She winked at me.

"Really?" Isidora looked skeptical for a moment before deciding to take Julia's statement at face value. "Then I suppose I do not mind being called a flea." She pulled Julia down to embrace her, knocking the book to the floor.

SIXTY-FOUR

October 1963

It was just before midnight on the eve of día de Todos Santos, the Bolivian day of the dead at the start of November, when the diaphanous veil between the world of the living and the world of the dead is at its most porous, allowing spirits to drift between realms.

I was in the guest room over the kitchen, Isidora curled by my side. We had stayed so late baking tantawawas with my mother that we were too tired for the journey home. Todos Santos was one of my mother's biggest days of the year, when people flocked to her shop for the provisions they needed to prepare sumptuous feasts for their dead relatives. As I had done since my adolescence, I helped to knead the tantawawas, pushing the little painted clay faces into the dough figures. This year, Isidora had worked alongside me, tenderly tucking each tantawawa into its bed of papers, filling twenty-seven tins for my mother to sell.

A noise startled me from an uneasy sleep. Perhaps it was the clatter of the padlock to the counter, or the rattle of the tin itself. Perhaps my father, whose knees had recently become unreliable, had stumbled on the stairs.

I sat up on the edge of the bed, my body tensed, as if it already knew. I glanced down at Isidora, touched her sleep-warmed hand, her stubby brown plaits, but she did not stir. She was untroubled by the nightmares that still plagued the rest of us. When she closed her eyes, she did not see armies of spiders or piles of doll-size clothes.

Without stopping to search for my slippers in the dark, I crept to the top of the stairs. There: a rustle of paper, a drawer sliding open. I smiled, exhaled. He was at it again, raiding my mother's wares like a little boy. Slowly, I stepped down.

In the kitchen, a bulb buzzed in the overhead light — the electricity in Sopocachi was working, for once — and the clay tiles were icy on my bare feet. Shivering in my nightgown, I saw my father bent over the sink, a forkful of Palatschinken halfway to his mouth. Beside him on the counter was a rusting cookie tin, one of the dozens my mother used to store the food she sold in her bakery and in the markets of La Paz. The padlock that had fastened the tin lay open beside it, a slim bit of metal still inserted, the lid thrown back on its hinges. I stepped closer, alarm quickening my pulse. Despite the opened lid, the shape of the tin was clear: a Christmas tree.

"Vati, no!"

Jerking upright, my father dropped the fork into the sink and turned to face me. *"Orlita!* My heart. Are you trying to kill me?" He pulled his robe more tightly across his thin chest. "I'm sorry I disturbed you. I didn't hear you come down. Go back to bed now."

I grabbed his arm. "You don't understand. *How much did you eat?"*

"Not so much! What's the fuss? A bite of pancake more or less?"

"Mutti!" I wanted to run upstairs to get her but I didn't want to leave my father alone. "Mutti, *get down here!"*

My father looked bewildered. "Orlita, I'm sorry. Why do you want to wake your mother? Get me in trouble?"

"It's not you in trouble, Vati, not in the way you think —"

My mother appeared then, motionless on the bottom step, nightgown drifting around

613

her like a ghost. She stared at me, her silvery curls snaking straight out from her head. I hadn't heard her footsteps.

"He ate some, Mutti. The German food. Why is it there? *Why is it in this house?* I'll go for a doctor. What have you *done?*"

Her eyes conducted a rapid calculus of terror as she absorbed the tin and the missing chunk of pancake. *"How much did he eat?"*

"Just a corner. A bite or two. Julia, please, someone explain to me —"

My mother was already reaching for the earthen jars of herbs she kept above the sink, her personal pharmacy. "Light the stove. And get me the horsetail and milk thistle from the pantry. Where is my palo de aceite?" She opened a jar and sifted green leaves into her mortar.

"Shouldn't I get a doctor?" I needed to do something. I needed to save my father. I fetched her the herbs she had asked for.

"A doctor won't know how to undo this. I know the antidote."

"Have you ever used it?"

"Of course not."

"Mutti!" A tide of fury rose in me. But I could not risk distracting my mother now.

"Julia!" My father still stood in the middle of the kitchen in his dark-blue dressing

gown. "Stop, please. Stop. What are you doing?"

"I'm saving us," my mother said, pound-
ing the herbs into dust. "I am saving you."

My question for her was different from
my father's. My question was: *Who have you
become?*

As soon as my mother had finished mixing
up the antidote Wayra had apparently taught
her decades ago — just in case — she placed
the mug of dark foaming liquid on the table.
"Sit, Jakob. Drink this."

My father sat down, but refused to pick
up the mug.

"Vati, *please* drink." I sat down next to
him and nudged the mug closer to his hand.

"Jakob, there's no time to waste." My
mother hovered over him as though he were
a recalcitrant toddler refusing his milk.

He looked calmly up at her. "Then you
had better start talking."

"Stubborn fool! I'm talking. I'm talking
now. Where to start. Wayra. No, Thekla. Do
you remember the guard, the one who
Thekla knew . . ." As soon as she began, my
father picked up the mug and began to take
slow, careful sips.

The story she told was similar to the one
she had told me more than fifteen years ago

in a different kitchen. She spoke quickly, as if to get it all out in one breath.

My father kept his eyes on hers as he tilted up the mug. She paused after the second death and my father stopped drinking. "Orly *knew*? You made my daughter complicit?"

"She guessed. She made me promise to stop. She said if I didn't she would tell you."

For so many years she kept her word to me. I had heard of no suspicious deaths, had not had any bits of food knocked out of my hands or those of my daughter. I had watched her carefully. I would never have forgiven her had she put my daughter at risk. But now — hadn't she? Isidora was a curious, intelligent child. It would not be long until she was finding her way around locks.

My father looked at me. "She should have told me anyway."

"Why? What would you have done, turn Mutti in to the Bolivian police?" The last thing I wanted to do was defend my mother or myself, yet I could not see a clear benefit to reporting my mother's crime.

"So I could maybe not end up *poisoned by my own wife*."

"Don't blame Orly. She made me promise to stop. I kept that promise for so long, even when I knew Barbie was in the country. He was living far away anyway, it wasn't a possibility. It was only after I saw him in La Paz that I couldn't be idle anymore. Jakob, how could I sit there and watch a movie in front of the man who ordered the murder of our son?"

My father tipped up his mug until it was empty and then he stood. "You didn't have to watch a movie with him. That isn't what this is about." His hands curled in fists by his sides, shock turning to rage.

"No. You're right. But no one else is coming for him. Jakob, can't you understand? *He is leading a happy life.*"

"So these pancakes, these Palatschinken I have always loved, that have always been my favorite thing you make, these are what you choose for him? *My pancakes?* Mine?"

My mother's voice faltered. "They — they weren't the first thing I chose. The first thing I made was a strudel. But he gave it to one of his food tasters, one of his bodyguards."

"Who is no longer with us."

"Who is no longer with us," my mother conceded.

"Then you decided to try the pancakes." His voice fell flat, inflectionless.

"No, then it was Schnitzel. They always love the Schnitzel."

My father cleared his throat. "And who tasted the Schnitzel for him?"

"Another guard."

"I see. And no one was suspicious about the Austrian woman serving food to these guards?"

"They weren't in La Paz that often. And it's slow-acting poison. It can take days. They would have eaten several more meals by the time it took effect, and they were never sure which to blame. Plus, foreigners are always getting sick here."

"So no one was punished for those deaths."

"I don't think so. I didn't hear anything. And then I thought, pancakes . . . well, they've always tempted you. . . ." Her voice trailed off. "He is going to be the last one, I promise. Just him."

My father seized her shoulders. "No," he said. "You cannot."

"Jakob, what about Willi! What about those children!"

"You want to become like him? Damn you, Julia!" He pushed her away, causing her to stumble backward. He was shouting. I watched them, frozen. I had never heard him swear at my mother. "I married you because there was beauty in you, there was music and life. *What have you done with that woman?* What have you done with her?" He began to weep. "I learned how to live without your voice. But I can't live with who you are now. I have had enough of murderers."

He turned and walked upstairs, a hand on his stomach.

The sun rose, even on this day, at the exact time it always rose.

It was still cold in the kitchen. My mother and I sat for some time without speaking, having nothing more to say as we waited to see if my father would be joining the other souls adrift today, crossing the wrong direction.

"When will we know?" I finally asked.

She turned glassy eyes to me. "If he hasn't started getting ill by tomorrow, he'll be fine."

"Tomorrow?"

"I said it was slow."

She got up and carried the mugs to the sink and stood there a moment, as if wondering what to do next. "I suppose I'll go upstairs."

"Isidora will be up soon." Miraculously, the shouting had not woken her. She had not heard the story of her grandmother's crimes.

"I could make her breakfast." There was hope, there was pleading in her voice.

"No," I said firmly. "I'll do that."

Alone in the kitchen I scraped the sodden herbs into the trash and washed the dishes three times. I threw out the pancakes and scoured the tin. I worked quickly, wanting to get rid of all of it before my daughter came downstairs. I rang Miguel quickly to say we'd spend an extra day with my parents, and to ask if he could look after Julia, whom we'd left behind because she had a cold. "I'll explain once I'm home."

Weary and panicked, I started up the stairs. Isidora was still sleeping, sprawled diagonally across the entire bed. Thankful for her oblivion, I tiptoed to my parents' bedroom. My father was asleep. My mother had curved her body around his on their bed, careful not to touch him, knowing what would happen should he wake, but near enough she could probably feel the warmth emanating from his skin. Suspecting, perhaps, that she would never again be allowed so close.

Unaware, he slept on. I stepped over the threshold.

As I stood over them, I had a vision of myself at seven or so, standing over their

620

bed in Vienna, their lace curtains fluttering in a spring breeze. While they rarely let me stay in bed with them if I woke in the middle of the night, often they would let me sneak in in the morning. If I crept in quietly enough, sometimes they wouldn't even wake. But one morning, this morning that came back to me, I had found them like this: my mother curled around my father, but their arms and legs intertwined so closely that their intimacy seemed inviolable. Sometime in the night they had thrown off the pile of sheets and blankets that lay twisted at the foot of the bed, as if they wanted nothing between them. I stood for a moment, watching them, before turning to go back to my own bed, feeling my solitude more acutely than ever.

Now, I felt the same resistance to disturbing them. My mother hadn't stirred when I came in. I wondered if she were asleep. How could she sleep? But then, she had been sleeping for years.

Sixty-Five

Isidora and I returned home as soon as we were reassured that my father would live. On the second day after the pancakes, he was feeling so vigorous that he packed a suitcase and left to spend the night at Gregor's apartment. A damp grey mist was sifting down through my rib cage.

Isidora was upstairs with her rabbits when Julia came down from her room to make tea. She wore a purple cotton sundress that somehow made her look even younger.

"Julia." I stopped in the doorway of the kitchen, where she was filling the kettle.

"Sí?"

"Come sit down with me when you're done?"

She came to perch beside me on the living room sofa, cupping the mug between her palms. It wasn't any easier in the retelling, not any of it. Julia cried like Isidora often did, only quietly, with less abandon.

She cried as if she were accustomed to crying in secret.

"My grandfather — he's really okay?" Julia looked up at me, pink mottling her cheeks. She finally set down her mug and pressed her hands together between her knees.

"He seems to be. He went to stay with a friend for a while."

"He looked fine?"

"He looked fine. I don't think his stomach was in very good shape but he's alive. Alive and furious."

"I only just found them."

"I know."

"It's so weird that Barbie ended up here. I mean, where we are. The family of someone he ordered killed."

"Not that weird. He murdered thousands of people, Julia. There are families of people he murdered in almost any country you could mention. He's always going to be passing families of his victims on the street. Though not all of them will recognize him."

She turned her head to look at me, a lock of dark hair falling across her eyes. "Do you think she'll try again?"

"For Barbie? I don't think so. She knows we're watching. And it's now unmistakably clear she might have killed any of us." Even as I said this, I knew I would never again feel easy about sending Isidora to stay with her grandparents.

"Not just Barbie, but in general . . . ?"

"She promised my father she would stop. Though there seems to be no shortage of Nazis, here or anywhere in South America. The temptation is always there."

"But he still left. My grandfather."

"Yes. But maybe he'll change his mind." I shifted on the sofa to face her. "Am I wrong?"

Julia was quiet for a moment. "Isn't there a part of you that wishes she had succeeded?"

I didn't need time to think about that one. "Of course. He doesn't deserve to live. But I don't want my mother to be the one to do it. I don't want it to be on her soul."

"Do you believe in souls?"

"I don't know. But it would make her more like them. And it wouldn't bring Willi back, or the children."

Julia nodded.

"Do you think my grandmother is a little bit like them?"

My own tears came then, the knife of the question slicing me open. I thought of my mother at *Les Huguenots,* talking to me of the dangers of war, of religion. I heard her voice singing to Elektra, begging for peace. I remembered the way she curled around me on Pogrom Night, blocking my ears with her song.

And I thought of her now.

"I can't — That equation. It's not —"

Julia look chagrined. "I'm sorry."

I took her hand between mine. "The problem is older and greater than these men. A poison has been spreading through Europe for centuries. Someone else might have done what Hitler or Barbie did. It's dangerous to believe that it's just about these men. Their ability to manipulate ancient hatreds is not unique."

Julia leaned into me, resting her forehead on my shoulder. "I don't want my grandmother to hurt anyone," she said in a small voice.

"All right." I rested my hand on her back. "We won't let her hurt anyone."

Barbie lived long enough to be extradited to France in 1983. Justice had finally arrived, if only after Barbie had had the luxury of a long and happy life.

Six months after my mother nearly killed him, my father moved back home. Maybe it was too late for him to start again. Maybe he had forgiven her. He did not immediately move back into their bedroom, but slept in his office.

"Vati, I'm glad." What I didn't say was, I'm glad someone will be watching her.

A few weeks later he and I sat in the living room together, mostly quiet, watching my mother and Julia through the kitchen doorway as they moved back and forth across the tiles.

"She promised me all that is over."

"And you believe she means it this time?"

My father's long, thin fingers traced patterns on the surface of the coffee table. "I can't bring myself to give up hope. When I thought I had, I realized there was nothing else holding me up. Just the hope that she would be herself again."

"Even now?"

"Even now."

"You don't think maybe you should do the cooking?"

He laughed. "No. That's how lazy I am. Not even fear of poisoning will drive me to the kitchen."

"Vati —"

"I know. I'm a foolish old man, Orlita."

"Not foolish. Illogically tenacious, perhaps." I smiled at him. "What are they making in the kitchen?"

"Pancakes."

I leapt to my feet, but he laughed. "I'm joking. They're making cinnamon rolls. I think the first batch is out of the oven if you feel like stealing a few for us."

"You're sure."

"I'm sure."

I picked up our teacups from the table and started for the kitchen. In the doorway, I paused. My mother was rolling strips of spiced dough into pinwheels, which Julia took from her hands and settled onto metal trays. As I stepped closer to them I heard something strange. A foreign yet not unfamiliar sound that disinterred something inside me. I couldn't believe it. My mother was humming.

SIXTY-SIX

I was stepping into a bath when I heard the knock at the door. It wasn't even 7:00 A.M. No one in our neighborhood paid a social call at that hour. Pulling my dressing gown from its hook and wrapping it around me I ran to look out the front window. Below me I saw only the top of a dark head, a small, vaguely female form. Perhaps she was a beggar. Or maybe there was an emergency. An antigovernment manifestación. Flooding. A sick friend. My parents. Worried something had happened to my mother or father, I ran down the stairs. Passing Isidora's room, I checked to make sure she was still there, snoring gently under her covers.

I remember everything about the moment that I opened the door. The sun blazing red on the cliffs above us, the deep blue of the sky, the slim crescent of moon still visible. I remember the metallic, post-rain smell of

628

the air. The breeze cold against my right foot, the only part of me I had dipped into the bath. I can still feel the pull of the hairpins stuck into the top of my head, the bareness of my neck.

And I remember the girl, the woman, before me.

Her black hair was streaked with white and cut chin length and deep lines scored her forehead. At the left corner of her lip, a smile quivered. Her brown eyes were bigger, her face narrower, her skin unnaturally pale, almost blue. Otherwise she was the same. Short, slim, eyes stormy with some subterranean feeling.

We stood there, staring at each other across the threshold, saying nothing.

Saying everything.

I had opened the door into another life.

As I stood there, trembling in my dressing gown, she linked her thumbs and raised them over her head, her fingers fanned out on either side, like wings. My arms rose to mirror her.

Then she vomited onto my bare feet.

Because I wasn't sure that she could or should walk up the stairs herself, I scooped her up in my arms. She wasn't heavy. I could feel her ribs pressing against my right forearm, her heart staggering. A reek of perspiration, bile, and staleness rose from her dress.

At the top of the stairs I set her on her feet, keeping one arm around her shoulders. "Ana," I said — as if she were any other guest, as if years and wars and cruelty and ships and mountains had not come between us — "you need to rest. There's a bath ready, I was just getting in."

She nodded. "I smell, don't I? I'm so sorry, Orly. That wasn't how I pictured our reunion."

"It's hard to predict how altitude will affect you." I felt impatient with the altitude, for distracting us from the infinite things we had to say to each other.

"I've been vomiting all the way here. I could have waited until I was better, I suppose, but I couldn't wait. I couldn't. I've already waited too long. It took so long! I didn't want to tell you I was coming just in case I didn't make it. I have been disappointing you for so many years." She looked at me as she unbuttoned her dress and shrugged it to the floor. Automatically, I picked it up, averting my eyes. My hands, I noticed, were still trembling.

"I'll wash your dress."

"I brought another one." Ana lifted one

thin leg over the edge of the tub and sank down, the pink tips of her breasts floating up in the water. "I left my case somewhere near your front door. I might throw up again." Her brow creased, deepening the lines.

"Here." I dragged over the rubbish bin and set it next to the tub. "I don't think you had breasts the last time I saw you."

"Are you getting in?"

I smiled, remembering the times she had climbed in with me over Stefi's protestations that there was not room enough for two children in the bath. Poor Stefi. We had knocked over jars of my mother's creams and flooded the bathroom floor.

"Not if you're going to vomit on me again."

"Yes, I suppose you had better not. Would you push that bin a bit closer?"

As she hung over the edge of the bath, I slipped out to clean the hallway and to fetch her case. The front door still stood wide open, the case waiting expectantly on the top step. It was small, but heavy. I carried it upstairs to Julia's room and set it down. I should change the sheets.

"Orly?"

I hurried back to the bath. Anneliese was shivering on the mat. "May I have a towel?"

I had used mine to clean my feet and the front step, so I handed her Miguel's. Once she was dressed in an old nightgown, I made her coca tea and then made up her bed as she sat on the floor and watched, warming her hands on the mug.

"Will I feel like this forever?"

"Most people adjust."

"I feel like I might die. Will I die?"

"I don't think so. Not unless you try to run a marathon."

"Mamá?" Isidora stood in the doorway, wearing the bunny costume we had bought her for Carnival. She still liked to sleep in it. She stared at Anneliese sitting on the floor next to a bucket, and looked back up at me. "Do I have another cousin?"

It was hard to let Anneliese sleep. It wasn't only the never-ending questions pushing their way to the forefront of my brain, or the fact that Isidora wanted to play with her. I just wanted to listen to her voice, to make her laugh, to touch her hand.

She didn't want to sleep. I could tell by the way she clung to my hand, explaining herself in German to my daughter. But at last she fell back against the pillow. "It's getting the better of me," she said.

I closed the door to her room and shooed

Isidora downstairs. It was a Saturday and Miguel had left in the dark for the observatory. My head and heart reeling, I grounded myself in the mundane task of preparing breakfast for Isidora. All of the best things happen before breakfast, I thought. I had always loved mornings, the clean slate of them, the infinite promise. After lunch I was sometimes overtaken by a heaviness, a loss of hope. I have given up fighting this; there will always be darkness in me. How could it not remain in all of us? Only playing my charango with a group of other musicians, Isidora's return from guardería, or Miguel's arrival home from work could lift me back up.

Anneliese came downstairs for lunch, but couldn't manage more than a couple of spoonfuls of peanut soup. She sat at the table shivering in one of my alpaca sweaters, while Isidora asked her riddles. *What gets wetter the more that it dries?* she asked Anneliese in German. *What weighs more, a kilo of feathers or a kilo of bricks?*

"Sweetheart, let Anneliese rest."

"She's been resting all morning!" Isidora crossed her skinny arms across her chest.

"She's had a long journey and isn't feeling very well." I stirred my soup, not feeling

633

hungry myself.

"Like Julia? Does she come from where Julia came from?"

"No." I was still thinking of Anneliese as Viennese, as Austrian. But then it occurred to me that she had been in France now for a very long time. "Maybe, in a way. Ana, are you still in France? You haven't gone back to Vienna?" I was talking to Anneliese. *I was talking to Anneliese.*

"*Vienna?* You think I could still live in Vienna?" She almost spat the words. "No. France has been terrible enough, but Vienna, never. I could never." She pulled the sweater more tightly around her.

"I didn't know." I shrugged helplessly. "I don't know anything."

"No. Thank God. There is very little I would want you to know about those years."

"We've heard things. Many of us came here after."

"Did they?"

"Yes. My aunt Thekla."

"I remember Thekla!" She sat up straighter. "With Klara and Felix?"

I shook my head, glancing over at Isidora. I had tried to spare her too many of these stories.

"Not anymore. Not any of them."

"But you said Thekla came here . . ."

634

"Yes." I tipped my head toward my daughter. "But it was too much for her."

"What was too much, Mamá?"

"I'm sorry," said Anneliese. "This can wait."

"What can wait?" Isidora hated not knowing everything. "What can wait!"

"Nothing, lovie. Just talking. Anneliese and I have not talked in a very long time."

Anneliese smiled. "I think it may take us twenty-four years of talking to even begin."

"At least."

"I was hoping I would never have to speak German again," she said, in German. "I've wanted to change my name forever. But I knew that if I did you could never find me."

"If I had seen the book I would have known," I said. "Even if your surname had changed. If I had read the story about carrotmobiles."

"There was such a small chance you would. I wanted to be as findable as I could."

We sat smiling at each other while Isidora scraped up bits of carrot from the bottom of her bowl. I felt awkward, words clotting in my throat. Too many words. "Tell us about your village?"

"It's in the South of France. Near Nîmes. A very small village, on a river. Quiet. Lots of artists. We even have circus performers. A tightrope walker. A trapeze artist."

Isidora perked up. "Julia is from France!"

Anneliese looked questioningly at me. "Julia?"

"Willi's daughter. She is here now, she stays with us sometimes."

"Right! Willi's daughter! My brain isn't working. She is still here?"

"Yes." I was unable to stop smiling. "You will love her. And I promise I will tell you all."

Anneliese did not get better. She tried coming downstairs to the table for dinner later that day, to meet Miguel, but only sipped at her water. Miguel was welcoming and kind; while I got her back to bed he went out to buy the sorochi pills that helped some people with the altitude. "I'm so glad, Orly," he said. "It's like one of the stories you've told me coming true. Like I know her before she talks." Julia stayed with my parents so that Anneliese could have the guest room. They hadn't even met yet. There would be time. I hoped that there would be time.

Once Miguel left for work the next morning and I dropped Isidora at nursery, I got into bed with Ana, lying beside her as we had several lifetimes ago, pressing her cold hands between my palms. It felt so easy. We talked all morning, until she slipped back to sleep. Lying beside her, watching her eyelids quiver with dreams, I marveled that she was still Anneliese. That it could still be so simple to talk with her, almost like having a conversation with a part of myself, a part that had been missing and returned.

At night, after I had tucked Isidora in bed with Anneliese's book, which she wanted to read again now that she had met the author ("a real live writer!"), I returned to her, lying fully clothed on top of the covers beside her while she tried to sketch the missing years.

As I knew from her letters, in 1943 Anneliese had run away. Now, she filled in many details. "I couldn't stand it anymore," she said. "Living with them. Pretending I didn't hate them more than I have ever hated anyone. Not doing anything. Not doing anything to the people who had taken you away. How could I just stay there and do nothing? With the Nazis everywhere, taking everyone, everything? How could anyone?" She shook her head, as if to shake the very thought out. "You should have seen what Heinrich Müller became. You thought he was bad as a child!"

She refrained from telling me too many details of the years in Vienna that followed my departure. "You have enough memories to haunt you. You will already have read, already heard, more than anyone should have to."

The Resistance networks were growing stronger in 1943, especially among various Catholic groups. It was an Austrian priest from one of these groups who had helped her to travel to Switzerland and put her in touch with people from the Christlicher Friedensdienst, the Christian Peace Service, who took her in. She lived with religious women there, working with them to help Jewish refugee children find homes. There were labor camps for Jewish refugees, she told me. She had visited one, looking for Willi. "I didn't see him." She crinkled her forehead, remembering. "I looked for him. I wanted to see him, Orly. I wanted him to tell me where you were. But I didn't know where he had gone, or you, or anyone. No one knew where you were."

"No. I should have told you. I don't know why I didn't tell you. My mother had said not to, but I should have trusted you."

"You were wise, Orly. I might have been different. Or I might have been made to talk."

"They wouldn't have come after us to Bolivia."

"Maybe not."

"Then again, there are Nazis here."

"They came for you? Here?" She looked confused.

"For themselves. Escaping. Justice doesn't ever seem to reach South America."

Anneliese closed her eyes. "The Nazi diaspora," she said. "Just what the world needs." And she was asleep again.

After the third day, Miguel suggested I take Anneliese to Tarija. We were lying in bed reading, our bedside lamps still burning. "You could stay with my aunt there, or even in a hotel. It won't be expensive. It's lower, she won't be as sick."

This had occurred to me, but seemed too much to ask of my husband. I should have known better than to underestimate him, his generosity.

"I can do some of my work from home after I pick Isidora up from guardería."

"You don't cook." Most Bolivian men did not cook. You were lucky if you could find yourself a husband who could make his own coffee. They stayed with their parents until they married, and even after marriage they went home every Sunday. This had caused us a great amount of conflict in the early years of our marriage. Though I loved Miguel's family, once in a while I wanted a Sunday to myself.

"I'll buy salteñas! I can slice fruit and buy marraquetas. We'll cope." He closed *The Feynman Lectures on Physics* and turned toward me. "You need to go, Orlita. Aside from the altitude sickness. You can't talk properly here. Take a few days away from us and all of our distractions."

I shut my own book, a collection of French poetry. "Miguelito." My throat closed and I could not say any more.

He reached for me. "There is so much I can't understand," he said. "So much I will never understand."

Eventually I felt his arm around my ribs grow heavy, his breathing turn to snores. "Thank you," I whispered. "Gracias."

Sleep refused to come. Our blankets were too heavy, too hot. I pushed myself into a sitting position and walked to my dresser. I was wearing wool socks. I always wore wool socks to bed here. Miguel had laughed the first time I had undressed for him but refused to take off my socks. "Gringa chic," he said. "So alluring." Crouching, I pulled open the bottom drawer, took out the sealed tin I kept there, and carried it down the hall and up the stairs to the small attic room where we stored our suitcases. By the time a sliver of pink appeared on the horizon, I was packed.

We took the train to Tupiza and a bus from there. Anneliese slumped against me, ill nearly the entire journey, while I stared out the window imagining our car tumbling to the cliffs below the road. It was a relief to arrive in the green of Tarija, in its thick sweet air, its red earth. After a few faltering steps, Anneliese found her footing and wanted to walk to the hotel. It wasn't far from the train station, but I was surprised at the speed of her recovery.

"It was just the altitude, I think. I feel marvelously better already!" She swung her arms as she walked. "I can feel the oxygen whooshing around inside of me."

I looked at her face, transformed for a moment into a younger Anneliese I recognized. For a few moments, I felt uncontaminated joy. I reached for her hand.

"I'm sorry. I should have brought you here sooner. Most people do adjust though, eventually."

"I guess you didn't have a choice."

"Some of us did go down to the jungle.

There was a colony, a farming colony of Jews."

"You're joking."

"I'm not."

"Farming Jews?"

"Don't you remember what I wrote about Rachel?"

"The orphan girl who got sent to the jungle?"

"Yes. My friend."

"Who died?"

I nodded.

I told her the rest of the story, about Mauricio Hochschild, the crop failures, and disease. I didn't tell her everything about Rachel.

Anneliese was silent. "That poor girl."

I nodded. Rachel's death was one more reason prayer felt futile. I didn't understand why my father had continued to go to synagogue. If there was a god, he or she was guilty of such gross negligence I hardly knew where to start, how to voice my bottomless fury and grief. These mountains were all the synagogue I needed. Even if I believed in God, why would I go inside to worship when all of creation was outside? These rocks, this red earth, this pale blue sky. Whoever made these, whatever force of nature, inspires in me greater faith than man-made buildings or worlds ever did.

"Are there many of you here?" Anneliese asked. "How many are left?"

"Not so many. Me, my parents. There can't be more than a hundred others." There had been so many thousands of us in 1939. And in 1946, when the survivors were washed up here by the war.

It hadn't occurred to me that we would need to call ahead to make a reservation, but by the time we arrived at our chosen hotel, the one Miguel had recommended, almost all the rooms were full. "I have one room left near the pool," the young clerk told us. "But it has only one bed."

Anneliese and I looked at each other.

"It's fine," said Anneliese quietly. I repeated this in Spanish to the hotel clerk, who looked unsurprised. Entire Bolivian families often shared a bed.

The room felt enormous and empty. Anneliese walked over to the window and drew the curtain aside. "It's so strange," she said.

I came to stand next to her. She smelled like lavender, like her French shampoo. She had washed her hair that morning in my bath. Outside in the wild gardens, a bright green bird paused atop a palm tree.

Anneliese turned to me abruptly. "Can we

go for a walk?"

"Of course!" It was the first thing I did anywhere I visited. It calmed me after the anxiety of travel. So great was the diversity of Bolivia's lands, I was discovering with Miguel, that we could find ourselves in an entirely different landscape and climate in a matter of hours. Walking oriented us.

After getting lost in the streets near the hotel, we finally found ourselves on a dirt road heading outside of town. If we continued on it for forty minutes or so, and took a right, it would cross a river, the hotel clerk had told us. A path on the other side would take us back.

Anneliese wasn't the only one who perked up closer to sea level. While I had never experienced altitude sickness and felt myself to be as adapted as any native, I could not deny that a few days at lower altitude gave me superhuman powers. I could drink more than one glass of wine, I could run twice as far, I could go an entire night without sleep.

For a while, we walked without talking along the rutted road. Despite our silence, it wasn't a quiet walk. Birds squawked, winds rustled the leaves, bits of music leaked out of the few houses we passed.

"Oh!" Anneliese cried suddenly, stopping. "Are those *vineyards*?"

I followed her gaze. "We're in Tarija. It's the wine region."

"There's a wine region? Here?"

"For at least a few hundred years or so. France didn't invent wine, you know."

"I know, it was Bacchus, in Greece." She grinned at me.

"Do you see that?" I pointed to the trees growing across the fields. "Those are muscat grapes. They plant the vines around the molle trees, and the resin protects the vines from fungus."

Anneliese stopped and gazed out at the green fields. "I wonder if France has molle trees?"

I shrugged.

"No, I guess not." She turned back to the road. "We wouldn't want all wines to taste the same anyway."

That night we ate a simple meal of local cheeses and hams in a small café near the hotel. "It's not terrible." Anneliese swirled the red wine in her glass. "Ça se boit."

I poured myself a second glass. "I don't think I've ever had anything but Bolivian wine. There's some here from Argentina and Chile, but it's more expensive and Miguel won't buy it."

"Patriotism over palate."

"Something like that. Though there is very good Bolivian wine."

When we got back to the hotel I rummaged around in my bag until I found the tin. "I've been saving these to show you."

Anneliese sat on the edge of the bed, holding the tin in both hands. I stood before her, too anxious to sit. "Most of the stories are Nayra's, some are mine, and some we mixed together. The poems are all mine."

She ran her fingers around the rim of the tin, dug her fingernails underneath the edge. "Wait. I have something for you too — if you want. They're just stories. For the next book."

"Of course I want!"

She set my tin down to rifle through her bag and pulled out a packet of handwritten pages tied with string.

That evening, she read every poem, every story, taking breaks only for a drink of water or to use the bathroom. Even Miguel had never read all of these stories and poems. Reading things unrelated to science made him restless.

She cried as she read.

I sprawled on the floor with her packet. The stories were good. These were not childish tales of a magical land, but stories of Frenchwomen working in the Resistance, of trapeze artists falling into rivers, and of a charismatic ceramicist who seduces a young Austrian girl. But while I appreciated their artistry, reading them made me feel far from her. They reminded me of the length of the years we were apart, the discrepancies in experience. It's not that her life had been easier; that would be too simple. It is just that it was a life, a full life, that I knew nothing about.

I finished before her and paced the carpet of the room, pausing to stare out into the dark night. But the glass was reflective, and all that stared back was my own shadow and Anneliese's.

Late that first night, our pages scattered around us, Anneliese lay back on the bed, her face contorting as tears streamed down her temples. I watched the tears roll into her ears and worried that something would happen to her hearing. "Ana?"

She just lay there and sobbed. I knelt on the cover beside her. "Ana? Why are you crying?"

"Why aren't you? Why isn't everyone, all the time?"

"I don't know." Surely if anyone has a right to cry all of the time, it's us Jews. But is that what we survived for?

"I missed so many stories. I had to write

them all down on my own and it isn't the same. I should have had you. We should have had each other."

I nodded, but she didn't see me because she kept staring at the ceiling.

"There is just so much that is terrible. So much. In Vienna I saw a man throw a little girl off a roof, Orly. I can't stop seeing her, with her little blue dress and little plaits. Someone had plaited her hair that morning, someone had combed it out and plaited it and put ribbons on the ends and made her look neat and pretty. And someone else just *threw her out.*" Those last words choked her. "I'm sorry, I'm sorry, I swore I wasn't going to tell you."

A wave of nausea and heat flooded my abdomen. For so many years, these were the images I had been avoiding. I sat beside her on the bed and picked up one of her now-warm hands, holding it between mine.

"Knowing that we are capable of all of that, how do we go on?"

I didn't have any answers. Weren't these the questions I had been asking my mother ever since we left Austria? Maybe even before? I don't know how we go on. But we do. Some of us, anyway, go on.

"I don't think *you* are capable of that, Ana. Of cruelty. You never were. You could

648

have been, so easily you could have been, but you weren't."

Her breath slowed. "No." She rolled on to her side to look at me. "No, I don't think I am."

"You could have been like your parents. Or like Heinrich Müller. I still don't know why you weren't."

She was quiet. "Because I loved you?"

"There must be more to it than that. I think you would have been kind to anyone Jewish even if it weren't for me."

"It's impossible to know who I would be if not for you. I didn't exist before you."

I lay down facing her, my knees curled to touch hers, and looked at the eyes I had known since birth. Listened to the way our breaths fell into rhythm.

"All those wasted years, Orly. Think what we could have done with them if we were not all murdering each other."

"We haven't been murdering anyone."

Anneliese smiled, tiny lights coming on in her eyes. "You did the opposite. You created a person."

I smiled. "I did. With a little help."

"Isn't it scary? Sending some part of you out into this world?"

"Yes. It's terrifying. All the time. Is that why you never had a child?"

"I couldn't bear the thought of watching anyone else suffer. And the way the world was going, has been going, suffering seemed inevitable."

"Suffering has always been inevitable."

"Yes." She closed her eyes. "I don't know what I am doing with my life."

I touched her cheek to make her open her eyes. "Alleviating my suffering." And I kissed her.

A new version of me emerged that night, a version that might have sprung to life decades earlier. What we did was neither better nor worse than what I shared with Miguel. It was a thing apart. He was gentler, more careful than Anneliese, more afraid of hurting me. Making love to Anneliese did new and shattering things to my body, things that left me sobbing and inside out. Things that left our sheets soaked and tangled, so that we had to get the towels from the bathroom and spread them all over the bed.

The thought of hurting Miguel was unbearable to me. But so was the thought of leaving this part of me, secret for so long, forever unexplored. It wasn't fair that she had come so late. It wasn't fair to Miguel that she had come at all. Yet here she was.

And there were things I had to know about myself. And about us.

"I wasn't sure," she told me in the dark of early morning. "I wasn't sure this was part of what we were to each other."

"It always has been, Ana, always, even when I didn't understand." I told her about *The Scorpion,* about falling in love with Rachel. That after Rachel died I had caged those emotions, the secret responses to girls that brought both the pain of loss and the fear of discovery. I had never heard anyone here talk about falling in love with someone of the same sex unless it was to condemn it as an unforgivable sin. Admitting a passion for women would put me in almost as much danger as being Jewish had in Vienna.

Then there had been Miguel. Guilt flashed through me. Anneliese had an earlier claim, but I had promised him the future.

"Come back with me. Come to France." Her arms tightened around me. They felt strong, as though she had been pushing a plow in France rather than plucking at typewriter keys. Maybe she had been pushing a plow. She had probably done a lot of things I didn't know about.

I let myself imagine it. Getting on a plane with her, going to her French village, moving into her little house. Sleeping next to her skin. Waking up next to her skin. Telling stories with her. Lying in lavender-scented sheets while she went out to buy bread for our breakfast. For a moment, I glimpsed the life I might have had. That I could still perhaps have, if I were willing to give up everything.

"Ana, don't ask me, don't ask me now." I buried my face in her neck, her celery-smelling neck. How could it be that her neck still smelled the same?

At night while she slept I tried to find ways to make the pieces of my life fit together. Even from the start I knew it was futile. Life without Isidora was not possible. For me, there was no life without Isidora. Nor could there be life without Miguel. I had grown into his contours, the contours of his country.

"Stay here," I pleaded, desperately, stupidly, and without hope. My city made Anneliese sick. My city contained my family.

"Leave here," she replied, her breath hot on my ear.

We had been there three days when I asked her if she lived alone in France. It was late morning, the sun long up, and we still lay in bed. Anneliese rolled onto her back.

"I live with someone."

"A woman?"

"A woman."

I considered this. "She knows where you are?"

"In a way. She knows you are a childhood friend who was lost."

A childhood friend. I felt myself disappearing into insignificance.

"Is that acceptable there? To live with a woman?"

Anneliese laughed. "As long as no one looks in our windows at night."

That tore at me, the image of Anneliese with another woman.

"The villagers think we're spinster roommates, I suppose. Or relatives. I don't know what they think. We keep to ourselves. I would have written to you about it, but I think you know how dangerous it is to admit something like this. Even with you, I couldn't be sure you wouldn't turn away. That's why I haven't told you."

"What is her name?"

"Henriette. She is a ceramicist and runs a gallery. I write their publicity materials."

I imagined their life, their idyllic life in this French village. Their nights together, their days spent working companionably at things they loved.

"So what would you do if I said I would come with you? Or didn't you mean it? What would become of poor Henriette?"

Anneliese turned to look at me. "But you won't come back with me, will you?"

"But what if I did?"

"You know what would happen if you did, my Iphis." She ran her fingertips along my side, from my ribs down toward my hips, then lower.

"Shall I turn myself into a man for you?"

"Please," she said. "Please don't."

"Would we live together?"

"Why are you tormenting me?"

"I just want to know. I want to be able to picture the life I am missing."

She sighed. "If you came back with me, we would find another village. Maybe even a city. Villages are full of curious people. I would write books and you would write your poems and play your charango. We would drink wine at night and then we would do this. . . ." She bit the skin on the inside of my thigh.

I caught my breath. "And Henriette?" I managed.

Anneliese rolled her head so she could see my face. "I would write her a letter. A kind letter. Saying that you had a prior claim. That I was sorry. Henriette would find someone else. There are many women in France."

Her mouth moved down my skin until it replaced her fingers. And we could say no more.

When I woke the next morning she was already up, sitting in the chair by the window. "Ana?" I stretched out an arm.

She turned to look at me, her black hair glossy in the sunlight, her eyes serious. "Why did you never leave here? There must have been a time you could have."

I pulled my knees to my chest under the blanket. "Where should I have gone?"

"Not back to Austria, that wasn't what I was suggesting."

"So where?"

"Anywhere. The U.S., Israel. Somewhere, maybe, not so backward, more advanced . . ."

For the first time, I felt angry with her. I got out of bed and began pulling on my clothing. "Is there a reason I need to be somewhere *advanced*? I write poems. I own a bookstore. I play charango. Do these require a state-of-the-art country? Scientific progress didn't do us much good in Vienna."

She was silent for a moment. "I know. It's just, what is there for you here? In a run-down little city with no oxygen and no theater, no opera, all the culture you love. You're so far from the world."

Her words stunned me. "You don't think Bolivia has a culture?"

"You know what I mean."

"I'm not sure I do. Ana, La Paz for me is not far from the world. It *is* the world."

She looked chagrined. "I'm sorry. I guess you've been here so long . . ."

"Everything important that has happened to me since I was ten happened here. Isn't it the same for you? Isn't France yours now?"

She looked back out the window, as if she could see France from there.

"I don't know. Maybe. But at least France has art, publishing, doctors, everything. Opportunities to do something with your life."

"Am I not *doing something with my life*?" Furious now, I began picking up items of clothing from the floor and folding them into my suitcase.

"That's not what I meant!" She sprang from the chair and came toward me. "I'm sorry, Orly. I guess I don't understand."

I stopped packing and looked up at her. Her dark eyes, so clouded, so near me.

"Ana. My daughter is Bolivian. My husband." I say this as if maybe she hadn't

656

noticed.

She reached for my hand and I stepped away. Her eyes filled with tears. "I guess you're Bolivian now too."

"I guess I am."

Anneliese bent to pick up a discarded nightgown from the floor, folded it, and tucked it in her suitcase, avoiding my eyes. There was nothing more we could say. Thousands of stories were left untold, but none that could resurrect us.

Not until we had finished packing our bags and taking a last look around the room did I notice that on the wall above our bed was a woven tapestry of birds. Beautiful black birds, woven into a sunset-striped background. I climbed onto the bed in my stockinged feet to examine it more closely. Thin threads bound the birds to the earth. They were not free to fly. Below the tapestry to the right a tiny card was pinned to the wall. *Song of the Earth,* it said. By Nayra. My heart lifted. A connection to Mahler after all.

By the time we arrived back in La Paz, Anneliese was sick again, limp against my side. I walked her to her train and watched as a man tied ropes around her suitcase and hauled it to the top of the car. She turned to me, curled herself into my side, closed her eyes against the people swarming around us. I inhaled the scent of her neck one last time. *My Anneliese.* Despite everything, for a moment I wasn't sure I could let her go.

She was the first to loosen her arms. "Maybe in some other lifetime we could exist, Orly? Some other universe." Tipping her face up to me, she looked almost hopeful.

I brushed a few stray hairs from her face, tucked them behind her tiny ears. "We have always existed, Anneliese." The tears came then, finally, like rain. "We will always exist."

She turned to climb the stairs to the train car and was gone. Gone, just like that. I stood there letting the tears roll down my lips and into my mouth, tasting the salt. Looking for her in the windows. She was in none of them. She was gone, severing that last thread between me and the land where I was born.

I watched as the man in the white shirt leapt down to unlock the metal gates to allow the train to leave the station. Stood there watching as the whistle blew and in a cloud of steam it lurched down the tracks. Stood there, my feet unwilling to take a step away, until a station cleaner chased me out with a broom.

Though I had been traveling all day, I needed space before I returned home. Time. Yet I could not bear the thought of a solitary night, another night away from Isidora. From Miguel. I needed to be moving toward them; I needed time.

I walked home.

I stood in the doorway of our house, my suitcase still in my hand. It was quiet and dark. Were they both asleep? From the kitchen came the scent of rosemary and garlic. Sweet potatoes. Camote. Miguel had cooked. From my left came Izzy's voice. Setting my suitcase down by the door, I stepped quietly across the living room to the open doors to the terrace. There they lay, side by side, their heads on sofa cushions, covered by an alpaca blanket María Teresa had made for Isidora.

"Will we ever go there, Papá? To Pluto? To Jupiter?"

"It's not inconceivable." This was Miguel's answer to nearly everything. He could conceive of it all. He thought in potentialities. "We are already closer than almost anyone. Imagine, manicita, little peanut. Who is as close to the sky as we are?"

"Aren't mountain climbers close?"

"Only the bravest and most foolish of mountain climbers. But most are below us."

"Can I touch the sky?"

"We touch it all the time, Izzy. You are touching it now, with your face and your hands."

"Can it touch us back?"

"Can't you feel it?"

Leaning against the doorframe, I closed my eyes and I could feel it. The sky had infinite fingers. They were cool on my hair at night, they burned my eyes in the morning. The sky was powerful and not always kind. Yet I wanted to press myself against it, pushing upward, propelling myself into space.

How could I have contemplated leaving them, leaving this? Yet I had, if only for one wild moment. I had wanted to live two lives, love two — three — people. I wanted to be everywhere at once. I didn't want to miss anything.

Miguel turned his head, saw me standing in the doorway. Even in the dark I could see his smile. "Mira, Izzy. Mira. Your mamá's home."

He lifted the blanket and I walked to them, slipped into the warmth between them. I kissed Izzy and pressed my face against Miguel's. "Please don't go to Jupiter," I whispered. "Please don't go to Pluto."

"As long as you're here, we won't go anywhere," he answered. "Not without you."

When they were both asleep, I tiptoed inside and walked in the dark to the corner shelf where I kept my charango and unzipped its case. Sitting on the sofa, my heartbeat loud in my ears, I plucked a few strings. But I didn't want to play alone. I walked back to the terrace and lowered myself onto the tiles. They didn't turn their heads. They were dreaming. I rested the fingers of my right hand on the strings and thought. How to begin?

Think of two people or objects or ideas or places that have nothing in common. Anneliese and Miguel. Austria and Bolivia. Quinoa and croissants. Sky and earth. Friedenglückhasenland and Krokodilland. Words and music. France and Tarija. Anneliese and me. Miguel and me. Isidora and me. The world and me.

Now, write the connection.

ACKNOWLEDGMENTS

Entire countries of people contributed to the creation of this book, far too many to thank in these pages. But I will try. I want to acknowledge my debt to all those who allowed me to interview them or who penned memoirs about their experiences fleeing Austria and/or finding refuge in Bolivia, as well as to the historians, novelists, and Holocaust experts I consulted. I could have researched this book until the end of time, were it not for editorial deadlines. At times I have forced history to bend to my narrative — as far as I know, no one named Willi was deported with the children of Izieu, none of Klaus Barbie's bodyguards was poisoned, and Erich Eisner never conducted Jakob. But I have done my best to accurately portray the context in which my characters lived.

Infinita Gratitud A:

John Gelernter, whose assistance and experiences guided my first shaky steps. My Bolivian readers, Raul Peñaranda, Ana María Yapu Flores, and Wayra Anahi Ramos Yapu. My Bolivianish friends Violaine Felten and Susan Frick, whose thoughtful notes and corrections on early drafts were invaluable. Guillermo Wiener S., for his story. Angela Estenssoro for her friendship. Tito Hoz de Vila for his warmth and support from our first days. María Teresa Torres, for friendship and sanity in uncertain times. Walter Mur Bardales, for his ever-smiling assistance. Karola Guzmán de Rojas, for spinal support. Vico Figueroa, for his patience with the erratic progress of my Spanish. Diana Syrse, who corrected my many musical mistakes and helped me to hear this novel.

Danke Vielmals Zu:

Dietrich Hausherr, Austrian honorary consul in Bolivia, for research assistance and friendship. Ian Wekwerth, pianist for the Max Raabe & Palast Orchester, for his expertise on the music of the era, and for Orly's recital piece. Anna Goldenberg, for help with Austria research. Walter Juraschek for the stories and Stones of Remembrance.

Gregory Weeks, for responding to each of my emails with five of his own, and for generosity with time and resources. Ruth Mateus-Berr, for her Austrian expertise, especially about Fasching. Michaela Raggam-Blesch for her emails.

Grazie Infinite Per:
Barbara of Milk & Honey, my Genoa guide.

Infinite Gratitude To:
Everyone at Craigardan but particularly Michele Drozd, whose passion for the arts and commitment to creating a supportive and inspirational environment for writers and artists is exceptional. I was given not only time and space to write and piles of organic vegetables but an unforgettable residency with my daughter, who spent her days climbing mountains while I wrote. It's rare to find a residency that acknowledges that some writers have families, don't have child care, and that children can be part of the creative process. We love you. And your car.

Kate Moses, for the invitation. Megan Moody, for the farming. Zachary Gerhardt Clemans for the food. Alison, Lorene, Christian, and Ellen, for guineapigging with me.

Kimmel Harding Nelson for the time and space to finish the first complete draft of this novel. Also for the writerly and artistic companionship I found there. Thank you, Holly, Pat, Yaloo, Yukari, Julia, Junyi, Rachel, and Jennifer.

Leo Spitzer, for his brilliant books and his willingness to talk me through his early experiences as a child in Bolivia. Joy Haslam Calico for opera expertise. Wendy Reiss Rothfield for the interview and Maggie Worsdell for the book. Brigitte Sion, Elizabeth Anthony, PhD, of the United States Holocaust Memorial Museum, Bill Ecker of Harmonie Autographs and Music, Inc., Christine Schmidt of The Wiener Library for the Study of the Holocaust & Genocide in London, the JDC staff and New York archives, and the Leo Baeck Institute and Center for Jewish History in New York City for research assitance. Olivia Katrandjian, for inspirational conversation and books. My students, for new perspectives and for the constant reminders of craft. Seraphima Kennedy and NAWE for the community. Jill and Marc Mehl for treating us as family.

My beloved agent and friend Brettne Bloom, whose passion for this book almost before I got words on the page has been an unstoppable force. Brettne, I owe you everything.

Sarah Stein, for being among the first to believe in this book, and for her wise early edits.

Laura Tisdel and Amy Sun for patient, enlightened, and just plain genius editing. Also Jane Cavolina for making sure all the trees in my forest were in the right place and the entire team at Viking for their diligence and enthusiasm.

Last, nothing I do is possible without my family. Theadora, my firework of invention, your spirit infuses every page. I owe you infinite bunnies. Tim, my love, you provide the architecture of our existence, a never-ending stream of literary inspiration. To me, you are more home than man. (Without you, who would iron our underwear?)

ABOUT THE AUTHOR

Jennifer Steil is the author of two previous books, *The Woman Who Fell from the Sky,* a memoir of her experience as a journalist in Yemen, and *The Ambassador's Wife,* a novel about a hostage crisis that was also inspired by Steil's own experience. She currently lives in Tashkent, Uzbekistan, with her husband and daughter.